THE CHIRAL PROTOCOL

ALSO BY LL RICHMAN

The Biogenesis War Series

The Chiral Agent

The Chiral Protocol

Chiral Justice

Chiral Agent/Chiral Conspiracy audiobook set

Chiral Protocol/Ambush in the Sargon Straits audio set

The Biogenesis War Files: The Early Years

Operation Cobalt

Ambush in the Sargon Straits

The Chiral Conspiracy

— BOOK 2 —
THE BIOGENESIS WAR

THE CHIRAL PROTOCOL

LL RICHMAN

Copyright © 2020 by L.L. Richman

This book is a work of fiction. Names, characters, businesses, organizations, places, events, and incidents either are the product of the author's imagination or are used fictitiously. Any resemblance to actual persons, living or dead, events, or locales is entirely coincidental.

THE CHIRAL PROTOCOL
Published by Delta V Press
The Biogenesis War™ is a registered trademark of L.L. Richman
Cover copyright © 2020 L.L. Richman

All rights reserved. This eBook is licensed for your personal enjoyment only. It is protected under the copyright laws of the United States of America. No part of this book may be reproduced in any form or by any means, without the prior written consent of the publisher, excepting brief quotes used in reviews.

ISBN-13: 978-1-7373636-1-3

0 9 8 7   5 4 3 2 1

Produced in the United States of America

CONTENTS

Also by L.L. Richman iii

Copyright page vi

Contents vii

Foreword 10

Epigraph 12

PROLOGUE 13

TRAITOR 16

POWER PLAY 22

REPORTED THEFT 33

LIBERTY 40

COMPLICATIONS 56

TEMPTATION 58

BRIEFING 68

NATIONAL DUTY 81

HIDDEN LAB 88

MERCER 95

SYNTHETIC INTELLIGENCE 102

PREVENTIVE MEASURES 110

YACHT 118

BAD INTEL 123

DEAD MAN'S BLUFF 130

CONTAGION 139

MISLABELED 144

DAMAGE CONTROL 151

STAKEOUT 161

BACKUP 166

OLD ENEMIES 171

ENTANGLED VIALS 181

MISSING TRIGGER 187

EPIDEMIC 192

HANTA IN HIDING 195

FARADAY TATTOO 209

SLEIGHT OF HAND 216

DERELICT SHIP... 220

REVEALED.. 223

BREADCRUMBS.. 229

TEST SUBJECTS... 235

ANTIGEN DROP 242

MISSION PREP 247

NIMITZ BASE 251

LIVE FIRE.. 260

PANDEMIC... 267

DEADLY SHIPMENT.. 272

STRIKE FORCE 276

PITCHED BATTLE.. 283

STEALTH ESCAPE 298

DEATH TRAP.. 302

SECURITY SWEEP... 308

A LUCKY BREAK.. 318

SHADOW SHIP 323

SUSPICIOUS FIGURE 325

UNEXPECTED ALLY 329

BLINDSIDED 335

TO SAVE HAWKING... 341

DEBRIEF... 350

PREVIEW: CHIRAL JUSTICE.................................. 362

    EPIGRAPH 363

PART ONE: DISCOVERY.. 364

    TURNING THE ASSET 365

    A STRANGER'S PLEA.................................... 371

Terminology 386

Weaponry and Armor 390

Major Players in the Biogenesis War Universe.......... 391

Acknowledgements..393
Also by L.L. Richman...394
About the author 395

FOREWORD

The first three books in this series were imagined in the summer of 2019. This book, with Akkadia's plan to weaponize a chiral virus, was both concepted and fully outlined at that time.

I could not have predicted how things would transpire in 2020. I have to admit, it's an eerie feeling, seeing events unfold months—in some cases, mere weeks—after I wrote my fictional version of them.

I thought about postponing the book's release, since as of September, the pandemic was still a very real thing. There is hope on the horizon, but we struggle to see a true end in sight.

I thought about adding a trigger warning to this book, because on top of everything else, 2020 hammered us with devastating fire along the western half of the U.S. As luck would have it, this book also includes a very detailed description of how dangerous a wildfire can be.

I wrote the chapter "Liberty" in February, months before the first fires broke out. I included it because I'm a pilot, and because there is nothing I love more than writing an action scene from a pilot's point of view.

It's not commonly known, but there are very, very few things that have the potential to be as action-packed and dangerous as flying against fire.

As with all my books, the numbers are as accurate as I can make them. A burnover truly can reach temperatures more than five times what an astronaut on an EVA might experience in full sun.

"Liberty" is my ode to the valiant men and women who battle the blaze worldwide. They have my deepest respect.

Aerial firefighters aren't the only heroes celebrated in these pages. I also wanted to celebrate the quiet work of another kind of hero: virologists and medical scientists.

These people work tirelessly day in and day out, seeking new methodologies to eradicate disease. They are making great strides toward that goal, yet they remain unsung heroes, often widely overlooked.

Although the conflict in *The Chiral Protocol* centers around an evil empire that seizes a virus and weaponizes it, I wanted you to see both how viruses function, and how they can be used for good.

You'll find an explanation in the chapter "Briefing" that describes how chiral supraparticles can be used on the battlefield to deliver healing medical nano and save lives. Though it might seem like science fiction, that technology is being developed right now. Scientists today are building chiral supraparticles, they're coupling them with nanomedicines, and they're deploying them on a different battlefield: the fight against cancer.

I hope you enjoy this book. More, I hope there are passages in it that help you appreciate the heroes we have among us. With every book I write, I strive to honor those who stand between the innocent and the profane, who work each day to ensure that good triumphs over evil and the weak are defended by the strong.

Such heroism is found in soldiers who charge forward into hostile territory, and in warriors who fly combat missions while under a hail of bullets. In hotshot firefighters who battle the blaze, and in scientists who battle those attacks we cannot see.

I'll admit, this book has a tone that is not seen in the previous book, nor the ones that will follow. In a way, perhaps this is entirely appropriate for 2020.

LL Richman
Leawood, September, 2020

All warfare is based on deception.
The whole secret lies in confusing the enemy,
so that he cannot fathom our real intent.
~ SUN TZU

PROLOGUE

In the twenty-second century, humanity reached the stars.

With colonies established throughout the Sol system, pioneers hungry for new ventures traveled beyond its borders to nearby Alpha Centauri. There, they planted the first seeds of what would become three independent star nations—two around its binary stars, a third orbiting nearby Proxima Centauri.

Not long after, a theoretical form of propulsion became a reality. The experimental new drive's Casimir bubble magnified the Scharnhorst effect, allowing velocities up to three times the speed of light.

A brave band of explorers took a chance on the new tech and launched a pair of colony ships toward the binary stars of Procyon and Sirius. Their descendants flourished, forming the Geminate Alliance.

While the Scharnhorst drive made it possible to reach stars as distant as Sirius and Procyon, travel between the fledgling colonies and their parent star was still measured in years. The Geminate settlers were on their own, and they knew it.

Three hundred years passed. In the mid-twenty-fifth century, a pair of Alliance scientists discovered a way to fold spacetime, bending the compactified branes that were stacked within the Bulk of extradimensional space. Thus, the Calabi-Yau gates were born.

These specially tuned, 'pair-partnered' gates provided instantaneous travel between star systems, regardless of distance. For the first time, far-flung civilizations reconnected in real-time, and true interstellar commerce became a reality.

Those back in Sol had formed a loose association known as the Coalition of Worlds. The Coalition eagerly embraced the Alliance's gate tech. Treaties were signed, leases granted, and soon, the Geminate government had gates at each heliopause.

A robust and vigorous trade developed between the settled worlds, ushering in a prosperous new era for every star nation involved—with one exception: Akkadia.

The star nation orbiting Rigel Kentaurus had built an export economy around handcrafted materials whose value was based on scarcity, forced by Scharnhorst limitations and slow trade routes. This was utterly disrupted by the gates.

Akkadia plunged into a recession. Desperate circumstances allowed an oppressive regime to wrest power from its premier. The planet went from an artisan's enclave to a totalitarian government.

The current Ministry of State Security was rumored to have its hooks in every star nation from Terra to Sirius. It stole tech where it could, sabotaged when it couldn't. Such actions propelled Akkadia into a state of cold war with the rest of the settled worlds.

And then the Akkadian premier set his sights on the Geminate gate tech.

The Alliance has no idea how far Akkadia is willing to go to achieve this goal. They're also unaware how thoroughly they've been compromised, but they're about to find out...

Protocol (*n.*) In scientific research, a protocol is a predefined procedural method used to conduct an experiment. Protocols are written in order to ensure successful replication of results by others.

When treating with fellow star nations, or within one's own military, protocol is defined as the adherence to a specific and often elaborate code of conduct.

Under certain conditions, to break protocol can be tantamount to declaring war.

TRAITOR

Leavitt Station

Procyon Calabi-Yau Gate, Heliopause

Geminate Alliance (Procyon System)

THE AGENT WAS stretched prone along a section of catwalk, scope held steady against one eye, intent upon his target. The narrow steel walkway felt cool under his lightweight shirt, its raised crosshatch pattern cushioned somewhat by the duffel he'd propped under one forearm.

The catwalk was suspended several meters in the air, welded to the side of a massive arch that rose high above his head. It was one of many that curved upward to form the cathedral-like expanse of Leavitt Station's Concourse D. The catwalk's height provided the perfect vantage from which to observe the people passing below—and to wait for one in particular.

Leavitt was a smart choice for an anonymous meet. As the binary system's lone customs entry point, it was a crowded place, one that provided good cover. It held station just beyond the threshold of Procyon's Calabi-Yau gate.

The fortress was built to withstand the stresses placed on local spacetime when the gate punched past the surrounding dimensions to access its pair-partner on the other end.

Operating costs, coupled with rigorous policing by the Alliance to safeguard its intellectual property, limited the number of gates built. There were currently only five in existence, each anchored at the heliopause of a stellar body.

Procyon's nearby neighbor, Luyten's Star, was the most recent gate constructed. It also held the distinction of being the one most distant from Sol.

From there, the gates marched inward toward the birthplace of humanity. Sirius was next, followed by Proxima Centauri, Alpha Centauri, and finally, the yellow star around which Earth orbited.

The agent cared little about such things. They got him to where he needed to be in order to do his job, and that was good enough for him. At the moment, that job was to find out why an Akkadian agent was on Leavitt, and to discover who he was there to meet.

Beneath him, ticketed passengers flowed past. They marched in predictable patterns, sparing quick glances at holodisplays spaced along the concourse. The screens served as navigational aids. They announced departure and arrival times, delays, and gate changes.

Citizens of his own Geminate Alliance mingled with visitors from the Coalition of Federated Worlds. Most had some form of luggage floating behind them or slung over a shoulder, filled with purchases bought in far-flung star systems. A few off-duty naval personnel hauled duffels on their way home for a bit of leave.

Savory smells from food vendors three levels beneath him tickled the agent's nose. Very little sound reached him, though, thanks to the structure's nanoacoustics. They worked in concert with metamaterials to dampen the impact such a large mass of humanity had on the cavernous facility. What should have been a loud din was transformed into a soft susurration that enveloped all who transited the concourse.

Given the number of travelers on station, the agent was lucky to have spotted the Akkadian at all. The man certainly hadn't made it easy. The meet's location—and the agent was certain it was a meet—was obscured by a cloud of light-bending nano. It permeated the short side passageway that had been blocked by an 'under construction' sign, warning visitors to stay clear of the area.

When the Akkadian disappeared into the nanocloud, the agent had been forced to retrieve from his pack the scope he now held. The scope compensated for visual attenuation and allowed him to record the developing scene below.

The station's sound-dampening prevented the agent from recording audio, but he knew the Synthetic Intelligence program embedded in the base of his skull would be able to glean some of what was being said by dint of simple lip-reading. The agent would have to be content with what his SI could capture for now, until opportunity presented itself to detain and interrogate the man.

A woman materialized out of the shadows to stand beside the Akkadian. She looked like she might be a partner of sorts, or perhaps a bodyguard. Her head was on a swivel, her hand hovering near the butt of a weapon holstered by her side.

The two stood quietly, waiting. The agent waited, too.

It wasn't long before a third joined them. The agent's jaw tightened as he saw the uniform the man wore—that of a Geminate Alliance naval officer. A lieutenant, by the holopips on the collar. The wings beneath indicated he was a pilot.

Traitor, or spy? the agent wondered.

His gaze sharpened as the naval aviator handed a case over for the Akkadian to inspect.

Traitor, then.

The agent shifted to keep the case within the scope's sights as the Akkadian propped it against a nearby wall and lifted the lid. The man's shoulder partially obscured the case's contents, and the agent moved once more to get a better view.

For one brief moment, he could clearly see the hazard icon emblazoned on the three sealed metal cylinders resting within. He readjusted the scope to try to capture the serial numbers embedded in the icons, but a hand obscured them as the lid closed. What he'd managed to capture would have to do.

The agent used his neural wire to interface with the Synthetic Intelligence in his skull, ordering it to initiate a data upload to the Special Reconnaissance Unit's headquarters element, back on Ceriba.

The wire's evanescent wave nanocircuitry connected him directly to the Ford-Svaiter node held in orbit around Leavitt by a Starshot buoy. It was one of many such buoys seeded throughout the Procyon binary system. Their placement allowed for near real-time communication to anyone, anywhere within the system.

Not that the agent understood how it all worked. He couldn't care less about quantum tunneling, or photons as evanescent waves, nor how they allowed for instantaneous transfer of information. It was enough that his encrypted transmission would be intercepted at the other end by people who would know what to do with the information he held.

Sudden action through the scope had the agent readjusting his focal length once more. He caught a brilliant flare of light, indicating the edge of a plasma blade. The Akkadian had pulled a weapon on the traitor. He slashed, and the knife bit deep into the pilot's throat.

The agent had seen enough. He lowered the scope, intent on breaking it down and storing it back in its case, when his own internal alarm went off.

He hadn't registered the woman's absence. He'd been so focused on the contents of the small case the courier was handing over that he'd missed her sudden head turn, the sharp look she shot his way as her eyes searched the truss overhead. Had he seen, he might have guessed the truth—that light had reflected off his scope's optics, drawing her attention.

It was a rookie mistake.

A soft scraping alerted him that he was no longer alone on the catwalk. He dropped the scope and rolled, reaching for his weapon. He felt something smash against the base of his head, just as his fingers wrapped around the pistol in his shoulder holster. His skull, reinforced with a stacked lattice of single-layer magic-angle carbyne was virtually impenetrable, although the impact hurt and it bled like hell.

The pistol dropped onto the catwalk's steel deck; his hand scrabbled to reacquire it as he kicked out at his attacker. At the same time, he realized his transmission had been cut off. Whatever she'd hit him with must have had a suppression web attached to it.

His foot met air as the Akkadian woman sidestepped. He flung the duffel he'd been using to prop the scope at her head, and twisted, fingers wrapped around his weapon once more.

A soft click and a whoosh cut through the air as he brought the pistol around. His brain catalogued the sound as that of a pressurized cartridge powering a flechette pistol at the same time searing pain traced its way across his lower back and up through his bicep.

His arm flopped uselessly beside him, victim of the vaned, pointed-steel projectiles the weapon had fired. A nauseating agony settled where his kidney had once been before the nano reserves controlled by his SI implant began triaging his body. Blessed numbness descended as pain-blocking medication was pumped into his system.

The stimulant that automatically triggered on the heels of the anesthetic was intended to provide the necessary boost to help him evade his opponent and get to safety. It might have been effective had another round of the tiny metal arrows not torn through his back.

His mind distantly registered that the pool of warmth spreading beneath him was his own blood. He commanded his body to move—and realized he was paralyzed.

His head rolled to one side, his cheek coming to rest against the cold deck of the catwalk, the woman's form blurring as he blinked away the blood dripping into his eye. She crouched beside him, nudging him with the barrel of her weapon as if annoyed that he was taking so long to die.

The agent's SI flashed a warning onto his retina that his wounds required immediate intervention. He wheezed a laugh at the obviousness of that statement. Like he could do anything about it at the moment.

The woman stood, holstered her weapon, and turned to walk away. As her steps receded from his hearing, he heard the *plink* of something dropping nearby, but could not turn his head to see what it was.

A deep chill settled into his core, and he found his mind wandering. An image of his wife and son drifted across his consciousness, a vague remorse coloring his thoughts.

His eyelids fluttered closed, his body succumbing to the injuries inflicted. As he drew his last breath, a single tear slipped from the corner of one eye, trailing across his cheek and dripping onto the catwalk to mingle with the ever-widening pool of blood.

POWER PLAY

Headquarters, Ministry of State Security

Central Prefecture, Eridu

Akkadian Empire (Alpha Centauri A)

CITIZEN GENERAL CHE Josza hadn't seen the inside of the State Security building in months. Eight and a half, to be exact.

The last time he'd walked its halls, he'd been brought before the minister of state security, Rin Zhou Enlai, to explain his failure to acquire the Alliance materials stolen from Luyten's Star. The minister had allowed him to keep his position as the leader of the Junxun, but had reduced his rank from general first-class to general third-class.

The demotion made his job difficult, doubly so since his humiliation was public record. Anyone in the Junxun could access it.

The Junxun, or military training regimen, was compulsory for all citizens. Its curriculum was Che's creation. All Akkadians of age were required to spend the first year of their adult lives under his tutelage. It was a crucible of indoctrination, a way to forge young minds and bodies into the perfect weapons the State could wield.

Che had a talent for finding the most gifted among them, but his skills had been sorely tested in recent months.

His students did not know the specifics; they only knew he'd been demoted. Some took this to mean he was unworthy, as life had not yet tempered the hubris of their youth. They'd not faced their first real trial, did not understand that sometimes a battle was unwinnable. These were the ones who tried him and found him wanting.

It was difficult indeed to refine the edge of the carbyne blade when the blade itself refused to cooperate.

Rin Zhou knew this, of course. It was part of the punishment she had meted out. He thought he'd accepted it with stoic equanimity, gratitude even. His behavior since that time had been exemplary. He'd carefully avoided the spotlight, toed the line, rendered his obeisance with dignity and respect. Or so he thought.

He strode down the cold, stark corridors, keeping pace with the guard sent to escort him to the minister's chambers. The escort symbolized another privilege that had been stripped from him during his demotion, as only generals first-class were granted clearance to enter the State Security Building unescorted.

Outwardly, his countenance remained impassive. Inwardly, his mind worked feverishly to figure out what he'd done, where he'd gone wrong.

He could think of nothing.

Che's thoughts drifted to his small holdings, just outside Central Prefecture—all that remained of his fortunes since his fall from grace. He wondered if he'd be returning to his home, or if that, too, would be stripped from him.

Perhaps this time, his luck had finally run out.

What luck? he asked himself bitterly. *Surely what little I had abandoned me on that suns-cursed station in Procyon nine months ago.*

The imperialist bastards who ran the Geminate Alliance had waged an aggressive campaign against the small tactical team he'd led that day.

It should have been a simple extraction. An in-and-out job. Retrieve a valuable sample case filled with research material carefully culled from deGrasse torus. Bring it back to Akkadia, where it would be used to further the empire's goals.

His decision to oversee the operation personally was one he deeply regretted. Had he stayed behind on Eridu, he could have distanced himself from the operation, cast blame upon the ones who led in his stead. But this was a high-profile case, one that held the minister's complete attention.

He'd made a tactical error that day. When a supposedly dead man—one that an Akkadian sleeper agent had experimented on—showed up very much alive, he'd split his team.

How difficult was it to capture one man?

He'd thought it was a sure bet. He'd rolled the dice and lost. Both the man and the stolen material had slipped through his fingers, and he'd been left to bear the burden of responsibility.

Part of him had been surprised to come out the other end with his life. Another part recognized that Rin Zhou was harsh, but fair—more so than any of her predecessors he'd worked with during his career. She knew, as well as he, that the weak link in the operation had been that same sleeper agent.

Clint Janus was both a narcissist and a sociopath, and just a little bit unhinged. The man had nearly cost Che his very best agent, Dacina Zian, his Fierce Dagger.

The assassin he'd assigned to Janus as his handler was very nearly lost to him—and for what? An egocentric scientist whose goals only aligned with his motherland when he found it convenient.

Che allowed a small, grim smile to play about his lips. His Dacina had taken care of that last. She'd run Janus through a deep indoctrination program during their return voyage. The man would not soon slip his leash.

Small comfort, at this point. His mind returned to his current problems and he wondered anew why he still lived.

Likely, she thinks death would be too much of a mercy, he thought with asperity. Living with shame in Akkadian culture, to lose face... Death was preferable.

His musings crashed to an abrupt halt as they stopped before the minister's office suite. The Synthetic Intelligence embedded in his skull proffered his security token to the SI that stood guard over Rin Zhou's chambers. Once accepted, the doors slid silently open.

The guard retreated, leaving Che alone to face his minister.

His pulse thundered in his ears, testament to the tenuous nature of the situation. He stepped forward, the doors sliding shut behind him.

The minister stood before a floor-to-ceiling expanse of clearsteel windows, looking out over the hazy skyline. Beyond her, Che could just make out the silver ribbon of the planet's main space elevator glinting in the distance.

Rin Zhou looked up as he halted just inside the entrance. With an impatient wave of her hand, she motioned him forward.

He found his feet responding instinctively to the unspoken demand. "Citizen Minister," he murmured, head bowed.

"Citizen General," she said. "Your premier has need of your services once more."

He looked up at that. His surprise must have shown; it brought unexpected humor to her eyes.

Lips twitching slightly in amusement, she asked, "Not what you anticipated?"

Che chose to be candid. "No, Citizen Minister. Given my circumstances...." He let his voice trail off, and she nodded her understanding.

Rin Zhou waved him to a low table where the setting for a ritual pour had already been laid. He settled into the cushion she indicated and waited for her to join him. To his utter shock, she picked up the steaming carafe of water and began the service herself.

"I...." His voice trailed off.

They were in uncharted territory.

He swallowed, his gaze locked on her hand as it wove gently over the freshly-ground coffee, swirling the water in smooth arcs. He tried again. "Citizen Minister, please. Allow me."

He froze as she brought her free hand up sharply.

"Is it not true that all Akkadians are equal?"

"I—Yes, but…."

How does one refute the party line to one's superior? Everyone knew some were more 'equal' than others. There would always be the need for leadership, and yet—

"As Minister of State Security, *all* Akkadians are in my charge," Rin Zhou continued, tone mild. Her eyes cut sharply to meet his. "Even those who have fallen and are working to atone."

He inclined his head respectfully.

There was nothing he could say to that, nothing at all.

Rin Zhou finished the ritual pour and sank gracefully into the cushion across from him. He waited for her to pick up her own cup, hand waving gently across its surface to release its aroma. It was customary to inhale prior to the first sip; it prepared the mind to properly appreciate the drink.

He followed suit, his hand bringing the coffee's bouquet wafting to him. He breathed the bean, his hand lifting the cup.

"You said the premier has need of me," he began carefully, after his first swallow. "How may I be of service, beyond the training of the Junxun?"

Rin Zhou sipped thoughtfully, taking her time before she replied. Her mouth moved, tongue rolling the coffee around to experience its full flavor profile before swallowing. When her words came, they weren't an answer to his question. Instead, they posed another, more disturbing one.

"How far would you go, Che Josza, to restore your honor, I wonder?" she mused. "Would you embark upon an unsanctioned mission, one the premier would surely disavow, should news of it reach his ears?"

Che's hand stilled, cup halfway to his lips. Very carefully, he set the cup back down. His hand smoothed the fine linen serviette lying to one side of the ritual place setting, his mind racing.

The minister was well aware of his service record. She knew Che was an exceptional strategist. The number of complex, high-risk missions he'd successfully completed on the people's behalf were known only to a select few, due to their sensitivity.

"I would take on any task, regardless of its difficulty, if it served the people." His words came slowly as he measured each one out. "My life is Akkadia's. It would be an honor to spend it in her service, Citizen Minister. I would hope you know that."

Rin Zhou nodded, and he saw satisfaction blazing in her eyes. "Good," she said, the flat of her free hand coming down to slap sharply against the table's surface.

The action triggered a series of preset functions the room's Synthetic Intelligence was programmed to execute. Che suddenly found himself cut off from both the planetary net and the encrypted people's military subnet. Intrigued, he waited for her to speak.

"As you know, the premier is closing in on his two hundredth birth date."

She lapsed into silence, one brow raised expectantly.

Dutifully, Che considered her words, turning over what he knew of the premier. This was the man who had wrested control from the floundering of the colony's original settlers when it had become clear that the financial impact of the Calabi-Yau gates was decimating Eridu's economy.

The man had singlehandedly forced Akkadia into a new world order. He'd marshaled the disenfranchised, the desperate, and the homeless into an army, overthrown those who held office, and established martial law.

The new Akkadia was a world where everyone was equal and each citizen worked toward the betterment of the colony—or they were quietly disappeared. Only the strong survived; the premier hammered that into the minds of impressionable youth, along with the maxim that hard work and service to the homeland were what made life sweet.

The premier's brute force approach had been harsh, but the planet had survived. More, the military under the premier's guidance had become aggressive and expansionist, appropriating privately held business concerns that worked nearby asteroid mines. The monies that came from such ventures funded the struggling colony until Eridu's infrastructure adjusted to the totalitarian regime the premier had put into place.

His advanced age was something no one ever spoke about openly, but there had been much speculation about who would succeed him, and when. He had a daughter, Yachi. The woman cut her teeth on statesmanship, learning the art of political warfare at her father's knee. Everyone knew she was destined to be her father's successor, next in line for the premiership, but had assumed a peaceful transfer of power would ensue at some point.

Che jerked his head back, eyes narrowing. "Yachi will challenge?"

Rin Zhou shook her head. "There will be no challenge," she said slowly. "There is another whose aspirations eclipse hers."

Che's brows drew down. "Who?"

"The ministry has already intercepted two assassins who were foolhardy enough to accept a contract for the premier's life." Rin Zhou gestured to his cup as she lifted her own. "We interrogated them. It turns out they had been hired by Asher Dent."

Che rocked back on his cushion in surprise. "Your predecessor's son."

Rin Zhou nodded.

"But Dent chose to run for Akkadia's seat in the Coalition's General Assembly. He has power, influence."

The minister nodded again. "That does not negate a bid for premier."

"He's the minority leader for the Coalition of Worlds. He's made no secret of his ambition. His stated goal has always been to become council president."

Rin Zhou smiled. It did not reach her eyes. "His *stated* goal, yes."

Che gestured with one hand. "Why would he try for the premiership when he could hold sway over far more than just one world? Council president would bring him much greater influence than Akkadian premier."

Leaning forward, the minister clasped her hands around her steaming cup. "He doesn't see it that way, I'm told. Power within the council is a much different thing than the authority of the premiership. Here, on this planet, the premier's word is absolute. The General Assembly, on the other hand, was established with a set of checks and balances. The president's position can be overruled, his decisions questioned."

Reluctant understanding flared.

"I see," Che murmured. "You're right, of course. But what does any of this have to do with me?"

"Power has always been something Asher sought. He craves it. It was seared into his brain, branded there by his parent at a very early age." Rin Zhou lifted her coffee's stir stick and began to draw it through the hot liquid in a lazy figure-eight. "In order to ensure Yachi inherits her father's position, we must act preemptively."

"You intend to back her?"

Rin Zhou looked directly into his eyes. "She will need a great deal of guidance. Advisors she can trust."

Everything came into focus with sudden clarity. Rin Zhou wasn't concerned about preserving Yachi's rightful place; she intended to make the woman her puppet, to rule from the shadows.

The only question now was, would Che back Rin Zhou's power play, or not?

Che sipped at his drink as he thought through everything he'd been told. It was no secret that Rin Zhou had a hand in ousting the previous minister of state security. If Dent were to succeed in his bid for premier, Rin Zhou's career—most likely her life—would be measured in days, if not hours.

For better or worse, Che's own career was closely tied to that of Rin Zhou. If she went down, he certainly would, too.

"What do you propose?" he asked.

Something shifted in Rin Zhou's expression, her eyes gleaming in the soft glow of her office's muted light. It caused the hair on the back of Che's neck to stand on end.

"An operation that will assure Akkadia's military supremacy while dealing our sister colonies a crippling blow," she stated. "A success of such magnitude, orchestrated by the premier's daughter, would make Yachi untouchable."

And there it was. By crediting Yachi with the success, Rin Zhou was cementing her position within her fledging regime, all but assuring her own career path.

On its heels came a troubling thought.

But am I witnessing history repeat itself?

Asher Dent's own father, the man who'd held the office prior to Rin Zhou, had thought to attempt an equally daring gambit. He'd failed, and the woman before him had been instrumental in his removal from office. And yet....

"What kind of operation?" he found himself asking.

"The Alliance has been experimenting with the samples brought back from Luyten's Star. I have a team working to acquire them."

Che nodded, unsurprised. He waited while Rin Zhou took another sip. When she didn't continue, he asked, "What do you intend to do with the samples, Minister?"

"I intend for *you* to put them to good use. The samples are viral in nature." Her gaze bore into him. "Make me a weapon. It must be swift, and it must be deadly."

Che jerked his head in a nod of obeisance, unable to do more at the moment. His mind was swimming. He had so many questions, all vying inside his head to be the first posed, but he waited to see what else she would say.

"One thing." Rin Zhou's words had him raising his brows in silent question.

"If we are to defeat Asher, we must proceed with great

caution. He has informants everywhere. No whisper of this can reach him."

Che considered that. It would be difficult to bury such an operation while using Akkadian resources. Even within the ranks of the Junxun, his own formidable army, there was a robustly healthy rumor mill. There was no way to guarantee he could keep it from them, and still make use of their vast resources.

He nodded slowly, thoughtfully. "You're saying this would have to be completely off the books."

Rin Zhou's gaze never left his face. "A black operation, yes. Select a handful of your most skilled warriors, but be careful who you choose. You must be very sure they can be trusted. The rest must be sourced from outside Akkadia. Nothing of this operation can be traced back to this ministry."

They sat in silence for long minutes, Che turning the problem over in his head. "I'll need to secure a laboratory for the research and experimentation," he murmured.

Rin Zhou lowered her chin. "It cannot be housed within Akkadia's borders."

Che inclined his head, acknowledging that truth.

"There is a place," he murmured finally. "An abandoned laboratory, deep in the dust belt of Proxima Centauri." He knew his eyes held warning as he added, "Even though it is several dozen AU from Shang, it's still squarely within An-Yang territory."

"Then I suppose anyone using that facility would need to proceed with care to ensure they are not discovered," she said mildly.

She set her cup aside and rose in one smooth motion. She waited for Che to join her before continuing.

"You have fifteen days. Once you have achieved your objective, contact me. I will make sure arrangements on this end are ready."

He blinked. "Fifteen *days?*"

Rin Zhou's look froze him in place. "Is this a problem?"

The task was impossible. It would take fifteen days to obtain the scientists and staff the laboratory. One look at Rin Zhou's face told Che it would do him no good to argue.

Ancestors, help me...

Outwardly, his face remained implacable.

"No, Citizen Minister." He dipped his head. "I live to serve."

* * *

Rin Zhou stood motionless until the doors slid shut behind Che Josza. She ordered the SI inside her head to bring up the security feed as she moved to her desk.

She watched as Che was escorted from the State Security grounds. The citizen general's demeanor was impeccable, rendering the required salute to a former peer, despite the other man's subtle rebuff.

Her mouth tightened. She understood what necessitated the snub; none who served the premier dared to be friendly with those whose names were under a cloud, for fear the association might reflect poorly on their own careers.

Rin Zhou hated that she'd had to demote Che. He was one of her most brilliant and capable generals, and yet the situation had dictated no less.

She'd chosen him for this particular operation because Che had always done as ordered, and given his current situation, he was more motivated than most. The opportunity to redeem himself was one he could not refuse. If it was humanly possible to deliver the weaponized material within such an aggressive time frame, he would.

Rin Zhou knew Che thought she had set him up to fail. Yet, fifteen days from now...

She dismissed the feed as Che disappeared into the crowded streets below and returned her attention to the intelligence report that had put today's events in motion.

Coalition Defense Summit, October fifteenth. Host: Geminate Alliance, Hawking Habitat.

Her eyes scanned the list of high-ranking military and intelligence personnel that would be attending. They were all key people from powerful governments, including one Asher Dent.

A strike at that event would not just eliminate her own personal threat. It would bring the rest of the settled worlds to their knees.

REPORTED THEFT

NATIONAL SECURITY AGENCY
ST. CLAIR TOWNSHIP, CERIBA
MYR (PROCYON B)
GEMINATE ALLIANCE

THE PLAYBACK OF the feed sent by the agent on Leavitt Station ended abruptly.

Duncan Cutter, director of the Alliance's National Security Agency, turned from the holoscreen to regard the woman seated across from him. They were in a Sensitive, Compartmentalized Information Facility—a SCIF—beneath Parliament House.

SCIFs were rooms that suppressed all forms of surveillance, allowing the exchange of sensitive security and military information between authorized personnel. After viewing the recording, Duncan understood why the woman who'd scheduled the briefing decided to hold it here.

"Pilot's body was found. No trace of the Akkadians." Colonel Tala Valenti turned from the frozen image on the holo to meet his eyes as she added, "Our agent's been found, too."

The economic spate of words was classic Valenti. The woman had a lean, muscled warrior's build, as befit the head of the Special Reconnaissance Unit.

"Alive?"

The question came from the only other person in the room. Admiral Amara Toland led the Navy's Advanced Research Agency. Her presence here was at Valenti's request.

The colonel's lips compressed into a thin, hard line. "No," she told Toland.

"Who was it? Ladue?" asked Duncan.

Valenti nodded.

Duncan's jaw tightened. Ladue was one of Valenti's best men, highly skilled at technical surveillance and sensitive site infiltration. He'd supplied the images they had just seen, of the pilot passing the vials to a known enemy.

"He was a good agent." Duncan scraped his hand across the stubble lining his jaw and swore softly. "I'll get in touch with his family. Damn, but I hate those conversations."

"He died under my command." Normally taciturn, Valenti's voice held rare emotion. "I can do it."

He shook his head, giving her a brief, non-smile.

"I know you can, and I appreciate the offer. It's ultimately my responsibility, though." He nodded toward the frozen image on the screen. "How did this happen?"

"The pilot, or Ladue?" Valenti asked.

Cutter lifted a hand. "Either. Both."

Valenti's eyes returned to the screen. "Pilot was listed AWOL a week ago."

"Akkadian asset?" Duncan asked sharply.

It was Toland who answered. Shaking her head, she said, "I don't think so. He had a known gambling problem, and I think they blackmailed him into it. He certainly paid for his sins," she added, with a glance toward the frozen image of the dead body, its throat slit.

"And Ladue?" Duncan's gaze shifted from Toland to Valenti.

The colonel nodded to the SCIF's holodisplay. "Takeko," she

ordered, "display file Leavitt Three-Five."

Duncan kept his expression neutral as Valenti addressed the Synthetic Intelligence implanted inside her head. He wasn't entirely comfortable with the concept of SIs being embedded within active military personnel.

"We'll wall the SI off," the Navy's chief scientist had assured the intelligence subcommittee when the initiative was first proposed. *"Think of it as being confined to a miniature SCIF inside the brain."*

The argument was a persuasive one.

Duncan sent a quick glance around the secured room where they sat. This particular SCIF was not only secure, it was fortified. A foreign agency would have to overcome insurmountable obstacles to breach it.

The analogy resonated with the subcommittee, and they'd approved limited deployment within the Alliance's defense command. The SI implants had been green-lighted just a handful of weeks ago. Colonel Valenti was one of the program's first recipients.

{Image Leavitt Three-Five.} Valenti's SI projected its voice over the SCIF's audio feed, and the holoscreen lit up once more.

A different visual appeared on the display, this one, with the watermark of NCIC, the Navy's Criminal Investigation Command.

{This was taken today by NCIC investigators, at oh-two-forty-seven, local time. Leavitt Station, concourse D.}

All thoughts of SCIFs and SIs fled when Duncan realized what he was looking at. The camera panned across the downed agent's slumped form, his slack hand resting beside a partially disassembled sniper's scope.

The recording changed angles, and suddenly, Duncan was looking at the crosshatched surface of the catwalk where Ladue's body lay. He could see a pool of reddish-brown staining its surface.

Ladue's blood.

Beside it was a small, round object. Valenti reached out, and with a gesture, highlighted it. That portion of the image sprang forward, revealing the object in greater detail.

An assassin's bead.

"They found him," Duncan stated heavily.

"It would seem so."

Valenti did something more with the display, and the feed reverted back to what Ladue had sent to NSA headquarters. She scrubbed through it until she came to a closeup of the case held in the pilot's hand.

"I suppose it's too much to hope there was nothing of value in those metal cylinders," Duncan murmured. "What did they steal?"

Toland took up the narrative. "Those cylinders are protective vaults. Each one holds a glass vial with material from the Center for Infectuous Diseases. They were reported missing earlier today."

Her gaze shifted from the case and its contents back to Duncan. Her expression was grave. "Those vials belong to Captain Moran."

Duncan felt the blood drain from his face. His eyes jumped back to the frozen visual. "*Addy* Moran? The doctor who was at Luyten's Star?" he clarified.

"Yes," confirmed Toland. "Those vials contain chiral material, held in suspension."

Duncan whispered a low curse. *Chiral material.*

Few outside those involved in the first exploratory mission to Luyten's Star knew what had been found there. The star system annexed by the Alliance a few years earlier was uninhabited and boasted a lone planet.

Vermilion was a super-earth, orbiting the red dwarf in a 3:2 resonance just inside its goldilocks zone. It also harbored a secret so shocking, the Alliance had immediately interdicted the system.

That secret was naturally occurring chiral life.

The concept of chirality dated back to pre-diaspora Earth, when scientists first realized that the building blocks of life all had a certain molecular structure. Each molecule had a mirror-image twin, but just as a right-handed glove would not fit on a person's left hand, none of these mirror-image molecules could sustain life.

The preference biology had for one 'handedness' over another became known as chirality, based on the ancient Greek word *kheir*, meaning 'hand'. The phenomenon was present in every living organism.

In the twenty-first century, chiral molecules were found in interstellar space. Later, when humanity expanded beyond their home star system, their exploration of other worlds revealed the same thing: native organisms everywhere all shared the predilection for left-handed life.

By then, it was understood the phenomenon was caused by cosmic rays, interacting with a planet's atmosphere and inducing a magnetic, polarized spin onto living things. Still, scientists hoped to one day stumble upon a sector of space that had been spared the influence.

The red dwarf that was Luyten's Star proved to be just such a breeding ground. The star had a history of emitting circularly polarized flares.

The right-handed photons that bombarded the system's lone habitable planet influenced its developing life in much the same way cosmic rays had done elsewhere in the explored galaxy. They created chiral life.

Such a discovery had rocked the scientists at the Navy's Advanced Research Agency, and they had rushed to study the world teeming with mirror organisms.

DeGrasse torus, one of three black-site research stations under NARA's umbrella, had been relocated to Vermilion so that Geminate scientists could study it. Amara Toland, a scientist in her own right who held degrees in both condensed matter and materials physics, commanded all three.

The torus had been subsequently destroyed by an Akkadian agent, virtually all hands lost. The admiral had been away from the torus at the time; it was the only reason she was still alive.

Duncan knew survivor's guilt still haunted her.

"How did this happen?" he asked quietly.

"The chiral material was on its way from our facility in Montpelier to the Hawking Habitat for a series of planned experiments," Toland said. "It never arrived."

Montpelier was one of the research centers under the admiral's command. This one, unlike deGrasse, was planet-bound, a few hundred kilometers away from their current location.

"Go on."

"The vials were logged out of Level Two containment three days ago. They were supposed to arrive on Hawking today." Her voice turned grim. "Someone swapped packages."

Duncan ripped his gaze from the vials resting inside the case to spear Valenti with a look. "Have you notified the team?"

He knew he didn't need to clarify which team. There was really only one capable of handling a chiral situation, and they all knew it.

Duncan had given Valenti carte blanche when he'd ordered her to create Task Force Blue. She'd assigned Captain Thad Severance to lead it, and had stolen Gabriel Alvarez from NCIC to be his second. Severance had brought along two people from his former recon unit to complete the fireteam. Boone was Blue's sniper, and Asha, its medic.

In addition, rather than rely on the Navy's Shadow Recon teams to ferry the task force to and from its covert missions, Valenti had retained Jonathan and Micah Case for the job. After a bit of negotiating with Major Snell, the man in charge of Shadow Recon, they'd brought in the remainder of the flight crew as well: Will, Nina, and Yuki filled the roles of crew chief, gunner, and copilot, respectively.

She nodded in response to his question. "Ladue's intel came in at about the same time the admiral contacted me," the colonel said with a nod toward Toland. "I sent Captain Severance a recall message right after. He should be getting it shortly."

"Getting it shortly?" Duncan repeated, feeling a bit confused.

"I don't recall them being on an active mission right now."

She shook her head. "They're not. Thad brought Micah and the rest of the crew planetside."

He felt his brows rise. "I can't think of many places where they'd be unreachable here on Ceriba," he murmured, "and I know for a fact you have priority override on their wires."

"I do." Valenti's response was short and to the point. Her next words, however, were a bit mystifying. "Let's just say things are getting a bit hot where they're at right now."

LIBERTY

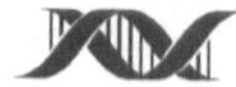

Huntington National Forest
Ceriba
Geminate Alliance

THE AIRCRAFT PITCHED, slewing sideways, the controls in Micah's hands shuddering under the tumult of superheated air that enveloped them. He held the yoke loosely, riding the currents that gripped the decommissioned military craft as updrafts and microbursts tossed the armored fighting machine about like an angry toddler flinging his toys.

The sudden displacement was met by a crazed whoop from the man seated to Micah's left.

"Hell of a ride, Navy! Bet you don't have this much fun in that fancy-ass Helios you usually fly, am I right?" The big man's grin was infectious, flashing bright white in his dusky face.

Micah grinned, gaze fixed on the controls as the ship buffeted once more. "Cannot confirm or deny."

Thad snorted. "Won't, you mean."

Micah's lips twitched as the man beside him leaned in to look at the Novastrike's forward holodisplay.

Thaddaeus Severance the Third. With a name like that, the man should look like some college professor, or a high-credit lawyer. But Thad was a jarhead, a hulking Marine who barely fit into the co-pilot's seat.

The leader of the Unit's newest special operations team had a side gig that few outside the close circle of Task Force Blue knew about. During fire season, he volunteered with the Ceriba Forestry Service.

"Why are you slumming with us, instead of up there, dishing out the orders?" Micah asked.

Normally, Thad would be high above the flames, working as the firefighters' air attack command, instructing aircraft where to most effectively release their loads. Pilots like Micah would fly over the conflagration in modified Navy vessels, their low-slung belly tanks filled with nano-laced smart fire retardant, ready to drop at Thad's direction.

When released, the nano separated into two materials. The heavier nano dropped, coating surfaces and making them impermeable to combustion. The lighter nano saturated the air ahead of a fire, depleting it of the oxygen the flames needed in order to feed.

Both were click-assembly bots, programmed to rapidly replicate themselves, given enough raw formation material. There was plenty of that in a fire, with carbon floating freely in the air currents. The trick was to flood the area with enough nano that the very winds that were feeding the fire would help seed its demise.

"Comm malfunction." Thad said in answer to Micah's question. He nodded to the wall of smoke and flames that obscured the towering Ceriban pines. "Adrenaline junkies like you depend on us bein' able to see the big picture, direct you to the spots that need it most. Can't do that if we can't talk at you."

"Someone's up there, subbing, though, right?"

Thad nodded again. "Davis commandeered a civilian shuttle," he explained, mentioning the other Air Attack commander who worked shifts opposite him. "Just as we landed, the report came in on the trapped smokejumpers. I diverted you and the rest of the team to SAR duty, soon as I heard."

SAR. Search-and-rescue.

Will and Yuki, the other half of their flight team, were circling south of the conflagration in another converted Novastrike, while he, Thad, and Nina circled north.

It was anyone's guess as to who would make it there first. And it was going to be a very bumpy ride.

The Novastrike—or Firestrike, as it was now called—was smaller than the ship Micah flew for the Navy. Stripped of its magnetic shield generators, the former attack craft had been converted to atmospheric flight, its drive altered to meet planetary emissions standards.

The fuselage aft of the cockpit had been reconfigured, too. Where once it had carried fully-kitted Marine fireteams, now it was rigged with an inflatable bladder that could deploy five thousand liters of red goo over a swath of burning land.

Thad wasn't a gearhead. The first time Micah had mentioned the changes the forestry service had made to the ships, Thad had shaken his head.

"Don't much care, hoss. Only thing that matters to me is how fast that thing can dump its load, turn around, an' do it again."

Today, it was all about how fast they could get to a pair of downed firefighters.

"You know," Micah called out as the aircraft bucked yet again, "using your liberty to volunteer with the Forestry Service is kind of like jumping out of the frying pan and into the fire..."

The woman behind him groaned and nudged the back of his seat. "We already know why he did it. He's batshit crazy."

"Careful, *cher*," warned the big Marine, shooting Nina an amused look, "you know what they say about pots and kettles. I don't call you crazy for flying with this lunatic day in and day out, do I?"

"*We're* not flying into thousand-degree fire on a regular basis," she countered. "That would be suicide. Aerial firefighting's scary shit. Just as dangerous as combat."

Every military pilot who flew against fire would agree with the gunner's assessment.

Thad inclined his head, conceding the point. And then he said, "That's because we don't pull you humans into the mix until the drones can't handle it any longer."

"We *know*." Micah infused the words with sarcasm. "Marginal conditions: check. Poor visibility: yes. Spooky, unpredictable weather patterns: hell to the yes."

"Too much for your pilot's augments to handle, 2.0?"

Micah didn't rise to the bait, or the nickname. "You're just going to have to deal. They're all I've got. Don't like it? Take it up with the Alliance Navy."

He fell silent as the Firestrike went through another rollercoaster-like gyration. After a moment, he glanced over at Thad once more. "You know, we could've dropped a load along the way."

Thad shook his head. "Couldn't wait. Every second counts." Micah couldn't argue, especially when your foe could leap a hundred meters in a single second.

He looked back down at his SyntheticVision feed, willing it to give him more actionable information. It didn't. In the midst of a wildfire as big and deadly as this one, enhanced-spectrum thermal imaging wasn't of much use.

Micah's infrared was just one big, superheated smear, the fire turning the aircraft's sensor suite into a riot of color. Topology was rendered in harsh yellows, oranges, fuchsias, and reds, as brush and trees fell beneath its fury.

Real-time surface-from-motion mapping wasn't much better. The currents and eddies within the heart of the fire were fierce and violent, whipping loose materials into a frenzy and uprooting even the sturdiest of trees.

"Nina's right," he murmured. "It's getting worse. This is suicidal."

The fire's instability had progressed. Thad whooped once more as the vessel plummeted, caught in a downdraft. Micah sent the Firestrike climbing once more.

"Still wishing we were carrying?" came Nina's tense voice.

"Nope." Micah bit the word out, his focus entirely on the ship. "I'd have had to turn around by now, if we were configured heavy."

Thad made a sound of agreement.

"What were these smokejumpers doing that they need rescuing?" Micah asked, as he thought about the challenge ahead.

Retrieving people trapped on the side of a mountain, in the kind of extreme weather brought on by a conflagration was risky, and demanded precision control. It would stretch anyone's abilities.

"They're with a crew of hotshot firefighters," said Thad. "They were working ahead of the fire's leading edge, cutting trees and creating a firebreak, upslope."

Micah could visualize what Thad described. Trees were cut so that their crowns fell downslope, back in the direction of the flames, leaving a bare area the flames could not cross. The plan was a solid one: starve the fire out, deprive it of the fuel it would need to travel past that point.

"Terrain?"

"There's a cliff above the firebreak, rises about fifty meters. Very little growth."

"What went wrong then?" asked Nina. "That sounds like it should have worked."

"Should have, *cher*, you're right about that. The fire broke through on both sides. Tree came down in exactly the right spot. It bridged the firebreak they'd built." Thad's voice was filled with remorse. "The way it fell, it cut those two off from the rest of their crew."

"So they're trapped," said Micah.

"And one of them's injured," Thad confirmed. "And they're directly in the path of the hottest part of the fire."

"Damn," Micah swore. He knew what that meant.

Despite the fact that firefighters in this century had far better equipment than their pre-diaspora predecessors back on Earth, the two trapped firefighters weren't well equipped to ride out a burnover of this intensity.

Firesuits had the capacity to shield the wearer from temperatures as high as two hundred fifty degrees, Celsius. That was equivalent to the protection provided by the EVA suits maintenance workers used on Humbolt, Ceriba's primary space platform.

A firefighter having to shelter in place as *this* wildfire burned over him would be subject to temperatures more than five times that amount. Not even current technology could shed heat that efficiently.

That left the Task Force Blue flight crew as their only hope.

{Foxtrot Seven! Fire whirl, dead ahead!}

That was the call sign for their ship. It came from the forestry service's Air Attack, flying nine kilometers above the fire.

A quick glance at the external sensor suite showed Micah they had plenty of clearance above, but a scant hundred meters below. "Shit. Hold onto something…"

With a fire whirl, a fierce and unpredictable tornado-like vortex that could spring up in a wildfire as big as this one, such a small amount of separation could become problematic.

The wall of smoke parted, and a twisting column of flame erupted ten meters in front of the Firestrike's nose.

"Brace for shear!" he shouted.

The hundred-year-old aircraft bucked as it hit a wall of turbulent air that surrounded the wildfire-induced whirlwind. It shot the Firestrike forty meters straight up, its internal temperature rocketing well past what the cockpit's climate controls could handle. The fiery vortex's thousand-degree heat made those inside the fuselage feel like they were on a close pass to Procyon's main-sequence star rather than flying search-and-rescue on Ceriba.

The sudden upward displacement was met by a muffled curse from the woman behind him, near the Firestrike's side door. Seconds later, the tornado-like fire whirl sent the craft plummeting.

Micah winced as he heard Nina's helmeted head slam into the top of the fuselage.

"You okay back there?" he asked as he compensated for the loss of altitude, redlining the drives as the ancient aircraft clawed its way to higher altitude.

He didn't wait for a response. A mental prompt called up Nina's biosig telemetry so he could see for himself that his gunner hadn't broken her neck.

"Spend your leave fighting fires, they said. It'll be fun, they said." Nina's dry comment caused his lips to twitch with amusement while at the same time easing his concerns.

{Closing on location,} he sent, switching their conversation to the ship's combat net. It was the only way they'd be able to communicate, once Nina opened the hatch. *{Fifty meters ahead, in a clearing just below that ridge.}*

{I see them.} Nina sent him a visual.

As he banked the Firestrike toward the ridge, he highlighted the temperature the aircraft's external sensors registered and pushed the data to Nina. *{Hot out there. Be sure you're fully suited before opening that door.}*

{Sir, yes, sir!} came the smart retort, and Micah could feel the eyeroll that accompanied the words.

Thad handled the comms, contacting the trapped firefighters and prepping them for extraction, while Micah concentrated on steadying the craft at the necessary altitude for Nina to drop the ropes to the figures waiting below.

She signaled her readiness, and Micah saw the indicator for the side door flash from green to red as Nina triggered the hatch. The craft's internal temperature rose as hot air billowed into the opening along with the smells of burning timber and hot ash. The deep throated roar of the fire swept in along with it, making it impossible to talk over.

{Foxtrot-Seven, we're sure glad to see you!} The relief in the smokejumper's voice that came over the wire was evident.

{Happy to be able to help. Status?}

{Smoke's done a number on us. Medical nano can't keep up.}

The firefighter's voice cut out, but was soon back. *{Sorry. My partner's femur's broken and I'm a bit banged up. We had to dive off that cliff to keep from being crushed by that tree.}*

{Dropping lines to you now. You see 'em?}

{Connecting to them now.} A brief pause. *{Good to go. Ready to get the hell out of here!}*

Micah's hands and feet worked in tandem with the onboard Synthetic Intelligence, the craft's autopilot automatically deferring to his own pilot's augmentations that superseded its native capabilities. An updraft buffeted the Firestrike, and Micah corrected for it while Thad called out the status of the two firefighters, now airborne and approaching the fuselage.

Nina had the winch cranked to the maximum safe speed, one gloved hand guiding the rope's ascent, the other braced against the aircraft's open frame. Her helmeted head breached the opening as she kept a direct visual on the two they had come to rescue.

A resounding *crack* sounded aft of the Firestrike as a tree exploded, sending limbs rocketing like shrapnel through the air. Micah registered a tree speeding toward them like a wooden javelin at the same time Thad's voice thundered *"Incoming!"* over the sound of the fire.

The Firestrike's SI brain began to lift the vessel, the proper evasion maneuver for an object hurtling toward them—except Micah instantly realized the move would be disastrous for the firemen hanging from the line below.

His hand snapped the controls to the left, overriding the autopilot as he yelled at his crew chief. *{Nina! Head inside! Now!}*

The Firestrike responded, rolling sharply to the left before falling into a slip, moving the rope holding the firemen to one side, instead of up into the path of the blazing spear that was once a pine tree. The crew chief's head fell back, gravity pulling her inside the fuselage just as the pine's fiery trunk shot past. The cloud of debris accompanying the tree peppered the water bladder attached to the Firestrike's belly like miniature missiles, the empty reservoir preventing them from penetrating the fuselage.

He heard Nina's sharp inhale. *{Damn, that was close. Forgot how volatile those trees can be when superheated like that. Thanks, Cap.}*

Micah didn't bother to respond; he was too busy flying the ship. Nina resumed winching the smokejumpers into the Firestrike, the uninjured man assisting his injured partner into the aft of the vessel where medical triage kits were stored.

Blessed coolness returned once Nina resealed the hatch, although the bitter scents of ash and burnt tar lingered. He held the Firestrike as steady as he could, waiting for Nina to confirm their passengers were secured. Scraping sounds from behind told him the gunner was crab-walking back to them, unclipping and reclipping her harness as she went.

After a moment, she called out, *{They're webbed in. Beginning triage. You're good to maneuver, Cap.}*

He sent her a two-click acknowledgment, then pulled up, increasing the ship's rate of climb and sending it back the way they'd come.

The Marine beside him patted the console almost paternally. "Told you she'd get us through. She's got grit." His tone was a blend of confident affection. "Not like a civilian airframe."

Micah's mouth curved into a smile. "Since we'd have been toast—"

"Literally," Nina interjected dryly.

"—in a civvy, I'm not going to argue that one."

"Been a while since you've flown a Firestrike?" Thad cocked his head toward Micah.

Micah shook his head, amazed at how unfazed the other man was by the maelstrom surrounding them. "Yeah. A few years, give or take."

Micah hadn't thought he'd ever find himself flying a Novastrike again. *Firestrike. Whatever.*

The ship he usually flew was much bigger. He'd flown the DAP Helios for several tours. Until a mission to Luyten's Star changed everything.

As if the thought had conjured it, a voice insinuated itself into his mind. *Having fun?*

Micah grunted as a particularly strong shear sent them shooting skyward.

Better'n being stuck inside headquarters, he shot back.

He received the mental impression of a grimace. *Don't remind me.*

Micah had first heard the voice when he'd awakened nine months earlier on a slab in deGrasse's morgue. The person behind the voice had saved Micah's life, helping him to escape those bent on his destruction.

He'd known there was something odd about the voice from the start. It needed no network connection, and it sounded hauntingly familiar. It was only when he'd come face to face—with himself—that reality had set in.

Micah had fallen victim to unethical experimentation. He'd been illegally cloned, without his consent. Worse, he was not the original, though he felt like it. He had the same memories, the same mannerisms, the exact same skills.

But it was *Micah* whose genetic code had been altered. He was the mirror twin. Or, as Thad called him, 2.0.

The process of making him into his own chiral doppelganger had an interesting quantum side effect. Spooky action at a distance entangled the two men, enabling them to communicate telepathically—anytime, anywhere.

He and his other self could share thoughts, feelings, and images. Nothing seemed to break that connection. Shielding didn't affect it. Neither did distance. The only thing that severed it was if one or the other was rendered unconscious.

It was a phenomenon the Alliance was still trying to understand. It was also a capability the Geminate Navy had decided was best hidden from the known worlds.

Officially, there was only one Jonathan Micah Case. Unofficially, there were two. One remained at headquarters, while the other deployed.

Not only did that serve to hide his existence from others, it also gave the team an edge that others lacked—constant contact with an untraceable, unassailable resource.

Today had been Micah's first opportunity to get away from the base in a month. It was Jonathan's turn to remain back at the black site, the place Micah now called home.

And instead of finding myself a nice, quiet beach and enjoying the sand and the surf, I get talked into another suicide mission.

A chuckle inside his head reminded him that his thoughts were no longer exclusively his own.

We love this shit, and you know it, so quit complaining. You're in the air, under blue skies—

Hardly, he shot back, a quick glance at the forward holoscreen showing nothing but smoke and flames.

Stow it, bro. You can't fool me.

An unwilling grin tugged at Micah's lips. This flight was right up there with some of the most dangerous missions he'd ever flown.

Jonathan was right; he—*they*—loved it.

Forty-five minutes later, Micah brought the Firestrike to a rest, wheels gently kissing the tarmac at Mount Huntington Aviation. On-staff medics were standing by to receive the two smokejumpers, both of whom had already received meds and nano for smoke inhalation and blood-clotting.

Micah hopped out and began to shrug out of his fire-retardant flight suit. He let the arms flap behind him as he joined Nina at the vessel's side entrance and began restocking the medical supplies the medics had brought along with them.

Movement behind the medics caught his eye, and he saw the sleek form of a large cat emerge from the tree line. It came streaking toward them across the clearing.

A piercing whistle split the air moments later, a heads-up from the tower. The cat's ears flattened in annoyance, but he didn't break his loping stride. Thad pivoted at the sound, and then erupted in a string of low curses when he saw the animal arrowing toward them.

Micah smothered a laugh at the Marine's reaction. "Let me

guess," he said, stepping up beside Thad and clapping him on the shoulder. "You still owe him some steaks, and he's here to collect."

"Damn extortionist," Thad muttered.

The black panther closing on them was a working cat, trained to attack targets and identify hidden threats. Pascal had been allowed to come along as a reward for the work he'd done on their last mission. Like Micah, he was the product of an illegal cloning. Pascal was Joule's mirror twin. The panther's brain was as entangled with his twin as Micah's was with Jonathan.

The scientist responsible for their chirality hadn't let ethics stand in the way of the implants he'd inserted into the animals' brains. The simple E-V circuitry allowed for limited range communication. The panthers didn't often make use of them... except when working, to acknowledge their handlers' instructions.

Or to needle certain humans, like Thad.

Pascal slowed to a prowl, chuffing as he drew to a stop in front of them.

{Deal's a deal,} Micah heard the cat say as he lifted baleful green eyes to Thad. *{Fifty steaks. I've had three.}*

Thad's eyes narrowed, and he jabbed a finger toward the large animal. "You've had six, you mangy bastard."

{Too small. Had to double up,} the cat replied, batting away Thad's finger with a massive paw.

An exaggerated cough erupted from Nina, causing the man to pivot and pin her with the kind of glare only a Marine captain could dish out.

"You have something to say, Chief?" he demanded.

Micah cupped a hand over his mouth and turned to the side as Nina straightened into a mock semblance of attention.

"Sir, yes sir," she said. "Just wondering if the captain bothered to negotiate the size of those steaks before he entered into the agreement, sir."

One of the medics paused on her way past. "Chief's got you there, Thad," the woman said. Nodding to the black cat, she added, "Pascal's a pretty savvy negotiator. He's already conned Cook out of ten kilos of bison jerky and two bags of catnip."

"Catnip?" Micah's brows rose. He turned to face Pascal. "I didn't know panthers liked catnip."

{Not a panther,} Pascal responded.

Micah's brow furrowed in confusion. "What?"

The medic tilted her head to indicate the ranger station. "A Huntington park ranger dropped by while you guys were rescuing the smokejumpers. Took one look and recognized Pascal's build and markings."

{Ceriban hunting cat,} the cat under scrutiny supplied, and then slitted his eyes at Thad once more. *{Require **lots** of fresh meat. More than panthers. Deal's now for seventy-five steaks.}*

"Whoa, hoss, hold on there just a goddam minute." Thad crossed his arms and stared down at the big animal. "Ain't nobody ever told you? You can't renegotiate a contract after the fact."

{Was negotiated based on panther intake.} Pascal gave the big Marine the feline-equivalent of a smirk. *{Ceriban hunting cats require more calories.}*

Thad glowered at Pascal for another few seconds, and then turned on his heel and marched toward the ranger's building.

The whine of an approaching aircraft had Micah scanning the skies. Nothing showed over the treeline, though he could tell by the sound that it was an incoming Firestrike.

His gaze settled at the far end of the runway, where he could see a steady stream of drones alighting beside the tanks of fire-retardant nanofoam. As soon as their payload was full, they were up again, heading back out to the front line, to coat unburnt brush and trees, doing their best to deny the raging beast the fuel it needed to sustain its fire.

His view of the departing drones was obscured by the appearance of a Firestrike that matched the one he'd flown. He lifted a hand in greeting as it neared, and then turned to rack his helmet behind the pilot's seat before triggering the hatch closed once more. The cockpit's windlace sighed shut just as the

Firestrike carrying the other half of Task Force Blue's flight crew touched down a dozen meters to his right.

A gust of warm air greeted him, kicked up by the vessel's landing. It brought with it a fresh wave of ash and burning wood, the scents mingling with the smells of dinner someone had scared up for the hungry, returning crews.

As he glanced over, the second Firestrike's side doors cracked open and disgorged two figures. The first was the team's flight engineer and crew chief. Will's sandy hair glinted in the Ceriba sunlight as he turned to do a post-flight walkaround of his bird.

The other pulled her pilot's helmet off, releasing a cascade of blue-black hair, before setting it back onto the pilot's seat. Her body fairly buzzing with energy, Yuki grabbed the handholds inset into the frame of the aircraft and hauled herself up to inspect the air intake on the modified turbofan motor that had been added when the craft was converted to atmospheric flight.

Hey, bro. Jonathan's voice broke in. *The colonel wants the team back up here, ASAP. Says it's urgent.*

Micah's gaze swung back to Thad. Although Micah captained the vessel that flew the task force to its missions, the team itself was under Thad's command. The Marine's expression indicated he'd intercepted a similar message.

He caught Micah's glance and nodded once.

Yeah, looks like someone's just given Thad the head's up, too, he told his other self. *We're on our way.*

He looked over at Nina. The gunner pushed her hair back from a soot-covered face, an equally grimy hand trailing a smear up one cheek, into the hairline of her unruly, red hair.

How urgent is it? he added. *We're not exactly spit-shined here.*

Amusement surged over their connection. *You smell like a campfire, you mean?*

Been there, done that. Almost got skewered for our trouble, too. He sent Jonathan a mental snapshot of the fiery conifer-turned-javelin that had tried to take them out.

A low mental whistle was the other man's reply. *I'll tell them you need twenty minutes once you arrive to make yourselves presentable.*

Micah pushed a mental thanks toward his twin and turned back to the Firestrike to complete his own post-flight. Fifteen minutes later, the bird was as clean as they could make it; the aviation company's cleaning crews would take care of checking the drives, restocking the ship's stores, and ensuring all air intakes were clear of ash prior to its next flight.

"You ready, sir?" Nina asked as she shouldered a duffel from the back of the Firestrike. She nodded toward the ranger station. "Transport just pulled up."

Micah nodded at the other Firestrike. "I'll grab Yuki and Will." He waved her on. "Don't let them leave without us."

"You got it." She hefted the duffel higher on her well-muscled shoulder and walked toward the building that Mount Huntington Aviation called home.

Several minutes later, they were watching the ranger station recede into the distance as the transport headed south toward Ceriba's capital city of St. Clair Township.

As they left the forest range behind, Micah could see the wildfire's dense, black cloud base, formed from hot embers and ash. Topping it was a seething column of clouds with a plumed top that flattened where it hit Ceriba's jet stream.

"You do take us to the nicest places, Cap." Yuki's eyes were fixed on the burnt landscape.

"Yeah, but it's good to know we're contributing, even if it's just in a small way, to beating that monster into submission," countered Nina.

Will's smile was brief. The flight engineer was by far the quietest member of the team, but he more than made up for it by being the best damn mechanic ever to work on a Helios.

"I don't think those two smokejumpers would call your contribution today insignificant," he protested in a mild voice. His gaze turned from the view out the transport's window to favor Nina with a raised brow.

Nina shrugged. "Still, wish we'd been able to stick around until that bastard was fully beaten down."

"We'd be done by now anyway," Thad said. He was stretched out several rows in front of them, cap drawn down low over his eyes, his head resting on Pascal's flank. "Air attack just announced containment. Only thing left is to take care of hotspots for the next few hours."

He pulled himself up, settling his cap back onto his head as he eyed Nina. "That's mainly drone work, *cher,* plus SI and human crews following up to spot-check. Besides," he added, settling his head back down onto Pascal's flank and ignoring the hunting cat's grunt, "something tells me we have a much bigger fire to put out than the one we just left."

COMPLICATIONS

NATIONAL SECURITY AGENCY
PARLIAMENT HOUSE
ST. CLAIR TOWNSHIP, CERIBA

DUNCAN CUTTER'S ASSISTANT had just shown up at his office with lunch when a comm request came in from Valenti.

"Thanks, Rob," he said. "Just set it down, and I'll get to it in a few."

Rob hefted the wrap in his hand. "Just so you know, this isn't just any sandwich," he told Duncan. "It's Chef's signature. Ceriban quail smothered in chutney made from real night-blooming mockberries. It was their last one, and I had to fight Senator Regier for it."

Duncan held up a hand. "I appreciate it, believe me. But this is important."

Rob shot him a pointed look as he set the wrap and a container of water on the corner of Duncan's desk. "Everything's important. Can't recall the last time you ate a lunch that required two hands, sir. Just saying."

"Hazard of the job, Rob."

His assistant dipped his head, acknowledging that fact as he backed out of the room and left Duncan alone.

With a longing look at the wrap, Duncan reached for the water as he accepted Valenti's ping. As hungry as he was, he refused to chew in someone else's ear, even if it was over the wire.

You'd think, after twelve years at this job, I'd be used to it by now, he thought. *Rob's right. Someday, I'm going to find time to eat a lunch that requires a knife and fork....*

Valenti's avatar popped up on his overlay, joined seconds later by Amara Toland. He sent them both a quick mental greeting as he uncapped his water and took a long drink.

{Just wanted you to know the team should be arriving at the base within the hour,} Valenti sent. *{Are you free to join?}*

{Hang on. Let me check.} He set the water down as he pulled up his calendar. He'd have to rearrange a few meetings, but it was doable.

{I'll be there.}

{I won't be,} Toland said. *{I may have a lead on those four vials. I'm going to chase it down. I'll send you whatever I find.}*

Duncan paused, water halfway to his mouth once more. *{Hold on. You said **four** vials?}*

{That's what Doctor Moran's report indicated. Why?}

His eyes narrowed as his mind worked furiously to recall the image he'd seen in the SCIF earlier that day.

{Pull up the feed Ladue sent,} he instructed Valenti. *{Take a good look at that closeup he captured of the case. Tell me what you see.}*

The colonel's avatar froze, and Duncan could tell she'd put them on hold. Moments later, an icon flashed on his overlay. It was an image capture of the open case.

Three vials rested within, the hazardous materials icon prominently displayed on each.

He heard Toland's swift intake of breath.

{It seems we have two problems on our hands,} he told them, eyes glued to the frozen image. *{If the Akkadians only have three*

vials, then where's the fourth one?}

TEMPTATION

HACKER BAR
OUTSKIRTS OF TOWN
ST. CLAIR TOWNSHIP, CERIBA

THE THIEF SPIED the hacker the moment he stepped inside the underground speakeasy. He waited for her to see him before moving in her direction. Her eyes widened a fraction in recognition, and she raised her glass in greeting.

Tilting his chin in acknowledgment, he let his gaze sweep the darkened area until he found a server. He caught the woman's attention and waited for her to navigate her way through the crowd to where he stood.

Leaning in so that she could hear him over the pulsing music, he placed his order and then pointed to the table where the hacker sat. Flipping the credit chit he held in his hand so that its smooth surface caught the light, he proffered it with a flourish so that she could scan it.

Seconds later, he'd crossed the room. Smiling, he slid into the booth beside the hacker. "So, how'd the handoff go down?" he asked by way of greeting.

"The package for the pharmaceutical company, you mean?"

At his nod, she tossed back the last of her drink and set the glass down onto the table with a decisive thud.

"Slicker than shit," she bragged. She interlaced her hands behind her head and leaned back with a proud grin. She waggled an elbow in the direction of the bar. "Saw you stopping the waiter. Didn't happen to order me one, did ya?"

He nodded. "I did. Ordered an entire pitcher, in fact. Thought you might be in the mood to celebrate."

He saw her eyes narrow in suspicion as she dropped her arms. He grinned and with the flick of a hand, held the chit up between his fingers for her to see. "It just so happens that I came into a bit of a windfall today, so I thought I'd do the honors."

She squinted at the stolen chit he'd lifted from some hapless pedestrian, and then reached for it. He pulled it from her grasp.

"How long before they notice it's missing?" she asked.

He buried his annoyance at her implied slight behind another blinding grin. "Oh, it's not missing, luv. I cloned some fool's unprotected credit chit."

"What in the stars was someone doing with one of those?"

The chit went spinning into the air as he flipped it. Just as quickly, he snatched it back, fingers curving around it possessively.

"My guess, something illegal he didn't want traced back to his ID token, otherwise it woulda been encrypted. So, see? You could say I was just doing my part to keep crime off the streets."

She settled back with an amused look. "Well, then. I accept your offer to foot the bill for this little celebration." She inclined her head as if she were bestowing some great privilege upon him.

Ignoring her airs, he leaned forward, bracing his forearms on the table. "So, those government types over at the CID never caught on that someone nipped their package?"

Her expression turned smug. "You were with me," she said, her voice breezily confident as she nudged him on the shoulder.

"You saw, same as I did. It went off without a hitch."

His brows drew down. "Initially, yeah, but this is the Centers for Infectious Diseases we're talking here."

The hacker sat up, offended. "So what? Did you think they had some sort of tracker embedded in the case the vials were in that I wouldn't catch?"

"Well…maybe," he admitted.

She shrugged. "The shipment was legit. There really was a package scheduled for pickup by the courier service that day," she reminded him. "You were in the delivery van with me. You saw the dispatch come through for it. You saw me go in and bring it back out. What's with the third degree?"

He lifted a placating palm. "Just curious, is all. You usually don't go for the jobs that require anything beyond cracking into a server and moving electronic shit around. Hell, I rarely see you outside your studio. I just wondered what made you break your routine."

She slitted her eyes as she leaned into him. "Credits," she hissed, her voice low. "Lots and lots of them."

She broke off as the server approached, pitcher in hand. It wasn't until they were alone once more and he'd poured them both a drink that she continued.

"It might have been outside my standard portfolio, but it's not something I've never done before," she added, and he heard the asperity in her voice that warned him to back off. "It was easy enough to hack into the delivery company's database, add myself to their roster, and assign the job to me. The transport was waiting for me, keyed to my forged employee ID. Passing the package off to Brower Biologic's agent was even easier. They had a substitute package ready. I just added it to the delivery pile, and then walked off the job."

She paused to take a sip of her drink. He felt her studying him as he fiddled with the credit chit. "He got the package, I got the credits, end of story. So why don't you tell me what this is really about, hmm?"

Still, he was reluctant. "And no one opened the case? No one scanned the contents, or questioned what was inside? They were satisfied with what you delivered?" he persisted.

"Jake, what is *wrong* with you?" she snapped, setting her drink down a little harder than necessary.

The thief pulled his hand out from his jacket, cupping an object that he waggled in front of his friend's face. "Well, if they're satisfied, then it's unlikely they'll care that I helped myself to one of these, then."

She sat up abruptly and hissed, "Holy shit, you *stole* from me?"

She swiped at the vial, but he jerked it away from her grasp, pocketing it once more.

"When? How—?" She sagged back in her seat, scowling at him. "It was when I handed you the case, wasn't it? When you placed it in the storage locker in the back of the delivery transport."

He nodded once. "Thanks for letting me tag along." He pitched his voice low and let admiration seep into his tone. "It was a real rush, watching you work."

Her ego had always been her weak spot; she was so easy to manipulate. This time proved no different.

She preened under his compliment, anger melting away, as he knew it would. "What are you going to do with it?" she asked grudgingly.

The thief shrugged. "I found a buyer. Want in?"

* * *

The next morning found Jake seated in his ship's cockpit, staring at his face on the forward screen. Except it looked nothing like him, and was menacing as hell. Intimidating enough that *he'd* think twice about crossing himself. He turned his head, and the image on the holo did the same.

"So, you think he'll buy it?" he asked.

As he watched, the image in the holoscreen before him parroted the words back.

He heard an inelegant snort come through over the connection. *{I'm the best,}* the hacker reminded him, and he could hear the self-assuredness in her tone. *{He won't have any way of tracing the ping, and he certainly won't know that the image on his holo isn't of you. Relax. You've got this.}*

Jake grimaced, the image before him mirroring his actions. "Okay, then. Well, wish me luck. I'm pinging him now."

He used the encrypted, untraceable connection the hacker had set up for him to connect to the Drug Lord.

Self-styled 'Drug Lord', he reminded himself with a sardonic twist to his lips. *Guy's a legend in his own mind. Who would name themselves something like that, anyway?*

An SI answered on the other end. The thief introduced himself—using his alias—and let the SI know he had valuable material the Drug Lord would want to have.

After a few moments spent haggling, with the hacker lurking in the background and listening to the entire exchange, the SI agreed to put him through to the Drug Lord's properties manager.

A thin-faced woman appeared on the holo, impatience etched into her visage. *{What do you want?}* she demanded.

The thief didn't respond. He merely lifted the vial in one hand, the hazardous material icon clearly visible to the holorecorder.

The woman's expression morphed from irritation to curiosity, and the thief knew she was hooked.

{What is it?} she asked.

The thief waggled the cylinder in his hand. "Something the CID's been studying," he grunted out, pitching his voice a half octave lower than his normal speaking voice.

{Cut it out,} the hacker hissed. *{My program's compensating for your speech pattern, too. Now just act normal. Well, whatever your normal is, anyway.}*

The thief cleared his throat and realized belatedly that the hacker's comment had distracted him, and he'd missed the woman's response.

She pressed her lips together and shook her head. *{Don't need any government trouble coming down upon us, not to mention the shit they're messing with in there is just as likely to kill you as not. No thanks.}*

She reached to disconnect, and he quickly raised a hand.

"It's also something a pharmaceutical company went to a lot of trouble to acquire," he rushed to say. "They paid big money to get their hands on three vials of this stuff. I...liberated...the fourth before they took delivery."

He saw the woman's eyes narrow at this, and he abruptly regretted his momentary lapse into honesty. If the hacker's sharp comment over his wire was any indication, she thought it was a particularly stupid move herself.

That was all quickly forgotten at the woman's next words.

{How much do you want for it?}

"Thirty million creds." He managed to hang onto his stoic expression even in the face of her derisive laughter.

{I see you have a sense of humor,} she replied. Amusement fled, and her eyes went dead. *{No.}*

He shrugged and, with a bravado he didn't feel, said, "Okay, then. Give me a counteroffer."

After several minutes of haggling, they agreed upon a price, provided the thief was able to deliver the vial's provenance.

That had taken him aback, and only a quick mental reassurance from the hacker had allowed him to keep his equanimity as he agreed to the properties manager's demands.

"Very good," he said. "Where and when would you like to make the exchange?"

The woman thought a moment. *{I can have someone at the Starshot buoy at the one-AU mark from Ceriba, toward the Klintis belt, by tomorrow, fifteen hundred local.}*

The thief considered his response. "That'll work. My man will be in a small, private runabout with this tail number."

He rattled off the number of one of the 'burner' transponders he'd had made, and the woman nodded.

{Until then.}

The comm signal severed, and the thief sat back with a sigh.

{See? Told you.} The hacker's confident voice surged inside his head. *{Don't forget. I get twenty percent, up front.}*

He sent her a breezy smile. "No worries, I have your account info. The minute the credits clear, they'll be transferred to you." He held up a hand. "Honest."

A sarcastic laugh was her only reply. *{Good thing I didn't invest a lot of time into your avatar. Just remember, it's as easy for me to undo that work and send them your real ID as it is for me to keep it hidden from them.}*

Jake blanched at the thought of the Drug Lord's people discovering his fabrication, but then mentally shrugged it off. The person the hacker thought he was didn't exist, either, so what did it really matter?

He was adept at slipping through the cracks and disappearing. If trouble found him, he'd simply disappear until things blew over and he could reinvent himself once more.

* * *

The thief had to disengage his drive's safety interlocks, redlining the ship in order to make it to the Starshot buoy in time for the rendezvous. To take his mind off his current circumstances—enduring ten-*gs* of acceleration wasn't much fun, even with his pilot's mods—he focused his attention on the elaborate security lock sealing the vial.

The vial itself was locked tightly into a protective vault, cushioned to withstand the forces exerted upon it. His wire was connected to nanofilaments he'd threaded through the vault, allowing him access to the vial's encrypted seal.

He fancied himself somewhat of an expert safecracker, and the vial was proving to be a fascinating challenge. He applied various combinations to no avail, but thought he might have just hit on the right combination of programming cues.

He dropped the nanopackage onto the seal just as his ship's sensors detected a Mercer Mining tug turning its nose ponderously toward the buoy. Moments later, the vessel was hailing him.

{Runabout seven-hotel-victor, any news on the championship game's score?}

The code-word challenge was just as the properties manager said it would be.

He replied in kind. "Nothing yet, sorry to say. Last I heard, it wasn't looking good for the Merki Meerkats, though."

Not for the first time did he wonder what in the stars a meerkat was, but the thought was a fleeting one, quickly forgotten as he dove into the intricacies of bleeding off speed and matching velocities with the other ship.

Hours later, the tug latched onto his small runabout and began inexorably hauling it in. He wisely chose to allow the beefier machine to handle synching the hatches. As he waited, he ran his thumb over the top of the vial as he'd done countless times.

His heart lurched when the lid moved.

Holy shit, that last app combo worked!

He peered closely at the glass container; the material inside looked like nothing more than distilled water. Curiosity overcame him.

{Hey, you said this stuff was harmless, right? Whatever's in it is totally inert?} He sent the thought privately along the encrypted channel the hacker had set up with him.

{Yes,} came her guarded response. *{Why?}*

He sent her a mental shrug as he uncapped the vial and looked inside. He was surprised to see the interior was separated into two partitions, an inner and outer chamber.

He thought about trying to hack the seal on the inner compartment, too, but thought better of it. What if the two liquids became volatile when mixed?

He dribbled a few drops onto the console in front of him. Nothing happened. He brought it to his nose and sniffed. Still nothing. Disappointed, he recapped the glass cylinder.

{Just wanted to reassure the buyer that it's safe to transport is

all,} he told her.

She cursed and sent him a vicious mental shove. *{Were you messing with it again?}*

{What do you mean, 'again'?} he asked.

{I saw you playing with it that night at the speakeasy,} she said. *{You were rubbing your thumb along the top like a worry-stone. What'd you do, try some of your lock-picking programs to see if you could crack the seal?}*

When he didn't respond, she groaned. *{You did, didn't you. Stars, please tell me you didn't use something as ham-handed as a Crowbar.}*

{Of course not,} he shot back, offended that she would suggest such a thing. *{My apps are much more sophisticated than that.}*

{Well, you'd better reseal it, fast, and pray they don't notice. They might suspect you contaminated it.}

The thief swore when a blinking icon appeared on his overlay, indicating the tug's hatch was cycling.

He ordered his safecracking app to rebuild the seal he'd just undone. Just as a thunderous pounding sounded on the outside of his own hatch, the app pinged, informing him the reprogramming was complete.

He examined it closely, pleased the vial showed no evidence of tampering. *{Okay, here goes nothing. I'm unsealing the hatch.}*

* * *

Fifteen minutes later, the ships had separated, the thief ten million credits richer—less the hacker's twenty percent. He breathed a sigh of relief, feeling almost giddy at his own success.

He punched up the local news net, and the holo flared to life. Emblazoned upon the screen was an advertisement for a cruise through the Atlieka Rapids on a luxury yacht run by Royal Ceriban Cruise Lines.

Leaning back in the pilot's seat, he interlaced his fingers, cracked his knuckles, and grinned. "I could use a vacation," he mused. "Now that, right there, is the proper way to celebrate a windfall."

He sat up, and with great relish, had the ship's net connect to the reservations line at Royal Ceriba.

BRIEFING

HUMBOLT BASE
GEOSTATIONARY ORBIT, CERIBA

MICAH DIDN'T OFTEN get ferried around in a Navy pinnace sent specifically to escort him to base. He had to admit, this was a far more efficient way to get back to Humbolt than hitching a ride on a shuttle, or taking the elevator.

If Jonathan hadn't already let him know the situation was urgent, the pinnace sitting hot on the spaceport's tarmac would have clued him in. He could tell the way they were being routed that the pinnace was being given a priority slot.

They shed Ceriba's atmosphere, slipping into Humbolt's controlled space in record time. From there, it was a short jaunt past the imaginary line that separated the station's commercial side from its military operations area and into the Navy's docking bay.

{Pinwheel-One, Humbolt Base.} Micah heard the local traffic controller contact the pinnace's pilot over the base's spaceport comm frequency. *{Cleared to Echo-Three.}*

The ship began to move gently forward, their pilot nudging them on thrusters in the direction indicated.

As the pinnace taxied to its berth, they began to gather their gear. Nina shouldered her kit while Yuki arched her back to work out the kinks.

The minute the pinnace settled into its cradle, the hatch cycled open. Thad stood with a groan and Pascal pushed past, flowing down the ramp and out onto Humbolt's dock.

Will shoved to his feet. "If that cat's not careful, he's going to get shot by some freaked-out airman." He ducked out of the pinnace to follow, Nina and Yuki at his heels.

Thad moved to the hatch, his big frame blocking the view of the bay just beyond. Shooting a look over his shoulder, he asked, "Comin', Navy?"

Micah nodded. *{Any idea what's awaiting us?}* he sent privately as the Marine's feet landed with a thump on the sole of the deck.

Thad grunted. *{Nothin' good, ami,}* he replied as they headed for the bay doors.

They lapsed into a silence that continued until they hit a restricted area deep inside Humbolt Base, reserved for the men and women of the Special Reconnaissance Unit. A security SI stopped them at the entrance.

Micah felt his heart kick a little faster, as it always did when his ID token was challenged at these security checkpoints. He knew his clearance had come from the highest level within the Alliance, but still, it was a forgery. There was only one Jonathan Micah Case.

He passed through, as he always did. The amused look Thad slid him told Micah his tension had not gone unnoticed.

{Quit being an asshole,} he grumbled.

{Quit freaking out every time you pass through security, Navy. You're not a fraud.}

{No,} came his acerbic response, *{just a freak of nature.}*

Thad shot him a mental eyeroll. *{Freak of **science**, hoss. Get it right.}*

They slowed as they approached the next checkpoint, buried deep inside the SRU. A shadow detached itself from the bulkhead. The soldier was dressed in Navy greys that sported a holopatch on its right sleeve. It was the SRU's seal, a stylized carbyne blade embedded in a flame. It confirmed she belonged inside this restricted zone.

This base of operations was within a sector so classified, it was categorized as a black site. It was the home of Task Force Blue.

Aside from the warriors billeted there, the people cleared to enter the area were few. All reported directly to Colonel Tala Valenti. She, in turn, reported directly to Duncan Cutter.

"Sirs." The lieutenant nodded respectfully. Her security token challenged theirs, and when they cleared, she gestured down the passageway. "The colonel's in the SCIF. Director Cutter's on his way. ETA, fifteen minutes."

"Thanks, LT," Micah replied.

Thad clapped him on the shoulder, waved his hand in the air, and gave an exaggerated cough. "C'mon Navy, let's get you cleaned up before you set off the base's smoke alarms."

"Not looking too pretty yourself there, jarhead."

Thad swallowed a laugh as they jogged toward TF Blue's housing.

Took you long enough. Jonathan's voice popped into his head. *Valenti's getting impatient.*

As if he knew Micah and Jonathan were mentally conversing, Thad's head swung his direction when they approached his quarters. "That lazy-ass flyboy on the other end of that woo-woo connection not telling you anything?"

Micah shook his head, pausing two doors down. "Nothing, sorry."

Thad shrugged. "Guess we'll find out soon enough, *ami.* Fifteen minutes," the Marine drawled, pointing a meaty finger in his direction. "Don't be late."

After a quick but much-needed shower, Micah slipped into the SCIF room behind Thad. A quick glance around told him the only other team members in on the meeting were the 'lazy-ass flyboy' and Thad's second, Gabriel Alvarez.

Gabe's eyes collided with his, and they exchanged a brief nod. Micah had met the former NCIC special agent nine months earlier, at the receiving end of the other man's weapon.

The naval investigator had been annoyed to learn he'd been played. The enemy had given Gabe false information, leading the then-agent to believe Micah was a wanted criminal. Gabe had cornered Micah at a critical moment, and they'd nearly lost one of their own in the process.

Both Gabe and Micah were determined that Akkadia would someday pay for that, one way or another.

Micah's gaze traveled past Gabe to where the colonel sat. He gave a respectful nod before making his way around the table. As Micah slid into his seat, he spared Jonathan a look and saw lines of pain bracketing his mouth.

Shoulder bothering you again?

Jonathan's eyelids flickered. *Leave it.*

Two weeks earlier, it had been Micah's turn to stay behind while his twin deployed. Jonathan had taken several rounds while providing covering fire for a hot extraction of an SRU team. He'd continued to return fire, bracing himself against the inside of *Wraith*'s hatch until every operative was aboard.

The team's medic had stabilized him during the return flight, but the wound had done enough damage that Navy surgeons had suggested simply growing a new limb.

Jonathan had refused.

Maybe you should take their advice, have them replace it, like they did your legs?

Jonathan's response was immediate, his words causing Micah to flinch.

I think they've cloned enough of me as it is, don't you?

The words hung there between them as the silence lengthened. Micah kept his expression neutral, but he could see guilt begin to play over Jonathan's face.

Shit. Didn't mean it like that. Sorry. Jonathan's voice was tinged with regret.

Just then, Duncan Cutter entered the room, bringing their mental conversation to a halt. With him was Admiral Toland and Captain Addy Moran, deGrasse's former chief surgeon. Upon their return to Procyon, Admiral Toland had added Addy to Project Rufus as its chief medical advisor. Together, their job was to pick up the shattered pieces of deGrasse's chiral research and make sense of it.

"Thanks for coming," Cutter said as the doors shut behind him.

The moment they sealed, Micah's connection to the base's military net was severed. The SCIF was active.

"The admiral is here to update us on a developing situation," the director told them.

The room's holoscreen flickered on. An image appeared of a container filled with metal cylinders. Each cylinder was marked with a hazardous materials icon.

"Admiral?" Cutter invited, waving a hand toward the screen.

Toland studied the visual for a moment before turning to face those assembled.

"As you may know, everything we brought back from Luyten's Star is at the Center for Infectious Diseases in nearby Montpelier," she said. "We have dedicated labs running tests on the material we were able to salvage. Some experiments can't be conducted planetside, however, so I sent a small team of trusted personnel to Hawking to set up a smaller, remote testing center."

She gestured to the screen. "Inside each cylinder is a glass vial filled with chiral material. They were supposed to be delivered by special courier today. The package never arrived."

Shock flooded Micah. "You're telling me we've misplaced chiral material?"

Toland nodded, her gaze shifting between Micah and Jonathan, her expression carefully blank.

"I take it this is more than a shipping mix-up, since we're here," Gabe said, shooting Micah a warning glance.

Micah could tell the former special agent half expected him to blow up at the doctor, and was ready to step in to defuse it if necessary.

Toland shook her head. "We checked, and there was no mix-up. Someone hacked the shipping company and stole the package."

Gabe nodded to the holo. "Did your team take that photo before the vials were packaged up, then, to document its contents?"

"No." Valenti gestured to the holoscreen. "That was taken yesterday, at Leavitt Station."

The image was replaced by another, this one showing a man in a Navy uniform, handing the case to a stranger in civilian dress.

"That person is a known Akkadian spy. The agent did not make it out alive."

Shit, brother. This is bad.

Micah nodded absently in agreement, eyes riveted on the hazardous materials icon emblazoned on each vial. "Is there any reason other than the obvious why you'd have them labeled hazardous?" he asked.

Toland flicked a glance at Cutter, who nodded for her to continue. She did, her expression clearly unhappy.

"These vials should contain nothing more than chiral samples, held in suspension, but there was a glitch in the labs' security feeds the day the samples were packaged up. It's probably nothing. Still, I'm having my people reconfirm which vials were shipped so we know for certain what material the Akkadians have."

Thad leaned forward. "Excuse me, Admiral, but that sounds like you're worried something bad got loose. What kind of experiments are you running over there?"

Micah looked over at Valenti and Cutter. Neither looked surprised by this. His gaze shifted to Toland when she spoke.

"The vials scheduled to be sent were straightforward samples," she told Thad. "Protein chains. DNA strands. But until we've run a full audit, I can't rule out the possibility they contain something a bit more complex."

"Complex, as in…?" Gabe asked.

"Depending on which lab the vials came from, they could contain supraparticles, or… something else."

Gabe lifted a brow. "Supra…?"

"A supraparticle is a grouping of nanoparticles that bind together to form a larger, more defined structure."

Gabe's expression turned thoughtful. "That sounds almost like you're building something with them."

Something shifted in Toland's expression.

Disbelief coursed through Micah when she didn't deny it. He rounded on Cutter. "*Building* something?"

Jonathan's angry voice cut in. "What, like cloning? You told us you'd shut down Stinton's research."

Valenti's hand slashed through the air. "Captains," her voice held a note of warning.

"It's not what you think," Addy said into the silence. Her eyes met Micah's, the expression in them equal parts frustration and entreaty. "Look, I'm a surgeon, not a scientist. The admiral would be better at explaining this from a scientific point of view, but I can tell you from a *medical* point of view why this is important."

He nodded for her to continue.

"If we're to understand what happened to you, we need to study how the chiral bias transfers from the molecular level up the chain, until the biological process takes over," she told him. "It's the only way we can determine where and how entanglement occurred during chiral cloning."

Jonathan leaned forward, his jaw jutting out angrily. "Why? So you can entangle more subjects?"

Addy shot him an exasperated look. "No, so we can understand how that process might impact you and the other chiral pairs. What if one of you were to—" she faltered.

"Die." Micah dropped the word into the sudden silence.

Addy's lips firmed as she nodded.

Toland took up the explanation. "Yes, we're looking into replicating the method of entanglement. But, *but*," she emphasized, talking over the incipient protests, "only at a microscopic level. We're working with organisms, genetic sequences, not emergent complex systems."

"Emergent complex—" Thad started.

Toland's eyes cut to him. "Life," she stated flatly. "Project Rufus has two mandates. We've been charged with trying to reverse-engineer Stinton's research, but we're also working to find a means to use this knowledge in ethical, beneficial ways." She nodded to the image of the vials. "Doctor Travis had an idea. Those vials are the result."

"*Sam* did this?" Micah asked, incredulous. "She'd never—"

"Science itself is not inherently bad. It's how you apply what you've learned that has that potential. Don't ever conflate what Stinton did with what we're doing here," Addy interrupted him, her tone sharp. "We're working at the cellular level, not to recreate living organisms. The material in those vials represents a potential way to save lives under battlefield conditions."

Valenti braced her forearms on the table, hands clasped. "How so, Captain?"

Addy fell silent a moment, gathering her thoughts.

"When a patient needs delicate surgery, the kind that requires nano repair techniques, the first step we take is to order a bio-ink that's genetically identical to the patient," she said. "We then use that ink to 3D-print nano repair bots unique to that individual. That way, I'm able to heal the damage without the patient's immune system fighting against me, or rejecting the bots as foreign substances. Are you with me so far?"

"Yes, but—" Micah began, but Addy overrode him.

"In triage situations, that's an impossibility. A corpsman trying to stop a soldier from bleeding out on the deck of a ship doesn't have the luxury of ordering out." Her voice took on a hard edge. "There's no bioidentical match, no 3D printer to spit out nice, compatible nanomachines on a battlefield."

She pointed a finger at the image on the holoscreen. "The

material inside those vials holds the promise of the next best thing."

She paused as if to allow the significance of what she had just said to sink in. After a moment, she continued.

"You all know the basics of chirality. You understand the concepts of handedness and mirror molecules. But you need to also understand how the human body reacts to chirally altered organisms. Chirality gives a pathogen immunity in the natural world, and vice versa.

"As the only chiral person in existence, Micah cannot be infected by a natural virus. By contrast, any mirror virus that could infect him can't hurt any of us. There is a mutual incompatibility. And while chiral bacteria can still replicate, it'll eventually die out, because the sugars they feed on are indigestible. They'll end up starving to death."

"But if they can't hurt their mirror counterparts, why bother studying them?" Jonathan asked.

"Chiral supraparticles offer a protective casing that not only stands up against the body's immune system, but confuses it long enough for the supra shell to deliver its payload of nano repair units directly to the wounded site. Get something like that into a medical corpsman's hands, and I guarantee you we can drastically reduce the number of lives lost."

There was silence as everyone digested what she'd just said.

Finally, Valenti nodded. "Thank you, Captain."

Addy returned the nod and settled back into her seat.

After a beat of silence, Gabe asked, "Okay, then, now for the elephant in the room." He looked up at the image displayed on the holoscreen. "What is the extent of the damage Akkadia can do if they get their hands on supraparticles instead of the raw material?"

Thad leaned forward, squinting at Gabe. "You talking biochemical warfare, *ami*?"

When Gabe nodded silently, Thad then turned his squint to the admiral, who sighed and leaned forward again.

"Depending on what was actually in those vials, that is a

possibility," Toland admitted. "It goes back to how an object can be used either for good or evil. That same supra shell that delivers healing nanobots could just as easily be used as a delivery system for something harmful."

"Like...?" Thad prodded.

"Like a deadly pathogen."

The words dropped like a miniature bomb into the room.

Gabe leaned forward. "Keep going, ma'am. But simple language, please. Something even a government lackey like me can understand."

Micah saw Toland's lips curve in a brief smile at Gabe's words.

"You know what a pathogen is. It could be a virus or bacteria, or another agent of infection. A supraparticle could act like a shield, hiding such a pathogen from detection. And if the supraparticle is preprogrammed to break down at a certain time...." She let her voice fade, allowing the team to draw the inevitable conclusion.

"As you can see, we need to get our hands on these vials—all of them—as soon as possible," Valenti stated.

"Rules of engagement?" Thad's voice was all business.

"Do what you need to do in order to accomplish the mission." The director's voice was level but firm.

All heads around the table nodded.

"What leads do we have?" Jonathan asked.

"Not many," Valenti replied. "The trail runs cold at Leavitt. We're working all channels to see what our agents in place in Alpha Centauri might be able to pick up, but the Akkadians are being extremely tight-lipped on this."

"There's one other thing," Cutter said. He nodded to Toland to continue.

She returned her gaze to the holodisplay. "I reconfirmed with my team. They shipped four vials to Hawking." Nodding to the frozen image, the admiral added, "As you can see, there are only three in that case."

"Any leads on where that fourth vial went?" Micah asked.

"Yes."

As Valenti spoke, the visual of the vials was replaced by a pinwheel floating in the black. A sea of asteroids was scattered in the distance behind it, giving Micah a fairly good idea where the station they were looking at was located.

"One of the border patrol agents stationed at the edge of the Atliekas intercepted a gun runner yesterday afternoon," Valenti said, confirming Micah's guess.

She swept a quick look about the table. "In exchange for a lighter sentence, the woman offered up information on a deal she'd heard was going down," she pointed, "on Mercer Mining Torus."

Thad looked skeptical. "How reliable do you think this information is?"

"Beggars can't be choosers, Captain Severance," Cutter responded. "At the moment, we're in a position that forces us to chase down every lead we get."

Valenti nodded. "According to our source, one of the drug lords operating out of the belt was bragging about acquiring something that might be worth big money."

"Drug lord?" Jonathan asked. "But it's not a drug."

"He doesn't know that," Gabe pointed out.

"And honestly, if someone like that ever learned about chiral supraparticles, he really could use them to cook up something new and different," the admiral said.

Gabe sat up abruptly, a concerned look on his face. "Admiral, how hard would it be for a scientist to crack the code on what you've been doing?"

Toland's brows drew together. "It would take time to reverse-engineer, but Akkadia would have a head start, since they know the material is chiral." Her smile didn't reach her eyes. "I imagine your drug lord might need a bit more time to figure it out."

Gabe didn't smile back. He leaned in, eyes intent. "And what if Akkadia gains access to one or more of the scientists who developed the material in those vials?"

Micah sat up, his gaze cutting from Gabe to Toland.

He's talking about Sam, he sent to his twin.

A mental image sprang up of the woman who saved his life, and Jonathan's, nine months earlier. A petite dynamo with blonde hair and green eyes, and a mind like no other. Simply put, Samantha Travis was the smartest, sexiest woman he'd ever met.

If she's in danger—

He felt Jonathan's hand come down on his arm, a non-verbal warning to stand down.

Toland frowned. "Are you suggesting that my team might be targeted? We have excellent security at the Center, a full squadron of Marines who rotate in every few months." Her expression turned wry, and she nodded to the holo. "I wouldn't go so far as to say it's impenetrable, given the circumstances, but smuggling a person out would be much more difficult than those vials."

Gabe nodded, eyes shifting to meet Cutter's. "Still, sir, the admiral's team doesn't sleep at the Center. I'd feel better if we had a protection detail on standby."

That sounded like a solid plan to Micah. He saw Cutter's expression grow thoughtful.

"Yes, or perhaps...." The director's voice trailed off, eyes snapping back to meet Gabe's. "I may have an idea. Let me work on it, and I'll get back to you in a few hours."

Deeply curious about the plan Cutter was formulating, Micah was tempted to speak up. Yet as much as his gut urged him to protect Sam, he knew his skills weren't the kind that would keep her safe. He was a pilot, not a warrior.

Valenti must have sussed out his intent; she adopted a stern look as she turned to him, and then pointed to his twin. "He's still benched until that shoulder's healed, so you're flying the team to Mercer."

Micah nodded his understanding as Jonathan spoke once more inside his head.

Don't worry. I'll keep an ear to the ground. If I hear anything about Sam, I'll let you know.

Micah grunted. *Damn straight you will.*

Oblivious to the mental exchange, Valenti's gaze swung to the other two men. "Severance, bring me that drug dealer. Alvarez, I want you to use those NCIC skills of yours to piece together what happened inside the CID. Take Kinsley with you."

One of military intelligence's top analysts, Harper Kinsley was seconded to Task Force Blue. She'd been undercover on deGrasse, along with Gabe, although neither had been aware of the other at the time.

With Valenti's instructions handed out, Cutter's gaze swept them one last time. He rapped his knuckles against the table and stood. "I know there's no need to impress upon you all the seriousness of this situation. Go recover those vials."

NATIONAL DUTY

PLANCK CENTRE FOR APPLIED PHYSICS
UNIVERSITY OF ST. CLAIR
ST. CLAIR TOWNSHIP, CERIBA

SAMANTHA TRAVIS'S CURRENT assignment had nothing to do with her work for the Centers for Infectious Diseases. At the moment, she was facing an oncoming coronal mass ejection from Procyon's main sequence star.

As a radiation physicist, it was Sam's job to explain to her audience exactly how life-threatening this would be. Fortunately, for today's purposes, the CME was hypothetical. The animation on the holoscreen was based off data captured by solar-monitoring equipment around a distant star.

"An X-fifty-plus solar event like the one you see here," Sam said, "can increase the integral dose equivalence a human is exposed to by as much as fifteen Sieverts. That dose will be equally hard on any unshielded equipment you have hanging around."

As the CME animation played, she turned to look at the

medical students assembled in the lecture hall. Today's class was a welcome reprieve from her normal duties. She'd spent so much time at the Center lately she'd not had room for anything else.

Motion in the back of the darkened hall caught her attention. She turned to follow it, and her eyes landed on two figures standing silently at the back. The way they carried themselves suggested that these were not students. So did their attire.

The man met Sam's gaze and gave a slight nod, while the woman scanned the room as if for some unseen threat. After a moment, both settled into the row of empty seats that lined the back of the far wall.

Military? she wondered, although their dress suggested they might be with her uncle's agency instead.

Sam's heartbeat kicked up, but she forced her mind back to her lecture. Focusing on the x-ray flare animation, she pointed out the series of coronal mass ejections that had accompanied the flare. Her voice carried easily to the topmost tier, even without the hall's intuitive audio interface, her husky contralto clear and strong.

"The initial CME will pave the way, allowing for subsequent CMEs to travel farther, faster, before slowing down. The closer in-system you are, the more energy these particles will transfer when they collide, and the more ionizing radiation you will receive. The dose equivalence continues to accumulate over the course of the multi-hour event."

Sam waved the animation away as she turned back to face the students. "That's why it's necessary to have temporary, heavily shielded sections within habitats and mining platforms. Any living creature and any sensitive unshielded equipment will need a safe haven to ride out the storm, so that damage to systems and living tissue can be avoided."

One of the students in the front, his stocky build clear evidence of his planetbound origins, lifted a hand.

Sam paused and pointed at him. "Yes?"

"Couldn't medical nano be used to repair the damage?"

Sam smiled. "Not at the rate at which these high energy particles would be coming at you, no. In the case of a solar storm of this size, it would be like trying to hold a plasfilm over your head in a torrential rain. If it was just a light mist, the thing would keep you fairly dry. If it's a deluge…" she shook her head. "You're going to get soaked."

Sam's overlay announced the ending of the class period, and she stepped back, blanking the holo. "Looks like our time's up. If you have any questions, feel free to reach out to me."

She moved to the lectern to gather her belongings as the students rose and began to file out.

The man waited until the crowd had thinned before taking the steps down to her level. The woman remained against the far wall, her observant gaze sweeping the students as if assessing their threat level. The vibe she was giving off had students shying away from her as they passed.

Sam's attention veered back to the man when he spoke.

"Doctor Travis?"

"What can I do for you?" she asked.

He looked over at the last few students exiting. "I thought you were a research physicist. I didn't expect to see you here, teaching." His inflection made his words sound almost like an accusation.

"What you saw was my annual radiation protection presentation. A friend of mine on the faculty likes me to give it to each new crop of medical students. Why do you ask?"

Nodding to the image on the holoprojector, he said, "Are you aware your lecture was incomplete?"

She turned, following his eyeline. "Excuse me?"

The agent stared her down. "You left out another way a person could be shielded from deadly radiation like that."

A bit bemused by his comment, she asked, "What did I miss?"

A thin smile flashed across his face. It did not put her at ease. "All you need to do to protect yourself from a high-energy solar event like that is jump into Scharnhorst space. The Casimir bubble will shield you."

Her suspicions about her visitors' origins crystallized into certainty. "You think I'm going to share that with students who don't know the military's still using those drives? Every one of these students here believes they've been outlawed for more than a century."

He shrugged. "Still, it's a valid answer."

Sam stared back at him. "I'm sure you didn't come in here just to let me know my lecture was lacking. Why don't you tell me why you're really here."

"We're your escort." With a slight tilt of his head, he indicated the shadowed figure standing in the back of the room.

"My escort? I'm sorry, I don't understand."

The man frowned. "You weren't notified of our arrival?"

"No. Should I have been?" she asked.

"Yes. The NSA should have pinged you. You've been activated."

She held up a hand to forestall anything else he might say as a priority override came across her wire, indicating a message was in the queue for her.

"I set my wire on Do Not Disturb while I lectured," she explained. "But something's coming through right now...."

She turned partially away from him as she accepted the incoming communication. The moment the connection snapped into place, she saw the seal for the National Security Agency, rotating against a sea of stars. A moment later, it was replaced by an avatar.

{Dr. Travis,} an SI said, {I apologize for the intrusion. Director Cutter has asked me to let you know your presence is requested. Please consider yourself activated, and look for your escort to arrive soon, to take you to a secure location.}

{He's here now,} she began, but her words were interrupted as the SI talked over her. She realized what she was hearing was a recording.

{Mr. Cutter regrets that he cannot escort you personally, but he had to attend to other matters that came up. I hope you understand.}

The communication cut off, and Sam swung her gaze back to the man standing in front of her. She crossed her arms. "You have some form of ID to show me?"

He nodded and held out a hand. Sam knew this was no ordinary handshake the moment her own hand clasped his.

Instantly, an encrypted icon appeared on her overlay. It unfurled, presenting the man's ID token as Agent McGee of the NSA. A second ID accompanied it.

Sam found herself looking toward the back of the room, matching the image on her overlay to that of the tall, stern-looking brunette who stood there.

{My partner, Agent Nissley,} the man in front of her confirmed.

The missive looked official enough, and was keyed to her personal ID token. Sam felt it handshake with a secret and highly experimental nanochip, recently inserted behind a secured partition in her wire's databanks.

The new processor attached to her existing wire implant. Both rested inside her skull, where temporal lobe met occipital. From there, fine tendrils of nanofloss branched outward, a neural lattice that went beyond the quantum encryption conventionally used across the settled worlds.

It employed a cipher that relied on holographic duality from Anti-deSitter/Conformal Field Theory correspondence. AdS/CFT processors were the stuff only elite military teams and persons high in government possessed. The encryption was impossible to crack.

She reached mentally for the document, and it opened on her overlay, revealing a mission brief sealed with Assistant Director Sullivan's personal ID token.

{Any idea why the SI mentioned my uncle, but the document itself is from Sullivan?} She sent the query over the direct link she shared with the man via their joined hands.

Agent McGee shook his head. *{Sorry, ma'am. This is Arcane class. Need to know, and compartmentalized. I'm just your transportation. Couldn't begin to guess.}*

Unease welled inside her. *{I'm afraid I'm going to have to verify this before I'll agree to go with—}*

{Actually, you don't have the freedom to refuse, doctor.}

The sharpness in the agent's voice had her pulling away, but the man's hand tightened almost painfully, forcing the connection to remain.

{I was instructed to tell you if you tried to back out that you signed a commission that places you at the Alliance's disposal whenever the NSA calls,} the agent said bluntly. *{That contract gives the Alliance the right to pull you away in the event of a national emergency. The CID has been informed you'll be taking a small leave of absence.}*

Before she had time to respond, the agent indicated the file sealed with Sullivan's token.

{I suggest you read this.}

Sam blew out a breath and nodded her agreement. With a curt nod of his own, he dropped her hand and stepped back.

She opened the file and then blinked in shock as she read the first line.

Vials stolen from Project Rufus. Agent killed, suspect Akkadian assassin.

McGee's pale eyes met hers. What he saw in them must have convinced him she would no longer put up a fight. "Ma'am, we're on a tight timeline. We need to go."

Sam allowed herself to be led up the tiered stairs as she continued to scan the document on her overlay.

Risking a glance at the man who walked beside her, she asked, "Can I at least let the university know I've completed my lecture here?"

McGee's expression didn't change. He shook his head. "Sorry, doctor. No communication allowed."

The silence remained until they exited the room. As they rounded the corner, she was surprised to see Clint Janus leaning against the wall.

She fought to hide the intense dislike her fellow scientist elicited from her. Sam was convinced the biochemist had been responsible for several deaths on deGrasse, and yet he'd come through the subsequent investigation unscathed.

She opened her mouth to ask what he was doing at the university, but McGee stepped forward, anger written clearly on his face.

Clint's hands snapped up, palms out, a wary expression in his eyes. Sam could clearly see the jagged scar that bisected his left palm, remnants of the torture he had endured at the hands of the Akkadians. "I was just leaving." He turned and sauntered down the hallway.

It occurred to Sam that he was the only other person around, and she wondered if the agency had anything to do with that.

Her thoughts were interrupted by McGee, who called out after the biochemist. "Dr. Janus." The words were sharp and held censure. "If anyone asks, the doctor is on a two-month exchange to a Coalition university. Understood?"

Clint paused and shot a look over his shoulder at the man. Undisguised hate rolled off him. "Oh, I can guess exactly where she's going."

A sliver of alarm whispered through Sam as Janus shot her one last, knowing look.

"See you around, Doctor Travis." With a sly look, he added, "Or maybe not."

HIDDEN LAB

CALABI-YAU GATE
AN-YANG HELIOPAUSE
(PROXIMA CENTAURI SYSTEM)

THE DRONE CARAVAN that emerged from An-Yang's gate at Proxima Centauri's heliopause carried dry goods and other trade merchandise made in Akkadia. The train was bound for the capital world of Shang. Its hidden tagalong was not.

Che had come to the bridge for the gate transition, something he made a point of doing at every opportunity. The gates fascinated him. Intellectually, he knew that the ethereal dance of light and color was merely a visual representation of the energies given off by the compactified branes when bent by the gates.

His gut, however, insisted on seeing it as a mystical, almost spiritual thing.

Che's gaze drifted from the caravan's aft view to the holo of the system before them. The star that glowed a deep golden hue at An-Yang's core was a good hundred astronomical units away.

Between it and them lay their goal.

The Proxima Centauri System sported two dense dust belts. The warm one circled just four AU from the star. The cold one was tilted forty-five degrees with respect to the system's plane, and was much further out—more than thirty AU from the red dwarf.

Most mining efforts had been concentrated within the inner belt. A few enterprising souls had begun to work the outer belt in the past century, but it was still a rough and largely unregulated sector of the system, where shady deals and the less savory hung out.

Those back on Shang, the system's capital, had too much on their hands to adequately police the Badlands, as the area had come to be known. This suited Che's needs perfectly.

Their ship had hitched a ride, maglocked between two of the caravan's massive cargo containers. Tucked thusly, the smaller vessel's EM signature was obscured by the caravan's more powerful thrusters. That, combined with the interference the gate itself generated, was enough to hide their presence from the Geminate technicians staffing the gate.

"Separation in twenty minutes," the ship's captain announced. "No indication they detected us."

Che gave the captain a sharp look. "You said you're timing this to a spectral event?"

With its unpredictable pattern of frequent flares and CMEs, Proxima's red dwarf provided excellent camouflage for vessels wishing to hide a ship's emissions, if maneuvers were timed appropriately to match. In addition, the asteroid that housed the abandoned lab was dense enough to hide any energy signatures that came from within.

The captain brought up a real-time emissions sensor feed of the star. "Indications are they'll be having a small solar event— well, small by An-Yang standards—within the next hour. It'll disrupt sensor feeds long enough for us to disengage and execute a quick burn before jumping to Scharnhorst space."

The captain did not mention the drives were banned. Such

restrictions might be considered law by the rest of the settled worlds, but Akkadia viewed them as more of a suggestion. Contact between a ship's Casimir bubble and a gate's field would be catastrophic, but as long as a gate wasn't in use, there was no danger.

Satisfied, Che stepped back, giving the captain a perfunctory nod of approval, and the caravan continued its sedate, one-and-a-half *g* push as it cleared the gate's star lanes.

Che knew that once the train exited the gate's no-wake zone, its acceleration would jump dramatically. With no humans to worry about, the SI-driven fleet of containers could push to fifty *g*s without harm to its cargo. Che planned to be long gone before that occurred.

He turned to the citizen soldier working the vessel's sensors. "Anything of particular interest between us and our destination?"

The soldier snapped to attention as best he could, given his seated position. "No, Citizen General. Everything is quiet. Nothing but routine traffic. Our route will place us several million kilometers away from the nearest ship, so they should not be a factor."

Nodding in satisfaction, Che stood. His eyes sought the woman seated behind him, and she stood with a subtle grace. He turned back to the captain. "Two-minute warning, please, before we depart."

"It will be done."

Che spared a glance around the bridge before wheeling and following the woman out the door.

He'd commandeered the vessel's CIC as a strategy room for this mission. It was a handful of steps down the passageway from the bridge. As he entered, he saw she already had the display up, an image of their destination projected onto the holoscreen.

The chunk of rock tucked in the outer belt they were approaching had a large facility hidden beneath its outer crust. The lab had been built by a drug cartel, and subsequently abandoned, decades ago.

A highly addictive hallucinogen had been manufactured there. It had been a hot commodity on the black market for a time. In recent years, the criminal underground had moved on to another darling, a psychotropic compound that promised better profits than the one this laboratory's distillation plant cultivated.

Before the cartel could upgrade the facility, it had fallen into the hands of the An-Yang National Police. A specially outfitted tactical group had raided the laboratory, seizing the drugs and arresting all inside. The cartel never recovered from the raid, and none had seen fit to follow in its wake. Since then, only squatters who had fallen on desperate circumstances had frequented the facility's frozen, barren corridors.

It was the perfect place for the mission Rin Zhou had charged him to fulfill.

"The laboratories have all been restored?" he inquired now of the woman who stood beside him.

Dacina Zian angled a glance his way. "Yes, Citizen General. The minister was quite free with the credits she funneled to our cause."

Our cause. Che suppressed a wince at her words. He'd not expected such loyalty from the assassin he'd trained.

She'd shown up mere hours after Che had been escorted from Rin Zhou's presence. She had pledged her allegiance to his mission before he could stop the words from tumbling from her mouth.

How Dacina had learned of Rin Zhou's plans was still unclear to him, and it caused him some concern. Though the assassin refused to explain how she knew, she'd insisted no one else was privy to the information.

The implication was clear: for some reason, Dacina was keeping tabs on him. He had yet to discover the method by which she'd tapped into his SI, but he was certain that's how she'd gleaned the information.

Che's shame was not hers, yet he understood that his Dacina, his Fierce Dagger, felt equally responsible for the Leavitt Station mission failure.

He also rather suspected Dacina saw in him a father figure. He knew the assassins' guild selected their initiates from wards of the state, unclaimed or abandoned children. The fact he'd invested so much time and interest in her training had obviously imprinted on her.

He cursed her sense of loyalty—a desirable trait, certainly, when referring to Akkadia, and the people. Not so desirable when it meant hitching one's star to an individual whose career could so quickly be found in decline.

Despite the unfairness of the burden she'd placed upon herself, Che was privately relieved that he didn't have to handle this project alone.

As for those scientists and doctors who would be carrying out the experiment....

Che's lips curled into a half-smile of satisfaction. His plan was brilliant in its simplicity, even though it required the reactivation of a sleeper asset, high up in the Geminate government.

It was a gamble, but this one, he felt confident would play out in the end. And pay out big for Akkadia as well.

"When can we expect our... guests... to arrive?"

Her deliberate hesitation over the word amused Che. The Dagger was possessed of a dry wit few had the opportunity to see. He knew she found his decision to trick the enemy into developing the means for their own demise particularly amusing.

"They should be here within the next two days," he told her.

"Four in all, yes? From where?"

Che grunted, his mind on the diagram of the laboratory she'd thrown up onto the room's main display. "One from Brower Biologics. Two from the Merki Institute. One from the CID."

"The CID?" she asked sharply. "Not anyone from the deGrasse mission?"

He favored her with a look of reproach. "Do not take that tone with me, Dacina Zian. Remember who forged the Dagger."

She made a rumbling noise in her throat, part groan, part growl. "My general," she said, and her tone held an exaggerated patience, "what if those people recognize me? Some, if I may be so bold, could recognize *you*."

He gestured vaguely, waving off her concerns. "Even if they could, they would never have the opportunity. The people staffing this operation will do all the work. I will merely observe, and review the data these scientists provide."

"And me?" Dacina asked, her voice dangerously soft. "You would hobble me? Stay my hand? My job is to ensure the mission is not compromised in any fashion. It will be difficult to enforce, if I cannot freely roam the facility."

Che chuckled lightly, rubbing a palm over the scruff that had begun to form on his chin. It had been a long day. "You need not be seen to be deadly, my child. I taught you to be invisible. You are a specter, a shade. You will persevere, despite the limitations the situation may place upon you."

Dacina stared back at him, her gaze dark and filled with foreboding. "I hope you are right in this, my general." Turning back to the holoscreen, she added, "For all our sakes."

The break from the caravan occurred without incident, the jump to Scharnhorst space seamless. Hours later, after the ship had come to rest in the asteroid's hangar bay and Che had toured the new facility, he found himself before a holoscreen in the asteroid's central command core.

The comm unit was connected to a stealthed Ford-Svaiter unit that held station a thousand kilometers above the asteroid's surface. The S-V communications system, in turn, was tied into Proxima's Starshot constellation, exploiting a vulnerability the older-model buoys on the outer rim were known to have.

This allowed Che to update the minister of state security in real-time, via encrypted signal sent directly to Eridu. He stood at attention as the connection was made, and when she appeared, he bowed his head once in deference.

"The laboratory is functional, Citizen Minister," he told Rin

Zhou.

"Excellent. You are in the location we discussed?"

"Yes, the same."

Rin Zhou's smile was conspiratorial. "I hear that area is rather difficult for An-Yang to police. I understand they have an issue with pirate raids on outer mining platforms to this day."

Che returned her smile with a predatory one of his own. "A shame, isn't it, that illicit activity has been reported to be on the upswing on the other side of the belt?"

"Indeed." She inclined her head, her finger tapping out a slow rhythm against the top of her desk.

Che hated it when she did that. It was an affectation she used, the proverbial clock ticking down, to inject tension into every meeting. It was a power play, a subtle way of reminding those seated across from her who was in charge.

Her finger halted abruptly. "What about those you used to obtain the samples? Is there any way to trace the theft of the vials back to us?"

"Our agent who intercepted the vials killed the courier pilot. As for the other...." Che smiled confidently. "The person working for us inside the CID will be eliminated, and her notes destroyed. They have no idea she swapped the chiral material for us."

"I had heard there were to be four vials. Is there any word on the whereabouts of the fourth one?"

"Not yet," Che frowned. "Unfortunately, our agent on Leavitt was unaware of the number of vials the case was supposed to have held, and so he eliminated the courier without questioning him about it."

"I trust you'll do what you can to find that missing material. It wouldn't do if that loose thread were to lead the Alliance back to us in any way," Rin Zhou warned.

"Understood, Citizen Minister," Che dipped his head in compliance.

"Very well. Do not forget your deadline. I expect regular progress reports from you. Are we clear on this?"

Che dipped his head once more. "Crystal."

MERCER

MICAH TIMED *WRAITH*'S exit from Scharnhorst space to occur at the same time the Starshot buoy nearest the mining platform fired its drives to adjust its heading. The buoy's energy signature easily masked the small EM flare the ship's Casimir bubble emitted as it dissipated.

Shadow Recon had been using the constellations' orbital adjustments for as long as he could remember. They were an effective and readily available way to mask stealth insertions.

Access to the Alliance's space traffic control system provided another method for concealing a ship's EM signature. As Micah scanned nearspace around the buoy, he found exactly what he needed.

A large tanker was lumbering toward Mercer, its five-*g* deceleration burn conveniently strong enough to mask *Wraith's* maneuvers. Micah tucked the Helios into the shadow of the larger and much noisier vessel, and followed the tanker in.

Up ahead, Mercer gleamed a dull gray against the blackness of space, a visual interruption that stood out among the tumbling stones of rock and ice that populated the fringes of the asteroid belt known as the Klintis.

{Transition complete,} Micah informed the team in the cabin.

Thad sent a two-click response, then followed it with, *{ETA?}*

Micah blinked through his overlay until the navigation screen popped up, showing time to Mercer. *{Two hours, fifteen.}*

{Copy that.}

Joining Thad were Asha, the team's medic, and Boone, their sniper. Since Gabe was back on Ceriba, Thad had borrowed one of the guys from his former unit to round out the fireteam. Micah didn't know the man's name; he'd just mentally tagged him as New Guy.

All four were gearing up, ready to slip onto the station once *Wraith* attached herself to Mercer's outer hull.

A moment later, a diagram of the mining platform popped up on the ship's net. Micah watched as Thad expanded it, rotating it until the service hatch where they'd insert into the torus was front and center.

{That's our LZ,} the Marine said. *{Dumps you right into one of the maintenance tunnels. Easy to breach, and less likelihood of anyone being around to see.}*

Micah glanced over at the swarm of drones his copilot Yuki was controlling. *{We on target to deliver the Heist?}* He leaned over to tap on the icon that represented one of her drones. It was closing on the lumbering tanker ahead of them.

She nodded. A small ETA flashed next to the drone. *{It should attach itself to their hull within the next few minutes.}*

Micah eased *Wraith* back a bit, increasing the separation between the two ships, and then settled in to wait.

{Drone lock,} Yuki announced. *{Unpacking the app now.}*

Micah gave her a quick thumbs-up and then pinged the team. *{Heist in progress.}*

{Copy,} Thad replied.

Movement on one of the internal feeds caught Micah's eye.

He saw New Guy shoot Boone a questioning look.

The sniper just shrugged and looked away.

Getting much the same reaction from Thad and Asha, New Guy turned toward the cockpit. "Hey, what's a heist?"

Micah grinned as Nina's boot rocked his cradle. Will coughed quietly from the station across from Nina. The four of them had flown together long enough to know Yuki's penchant for messing with new guys. Soldiers from the Unit were some of her favorite victims.

"A heist?" Yuki asked, swiveling her copilot's cradle to face the main cabin. She leaned back and stretched her legs out in front of her. "Well, now, there's a tale." She lifted her eyes to the overhead as if in thought.

Nina snickered, and Yuki shot her a quelling glance. Micah didn't dare take his eyes off *Wraith*'s cockpit feed for fear he would lose it if he saw Thad's expression.

Returning her gaze to New Guy, Yuki let out a long breath. "To truly appreciate the beauty of the heist, you have to understand that it comes from an old and storied tradition."

"Really?"

Micah dipped his head to hide a grin.

"Really." Yuki gave the new guy a solemn nod before settling back in to weave her tale. "It all began pre-diaspora, Old Earth, 20th century...."

"Can't believe something that old would have any value to the Unit," New Guy muttered disbelievingly.

Micah heard Thad clear his throat, and knew the Marine was using it to cover a laugh.

"Believe it." Yuki leveled a jaundiced eye at Thad. "Now, where was I? Oh yes, Old Earth, twentieth century." Her gaze returned to the overhead. "It was common in those days for thieves, criminals, and persons of ill repute—"

{Did she just say 'ill repute'?} Thad's voice sounded a bit strangled.

"As the story goes, back in those days, governments and private corporations used flat, two-dimensional video cameras to monitor vulnerable areas susceptible to being breached. A thief would have to overcome that in order to get past the security and take whatever it was he had come to steal."

"2D image feeds are easy to disrupt, though," New Guy said.

"They are, but if they wanted to pull off the perfect crime, and didn't want anyone to know that they'd ever been there in the first place, they'd hack the system, record enough of the feed to be believable, and then replace the live feed with their pre-recorded one."

"Why not just have them get past the security guys by subduing them first?" New Guy protested. "There are any number of ways you could do that."

"Yes, but then they'd all be *aware* that something had happened," Yuki said with an exaggerated patience. "And then it wouldn't qualify as a heist. The perfect heist is never discovered. You enter, swap the item of value with a high-quality facsimile, and then leave with no one the wiser. And looping the video feed is the first step to doing that."

"Okay, I can see that," New Guy nodded. "But what's the connection to the heist hack we're using?"

Micah saw the smug look on Yuki's face as she reeled New Guy in.

"Well, we're, in essence, stealing their magnetic-field-monitoring system, and inserting what we want them to see. Our heist insinuates itself into Mercer's systems the first time that ship out there communicates with Mercer's space traffic control. It waits until the ship docks, and then once a hard-link is set up, slips itself inside the torus's monitoring system, pretty as you please. They'll be completely unaware their magnetic field pattern has been falsified to appear as though no disruption has occurred."

"Heist," New Guy muttered, shaking his head and turning back to check his gear. "Damn, that's some real shit...."

A private connection sprang into existence between Thad and the flight crew.

{Who wants to wager how long it'll take New Guy to spread

that tall tale once we get back?} Nina asked. *{And how long will everyone let it go before someone lets him in on it? The hack's only called a Heist because the Navy's official designation for the app is HE–1ST.}*

{You know I don't take sucker bets, cher,} Thad replied.

{Hey, if New Guy's going to give me an opening like that, I'm taking it. Besides, my version's a lot more interesting than the truth. And way more convenient than calling out 'Hack Executable-1-Sierra Tango' every time we use it,} Yuki retorted.

{Not gonna argue,} Micah told her.

A notification snagged his attention as the tanker docked.

Yuki passed the HE-1ST's program over to Will, who tied the hack into *Wraith*'s systems status display. Its icon showed amber with a 'pending' status flag beside it.

Moments later, the telltale flickered to green.

The heist had successfully inserted itself into the torus's monitoring system and taken a snapshot of its magnetic field signature. It then synched with *Wraith*'s SI, isolating the Helios's approach vector. At the appropriate time, it would send a cancellation wave to counteract the ripple *Wraith* would cause in the magnetic lines when she intercepted Mercer's field.

No disturbance, no intruder.

{We're a go.}

At Will's words, everyone sprang into action. Micah nudged the ship to the edge of the no-wake zone and cut her drives, drifting silently through the torus's artificial magnetosphere.

While the ship closed on the station, the team moved aft toward *Wraith*'s hatch, and Nina and Will monitored the surrounding area for any indications the ship's disturbance of the magnetic field lines had been noted, despite the heist hack.

The hatch Thad had flagged grew as Micah used thrusters to close the distance, while matching the torus' rotational speed. He brought the ship to within a few meters of the opening and sent Boone a visual.

The sniper was alone in *Wraith*'s airlock, his drakeskin suit sealed for vacuum. Boone acknowledged receipt of the feed and then cycled the ship's hatch, exposing himself to space.

Micah spared a quick look at the feed to confirm the man was properly tethered. He saw the Bravo Charlie in Boone's hands, and knew the sniper was ready to make his move.

{Closing now,} he told the operative.

{Copy,} Boone replied.

Although a Bravo Charlie wasn't technically a weapon, the breaching canisters still fell under the sniper's purview. Once he affixed the BC to the hatch, the breaching program would subvert the torus's security system, convincing it that the hatch remained closed.

Only then would Micah bring *Wraith* into physical contact with Mercer.

He waited while Boone reached out, affixed the canister to the hatch, and then reeled himself back in. Micah waited for the BC to signal a positive lock before easing *Wraith* ever so slowly toward the torus's hull.

The moment the BC flipped from amber to green, he feathered the ship to a stop, the two hatches aligned perfectly. *Wraith*'s surface barely kissed Mercer's skin, but it was enough. The seal clicked into place.

{Done. You're up!} Micah told the team as he locked *Wraith*'s systems into station-keeping mode.

As always, separating himself from such a deep merge felt a bit like surfacing from a bottomless pond. His viewpoint flipped. His eyes were no longer tied into *Wraith*'s sensors; they were once again his own.

As the ship's interior came back into focus, Micah unwebbed and stood. With *Wraith* now sharing Mercer's centripetal force, down was now ship's starboard in the main cabin. The cockpit operated independently on its own gimbal and so was already positioned properly, but the rest of the ship needed a bit of tweaking.

Will handled it, sending the commands to restructure the cabin's modular walls and surfaces to reflect the new orientation.

It was something the Navy had worked out ages ago, sheathing its ships' interiors with ActiveFiber surfaces. Structures like interior walls, seating, and even plumbing were rearranged by simple programming.

Micah caught Thad at the hatch just before the Marine stepped through into Mercer.

"Good hunting," he told the man. "Let us know if you need anything."

"Will do, Navy." Thad sent him a quick nod and then sealed the hatch behind him.

Now, all the crew could do was wait.

SYNTHETIC INTELLIGENCE

CENTER FOR INFECTIOUS DISEASES
MONTPELIER, CERIBA

ADDY WATCHED THE Center for Infectious Diseases' headquarters complex grow larger in the shuttle's forward screens as they approached the outskirts of Montpelier. The sleepy suburban town was four hundred kilometers outside the capital city of St. Clair. As they neared, she could just make out the new wing that had been added to accommodate Project Rufus.

Up in the cockpit, she could hear Katie Hyer's energetic tones as the pilot conversed with Montpelier Tower. The few words Addy could make out indicated they were cleared for approach to the shuttle pad atop the Center's main building.

Chief Warrant Hyer was one of deGrasse's few survivors; Addy owed her life to the chief's actions that day. She was Task Force Blue's newest and youngest member, and had been brought in as a flight engineer. She'd been running sims in *Wraith*'s cockpit and would soon be fully mission-qualified as a backup pilot, as well.

"We'll be landing in a few," Hyer called out. "Colonel Valenti says I'm assigned to you today. Wherever you need to go, you just let me know."

"Thanks, Chief," Gabe said. "I think we'll be here a while."

The pilot considered his words, running a hand absently over her short-cropped, blue-tipped fuzz. "Soon as you're inside the building, I'll go find a place to park. Just ping if you need me." Hyer brought the shuttle to a stop and cracked open the hatch.

Heat radiated off the Center's roof as Addy and Gabe stepped out into Montpelier's summertime air. Blue skies were dotted with puffy white clouds. A warm breeze brought the smells of freshly cut grass. The pastoral environment seemed at odds with the urgency of their situation.

They crossed the few steps to the rooftop doors, cool air blasting Addy as her ID token granted them access. It heightened the contrast between the sun-drenched rooftop and the dimly lit vestibule.

The lift doors were open, with a car waiting to whisk them to the main lobby. It was empty save for a lone individual seated on a cushioned bench. Recognition flared in the woman's eyes as she spied Gabe.

"That's Harper," he said as she strode toward them, her long hair fanning out behind her, stirred by the brisk pace.

"Agent Alvarez," she said, and then turned to Addy. "I don't know if you remember me, Captain. We met once, on deGrasse. I helped Sam get out of there before—"

She broke off as Addy held out a hand. "There are precious few of us who are members of that particular survivor's guild. I'm glad you're on our team."

Harper gave her hand a quick shake, and Addy motioned them both toward the lobby's security kiosk. Once cleared into the building, another bank of lifts took them up to the more secured section that housed Project Rufus.

The NSA wing was protected by a much more stringent security system. Once the three were processed through, Addy led them to her office. One side of the hallway was lined with clearsteel walls that allowed them to see into each room as they passed. She paused in front of the first one and rested her hand on the transparent pane.

"Welcome to Project Rufus. Behind these walls lay everything that remains from deGrasse," she stated flatly. "As a precaution, Admiral Toland's ordered the work halted while we investigate the theft of those vials."

The proof of that was before them. The rooms were empty and dark, the only thing showing in the clearsteel was a soft reflection of her own features. She could thank the Akkadians' recent actions for the dark circles she saw smudging the hollows beneath her eyes.

She pushed away from the wall and turned down the hallway that led to her office. As they entered, she said, "Grab a seat while I access everything we have on the theft."

Gabe snagged a pair of chairs, dropped them in front of Addy's desk, and motioned for Harper to take a seat.

"Quick lesson on the differences between the three containment levels," Addy said. "Biosafety Level Two is for moderate hazards. Access to L2 is restricted, but all you need is to glove in a nano coating before you enter." She pointed down the hall. "It's on this same level, through a pass-coded entrance. We have two labs, and an observation room."

"An observation room?" Harper asked.

Addy smiled. "It's where we're keeping the chiral ferrets that Stinton cloned, so we can study them."

"Snotface and Sneaky Pete?" The analyst's brow furrowed. "What do you mean, study them?"

Addy could tell from Harper's tone that she suspected the worst. "It's not how it sounds," she reassured the other woman. "They're living in ferret luxury, I promise you that. The lab techs adore them and are constantly bringing them new toys or treats."

Gabe's expression turned curious. "Why keep them locked up?"

"The main reason is that one of them is chiral and wouldn't

survive without specially formulated food only we can provide," Addy said. "We very much want to understand how that entangled connection of theirs works. But everything we're doing is noninvasive and with their cooperation."

She shot them both a wry smile. "I can't begin to tell you how interesting *that* process has been."

Harper smiled wryly. "I can imagine."

Addy shook her head. "I have no idea what prompted Stinton to implant them with E-V comms, but I can't deny that even the basic communication they're capable of has been helpful."

Harper seemed satisfied with the explanation, so Addy continued. "The floor above us is home to the L3 and L4 labs. That's where we keep the materials that can pose serious to lethal risks. Both of these levels are under constant observation by medical SIs. Lab workers use full protection, and access is controlled at all times. She looked at Gabe with a wry expression. "Not that it stopped the thief."

Gabe shook his head. "Don't beat yourself up, Addy. Medical SIs aren't there for security; they're there for safety." He looked around. "This is your show. What's the best way to go about scanning those labs, so we can find out which vials are missing?"

Addy grimaced. "I know it's hard to believe, but the system isn't showing anything missing, and the serial numbers from the feed the agent sent us were partially obscured," she said. "We may have to do it physically, by hand."

Harper pointed to the secured jack built into Addy's desk that would allow hard-link access to the CID's mainframe. "May I?"

The captain waved her toward it. "Be my guest."

She reached for a stack of security-sealed plasfilm documents to make more room for Harper, but froze when she heard her office door slide open. She saw Harper swiftly blank the holo she'd just brought up.

Gabe's mental voice cracked like a whip across her wire. *{Captain, did you lock your door?}*

{I thought I did....}

Addy's mental voice trailed off as she spied the figure

standing there. It was humanoid in form, though clearly inorganic.

{That's Dave,} she told him. *{He's one of the Center's mobile SIs, and the one the tech department's been experimenting with the most. I'm sorry, I guess my door **wasn't** locked.}*

The Synthetic Intelligence housed inside the mobile frame came to a stop in front of Addy.

"Good morning, Captain Moran," Dave greeted. "Can I interest you and your guests in a fresh cup of coffee? I can whip up one of today's specials for you."

What the hell? Addy shot Gabe a swift look before moving toward the SI. "Dave, I'm in the middle of a meeting—"

"Today's special?" Gabe interrupted.

{Is this normal for it to just barge in like this?} Harper asked.

{No, he's never done this before. I've never had him offer guests coffee before, either. And I have no idea what 'specials' he's referring to.}

{Keep it talking,} Gabe instructed. *{Let's see what it does.}*

That wasn't hard to do. It seemed the SI had an agenda of its own.

"I've been experimenting with some of the specialty salts Jenna in L3 brought in," the SI said, its tone sounding oddly earnest. "I've been making caramel macchiatos with a sprinkling of the salts added to the top. The front desk loves them."

Addy sent Gabe a concerned look.

He held up a hand and turned to the SI. "I'd like some. Just straight coffee, please. Cream, no sugar." Gabe's gaze shifted to Harper, and he gave a subtle nod.

"Sure, why not? I'll try your special, Dave."

The SI beamed at Harper. "I'm certain you'll love it, Miss Kinsley. What about you, Captain? Would you like your regular, ma'am?"

How the hell would he know what my 'regular' is? Addy wondered, but followed Gabe's lead, and simply said, "Yes, please."

The SI nodded pleasantly, pivoted, and then exited the office.

"That was...weird," Harper commented.

"I agree. I suppose my drinking habits are stored in the break room machine's memory." Addy measured her words slowly as she thought it through. "He could have accessed the security kiosk to learn your identities, too. Still, that felt awfully... proactive for an SI."

Harper nodded, her gaze clinging thoughtfully to Addy's empty door frame. "Definitely the most modified SI I've encountered yet," she replied.

"The Center's lead programmer has been tweaking Dave's machine learning capabilities," Addy told them. "The intent was to make L4 experimentation safer by using SIs instead of humans, while still getting the results we need. I wonder...."

"You think someone meddled with his base code?" Gabe asked sharply.

"I think it would be a good idea to find out for sure," she replied.

"Let me insert a search worm behind the Center's firewall," Harper said. "I'll poke around and see what I can find."

A few minutes later, the SI reappeared, tray in hand. It was laden with three large, steaming mugs. Behind the mugs sat two small, espresso-sized cups.

Addy shot Gabe a mystified look as it came to a stop in front of her desk and set the tray down.

"Coffee, black, for the captain," Dave said, handing a mug to Addy.

"White for Agent Alvarez," the SI added, handing the next mug to Gabe.

Picking up the final mug, Dave handed Harper her drink. "And one special for you, Miss Kinsley."

"Dave, what's with the smaller cups?" Addy asked curiously.

The SI smiled and gave a half-bow. "I took the liberty of whipping up a few samples of today's special, on the house." He winked. "In case you changed your mind."

{That's some initiative,} Addy heard Harper observe over the wire.

Cautiously, Gabe reached for one of the cups. "On the house, huh? Where'd you hear that?"

Gabe's shuttered gaze flickered to Addy's as she reached for her own sample.

Her eyes widened as she took her first sip. "Wow, Dave. This is good. You've really missed your calling. Or exceeded your programming."

"Or both," she heard Harper whisper from beside Gabe.

"Ah, well, thank you for the coffees, Dave," Addy said quickly, to cover Harper's comment. "I'll let you know if we need anything else."

She expected the SI to respond and then leave, but Dave did neither. It just stood there, unblinking—as if frozen.

Addy leaned forward, peering intently into the SI's eyes.

Not eyes. Visual receptors, she reminded herself silently. *Don't anthropomorphize.* "Dave?" she called out, but there was no answer.

She exchanged a puzzled look with Harper.

The analyst's brows lifted. She rose and walked over to where the SI stood, and walked carefully around Dave's frozen frame. She had just reached for the frame's access panel when the SI suddenly came back to life.

Harper sprang back.

"I'll leave you folks to your investigation, then," Dave said pleasantly, as if the glitch had never occurred.

As the SI turned to walk away, Addy called out, "Wait. Dave, where did you go just now?"

The SI blinked. "Go?" he repeated. "I haven't gone anywhere, Captain. I have been here for the past five minutes, thirteen seconds."

"You froze," she said. "We could get no response from you for a good fifteen, maybe twenty seconds."

The SI made a humming noise. "I will run a self-diagnostic. Please do not concern yourself. I feel fine."

Addy let Dave leave, her eyes following the retreating frame. She palmed her door closed, locking it this time.

"Exactly how odd was that SI's behavior just now?" Gabe queried.

"On a scale of one to totally creepy? Pretty high," Addy admitted. "It wouldn't bother me so much, if he was either limited to our sector or banned from it altogether. I don't like that he's freely roaming the Center."

Harper pivoted around to face them. "You think your programmer's coming close to singularity?"

Addy tilted her head, considering the question. "You mean sentience? I... doubt it, but what do I know? We're been postulating that—and they've been predicting it was imminent—for three hundred years."

Gabe nodded toward the hallway where Dave had disappeared. "It's awfully coincidental that your SI would begin to act differently right after those vials were stolen." He frowned. "I don't believe in coincidences."

Addy stared back at him. "No," she said slowly. "Neither do I."

"Good, because you're not going to believe what I just found," Harper's gaze was fixed on the holodisplay projecting the hard-link connection.

She reached into the image, manipulating the data. A string of characters morphed into a visual feed of an office.

Addy stepped closer to the holo, something about the image teasing a memory. "That's Leah's office," she said as realization struck. "She's the Center's head programmer."

"She *was* the Center's head programmer," Harper corrected, her voice sounding odd.

She adjusted the holo once more, enlarging the picture.

What Addy had originally dismissed as a shadow behind the office's lone desk...wasn't. Leah's still figure lay slumped, her body placed at an unnatural angle.

Addy didn't need the feed's sensors to confirm what her medical training already told her. She knew what she was seeing.

Leah Harris was dead.

PREVENTIVE MEASURES

UNKNOWN LOCATION
UNKNOWN PASSAGE OF TIME

AWARENESS RETURNED TO Sam slowly. She realized she was resting on a soft yet firm surface. Her limbs felt weighted, which implied she was in a gravitational field of one sort or another.

As she wiggled her fingers experimentally, she could sense a diffuse light begin to grow in intensity from behind her closed lids.

Triggered by my movements, no doubt.

Her eyes fluttered open, confirming her suspicions. She was inside a tau-neu chamber. Stasis, in layman's terms. A place where all metabolic functions were suspended.

The soft white lighting and the slight breeze that blew across her face simulated the impression of expansiveness, a feature built into the tau-neu as a way to counteract feelings of claustrophobia.

The information poured into her brain from her med school days. Although Sam had eventually ended up working in the sciences rather than the medical field, she well recalled her first introduction to the chambers. All medical doctors were required to experience what it was like to be ensconced inside a tau-neu at some point during their residencies. It was deemed an essential part of learning about critical care.

On the heels of that thought, memory came flooding back.

Damned NSA agents, she thought in annoyance.

The one named McGee had been adamant that she travel to the secret base in this way. She'd refused, arguing that it hadn't been necessary when she'd gone to deGrasse.

"And you see how well that worked out," he'd stated.

Her thoughts had instantly flown to a dark-haired, blue-eyed man whose life had been forged at deGrasse. The act of terrorism had killed tens of thousands, but it had produced one very unique individual.

McGee hadn't known that, though, and she'd had no intention of telling him.

Sam placed a palm on the chamber's surface, a scant twenty centimeters from her face. Her touch activated the unit. The smooth, white surface split down the center, its sides retracting. One look around confirmed she was in a different location.

When the chamber's shroud had lowered, she'd been in the cargo hold of a small ship. Now, she was in a brightly lit laboratory of some sort.

Sam remained still, mentally cataloguing what she could sense of her environment before making any attempt to move. She inhaled, and the dry, slightly metallic taste of recirculated air hit the back of her throat. There was just a hint of ozone in the mix that told her she was on a station of some kind.

One without a hydroponics system, if they're using electrolysis to generate breathable air.

She started to sit up just as a face appeared within her view. The man was wearing a Navy ship's suit, the holopips on his collar indicating he was a medical corpsman.

"Doctor Travis," he greeted with a smile. His gaze shifted to somewhere above her head, and she realized he was reading the status display at the top of the tau-neu chamber. He nodded, as if satisfied. "Looks like you're ready to go, ma'am."

He held out a hand, and she grasped it. His accent suddenly registered as he levered her out of the unit.

"You're not from Procyon," she observed.

His hand tightened convulsively around her arm for a brief instant, before relaxing once more. "No, ma'am," he responded smoothly. "I'm an embassy brat. Raised at one of the consulates around the Jovian moons."

She nodded. "I'll bet that was an interesting childhood."

He made a noncommittal sound, and she turned her attention to her surroundings. The room was about as nondescript as a room could be, with plain, unadorned bulkheads. They were clean enough, but somehow gave the impression of age.

She turned back to the corpsman. "Where are we?"

The corpsman shot her an apologetic look. "Sorry, ma'am. I'm not at liberty to say."

She merely nodded, expecting nothing less. "Do I at least get some sort of orientation before you throw me into whatever project you brought me here to work on?"

"That would be my job," a smiling voice said from behind her.

Sam turned. "And you are?"

"Colonel Marceau." The man extended a hand. "Welcome to the Alliance's Rosen Laboratory. And no, I'm not going to tell you where it's located, either."

Sam's brow rose at that.

"Wheeler, Feynman, deGrasse, and now Rosen," she murmured as she took the man's proffered hand. "If nothing else, at least we're consistent, aren't we?"

Marceau laughed. "I suppose you're right," he said, releasing her hand and looking around at the sparse room. "Most of the Alliance's research facilities have been named after famous Old Earth physicists."

Sam kept her smile firmly in place, but cocked her head inquiringly. "I've never heard of a Colonel Marceau in the Geminate Navy. Why is that?"

"I suppose that's a fair question, given the circumstances," he admitted. "The past few years, I've been stationed here, running Rosen. Prior to that, I was based in Sirius, so unless you've spent a lot of time out there, I doubt our paths would have crossed."

"You don't mind if I confirm that for myself, do you?"

Rather than bristling at her, the man seemed to find her skepticism humorous. His grin widened and he chuckled. "You're exactly as Duncan described you, outspoken and candid. It's refreshing to have someone speak so frankly with me. Not many do around here."

He winked and leaned in as if confiding something. "I've heard it's not good for career advancement to behave like that to the facility's commanding officer."

The man was doing his best to make her feel welcome, and Sam felt her unease melt away.

"Now, to address your concerns. I apologize for the way you were brought here, Sam. Can I call you Sam?" he asked, spearing her with a questioning look. "The way your uncle talks about you, I feel as if I know you already. I know the agents who brought you here weren't free to divulge much. I assume they told you that you're needed to help us prevent a chiral disaster?"

His words had Sam hugging her arms around herself. Marceau mistook that for her being chilled, and abruptly stopped.

"I'm sorry. I completely forgot you're wearing civilian clothes," he apologized, and gestured toward the room's exit. "Here. Let me show you to your quarters. We've taken the liberty of supplying you with a few standard shipsuits that'll allow you to regulate your temperature. We'll stop by the mess hall along the way and grab you something warm to drink."

Sam nodded her thanks and followed him out the door. At least she'd get a chance to mentally map her surroundings, in case her misgivings turned out to be justified.

The corridor was as bland as the room they'd just left. The passageways were unrelenting metal-composite bulkheads, with no distinguishing marks of any kind.

Marceau ducked into an empty mess hall where a digital-to-biological converter had been installed. The DBC could replicate simple foods and drinks, and was most often used in offices or mess halls like this during off hours.

Heading over to it, he called over his shoulder. "Coffee? Tea? What's your poison?"

"Tulsi tea, if the unit's programmed for it," she responded. "No sweetener."

"One tulsi, coming up."

He must have accessed the unit from his wire's overlay, for the DBC immediately came to life. When it finished, he handed the insulated cup to her with a small flourish and then gestured to the passageway.

"Let's walk while you enjoy your tea. I can show you to your quarters so you can get settled." He placed a hand at her elbow, the contact allowing a request to flash on Sam's overlay.

She realized abruptly that her wire had been quiescent ever since her arrival. A swift look told her there was a single encrypted network signal available, and she was denied access.

Hesitantly, she accepted Marceau's connection request as they walked. A diagram, entitled 'Rosen Station' appeared, sections of it blacked out.

"The identified areas on that map are free for you to roam," Marceau told her, his hand dropping from her arm. "The rest are restricted."

Sam nodded wordlessly. "And network access?"

Marceau's hand struck his forehead. "Sorry," he muttered. "Completely forgot."

A few seconds later, the network icon on her wire flashed a status of 'limited connectivity'.

Sam angled a look toward the colonel. "Limited connectivity?"

Marceau's pleasant expression faltered. Looking down at her, he said, "That... requires a bit more explanation. However, it's a conversation that needs to happen in a more secure setting than this. How about I give you the tour first, and then we can head to my office?"

Sam took a sip of the tea, considering her options. "If you don't mind, I'd really rather know what's going on first."

"As you wish." He gestured to a cross-passageway coming up on their left. "My office is down here."

A few minutes later, Sam found herself hustled past a man with commander's holopips on his collar, seated in the anteroom of the colonel's office. Marceau issued his adjutant a curt, "Please ensure we're not disturbed," and then sealed his office door behind them.

"Have a seat," he invited, directing her toward a pair of low-slung chairs placed off to one side. He sank into one, and she in the other.

He leaned forward, hands clasped, elbows braced on his knees. "What I'm about to tell you is something not everyone here is privy to, so I'll ask you to keep this in confidence."

Sam considered him from over the rim of her mug. "That's saying something, considering how black this site already is," she murmured.

"Look, there's no easy way to say this. We brought you here the way we did because we received word that the Akkadians might be targeting scientists associated with the chiral study. We had reason to believe you were on that list."

Sam felt like she'd been punched in the gut. "They were going to *kill* me?"

"Not that kind of target, no. They were going to kidnap you." Marceau said. "Your uncle thought it best if we make a preemptive move. After your involvement with the deGrasse incident, you know we suspect sleeper agents have infiltrated our government. We were afraid they might learn our intentions. We wanted to get you to safety before they found out about our plans."

Sam's mind reeled. "Do you have any idea what they intend to do with the vials?"

"Surely you, of all people, understand the things Akkadia is capable of doing. They're not above testing such weapons on innocent people. They've been known to do so on their own citizens."

Sam weighed what he'd just said. "That's...."

Marceau's smile was thin. "Monstrous, I know. I apologize, but I can't afford to sugarcoat this for you, doctor. Akkadia plans to weaponize those vials. I need you to beat them to it."

"I'm not sure I follow. I don't see how weaponizing chiral material helps us to stop them," she said.

"It's simple," he said. "If we know the most likely vector their attack will take, then we can begin to formulate our own counterattack."

Sam pulled back, blinking in surprise. "Here there be dragons," she murmured.

He shot her a questioning look.

"That sounds like a recipe for mutually assured destruction," she said.

"I misspoke when I used the word counterattack. Our objective isn't to use your research as a weapon. We want you to find a way to neutralize an attack."

Sam made a sound as she began to speak, but then hesitated.

"What is it, doctor?"

"I feel I have to warn you. I'm a radiation physicist first, a medical doctor second. Yes, I know a lot about radiation biology, but I was sucked into the chiral study kind of by accident," she told him. "It really stretches credulity to call me an expert on chirality. I'm probably not the best person to help you out on this. You'd be better served to have a biochemist or a biophysicist instead."

Marceau held up a hand. "Don't sell yourself short, Sam. Duncan's told me how involved you've been with the program. I'm sure you'll have plenty to contribute."

"Okay, then, how about this? The number of possible methods they could use to weaponize this is incalculable. I don't know if what you're asking is doable."

"All I ask is that you try. You are our best hope, you and the other experts we're bringing in." He leaned back in his seat, studying her intently. "The staff here has been read into what we found in Luyten's Star, but not the work you've been doing at the CID. I'd like you to brief them."

He rose and strode toward the door. Opening it, he gestured to the commander seated outside. As the man appeared in the doorway, Marceau turned back to Sam.

"My assistant will show you to your quarters where you can get changed. There's an adjacent office. You can work there the rest of the day, undisturbed. Please pull together what you have on the Center's work, and be prepared to present it to the staff tomorrow morning at oh-eight-hundred."

YACHT

ROYAL CERIBA PIER
ATLIEKAS NEBULA PARK ENTRANCE

THE THIEF DIDN'T have far to travel to get to the Royal Ceriban Cruise Lines' main pier. The spacedock where the yachts departed was located just past the Starshot buoy, in the direction of the Atliekas.

An automated valet system ushered his small ship into port, maneuvering it into a parking position with little fuss. The shuttle that bellied up against his ship's hatch was well-appointed and more comfortable than any he'd enjoyed in quite some time. It dropped him off directly in front of the pier's entrance, the ship's SI welcoming him to 'the adventure of a lifetime' as he disembarked.

He paused to stare up at the welcome holo splashed across the archway that separated Royal Ceriba's passenger parking from the main pier. The promotional imagery flashed between colorful scenes of the Atliekas 'shoreline' to the rocky promontories of the Klintis. Interspersed between was a feed of the luxurious accommodations that passengers would enjoy aboard each of the company's yachts.

His face creased into a smile and he shouldered his overnight bag, stepping through onto the causeway that led to the various boarding stations. His smile cut off abruptly as a wracking cough shook his frame.

He covered his mouth with his hand as another one struck. When it subsided, he rubbed his chest, feeling a pressure there he'd not felt before.

Damn off-label medical nano, he grumbled to himself.

He rubbed his chest once again. He really wasn't feeling very well. He was young and reasonably fit, so he didn't bother wasting good creds on health nano. He'd rather invest in the best safe-cracking hacks and illegal nano apps he could find. At his age, he figured the biggest risk to his health was the pissed-off victims he'd managed to dupe.

He'd have to rethink his strategy, if some measly cold was going to ruin a hard-earned vacation.

It occurred to him that a Royal Ceriban yacht would surely have a medical department. He'd pay them a visit once he'd boarded, let them eradicate whatever bug he'd caught.

Eager chatter had him turning as a family with three young children came up behind him.

The youngest, a girl with a mop of auburn curls, went skipping ahead of them, giggling with glee. She skidded to a stop and stared up at him, one finger stuck up her nose.

"Angela!" the mother scolded, and the girl yanked her hand behind her back. She grinned up at the thief, and not wanting to be impolite, he smiled back.

"I'm going on a *cruise,*" she whispered, leaning in as if revealing a big secret. "I'm going to see all the glowy rocks an' big 'splosions an'—"

She threw her arms out, mimicking what he assumed was supposed to be the sound an explosion made.

"That big, huh?" he said.

She reminded him of his sister's kid. They were cute enough, as long as they weren't his and he could send them home when he tired of them.

Her eyes widened. "*Bigger* even!" She threw her arms out once more, overbalanced, and fell against him.

Instinctively, he reached down to stabilize her, the jarring action loosing another tickle from his throat. He turned his head away to cough lightly into his hand, and then used the same hand without thinking anything of it to set her back on her feet.

The young mother sent him an apologetic look as she pulled her daughter away, fingers firmly intwined with her smaller ones. Sternly, she addressed the girl.

"Angela, what did we say about staying together?"

The child gave her mother a stubborn look and remained mute.

Annoyance colored the woman's expression and she shot her partner a loo. The man gave an easy shrug as if to say *'Kids, what are you going to do?'.*

The thief smiled back at his newfound friend, reaching out to tuck one of her wild curls behind her ear.

"Enjoy the big explosions," he told her.

"You, too, mister!" She giggled once more, waved, and then went racing away.

"Angela!" the woman called out sharply as the child bolted into a nearby souvenir shop. That was followed by an exasperated "Rand!" and a few muttered imprecations that questioned his general usefulness.

The man waved her off, altering his trajectory to intersect the shop. "Calm down, Ana. We're on vacation."

The thief swallowed a snicker when the other two kids broke away to follow. The woman threw up her hands and stalked after them.

The shops lining the causeway were varied and colorful, and to the thief's jaundiced eye, were only a slightly more legal version of his own occupation. The exorbitant prices for cheap trinkets were universal at theme parks like this, capitalizing on a person's desire to memorialize a pleasant event.

Since none of this appealed to the thief, he decided to locate his gate agent, and tender his ID—fake, of course, but a damn good one.

He staggered as he stood, feeling a bit lightheaded. "Well, hell," he muttered. "Guess I shouldn't have skipped breakfast."

The cruise line had real humans at their security kiosk, and that amused him. Royal Ceriba's customer service really was the best, eschewing the impersonal SI interface most places employed.

"Hello," the woman greeted with a smile. "Welcome to the Royal Ceriba Pier."

"Thanks," he said.

She waved at the shops that littered the causeway. "The souvenir and sundries shops are creds only. They have prices clearly marked for your convenience. Restaurants, on the other hand, are part of your all-inclusive cruise package. Simply flash your cruise confirmation number at your waiter, and you're good to go."

She gestured to the kiosk beside which she stood. "Let me get you checked in, and you can be on your way."

He smiled and nodded, accepting the colorful folio she handed him. She asked to see his ID token, and then asked for contact information in case of emergency.

"Standard procedure," she explained. "We've never had a cruise liner leave port that didn't return safely home."

The thief thought about listing his sister, but he was boarding under a fake ID. Since this trip was possible due to the windfall of the stolen vial, he decided to give the hacker's name and contact information instead.

Won't she be envious if they have to contact her to tell her we've been stranded somewhere in the Klintis, he thought, amused. *If catastrophe strikes, at least we'll go out in style!*

That task completed, he moved up into the boarding line, eschewing the kitschy storefronts with their cheap trinkets. Soon, he was ushered through the hatch and into the ship itself.

The yacht was a luxury liner, beautifully appointed, with

lush decor and walls lined with holodisplays. These were currently advertising the many sites voyagers would see along the way.

The ship flashed a notification to his overlay, inviting him to join the entertainment network. He accepted, and a pleasant voice announced the location of the dining hall, as well as his assigned eating time. Other notifications flashed, with titles that read 'Poolside', 'Theater Showtimes', and 'Spa Reservations'.

He reached for the final notification, the one entitled, 'Your Deluxe Stateroom Accommodations'. This one brought up a map, complete with a 'You Are Here' icon.

He turned down the passageway the map indicated, marveling when he saw human stewards and maids pushing maglev carts, instead of the expected servitors. He'd never been to a joint this classy.

He rubbed his chest. The feeling of malaise was beginning to irritate the hell out of him. He coughed discreetly into his hand, and a nearby maid mistook it for a sneeze.

"Bless you!" she said, handing him a tissue.

He thanked her and wiped his mouth with it. When it came back, there was a small smear of blood on it. This alarmed him, and he looked over at the maid.

"Where's the ship's medical department?"

He waved a hand at the alarmed look that crossed her face, protesting, "Oh no I'm fine. My medical nano has expired, is all, and I think I need a fresh infusion."

Relief crossed her face. "Two floors down, and back the way you came," she said, pointing.

He smiled his thanks, and moved on to his cabin, just a few doors down. Setting his overnight bag onto the bed, he moved into the lav, the holomirror activating when it sensed his presence. His eyes looked blearily back at him, and he realized with a start that he was exhausted. Rinsing his mouth, he was pleased to note that there was no more blood.

I'll go see the doctor after a quick nap, he thought to himself.

The bed beckoned, and he fell down beside his overnight bag, asleep in minutes.

BAD INTEL

LOWER WAREHOUSE DISTRICT
MERCER MINING TORUS

THE FLIGHT CREW inside the stealthed ship clinging to Mercer's port maintained a watchful silence while waiting for the team to return. Will monitored the torus's chatter, while Yuki watched the station's STC feed. Micah split his attention between *Wraith*'s hatch and the steady stream of ships that came and went from the mining station.

On the Myr side of the torus, large tankers slid through the black, making their way from Mercer to the white dwarf's planetary nebula remains. On the other side, tugs nudged along their netted cargo of boulders, gathered from the asteroid belt that lay between Mercer and the system's F-class star.

Everything was business as usual, so Micah reached out to Jonathan for a sitrep.

Hey, bro, any word on Cutter's plans to protect the scientists?

He knew his casual attempt to get an update on Sam had failed when he heard the amusement in his mirror twin's voice.

No, nothing yet, Jonathan responded. *It's pretty quiet here, though.*

Micah thought about that for a moment. *I tried pinging Sam earlier, but her wire was on Do Not Disturb. Would you try reaching her for me?*

Sure, bro. I'll— Heads up, Jonathan's mental tone abruptly changed. *New intel just came in. Thad's not going to like it. Looks like the snitch played us.*

Micah cursed, wrenching his mind back to the mission. His words drew Yuki's attention.

{*What is it?*} Her voice came over the ship's net.

{*Possible trouble.*} To Jonathan, he asked, *Played us? How?*

The good news is that this 'Drug Lord' dude really is on Mercer to meet with a few dealers. Bad news? He's not where our informant said he'd be.

Any idea where, then?

Well, it's sure as hell not at that bar Thad's staking out, Jonathan told him.

His twin pushed an image his way. It was a diagram of Mercer's warehouse district, with a low, three-story building highlighted.

The meeting's scheduled there, an hour from now. You'll be interested to hear that one of the people attending is rumored to be an Akkadian.

Shit. Team's already inserted, Micah said. *They've gone dark.*

We suspected as much. Valenti said you'd better haul ass. Get in there and find the team, before this whole thing falls apart.

Micah nodded and began to unweb.

"Boss?" Nina looked up as he passed between her station and Will's.

"The team's stakeout's a bust."

Will looked up, alarmed. "That drug guy's our only link to the thief, and that thief's our only link to the Akkadians who stole those vials. Does Jonathan have a bead on him?"

Micah gave a quick nod. "Valenti's sending me out to find Thad and update him."

Will swiveled his seat back to face his console. "I think I can use the connection the heist made to the torus to backdoor into their internal sensors. Let me run his profile and do a search. If I can ID his location, I'll send it to you."

"Better route it through Jonathan."

The rule was no comm traffic while inserted into a location. Fortunately, Micah's spooky connection to his non-chiral twin allowed for a way to communicate that was untraceable and gave off no EM signal.

Will nodded. "Copy that."

Micah suited up, trading his Navy blues for a drakeskin suit of light armor. The synthsilk weave could dissipate most projectiles rated for a space environment. Its external nano coating was tunable and could render him invisible if necessary.

Palming the weapons locker open, he reached inside for a CUSP. The CUSP was a compact, ultra-short pulse weapon that delivered brief bursts of laser-induced plasma when triggered. Depending upon its setting, the pistol could be used as a short-range flash-bang or flash-blind. It could paralyze or deliver searing pain to its subject. Though it was technically a nonlethal weapon, this particular CUSP was illegal for civilians to own.

He holstered it, and then slid a carbyne-edged tanto blade into its ankle sheath.

"The ship's yours," he called out to Yuki.

He slipped through the hatch as she gave the customary, "I have the ship."

* * *

The torus was a bustling station, but it lacked the shine and polish of a place like Leavitt. This was a mining platform; those who'd built it hadn't bothered with finishing touches.

The thick bulkheads were exposed, unpolished metal. They arched up to meet clearsteel panels along the inner rim, which allowed illumination from the small, fusion-powered sun at its hub to shine through.

The torus was small enough that there was only a single pair of maglev tracks that circumnavigated the fifteen-plus-kilometer habitat. Trains operated in opposition to each other, the cars running along a synchronized, scheduled route.

The nearest maglev platform was a half kilometer from the hatch, and Micah broke into a slow jog, mindful that, with his suit on active stealth, he was now hidden from view. The last thing the team needed was for someone to report a cloaked intruder after they ran into an invisible wall.

There was a train stopped at the platform, but not a single soul was on board. The sign that normally showed departure times was dark.

That was odd. In all of Micah's travels, he'd yet to see an empty maglev car in a habitat of this size. There were always at least a few workers heading home after a long shift, or on their way to a late-night dinner.

Unless the car had been pulled into service for a special reason, by someone with the resources to make that happen.

His suspicions were confirmed a moment later.

Found him, but you'd better hustle, Jonathan advised. *Will says he just boarded that train, and it's about to depart. Guy has bodyguards with him, too. Assume they're running active scan.*

Micah began sprinting toward the train. *You have **got** to be shitting me. Which car?*

The last one.

Micah had a split second to make the call. He didn't dare risk entering that last car for fear their scan would pick up the disturbance in the air—despite him being fully stealthed—but the doors to the other cars were already sealed. Unless he could hack them in time.

Problem was, the train would be taking off at any moment, and he'd be out of luck.

He'd just reached the next to last car, the one in front of his quarry, when the maglev began to move.

Aw hell, he thought, and before he could talk himself out of it, made a mad leap. *Tell Will to bypass the sensors on the train's hull,* he gritted out, *or this party'll be over before it has a chance to start.*

A tense few seconds passed before Jonathan confirmed Will had successfully hacked into its system, bypassing safety protocols and allowing him to remain undetected.

As the maglev continued to pick up speed, Micah pressed his body closer to the car when air resistance tried to peel him off. The wind brought tears to his eyes, but before he could blink them away, his optical implants cleared his vision for him. His mods and the drakeskin's capabilities were the only things allowing him to hang on.

Unfortunately, there was precious little to hold onto. He'd wedged the fingers of one hand into the almost nonexistent indentation where the car's door met its frame. His other was splayed against the rounded edge where the train's sidewall curved into its roof. Both feet were balanced on the curved bump housing the car's superconducting electromagnets.

The SmartCarbyne lattice woven throughout his body that reinforced bones, strengthened muscles, and protected organs also had picosensors that ran along the axons of his neural circuitry. They functioned as supplemental nodes and signal boosters, enhancing his already well-honed pilot's reflexes far beyond the human norm. These allowed Micah to maintain his balance while the maglev rocketed toward the warehouse district.

The ionic threads woven into the drakeskin suit helped, too. Tiny organogel strands surfaced the palms of his gloves and the soles of his boots. The short nanofibers had electrostatic properties that allowed the wearer to cling to a smooth surface like a limpet to a rock.

The maglev went around a curve, and he sucked in a breath as he felt his balance shift. He shifted his center mass to compensate, then did so again as the train came out of the curve. The train began to slow as it approached the upspin end of a trainyard, and Micah braced to dismount.

As the doors of the car behind him slid open and his quarry

exited, Micah released a cloud of colloid audio chaff to mask his movements. He pushed off from the car's electromagnet casing and landed on the maglev's platform in a controlled roll to minimize the chance that vibration would telegraph his presence.

Reaching into a utility pocket, he freed a surveillance microdrone, waited until the drug lord and his bodyguards walked past, and set the drone to float silently in their wake. Micah could just make out the shadowed silhouettes of warehouses ahead of them.

They're headed for their meet, he told Jonathan. *I'm going to follow along.*

He activated his flight suit's magnetic field generator, drawing the colloid cloud around him like an invisible, soundproofed shell.

Micah kept to the shadows, not wanting to rely too much on the drakeskin's capabilities, in case they were running countermeasures he'd not detected, but no one gave any indication they suspected they were being followed.

The warehouse they led him to was on the trainyard's downspin side. Row upon row of maglev boxcars were parked here, rounded rectangular forms casting long shadows in the torus's twilight, their holds filled with ore awaiting shipment.

Micah spared a glance through Mercer's transparent dome at the dark, inner ring more than a kilometer and a half away, and then consulted the time stamp on his overlay. He still had a good three hours before the inner ring's complex mirror system reconfigured from its nighttime state to bring sunrise to the torus.

Plenty of time to snag a drug lord and bug out.

Micah had the surveillance microdrone halt just inside the warehouse's entrance as he performed a passive scan for electronic tripwires and other digital countersurveillance that might alert the drug lord that he had been followed.

He loosed a second surveillance microdrone and had it circle the perimeter of the building for external monitoring devices, but came up empty. Setting the second drone to monitor the far side of the warehouse, Micah moved into the shadows between two buildings across the street that had seen better days. He crouched behind a collection of pipes that ran alongside one of the buildings, his eyes glued to the warehouse door across the street.

The feeds from the stealth recon microdrones now occupied two quadrants of his overlay, their images reduced so as not to impede his view of the street, should anyone else show up to join the party.

Only two sentries had been on duty when the group Micah followed had arrived. The first was sloppy, clearly bored with his duty. His rifle was a modified design with a short barrel, and rather than holding it at the ready, the sentry had it slung crosswise, his hands occupied lighting a stem stick. Micah figured this guy was depending on the warehouse's systems to warn him of a breach.

The other was more problematic. Unlike her partner, this one seemed new to the role, if a bit jumpy. She appeared equally disinterested in both her employer and the Akkadian, opting instead to peer into the dark cavern of unlit warehouse stretching before her.

She had lousy trigger discipline. Micah zoomed the feed from the microdrone to a closeup of her hand, and watched as she kept up a nervous pattern. Her finger slid over the trigger, then down the stock to press-test the SC batt's strength indicator before returning her finger to the trigger once more. He'd need to time her dispatch carefully, else he risked her getting off a wild shot that could alert the drug lord and his bodyguards to Micah's presence.

He'd seen all he needed. He took in a deep breath, prepared to rise—

A shift in the air currents was the only thing that warned him he was no longer alone. Letting out his breath on a slow exhale and ensuring his heartbeat remained steady, he reached for the carbyne nano-edged blade strapped to his calf.

He froze as he felt the bite of a different blade against his neck.

DEAD MAN'S BLUFF

Leah Harris's Office, CID
Montpelier, Ceriba

HARPER STAYED BEHIND in Addy's office while Gabe swept the programmer's work area for evidence, and Addy had the body moved to medical for an autopsy.

Harper had gladly left the removal of the body and the physical investigation to them. She was more effective—and far more comfortable—with data anyway. As an analyst, information was her domain.

Bonus, it doesn't involve blood or bodily fluids.

Once the room had been swept and the body transferred, Harper moved in, hard-linking with Leah's data port for better access. She'd been rifling through material for the past two hours. She was drowning in data, and yet she'd only scratched the surface.

She'd just decided to ask Gabe to requisition some additional help when a voice sounded over the team net.

{Hey, Harper? Anything I can do to help?} The ID attached to

the voice indicated it belonged to Katie Hyer. *{I tried reaching Agent Alvarez, but he and the captain both have their comms set to 'busy'. Can you use a hand?}*

Harper jumped on the offer, knowing neither Gabe nor Addy would mind. Katie Hyer was part of TF Blue, so she was automatically read in on the situation.

Besides, there was something creepy about sitting all alone in a dead woman's office, and the chief could code a mean LockPik. Maybe she could help figure this out.

{I'd appreciate that, actually. Let me send you my location.}

She pushed a map of the Center to Katie, and then instructed the security kiosk to clear the chief warrant's token for immediate entry into Rufus's corridors.

Ten minutes later, she heard a running conversation outside Harris's office door, and realized Dave, the glitchy SI, had found Hyer.

"Would the chief warrant like to try a macchiato?"

"No!" Harper jumped out into the hallway before Katie had a chance to respond.

The other woman gave her a funny look, and Harper's eyes widened in a silent *'just go along with it'* message that thankfully, Katie understood.

"Very well, then. Have a nice day."

Have a nice day? Buddy, that flew out the window the minute you glitched and your programmer turned up dead....

Harper pushed Katie into Leah Harris's office and then activated the 'Police Line—Do Not Cross' holographic stanchions Gabe had given her in case she ended up having to deal with curious visitors. She turned to face Katie. The woman looked at her as if she had a few nanofilaments loose upstairs.

"Wanna tell me what *that* was all about?"

Harper pushed away from the door. "I think that SI's base code has been altered, and I think the Center's lead programmer had something to do with it."

"Well, why don't you just confront her with it, then?"

Harper grimaced. "Kind of hard to do when we just found

her body."

"She's *dead?*"

"Uh huh." Harper looked around uncomfortably. "And we're standing in her office."

Instead of mirroring her slightly freaked-out feelings, an intrigued look crossed the chief's face.

"Cool. So, what's the plan, and where do we start?"

Harper waved to the hard-link at the room's lone desk. "I've been going through the secured user data server the CID assigned to Leah. There's something interesting inside, and it wasn't there earlier today—I checked."

The chief wandered over to the desk. "What is it?"

"A ghost drive. Far's I can tell, it appeared right after she died. I think Leah Harris had a dead man's switch."

"A *what?*" Katie's head whipped around.

"You heard me."

Harper dragged a second chair up to the holodisplay. Gesturing for the chief to sit, she jacked back into the port and pulled up the secured data partition.

"Check it out. This is the network sector the Center automatically allocated to Leah when she was first hired, five years ago."

She waved a hand, and 'wayback' images began to populate on the screen, snapshots of the CID's network servers from one, three, and five years ago. She compared them to a snapshot of the current volume.

Highlighting an icon tucked in with the rest of Leah's work files, she said, "See there? That volume's data cache isn't listed anywhere in the past five years. It just suddenly appeared..." Harper checked the server's recent activity log, "two hours and forty-seven minutes ago."

The chief stared, speculation in her eyes. "Why do you think it's a dead man's switch?"

"The timing. Take a look. Addy's already uploaded her preliminary findings on the autopsy she's doing. Time of death occurred a little after oh-seven hundred this morning. Two hours, twenty-four minutes ago, to be exact."

The chief looked thoughtful.

"The one thing I can't figure out is, why the gap?" Harper continued. "I mean, there's almost ten minutes between time of death and when the volume suddenly appears. I suppose there might be a timed-delay thing, but I have no idea why—"

She broke off as a stunned awareness crossed the chief's features.

"Well, I'll be a plasma pissin' pulsar," Katie breathed. "I think...oh, wow. Yeah, that tracks." The chief warrant began to nod, eyes blinking rapidly as she thought through whatever revelation had suddenly hit her. "If I'm right," she said slowly, "there's a good reason why there's a ten-minute gap, give or take, between time of death and the dead man's switch."

She turned to the hard-link and began accessing data at a rapid rate. Streams of text and images of the human brain flew past, faster than Harper could follow.

Finally, after a few minutes, the chief grunted. "There," she said, enlarging one of the reports she'd pulled.

The file was a medical document on the web-like neural lattice that connected a person's consciousness to their embedded wire. The implant interfaced with critical spaces in the brain: information inputs at dendrites, data outputs at synaptic terminals. This was how people connected to local networks and communicated mentally with one another.

The file on the holoscreen showed what happened to the fine mesh of carbyne nanofloss embedded in the brain at the time of death. The lattice underwent a state of rapid decay once neural function ceased.

"So Leah's switch must have been tied to a sensor in her lattice," Harper murmured. "The sensor would have triggered an alarm when the woman's neural activity dropped to zero."

"Activating the dead man's switch, yeah," Katie nodded. "But it didn't do anything when it first detected the decay of your vic's neural lattice. It purposely delayed the seven to ten minutes it took for all brain activity to cease. Until there was no hope for resuscitation."

Harper blinked at the morbid imagery that evoked. "How did you know about the ten minute gap thing?"

"I overheard Doc Moran telling Gabe about it once. The delay you mentioned was what reminded me of it. The explanation tracks with what we're seeing here."

The chief tugged absently at a jewel-encrusted earlobe. The blue stone twinkled in the office's light. "So you think Leah might've left something on this ghost drive that'll lead us to the Akkadians who stole those vials?"

"Let's find out."

Harper brought the ghost drive forward on the holoscreen and they began scrolling through its holographic quantum register, sifting through its data hierarchy.

It took a while to coax information out of the volume of files the drive held, but after a few intense minutes of work, Katie sat back with a grin.

"Found something!"

What she had discovered were the meticulous records Leah kept of every interaction she had with the people who had hired her to steal the vials, but the feeds appeared untraceable.

Harper forwarded the information to Blue's headquarters to study anyway, in the hope they might see something she and Katie missed.

"Well." Harper sat back, frowning at the holo in front of her. "That was a bit of a dead end. And we still don't have any information on which vials she actually stole."

Katie shot her a curious look. "You said that SI of yours is acting up. Could she have hidden the information inside his base code?"

Harper opened up the SI file she'd flagged earlier. "Only one way to find out."

Pages of source code began scrolling past. The more she saw, the more she couldn't help but marvel at the deceased woman's skills.

"Pity her ethics weren't as strong as her ability to code," she remarked. "We could've used someone like this."

Katie sat up. "Hang on, did you see that?"

Harper scrolled back until a section that looked different from the rest caught her eye. "You mean this?"

Katie pointed to a section of code that was commented out, a method used by programmers to temporarily disable the code so that a remark or explanation could be inserted. "Yeah, that, right there." The chief warrant leaned forward. "But that notation makes no sense. It's like—"

"Like the commented section is encrypted?" Harper felt a stirring of anticipation. Maybe they were finally onto something.

"Yeah," Katie agreed. Her eyes narrowed. "Now all we need to do is crack it."

"If this ghost drive is any indication of how Leah Harris's mind worked, I'm betting it won't be a simple cipher."

"We have to start somewhere, though," Katie pointed out.

While the chief ran the commented section through standard decryption algorithms, Harper's mind drifted back to her discovery of the dead man's switch.

"I wonder...."

She reached out to Addy once more, relieved when the doctor answered.

{Does the CID keep copies of employees' DNA sequences in their medical records, by chance?}

{Yes. Why do you ask?}

Harper made a noncommittal sound. *{I'm not entirely certain yet, but it's possible Leah used her own DNA to encrypt something.}*

{I'll push the file to you here in a second,} Addy replied. *{Need anything else?}*

{Not now, thanks.}

Harper severed the link, and a few seconds later, a notification popped up on her overlay. She found a file waiting for her, filled with G-C-A-T tags and helical structures.

She grabbed the data, feeding it into the NSA's decryption

algorithm.

"Here," she told Katie, sending her the DNA crack. "Try this."

The chief warrant caught it and flipped it onto the holoscreen.

"Nope," she said after a few seconds had passed without any activity. "Got any other ideas?"

Harper's gaze landed on a holoframe, sitting dark on the corner of the programmer's desk. She reached over and toggled it on. An album appeared, filled with images of two people—Leah and a young man with similar features.

Harper sat back, studying the image.

"Brother, maybe?" Katie suggested.

Harper shrugged. "Feels right. Let me check her personnel file."

There, listed as next of kin, was one Charles Harris. He was a student at the U of Ceriba, St. Clair, studying machine learning, much like his sister had.

Leah's younger brother had also gone missing six weeks earlier.

"That right there could be motive," Katie remarked. "And maybe the DNA we need isn't hers, but her brother's."

Nodding her agreement, Harper's eyes swept the small office once more, something about it pulling at her memory. She stopped when she saw the U of Ceriba jacket that hung from a peg beside the office door.

"That jacket looks a bit big for a stick of a girl who's about fifty-five kilos, wouldn't you say?" she murmured.

Katie angled a look her way. "You think it's her brother's?"

"I think if I had a brother who'd gone missing under shady circumstances, I'd find comfort in having something of his nearby."

She reached for her bag, extracting a site survey microdrone and sample case, glad she'd thought to bring one along. It didn't take the small airborne machine long to identify three different traces of DNA on the jacket. Two of them were female, but the third was male.

She pulled the sample and uploaded the data to the Center's medical department, with a request that the sample be sequenced.

"That'll take an hour or two," she said, standing. "Let's go grab some lunch."

An hour later, they were back with fresh eyes and ready to tackle the rest of the drive. A few hours into the afternoon, a notification appeared across Harper's datalink.

"Got the DNA sequence back," she told Katie, opening a new window and importing the file that medical had sent.

She pushed it through the decryption algorithm and then applied the results to the scrambled sections of the SI's base code.

"Bingo," she said as the alphanumeric strings began reordering themselves into coherent sentences.

Both women read along as the code unpacked. The commented-out sections were a confession of sorts. Leah documented everything she'd done, and included a list of each of the stolen vials, by serial number.

"Holy—" Harper whispered. "She hacked Dave and then used the SI to steal the vials?"

"Looks like," Katie said.

As she scanned the information Leah had left, Harper realized the woman had done what she could to minimize the damage.

"Look," she said, highlighting a section. "She says they ordered her to steal L4 vials, but she sent L2 vials instead."

Katie looked up. 'Think that's what got her killed?"

Harper shook her head. "I don't think so. My credits are on them wanting to tie up loose ends." She leaned forward.Look. She sent Dave in to grab some empty L4 vials, and then ordered him to fill them with L2 material."

Katie looked at her. "Yes, but that doesn't explain why the L2 material's not showing as missing."

The chief warrant sat back and stared up to the ceiling, running blunt-tipped fingers through her short, blue hair as she thought through the possibilities.

"You think maybe she was skimming off the top, so to speak, to keep the theft hidden?" she asked slowly. "Maybe we'll find vials that have less volume than the rest."

Harper's brow furrowed. "The only way we're going to know for sure is to go into that lab and see for ourselves."

Katie jackknifed up. "Uhm, that's a hard no."

Harper smiled. "You weren't here for Addy's talk. No worries. L2's not the hazardous stuff. I'll do it."

The other woman shot her a doubtful look before she returned her attention to the folder with the SI's base code. She highlighted a companion file, one that recorded Dave's activities on that date. "Maybe you won't have to. This'll tell us what he did."

The SI's data record proved Katie's theory right; Leah had indeed ordered Dave to siphon material from some of the L2 vials. But then the record began showing error logs.

"Oh, damn," Harper said.

Katie reached for the command right before the error, and then scrubbed forward to the one immediately following it.

"This goes way beyond 'oh damn'," the chief said. "He glitched in the middle of the swap."

"Looks like she saw it and sent the command again."

Katie shot her a grim look. "Yeah, but look at exactly *where* in the process he froze. We're missing a good thirty seconds here. There's no record in his logs of Dave executing the command to acquire empty L4 vials. We have no proof, no way of knowing what he took."

Harper drew in a breath. "We do if I go down there."

Katie began to protest, and Harper waved her off.

"Look, I know we've already copied the ghost drive, but I'd feel better if you stayed here and kept this console active. I'll go check these serial numbers out in person, and you can cross-check me, okay? I think that's the only way to know for certain which vials are missing."

CONTAGION

ROYAL CERIBA YACHT *ATLIEKAN QUEEN*
ATLIEKAS NEBULA PARK

ZOYA NOLOTOV, THE yacht's captain, looked up from her holodisplay as a chime sounded, indicating someone was at her office door.

"Come in," she called out. When Josh, the yacht's chief medical officer, stepped inside, she indicated a chair. "What's up, doc?"

Serious eyes pegged hers. "We have a problem."

Nolotov was retired Navy. She'd spent decades captaining some of the Alliance's finest ships. Along with that came the responsibility of leadership, and she'd long ago mastered the ability to read her subordinates. She leaned back in her chair and studied him, noting his set jaw.

It was rare for the doctor to seek her out during the first few days of a launch, beyond the usual staff briefings. Usually, he was too busy with his staff, reviewing special passenger requirements for the seven-day voyage.

When he did drop by to see her, their relationship was more casual than the ones Zoya'd had while in the Navy. There, procedures were regimented. It had taken her a good year to get used to the fact that in the private sector, there could be three different ways to accomplish the same thing. That had resulted in a few disagreements between her and Josh.

Intellectually, she knew the cruise line catered to the affluent, and that they expected a certain standard of care. It was another thing altogether to learn that occasionally, passengers would use the trip to receive elective or cosmetic surgical procedures. She wondered if this was another problem along those lines, and reminded herself this wasn't a Navy ship.

"A problem?" Zoya repeated. "What kind of a problem?"

"One of our housekeeping staff has shown up in medical with respiratory symptoms," Josh said. "Her illness is resistant to standard treatment."

She thought about that for a moment. "The fact you're here talking to me suggests this goes beyond telling her to take the day off."

Josh nodded. "I might be borrowing trouble, but would rather err on the side of caution. It's possible she has a new virus. They mutate all the time, especially the RNA ones. If that's the case, she can't interact with anyone until she's no longer shedding the virus, so she's in isolation right now."

"Do we need to be concerned about people she may have infected?"

The doctor's worried eyes met hers. "That's really the reason I'm here. A family came in just an hour ago. Their six-year-old daughter is having difficulty breathing, same as my first patient. The kid's worsening, and nothing I've given her is helping. Whatever they have is pneumonic."

Her eyebrows rose. "Pneumonic?"

"Means it involves the respiratory system. The virus attaches to cells in the lungs."

Zoya sat back and thought a moment. "I'm sure you've done

a contact trace on everyone she ran into," she began, but broke off when he shook his head.

"Our sick staff member's not our patient zero. I already ran their ID tokens, and the little girl never came anywhere near her."

Alarmed, the captain stood. "How do we keep this from spreading, then?"

"That's going to be a bit more difficult. Both the maid and the little girl have interacted with thousands already. And then there's patient zero."

"Have you questioned your patients about where they've been recently? Did they recall running into anyone onboard who might be ill?"

"I have." The doctor looked down at his hands. "They both gave a description—it matches. The passenger our worker ran into asked for directions to medical, but he never showed up."

That concerned Zoya. "Does she recall where she saw this passenger?"

The doctor nodded. "Gardenia Deck, around stateroom G-47, she thinks. Her mind's a little fuzzy at the moment."

Zoya stared thoughtfully into the distance as she considered whether to initiate quarantine protocol.

"I don't want to overreact," she said slowly, "but do you think this warrants a shutdown?"

"I think it warrants contacting headquarters, and letting them know that we have a problem," Josh replied. "I have one of the nurses running a blood panel on both patients. Currently, they're being given fluids and are resting comfortably."

"Okay. I'll defer entirely to you on this, of course," she told him. "Whatever you recommend."

* * *

Two hours later, Zoya received a ping from the doctor.

{I think we found patient zero.} There was a pause and then he continued. *{I've taken the liberty to contact someone I know at*

the CID on Ceriba.}

The captain felt a shaft of surprise. *{Isn't that a bit...drastic?}*

{I can assure you, it's not. He's unresponsive, and in severe respiratory distress.}

She saw him initiate a request for a visual feed. She accepted it, throwing the connection up on her office's holoscreen.

His worried gaze stared back at her.

"How serious is it?"

"Serious enough," he said, ticking off the list with his fingers. "It's respiratory. It's fast-acting. And it's stealthy. It's able to remain hidden from my patients' immune systems while it replicates inside, until it swamps their defenses."

"Hidden?" Zoya repeated.

Josh nodded. "Some viruses are quite clever. They can mimic human RNA, fooling the body's security system into thinking it belongs."

"You talk about them as if they're alive, like some kind of enemy combatant."

Josh cocked his head. "In a way, they are. Well, they're not alive, like parasites or fungi or bacteria. But they're not technically dead, either. They're sort of like zombies."

She shook her head. "Now, there's an interesting mental picture."

Josh dipped his head in agreement. "A virus is like a really cunning thief; it'll attach itself to a certain cell type within the body and hack its way inside. Once there, it hijacks the cell, using the material inside to replicate itself."

"That sounds almost like guerilla warfare," Zoya said, thinking back to some of the more covert missions she'd flown with the Navy.

Josh nodded. "That's actually a good analogy. But this particular terrorist also has the ability to mutate or reassort its genetic material into new combinations." He looked pensive, as if he was reaching mentally for an analogy. "Kind of like if your terrorist came in with a flechette pistol but could change it to a CUSP or a frag grenade at will."

The captain blinked. As analogies went, the one Josh presented was damn scary.

"They're medicine's outliers. That's why viruses may be the one thing we never cure." Josh shook his head. "At any rate, I've sent everything we have on the patients to my contact at the CID. They should be getting back to me very soon. Until then, I really do think we need to initiate quarantine procedures."

Zoya pinched the bridge of her nose, a sudden headache starting behind her eyes. She nodded. "I'll make an announcement. Do you know how many people have been potentially exposed?"

A pained look crossed the doctor's face. "We ran a contact trace on everyone who's been within two meters of him, our maid, and the young girl's family."

"And?"

"And we're looking at upwards of five thousand people," he said.

"Stars gone nova," she muttered. "That's more than half of those on board this ship."

MISLABELED

LEVEL TWO CONTAINMENT, CID
MONTPELIER, CERIBA

HARPER LEFT KATIE behind in Leah's office while she ran up to the L2 lab to do an in-person visual check of the vials. True to form, the chief warrant kept a running commentary the entire way.

{You think maybe we should have waited to do this until Alvarez and the doctor came back online?}

Katie didn't sound nervous; Harper wasn't sure the chief warrant even knew how to *do* nervous. But she was questioning the wisdom of their actions. Harper could appreciate that, but she also knew the Akkadians weren't going to wait for them to catch up.

{All we're going to do is check the serial numbers on a few vials so we can identify what's missing. What can go wrong?}

Katie groaned as Harper entered the lift. *{Now you've gone and **jinxed** us, Kinsley. Don't you know nothing about ops?}*

Harper laughed. *{Hey, I'm an analyst, not an agent, remember? I don't go on ops. For a badass Navy pilot, you sure are* *superstitious.}*

The lift doors opened, depositing her onto the floor where the L2 labs were located. As she passed by Addy's office, she peeked in the open door. Neither the doctor nor Gabe were inside.

{Huh,} she said.

{Huh, what?} Katie asked.

{Oops, sorry. Didn't realize I'd sent that. Looks like Addy and Gabe are still in medical with the body,} Harper said.

When the chief responded, her voice sounded thoughtful. *{Feels wrong to call her 'the body' now that we've gotten to know her a bit, doesn't it?}*

{Yeah…. }

She came to a stop in front of the L2 containment doors, passed the security program her Mil-Int credentials, and stepped inside.

{Well, it's just like Addy described. Two labs, and a room for our favorite pair of troublemakers.}

The labs were dark, but the ferrets' room was lit. She crossed over to it, curious to see how the captain had set up their home.

{Okay, now I'm jealous,} Hyer said. *{I kinda miss those little guys. They sure made the trip back to Ceriba interesting.}*

Harper grinned at the memory. *{Try spending a few weeks sneaking through Luyten's Star with those two. Interesting's a mild way of putting it.}*

As she stopped in front of the door, she saw a digital placard announcing the room's occupants as 'chiral laboratory animals'. She frowned at the implications those words held, but as she looked through the windows, she had to admit the ferrets' setup looked pretty swank.

The clearsteel panes stretched from floor to ceiling, giving her an unobstructed view of the various layers and textures that filled the smaller room. Her eyes drifted across platforms and ladders, plush nests and tall cat trees. In one corner, she could just make out a small, wet nose, peeking out of a darkened, felted cave. Its whiskers and paws were twitching as it dreamed.

Harper craned her neck, searching for the ferret's mirror twin, and was disappointed she didn't see him.

She stepped away from the window and went over to the lab's door. This, too, required her credentials to access, as it was no simple entrance. The two-stage airlock system had a sensor suite that would sweep for contaminants on her way back out.

She passed through a light decon mist and then felt a pressure differential as the second set of doors opened. Harper paused on the threshold before entering the lab proper and uncapped a small cylinder, releasing a swarm of crime scene microdrones. She ordered them to sweep the area for material that would identify those who had most recently been inside.

To her mind, the sweep was more procedural than anything. Harper was convinced Leah had told the truth, and the vial's thief was, indeed, the Center's SI. That meant the drones should find nothing out of place.

Unfortunately, Harper had no proof to back up her theory, since Leah had erased the feeds that monitored the secured labs—all of them, L2 through L4—on the day in question.

An alert flashed as the swarm pushed a 'completed' message to her overlay.

{Drone sweep complete,} she told Katie, recalling the units to their cache. *{Pushing telemetry your way now.}*

{Got it,} the other woman confirmed after a moment. *{Cross referencing against the list of technicians cleared to enter the lab.}*

Harper took in a deep breath. *{That's it, then. I'm stepping inside.}*

Her gaze panned across the neat and sparsely furnished area. The room was pristine, not a thing out of place. Broad lab benches lined the walls, with a few long tables running down its center. Tidy rows of lab equipment were pushed against the wall or tucked into alcoves. The large preservation unit that contained the chiral specimens sat in one corner.

Other than a low hum from the unit, the only sound in the room came from Harper's heels, which clicked crisply against the tiled floor as she crossed over to the vials.

She heard a familiar chittering sound, followed by a voice that asked, *{You bring food? Sam with you? Micah? Micah too?}*

There was a scratching sound, and she turned to see a pair of tiny hands scrabbling at the door that separated the lab from the ferret's domain.

"Hey there, Sneaky Pete."

The ferret scrubbed his ear with one paw. *{Snotface,}* the animal corrected. He turned, arching his whiskers in the direction of the felted cube. *{Sneaky Pete asleep. Nest through there.}*

"Ah, sorry about that."

She turned back to the preservation unit, but Snotface wasn't done.

{Harper visit?}

"Sorry, little dude, I can't just yet. I have work to do."

{Work, work, work,} the ferret sighed.

Harper's lips twitched at the disgust in the creature's mental tone.

When she didn't respond, he upped his game.

{Bored, bored, bo-ored. Open door?} Snotface's voice was hopeful.

Harper glanced around at the lab and then back down at the ferret. "Something tells me they don't exactly let you roam around in here unsupervised. Not with all of the chiral samples they're working on."

{Not unsupervised,} Snotface reasoned. *{You here.}*

Amusement flared at his words. She'd learned on the return trip from Luyten's Star how futile it was to argue against ferret logic.

Steeling herself, she shook her head. "Nope, sorry, guy. But if you behave yourself, I'll let you in on a little secret. The chief warrant's here, too."

{Hyer? Hyer? Where?} Snotface stretched to his full height, palms patting the transparent door that separated them. *{Shiny blue! Wanna see!}*

She laughed at the ferret's enthusiasm. *{Hey, Chief,}* she told

Katie, *{you have a fan down here, asking about you.}*

{Awww, they remember me?}

Harper chuckled. *{And your earring.}*

{Tell 'em I'll come up and see them when we're done with this mess. Chief's honor.}

Snotface patted the door more insistently. *{Open! Need see Hyer now!}*

"Patience," Harper said with a smile. "I'll be in to see you in a minute, okay?"

{No fun, no fun,} he complained.

"You want fun?" She lifted a brow. "The chief with the sparkly blue earring says she'll come for a visit soon, but only if you behave."

The ferret dropped to a crouch, head tilted as if considering her words. Harper took that for compliance, and turned back to the unit, her focus once more on the job.

The samples were in a special case sectioned off within the preservation unit. It, too, required her credentials to gain access.

Well, I can't fault them for their security. How in the Suns of Sirius was Leah able to bypass all of this encryption to get to the vials?

She reached for the first one, and she and Katie began the tedious process of manually cross-referencing Leah's list against what was in the case.

{Okay, so far, nothing's in there that shouldn't be there,} Katie summarized as Harper reached the final row.

By the end, they'd identified three missing vials, but had only found one that shouldn't be there.

She reached once more for the one with the mysterious serial number. *{And you're sure it doesn't match anything from L4, either, right?}*

{Nope.} Katie sounded positive. *{That vial in your hand isn't in the system anywhere. Far's I can tell, it shouldn't exist.}*

As Harper's palm wrapped around it, she thought she could feel a difference in the label.

{Hang on. I think....}

She pulled it out to examine it more closely. Running her thumb against the label's seam, she pried a bit of it away. *{Yeah, this label's thicker than the others. I think it's not on the list because it's a fake label. Hang on, let me see if I can't get a look at what's underneath....}*

{Be careful,} Katie cautioned. *{If we go by Leah's notes, that thing's likely from L4.}*

{Almost have it....} Harper wiggled her thumbnail deeper into the groove she'd made, and the label began to peel back. "Gotcha," she murmured.

So intent was she on her discovery, she didn't hear the door that separated the lab from the ferrets' quarters open. Nor did she hear the soft scurrying sounds of ferret feet as they crossed to the preservation unit.

Tiny paws grabbed hold of her trousers and began to climb. Harper shrieked, the vial slipping through her fingers to crash against the floor. In the next instant, an alarm began to sound, and an ES field slammed into place, isolating her and the ferret inside.

Harper stumbled back, her foot slipping in her haste, and she went crashing to the floor.

Snotface quickly scrambled to her shoulders, his tail wrapping around her neck. *{Oh no, oh no,}* he snuffled into her ear. The ferret quivered as the shrill alarm continued to sound.

{Harper? Harper!}

Katie's voice rang inside her head, but Harper was too busy trying to figure out her next move to respond.

Her gaze raced around the room, looking for something, anything she could use to isolate the vial, lying two meters away. Spying a small transparent case, she scrambled to her feet, snatched it off the bench, and slammed it down on top of the specimen.

Tiny paws patted her cheek. *{You make noise stop now?}* the ferret asked anxiously.

Harper stared down at her hands holding the transparent case in place. A part of her mind observed distantly that they were trembling.

She reached up with one hand to comfort the creature, murmuring to him quietly. Inside, her gut was quaking every bit as much as the ferret was.

Katie's voice cut in once more. *{So help me, Kinsley, if you don't answer….}*

{I'm here. Sorry. There's…been an accident.}

{What do you mean? What kind of accident?} The chief's voice was sharp.

Harper gave a shaky laugh, but there wasn't much humor behind it. *{Take a look.}*

Her optics had recorded the serial number underneath the fake label right before she dropped it. She sent the image to Katie.

*{Ohhhhhhh **shit**.}*

Harper silently agreed.

The vial lying underneath that clearsteel case didn't belong to this lab. It was an L4 pathogen.

DAMAGE CONTROL

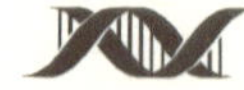

MEDICAL DEPARTMENT, CID
MONTPELIER, CERIBA

GABE SCROLLED THROUGH the data the sweeper bots had gathered from Leah Harris's office one last time before swiping the holoscreen off. As he suspected, they'd found nothing out of the ordinary.

Wanting to compare notes with Addy's findings, he left the room in medical that he'd temporarily commandeered, and went in search of her. They nearly collided as she bolted from the exam room that held Leah Harris's body.

"What's going on?" he asked as she sped past.

"Containment breach!"

"*What?*"

Shock held him immobilized for a brief instant, and then he turned and raced after her. He caught up to her at the lifts.

She paced in front of the doors like a caged lion, tension coiled in her compact frame. Gabe realized the woman before him was the same one he'd seen on deGrasse: a chief surgeon who took charge, barking orders like a drill instructor laying into greenie recruits. This woman was focused, at the tip of the spear, ready to engage.

Gabe also suspected she'd cut down anyone who got in her way.

"Talk to me, Addy. What kind of breach? Where?"

The lift doors opened, and he stepped in beside her.

She met his eyes as she input their destination. "It's Harper. She's been exposed to a pathogen."

"How bad?"

The doors of the lift closed, the brushed metal surface blurring their reflections. Even so, he could see her frown.

"I won't know until I get up there." Her voice was brusque, distracted.

"Pathogen," he repeated. "She wouldn't have been in L3 or L4 unless she suspected that's where the stolen vials were taken from. That's not good news."

"It's worse than that." Addy turned to face him, expression grim. "She wasn't in one of those labs. The spill occurred in an L2 lab."

Gabe's shock must have shown on his face.

Addy pointed. "That was my reaction, too. L2 *has* no pathogens. I don't know how it got there, but sensor readings don't lie."

Gabe worked his jaw as he considered how this might have happened. "I think it's time we lock that SI down," he said. "I'll go find Hyer and see what she can glean from his code."

The lift doors opened onto the Project Rufus wing, and Gabe held up a hand.

"Addy, wait."

Her head snapped to the side, anger flashing in her eyes at the presumed delay, but she held her tongue as he stepped out and kept pace with her.

"Is there anything else I can do to help?"

The captain shook her head as they raced past her office, toward the second checkpoint that separated the L2 labs from the rest of the floor.

"Let me see what she's been exposed to and get her the antigen," she called out over her shoulder. "Then we'll figure out how in hell this thing got loose."

He came to a stop, shooting her a quick salute before turning to retrace his steps. He paused when an alert flashed on his overlay. When he saw who was on the other end, he ducked into Addy's office and locked it behind him.

Toggling the room's privacy function, he took a seat as he accepted the transmission from Duncan Cutter.

{Sir. What can I do for you?}

The director's voice was grim. *{You can find my niece for me, Agent Alvarez. Sam's missing.}*

* * *

Addy had used her wire to trigger the L2 checkpoint, sending her credentials on ahead so that she could hit the doors at a dead run. Slipping through the moment they parted far enough to give her access, she sprinted for the lab where the containment breach alert flashed.

Her eyes went straight to the figure huddled on the floor behind the ES field as she came to a stop.

"Harper?" she called out, as one hand reached for the hazmat locker inset into the wall beside the lab's entrance.

The analyst looked up. "It was an accident," she said. "He didn't mean to...."

Her voice trailed off, and her head lowered.

Addy's eyes followed, and she saw the small form Harper held in her arms. A quick glance over at the habitat where the ferrets lived showed her an open door, and she could guess what had happened.

"He figured out how to unlock it."

Harper nodded. "He's still breathing. Will he be okay?"

Harper looked back up, and Addy could see the woman's eyes were glassy with fever. As she watched, a small trickle of blood began seeping from Harper's nose.

"Quickly, tell me what happened."

Harper swiped at her nose absently and nodded toward the preservation unit. "I was cross-referencing the serial numbers to see what was missing, and came across a number that didn't match. I'd pulled the vial out to examine it, when Snotface started climbing my leg. I hadn't heard him come in, and he startled me. I dropped it."

Addy had donned one of the protective suits while Harper talked. Slipping her left hand into the medical bracer she'd brought with her, she ordered the suit to power up. Its electrostatic properties were similar to those of a drakeskin suit, but in reverse. When triggered, it shed unwanted material like a dog shaking water from its coat.

She had the suit handshake with the ES field and stepped forward, allowing it to envelop her.

Harper watched, her hand coming up once more to wipe at her nose. When she noticed it came back bloody, she looked up, eyes wide. "Captain?" she whispered.

Addy held up a calming hand. "It's okay, I'm here. We'll get through this together."

She knelt beside Harper and cycled the bracer into diagnostic mode. Resting it against the analyst's neck, she injected a swarm of symptom checker nano, and then withdrew samples to analyze.

"Tell me more about that vial over there," Addy ordered as she moved the bracer over the ferret's flank and began treating him.

Harper moved her hands away from Snotface to give Addy room to work.

"The label felt thicker than the others," she said, "so I started pulling on it to see if I could expose the label underneath. I caught a glimpse before I dropped it. The number sequence begins with L4."

Addy nodded.

Telemetry had begun to filter in for both Harper and the

ferret. It confirmed her initial assessment: symptoms indicated a hemorrhagic virus.

"Let's see if it'll tell us what's in you, then."

Addy moved to the transparent case, bending to study the vial. She'd loaded the list of chiral virus pairs from the L4 labs on her way here and knew there were variants of Marburg, Lujo, and Sargon being studied. She was betting it was one of them.

She lifted the case covering the vial, and Harper gasped.

"What are you doing?"

As she examined the label the analyst had begun to pull away, Addy explained, "I need this serial number to confirm...."

She found the number on the list and breathed a soft sigh of relief.

"It's a Sargon variant," she said, "And it's one of the chiral pairs."

She crossed to the nearest lab station and reached into the cabinet that hung above it for a sterile dish.

"Is that bad?" Harper's voice was shaking.

"No," Addy said, looking up with a quick smile. "It's good, actually."

She poured the vial's contents into the dish. Along with the liquid came a second, inner vial.

She lifted it and showed it to Harper. "Every chiral pair we cloned had a secondary cylinder, tucked inside the non-chiral container. Inside this second vial is the virus's antigen."

She upended the sealed cylinder, pressing its lid into an ampoule socket on her bracer. Once the antigen was fully loaded, Addy returned to Harper's side. Kneeling down on the floor beside her, she ran her fingers through the holographic readout that hovered just above her bracer-clad forearm.

"It's loaded in here now. Let's get it inside you, shall we?"

Her wire's connection to the bracer allowed her to mentally prioritize the nano delivery system and dispense the antigen first to where it was most needed within Harper's body. Once she injected the woman, she repeated the process for the ferret.

Harper's gaze followed Addy's hand as she injected Snotface

with the antigen.

"Will he live?" she asked.

Addy smiled reassuringly. "You'll both be fine. It'll take a little bit for the medical nano to fully repair the damage the virus inflicted on both of you, so no strenuous activity for a few days, okay?"

The analyst nodded, stroking the ferret's fur. Addy reached for a tissue and handed it to her.

As the analyst wiped the blood from her face and hands, Addy asked, "You said you identified two of the missing vials?"

"Yes. All but two of the samples from this level have been accounted for, so I think it's safe to say that two of the stolen vials were from here."

"So that leaves two that were not," the captain reasoned, glancing down at the spill staining the floor. "Do you have any idea how this got in here?"

The analyst nodded with a bit more energy than she'd had moments ago, and Addy was happy to see her color improving. But when she moved as if to stand, Addy placed a restraining hand on her shoulder.

"Not just yet," she advised.

Harper nodded and settled back down to the floor, her gaze straying to the spill. "As we suspected, Leah Harris altered Dave's programming," she told Addy. "Her orders from Akkadia were to obtain L4 vials, or they'd kill her brother."

"Her brother? That's a pretty strong incentive."

Harper looked pensive. "In a way, it was very brave of her to try to substitute L2 vials by placing fake L4 labels on them," she said. "I think it was her intent to send something a lot less dangerous out the door. It would have worked, too, except for one thing."

"What's that?" Addy asked.

"He glitched."

"He? You mean Dave?"

Harper nodded. "Yeah, he glitched like he did in your office, right in the middle of carrying out her orders. When he froze, I think Leah sent the order a second time. The only problem was that the command came on the heels of the first one. So when Dave unfroze, I think he executed the command twice."

Addy nodded. "Gabe's on his way down to meet with the chief warrant. They're going to round up that SI and take him offline."

Harper waved a hand. "The chief's already done it. Dave's base code had a self-monitoring routine running. That's how we found the glitch that led to this." She gestured around her.

Addy's eyes moved back to the spilled vial. "If one L4 made it down here, then it's possible that the other two missing vials we've yet to identify are also L4s."

She saw Harper shudder. "That would be... awful."

Addy glanced down at her bracer once more, encouraged by Harper's rising health levels. She rose to her feet. Holding out a hand, she said, "Are you feeling well enough to stand?"

At Harper's nod, she helped the analyst to her feet, and motioned her to the decontamination chamber, inset beside the lab's entrance.

"Let's get you two through decon."

While Harper stripped and endured the chamber's sanitization process, Addy interfaced with the lab and ordered the room's automated systems to contain and neutralize the hazardous material.

"Quit fussing," she heard Harper scold, as a protesting squeak sounded from within.

Addy smiled her first real smile of the day when she heard a tiny voice sound over her wire.

*{Ferrets not **need** bath. Noooooo! Stopppp! Haaaalp!}*

"Well, if you hadn't used me for a ladder, we wouldn't be in this predicament. Now hold still!"

A minute later, Addy saw Harper step into the airlock. She was dressed in a set of fresh scrubs from the chamber, and held Snotface in her arms. When the little guy caught sight of Addy, he made frantic scrabbling motions.

{Addy doctor! Harper makes wet! I catch cold! Halp!}

Laughing, Addy motioned for the door. "Go on out," she said,

"I'll join you in a minute."

She stepped inside decon, and let the chamber seal behind her. Before she ran its sterilization procedure, she sent a pulse of electrostatic energy through the ionic threads of the hazmat suit, shedding all contaminants.

She felt the suit shiver as it activated, dispersing anything it had picked up within the L2 environment. A quick run through the decon sequence, and she was good to go. Picking up the bracer, she slid into the airlock, and then into the hallway to join Harper.

"All right, then," Addy reached out to steady the other woman, and began walking them back toward the exit and her office. "I think we can assume that the vial Thad and the team are chasing is an L4. I'll drop you two off and go up to those labs to find out what's missing."

* * *

Back in Addy's office, Gabe put Cutter on hold while he transferred their conversation to the more secured comm unit embedded in Addy's desk. He lowered himself into her chair as the holoscreen performed its handshake with the director's office.

"When you say she's off the grid," Gabe said the minute Cutter's visage appeared onscreen, "you mean she's not connected to the university's private network?"

"No. I mean I can't find her ID anywhere. Not on the university's net, and not on any sector of Ceriba's public net, either." Cutter's worried eyes met his. "Dammit. You were right to suggest anyone associated with deGrasse might be targeted. I thought I'd be able to get to her first. I thought we'd have time."

"You said she was DND earlier. Could she have—"

Gabe cut off when he saw Cutter shaking his head.

"She was on DND, but then she suddenly went dark." The director looked haggard. "She has me listed as next of kin/priority override. I should always be able to reach her in case of emergency. And... I can't."

Gabe's mind raced as he considered their options. "Have you searched for her out on the Constellation?"

If she'd left Ceriba, they should still be able to ping her ID. The Ford-Svaiter nodes within the Starshot buoy canvassed the entire Procyon System. She simply hadn't had time to get too far away.

"First thing I thought of, son," the director replied with a sharp look. "I might be NSA now, but I did my time in the field. I haven't quite forgotten everything in my doddering years."

Gabe almost laughed at that. Duncan Cutter couldn't be more than ten years his senior. The man had been a longtime operator before he'd been appointed to lead the NSA, and was a legend in the intelligence community. Of course he would have checked.

"I sent a few of Valenti's people over there to pull her out quietly, and they couldn't find her," Cutter was saying. "University's recorded feeds had been scrambled, too."

He looked down, hooking a hand around the back of his neck. When he met Gabe's eyes again, his words were much more subdued.

"I thought about what you said in the briefing about people like Sam being targets," Cutter confessed. "Thought maybe it'd be worth trying to set up another black site where we could outthink the enemy."

He stood and began to pace, the holorecorder pickups in his office following. "I made a mistake. I should have secured her immediately. Instead, I made a few calls, tried to get some things in place before approaching her about it. Now she's paying the price."

"Let's not borrow trouble just yet, sir," Gabe cautioned, although he privately feared the director was right. "There could be a logical explanation behind this. Sam's work is so far outside my wheelhouse, I can't begin to guess the number of reasons why she'd be blocked from the net."

Cutter chuckled, but to Gabe's trained ear, it sounded strained. "You're right about that."

Gabe rose to his feet. "I'll have Hyer fly me over to the university now. We'll get this sorted, sir."

Cutter's pacing stopped as he turned to face the screen. "She's like a daughter to me, Alvarez." His voice was low. "It nearly killed me, what she went through in deGrasse, and then on Leavitt. If they've gotten their hands on her again...."

They exchanged a silent look, and Gabe could see the other man's pain painted on his face.

"I'll get back to you as soon as I know something," he promised.

Cutter nodded. "Thanks."

STAKEOUT

Lower Warehouse District
Mercer Mining Torus

MICAH DIDN'T DARE breathe as the blade wedged against his neck moved from behind his ear to rest against his carotid.

"Don't bother, soldier. I've got you dead to rights."

The words were subvocalized, but he recognized the voice instantly.

Shit, he muttered to Jonathan. *Why didn't you tell me Thad was about to get the drop on me?*

He heard his mirror twin laugh. *Where's the fun in that?*

A short vibration inside his skull alerted him to an incoming com.

{You're AWOL, hoss.}

{I can explain—}

{Save it.} The Marine's mental tone was uncharacteristically amused. Micah was at a loss as to why, until Thad added, *{Boone caught sight of our friend skipping out on our meeting, so he followed. Imagine his surprise when he saw you playing*

Spiderman with a maglev.}

Micah felt his face burn with embarrassment. *{Hey, that guy's our only connection to the chiral material and Akkadia. You'd gone dark, and I couldn't risk them getting away.}*

{I'll file your reprimand for ignoring protocol in the same place I post your commendation for finding the target, ami.} His tone turned dry. *{In the circular file.}*

{Say what?}

At his blank look, Thad clapped Micah on the shoulder. *{Never mind. We'll take it from here.}*

{You'll be wanting these, then.} Micah sent Thad control of the two microdrones. *{The one that followed them inside did a passive perimeter sweep. Recording's attached.}*

Thad nodded, then turned to study the maglev spur line that ran from the trainyard to the docks. He pointed down the tracks. *{Tell you what. How 'bout you see if you can't find an unused dock over there for* Wraith *to belly up to. Word on the street is that a passel of people is headed this way. We'll drag this* cochon *out of his lair, but we may be comin' in hot. Call it half an hour.}*

Micah's eyes shot to the time stamp on his overlay. He nodded and backed silently away from the warehouse.

You got all that? he asked Jonathan.

His twin sent him a mental nod. *Will's been apprised. Yuki can float* Wraith *your way. Just feed me the coordinates once you find a slot for her.*

Copy that.

Micah took off at a ground-eating jog toward the spur line and the smaller dock that the line fed into. From what he could tell, it was currently unused. He vaulted over a cleaning bot and jinked around a train of automated maglev pallet-movers bound for a nearby warehouse.

The dock turned out to be one of the torus's maintenance ports, currently housing a few out-of-commission tugs that looked like they'd been pirated for parts. To the left, he saw an empty docking berth, the glow of a holo on standby indicating its ES field was functional.

Tell Yuki I found Wraith *a temporary home.* He sent Jonathan the location. *And tell Will I need his magic touch. Can he use the heist to backdoor me into these controls? I doubt they'll open for me.*

He plunged his hands into the interface, but his guess had been correct; it rejected his attempts to manually open the bay doors.

One hacker, comin' up. Would you like fries with that, bro?

Micah mentally flipped Jonathan off and waited for his twin to relay the request to the flight engineer.

Suddenly, into the silence, alarms began to sound, and he went scrambling back when the bay doors suddenly began to open. Loose plas sheets and empty cargo containers went flying, sucked toward the widening void, until an ES field sputtered and then belatedly snapped into place.

{Hoo-eee, Cap. Last time I saw someone hauling ass like that was when my sister's ex got chased by a gator down Atchafalaya way. Careful now. Be a damn shame if that fine ass of yours got sucked out into space, y'heah?}

Micah smothered a grin as *Wraith*'s ghostly image appeared on his overlay, the ship's nose just crossing the bay doors' threshold. *{Get your mind off my fine ass, Nina. And I wouldn't have been scrambling if this dock's equipment was functioning like it should have been.}*

He felt more than heard her ripple of amusement. He'd bet his next month's credits the woman had never been within a hundred kilometers of the Atchafalaya Bayou, either.

{Dare you to talk that way around Thad,} Micah said.

Nina laughed. *{Sir, no, sir. I value my life, thank you very much. Standing by to crack the seal. I hear we're in a hurry?}*

Micah checked his chrono as he circled around the ES field to the airlock where the field terminated. Nina already had the hatch open. He gripped her outstretched arm and nearly went airborne as the compact, muscular woman hauled him inside.

He regained his footing, leaving her to reseal the ship's side hatch as he closed the distance to the cockpit. Sliding into his cradle, he webbed up.

"Welcome back," Yuki murmured as he interfaced with *Wraith*.

As the Helios's sensor web registered his biosig, his overlay instantly populated with data: weapons, fuel, spaceframe health, and sensor feeds.

{Heads up,} Will called out. *{I have visual. They're coming in hot!}*

{Sealing her up,} Micah sent as he closed the doors between the ship's cabin and its cargo hold.

He grunted as Yuki juiced *Wraith*, sending the Helios skidding along the rails, getting the ship as close to the ES field as she could manage. At the same time, she lowered the aft ramp, venting all atmosphere from the cargo area.

Five figures were running toward them, their drakeskin suits sealing automatically as they crossed through the ES shield that held atmosphere in.

Boone and New Guy had the drug runner slumped between them, while Asha and Thad provided cover. Micah saw Boone slap a temp helmet meant for emergency EVAs onto the prisoner's head as they raced up the ramp.

Both Will and Nina were weapons hot, ready to engage any tangos who might be following on the heels of the inbound team. Their neural interfaces kept the ship's RAU-19 railgun barrels on a steady back-and-forth, while a surveillance drone hovered above the shadowed dock.

{...two, three, four—and one scumbag. All clear to raise the ramp. Go, go, go,} chanted Will.

{You have the controls,} Yuki's voice sounded in his head as she confirmed positive seal on the back ramp.

{I have the controls,} he responded, and then called out, *{Brace for maneuvers. Will, we still flying under Mercer's radar?}*

{Negative. Someone's noticed activity at the dock. They're sending a ship to investigate.}

Micah pushed thrusters hard, getting them as far away from the torus as possible before engaging drives. He really hated to light up inside the no-wake zone, but he would if he had to. *{Talk to me, Will.}*

{We're fully stealthed. No one's going to be picking us up on scan,} the flight engineer replied. *{I've gone in and erased the feeds from that dock, so they won't be able to identify us, but nothing's going to hide the fact someone was there.}*

{Let 'em wonder, hoss,} Thad interposed. *{We got what we came for, but the man didn't have the stolen vial. Spool up the drive as soon as you can. I want us back at base ASAP.}*

{Copy,} Micah replied.

At the no-wake boundary, he gave them all a warning heads-up and then drove the ship hard, pushing thirty *g*s. He felt his SmartCarbyne's accelerometer automatically engage the nanofilaments threaded throughout his body, encasing his organs in a protective shell as the agile ship sent them hurtling away from Mercer.

The mining torus's five-kilometer-wide profile was silhouetted against the bright blue-white of Merki as he pointed *Wraith*'s nose toward the white dwarf and the planet orbiting it.

{Prepare for Scharnhorst jump,} he warned. *{Engaging in thirty seconds.}*

BACKUP

CENTER FOR INFECTIOUS DISEASES
MONTPELIER, CERIBA

GABE'S CONVERSATION WITH Cutter had him worried. His gut was pinging him pretty hard, telling him that Sam had been targeted. He decided to make a quick detour before he ran up to the shuttlepad on the roof.

On his way, he reached out to Hyer. *{Chief, you still in the building? Need a lift. Rooftop in ten.}*

He kept his words brief as he pulled up the Center's map to locate its security division.

{Sir?} Katie's voice sounded distracted and a bit worried.

Gabe paused. He hadn't considered she might be involved with the containment breach.

{Sorry, Chief. Should have asked. Are you helping Addy? I can ping Valenti for another ride.}

{No, sir,} Hyer responded. *{I'm down in Harris's office, shutting down that damned SI and keeping the code open for the doc. Can it wait?}*

Gabe grimaced as he pulled to a stop in front of security. *{Hang on. Let me get back to you on that.}*

He entered, flashing his Unit credentials to the officer in charge.

The woman stood, surprise morphing quickly to professionalism. "What can I do for you, agent?"

"Do you have any spare weapons I can borrow?"

His unexpected request only threw her for a second. She nodded and waved him over to a secured room. As he stepped inside, he was gratified to see more than the standard operational security loadout.

Pointing to a CUSP sitting in the rack, he asked, "May I?"

She waved a hand and stepped back. "Take whatever you need, sir. Just sign it out with your badge, and we're good."

He saw a link to the Center's security node appear on his overlay, the checkout form highlighted. He nodded a wordless thanks and began to gear up.

He grabbed a CUSP and a pair of spare batteries. After a moment's hesitation, he found his palm wrapping around the grip of a ballistic handgun rated for safe use within both ships and space stations. Out of habit, he checked the chamber, safetied it, and fastened its holdout holster around his calf. A spare set of magazines went into his pocket.

He looked up and gave a brief salute to the woman. Nodding toward a dark office, he said, "Mind if I impose for a bit longer? I need to make a secured call."

She smiled. "Not at all. Let me know if you need anything else."

Thanking her, he stepped inside the room as he reconnected with Hyer.

{I assume Harris had a secured console?}

{The best,} the chief warrant confirmed.

{Good. I'm setting up a hard-link now with HQ. As soon as I get Valenti on the horn, I'll loop you in.}

He took a seat in front of the comm station, established an encrypted connection, and then pinged Valenti. As he waited for the comm to connect with the colonel, his gaze landed on what he could see of the Center's security division through the room's window.

The scene wasn't much different from an NCIC bullpen, and it reminded him of his life prior to being recruited to Task Force Blue. He'd been with Navy Criminal Investigation Command for fifteen years. For eight of those years, he'd been a special agent. During that time, he'd investigated mostly internal issues, crimes committed by military personnel inside the Alliance's borders.

There'd been plenty of spillover, though. He was no stranger to outside influences from other star nations. He'd handled his share of espionage cases, situations where Navy personnel allowed greed to trump their convictions. It seemed there was no end to the organizations—both private corporations and government entities alike—who sought the Alliance's secrets.

Still, nothing had prepared him for deGrasse. The scope of the operation the Akkadian Empire had unleashed to obtain the samples still boggled his mind.

So, are you truly surprised that they'd try again? he asked himself.

His attention snapped back to the holoscreen when the colonel's image appeared. She was down in the hangar, and he could see Jonathan and Major Snell, Shadow Recon's CO, standing in the background.

The two men must have been reviewing one of the ships. Jonathan had a grease-stained rag in his hands, which he was using to wipe them clean.

"Alvarez," Valenti greeted.

"Colonel," he nodded. "Wait one; let me bring the chief warrant in on this."

The moment her face appeared on the holo, Gabe started talking. "The director just told me Sam's missing."

Valenti nodded, confirming she'd already heard the report.

Her comm line must have been open, because Gabe saw Jonathan's head snap up, the rag he was using frozen mid-swipe.

The man's gaze swung to the holo. "Run that by me one more time?"

Gabe's eyes flicked back to Valenti, letting her take the lead.

The colonel looked from Gabe to Jonathan.

"We sent a team to retrieve Doctor Travis. When they arrived at her last known location, she wasn't there." Her eyes met Jonathan's as she added, "And she's not coming up on any ID sweeps, either."

Valenti held up a restraining hand as Jonathan stepped forward. "Do *not* tell your twin," she demanded. "That's an order."

The pilot frowned but nodded silent agreement.

"There could be a reason she's not showing up," she added, her attention returning to Gabe.

"Agreed," he said, "but Cutter's convinced there's foul play. I can hear it in his tone. He's always been able to bypass her DND, but he can't do it if her ID token can't be found."

Jonathan tossed the rag onto a nearby bench. "I'm coming with you."

Snell had been standing silently to one side up to this point. Now, he turned to pin Jonathan with a stare. "Against protocol. Micah's out with *Wraith*. You know the rules; if one of you deploys, the other stays here. That means you're ghosting, Captain."

Jonathan scowled back at Snell. Before he said anything that would get him in trouble, Gabe intervened.

"I appreciate the offer, Captain, but the major's right. Besides, Hyer's here with me at the Center. Mind if I borrow her for this?"

Jonathan's gaze bounced between Gabe and Valenti. "Correct me if I'm wrong, but this is time-sensitive. I know all the places she hangs out when she's at the Planck Centre. Besides, Micah's the only one on the team who's visited Sam there. He's done so several times, and what he knows, I know."

Valenti shook her head. "You're on an op, too, Captain. You're running overwatch for Mercer."

"They just jumped to Scharnhorst space, so there's nothing

left for me to do," Jonathan countered. "I can hitch a ride down in one of the Novastrikes. That way, I'm off the books with STC."

Valenti exchanged an unreadable look with Snell before shifting her attention back to Gabe, a question in her eyes. Gabe tilted his head to one side in an unspoken *'it's your call'* gesture.

Gabe could tell Snell was itching to deny Jonathan's request. He wasn't certain it was the best idea himself, but...

"I wouldn't mind the help," he admitted finally.

Valenti nodded. "Very, well, then. But don't make me regret it."

Snell's expression took on a look of annoyance at her words. Pointing his bladed hand at Jonathan, he warned, "You wear a cover at all times, you got me, Case?"

"Yessir," was Jonathan's quiet reply. He tossed a quick "Thanks" to Valenti and Gabe, and then launched himself across the hangar.

Gabe saw him scoop up a jacket, a billed cap, and what looked like a pair of ancient aviators from where they rested on top of a stool.

As he jogged out of range of the holo's pickups, Snell shot a look off to the side, where one of the Shadow Recon pilots stood, watching the exchange. He jerked a thumb in Jonathan's direction and pointed to a Novastrike, before turning to stalk off.

"We'll be careful," Gabe assured Valenti.

Her expression granite, she nodded. "See that you do."

OLD ENEMIES

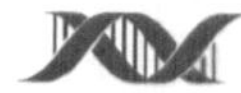

University of Ceriba, St. Clair

St. Clair Township, Ceriba

Katie Hyer's flight from the Center to the university was done in record time. At Gabe's direction, she brought the shuttle down right in front of the school's Planck Center for Physics.

Gabe unwebbed and stepped toward the hatch, and was surprised when Hyer joined him.

"I've got this, Chief," he assured her.

"If it's all the same, sir, I'd like to help. I'll stay out of trouble, I promise."

Gabe sighed. "All right. But do me a favor?" He pointed out the open hatch to where a shadowed figure stood, ballcap drawn low over his face. "Help me keep that guy off everyone's radar, will you?"

Hyer sent him a sloppy salute, swung her legs over the side of the ramp and hopped down. "You got it, boss."

While she retracted the ramp and secured the ship, Gabe walked over to where Jonathan stood. When he caught the other man's eyes from under the brim of his hat, Gabe held up a hand.

"My investigation. My rules."

Jonathan pulled a pair of aviators from his pocket. Donning them, he gave a brief nod. "Understood."

As Hyer joined them, Gabe brought them both into a three-way connection over their wires.

{Let's do this.}

He headed for the Planck Centre's entrance, and Jonathan fell into step beside him. Hyer came up on his other side, her long, coltish stride a counterpoint to Jonathan's cat-like grace.

{You think we might run into trouble?} she asked.

Gabe slid her a sidelong look. *{I think trouble already found Sam. I'm hoping she either left us some clues or has managed to evade them. If it's the latter, they might still be down here, trying to find where she holed up.}*

Jonathan's jaw worked from side to side. *{If they have her—}*

Gabe cut him off. *{That's one of the reasons we asked you not to tell Micah. He has his own mission he needs to focus on right now.}*

There was a beat of silence. *{I know. I don't like it, but yeah, I get it.}*

The university was surprisingly quiet, causing Gabe to check his wire's chrono. He realized they'd likely arrived during the break between regular and evening classes.

An invitation to join the campus network flashed on his display as they passed through its doors. He accepted it, shunting the connection to a firewalled public sector he'd partitioned off on his wire when he'd first joined NCIC.

He pulled up the school's directory, highlighted the lecture hall that was Sam's last known location, and then shared the map with the others.

{That's our first stop.}

Jonathan nodded and then pointed to a bank of lifts on the opposite side of the large, open atrium, and they headed in that direction.

They ascended in silence. Hyer stood comfortably in a loose

slouch; Jonathan shifted restlessly, flexing and clenching his hands.

{Let go of some of that,} Gabe advised. *{I need your head in the game.}*

Jonathan's nod turned into a mental growl when the lift doors parted and they saw a figure across the mezzanine that had no business being there.

{No can do, Alvarez. This here's the reason I came.}

Clint Janus looked up as they poured out of the lift, his eyes widening as he took in the three people approaching. Gabe saw Janus's gaze dip to his holster—and then the man was running.

The mezzanine circled the perimeter of the lobby atrium, terminating in wide, curving stairs, set opposite of the lifts, that led down to the ground floor. When Janus bolted for the steps, Gabe motioned Jonathan and Hyer to the left while he moved to the right.

"Doctor, stop!" Gabe called out, but his words merely served to push the man to greater speed.

When Janus saw Jonathan maneuvering to cut him off, Hyer hot on his heels, he leapt the railing and dropped to the atrium below.

Jonathan vaulted after him, and Hyer followed suit.

Gabe saw Janus dart through the door and cut right. A quick glance in the same direction inside showed a stairwell sign at the end of a hall. Gabe raced for it.

{Talk to me,} he ordered as he sprinted past closed, darkened classrooms.

{Janus is heading up the hill on the side of the building,} Hyer reported. *{Giving chase.}*

It was exactly what Gabe had hoped the man would do. It also meant his own gamble would pay off.

He hit the stairwell at a run, hooking a hand around the railing and dropping to the floor just beside the emergency exit doors. Pulling his CUSP, he burst outside just as Janus blew past.

The biochemist was agile for a person who spent more time with experiments than he did in a gym. He grabbed a nearby potted tree and toppled it, spoiling Gabe's initial shot.

Gabe hurdled the downed plant just as Jonathan and the chief joined him. Janus ducked around the side of the building, and startled shouts rang out. Gabe rounded the corner to see surprised faculty dodging out of the man's way.

"Police!" Gabe called out to them as he raced past.

Hyer pointed. "He's heading for that transport lot."

The enclosed lot held plenty of opportunity for cover. Gabe didn't intend to give Janus the chance to take advantage of it.

A fabric banner was draped across its entrance, secured by a group of papier-mâché flowers—a student art installation. Gabe let Hyer and Jonathan give chase while he reached for his holdout holster, pulled out the handgun, and aimed for the display.

He timed it for the moment just before Janus hit the entrance. The first shot had flowers raining down upon him; the second caused the banner to fall, wrapping the biochemist in meters of cloth.

Holstering the weapon, Gabe broke into a jog. By the time he caught up, Jonathan had Janus up, arms behind his back.

A CUSP had materialized in Hyer's hands, and the moment he spotted it, Janus stopped struggling.

"Why did you run, doctor?" Gabe asked as he drew to a stop in front of him.

The man's eyes were wild, his breaths coming in great gasps. "You were chasing me!" Janus pulled against Jonathan's hold.

"Doctor."

He turned at Gabe's voice, and recognition dawned. "You're that security guard from deGrasse. What are you doing here?"

"Look at you, doc, remembering us and all," Hyer's voice sounded from behind Gabe.

She slid past him, her CUSP now holstered. Stepping up to Janus, she brushed the shoulder of his suit as if to straighten it.

"Can you imagine that?" she drawled, accent thickening as she waggled a finger between the three of them. "What're the odds? I mean, really. All of us deGrasse survivors, bumpin' into each other on a college campus. Y'know I always did wonder what college life would be like."

The look on Janus's face told Gabe he was suffering from mental whiplash at Hyer's sudden familiarity. Gabe was wondering about it, himself.

The chief patted Janus on the cheek before waving a hand expansively. "Would you look at this place, sir? Swank, ain't it?"

Janus smoothed the front of his suit and glared at the chief warrant as if Hyer's touch had soiled it. "This is an institute of higher learning," he said. "It is not, nor has it ever been, *swank*."

*{Hyer, what the **hell**....}*

{Just like last time, boss,} she told Gabe as she stepped back beside him. *{One douchebag, tagged and tapped.}*

As she passed him the feed, her actions made sense. The spike she'd tagged him with would allow them to follow his movements. The surveillance bug would do the same, recording any conversations he might have, after they parted ways.

That wouldn't be any time soon. Gabe had questions he wanted the man to answer first.

He motioned for Jonathan to escort Janus back into the building. "What brings you here, doctor? I thought you worked for Brower Biologics. They don't have a research facility on Ceriba."

"Alma mater," the biochemist said, as if that explained everything.

When Gabe didn't give any indication that he understood, Janus appeared peeved.

"From time to time, the university invites some of its more successful graduates back, for a speaking engagement."

"Well, I assume you've just finished whatever it was you were doing, since it's the end of the day. Perfect timing."

"I'm afraid I can't—"

"I'm going to have to insist," Gabe said firmly.

Stopping by the side door he'd used earlier, Gabe lifted the back of his hand, engaging the holographic nanolayer that would display his NCIC credentials.

"I'm Special Agent Alvarez, Doctor Janus," he said, gesturing the man inside. "We're going to have to ask you some questions."

Janus jerked back as if he'd been stung. "Impossible. I'm late for an appointment."

"Reschedule it." Jonathan's voice came from behind Janus. It was pitched low and sounded menacing—and thankfully, nothing like Jonathan Micah Case.

Janus's eyes widened, and he craned his neck to get a look at the man behind him.

{Back off, Case. Dammit, if he recognizes you....}

{He won't.}

Gabe stepped forward, subtly crowding the man and forcing his attention away from Jonathan.

"You...you have no right to detain me," Janus spluttered as Jonathan pushed him up the steps.

Gabe lifted a brow. "Who said anything about detaining you? Did you do something you think would require such drastic action?"

Janus gave a nervous laugh. "Of course not. I just—"

"Then you should have no trouble helping out a naval investigation."

Janus had started nodding as Gabe spoke, but the nod quickly turned to a head-shake. "I'm sure you can find someone else—"

Gabe dropped a hand onto the man's shoulder, squeezing a bit harder than strictly necessary as he pushed Janus out into the second-floor hallway. "Now," he said softly, "why don't you show us where Doctor Travis is?"

And there it was. The telltale flicker Gabe had set Janus up to reveal. He'd worked to ensure the man was off balance, physical cues giving off a subtle threat while his voice remained cordial.

Emotion chased across Janus's face. Anger was replaced by a flash of fear that disappeared so fast, Gabe could have easily missed it. And then a crafty look settled in his eyes.

{He knows something.} Jonathan's voice sliced through his head.

{Yeah, he does. Stay chill, man. This is what I do. Now both of

you, back off and give me room to work.} Gabe pushed Janus forward, pointing down the hallway. "Is her office down here? Show me."

Janus had no choice but to follow the relentless pressure Gabe applied—at least, not without drawing attention to himself. Somehow, Gabe sensed this was not what the man wanted.

"Uh, yes. I believe it is."

He heard Janus swallow hard.

"Good. Good." Gabe began to move, and Janus had no choice but to follow. "So, how've you been since deGrasse? I heard you were tortured by those Akkadians."

Janus attempted a shaky laugh. "Yeah, uh, the way they treat people is pretty harsh. They're horrid human beings."

Truth... and a lie. Gabe sensed fragments of both in the man's words.

"What do you do for Brower?"

Janus cleared his throat. "Proprietary IP things. I'm not at liberty to discuss. I'm sure you understand."

"I can imagine," he said readily. "Did you know that Akkadia holds a controlling share in your company's firm? After what they did to you in Luyten's Star, I'd have assumed you'd want nothing to do with anything associated with those bastards."

With his hand clamped around the other man's shoulder as it was, Gabe could feel the involuntary shudder of fear that ran through the man at mention of Akkadia.

"Oh, really?" Janus's voice was faint.

He drew to a stop in front of a closed office door. Pointing to Sam's nameplate, he said, "There you are. I really have to go now." He attempted to pull away, and Gabe let him go.

Jonathan stepped up behind Janus once more, leaving him no room to maneuver.

{Hyer. Got a Crowbar on you by chance?} Gabe asked.

She shot him a saucy grin. *{Never leave home without it.}*

He tilted his head to indicate the door. *{See if it's unlocked.}*

Hyer's palm came to rest upon the access panel, and nothing

happened.

{Crack her open, Chief.}

A canister appeared in Hyer's hand, and she pressed it against the mechanism. The Crowbar activated the lock almost instantly.

As it slid open and the lights came on, the biochemist went stumbling in, propelled forcefully by Jonathan. He caught his hands on the top of Samantha's desk, and whirled to face Gabe as Jonathan sealed them inside.

"Now," Gabe said, nodding to a chair. "Have a seat."

Janus surprised him by growing a spine.

Drawing an air of effrontery about him, the scientist frowned at Gabe. "I will not," he stated firmly. "You have no right to detain me. I'll alert university security, and they'll—"

Gabe pulled his CUSP. "They'll understand my concerns when I tell them that Samantha Travis is missing, and you're wanted for questioning about it." He motioned to the chair with the CUSP's barrel as he slowly advanced. "Now, sit. *Down.*"

Janus sat.

Gabe spared a quick look at his team. Hyer leaned against the door, arms crossed. Jonathan was tucked into a shadowy corner, head down, face completely obscured by the bill of his cap.

He gave them both a quick nod of approval and then swung his attention back to the man seated in front of him. Holstering his weapon, he snagged a second chair, hauled it in front of Janus, and took a seat opposite the scientist.

"Now, let's try this again," he said in a low, even tone. "When was the last time you saw Samantha Travis?"

Janus cleared his throat, his eyes darting first to Hyer, and then to where Jonathan slouched before returning to Gabe. "I have no idea why you think I might know where Doctor Travis is, but as it happens, I *did* see her, about an hour ago."

Gabe nodded, but when he heard Jonathan shift in the corner, he barked, *{Stay **still**, or leave.}* He continued on aloud as if his teammate's restlessness was nothing of note. "What can you tell me about her whereabouts? I've been trying to reach her for a while now, and her wire's been set to Do Not Disturb."

He let the implication ride that he believed it was still set that way.

"I understand she was delivering a radiation lecture to the medical residents," Janus began after a moment. "When I saw her, she was on her way out."

"Did she stop to talk to anyone? Was anyone with her?" Gabe pressed.

Janus tried and failed to hide a smirk. Gabe sensed the man's rising confidence, and something else. Satisfaction, maybe? He knew the man held no love for Samantha.

"As a matter of fact, there were two people with her when I saw her last," he said. "A man and a woman."

Gabe leaned forward, propping his elbows on his knees. "Can you describe them for me, please?"

Janus's smirk deepened into a smile. "They were dressed in dark suits and looked official. The way they walked, I'd say they were from the government." His gaze swept Gabe's seated form. "You know, like you."

"Did you hear anything they said? Any mention of why they had come to visit her?"

"Oh, they weren't *visiting* her," the man corrected. "They'd come to escort her somewhere."

"Where?" Jonathan stepped forward, lifting his head to look at Janus.

The doctor looked up at Jonathan as he neared, and his eyes widened slightly in recognition. "Captain Case," he murmured, a calculating expression flashing across his face. "I see you made it out of deGrasse in one piece, too. Or should I say all *new* pieces...."

Inwardly cursing Jonathan's temper, Gabe nodded his thanks to Hyer as she moved to block their guest's view.

"You said they were taking her somewhere," he repeated, capturing Janus's attention once more. He leaned forward, getting right up into the other man's face. "*Where*, doctor?"

The smirk was back, only this time, it was accompanied by a

darker emotion. Triumph, maybe, or a vengeful gratification.

"They said to tell anyone who asks that Doctor Travis has been called away for a few months. Something about an exchange program at a Coalition university."

ENTANGLED VIALS

Rosen Base
Undisclosed location

Sam blinked in disorientation at the unfamiliar surroundings when she awoke the next morning. It took a moment before memory came flooding back.

The secret facility. Colonel Marceau.

Throwing the covers off the bed, she rose, her internal chrono telling her that she had half an hour before she was required to be at the lab Marceau had shown her yesterday.

She dressed quickly and exited, swinging past the small mess hall to grab a coffee and pastry first. Guards seemed to be at every intersection. They nodded politely, but remained watchful and silent.

As she turned down the corridor that led to the laboratory, she had her wire search for network access. There was only one network available to join, and it continued to display limited connectivity.

Marceau was standing outside the lab, conversing with a

guard in low tones. Their words were indistinguishable, but the expression on the colonel's face was severe, almost threatening. She heard him say something in a sharp voice just as the soldier looked up and saw her.

He must have alerted Marceau to her presence. The colonel pivoted to face her, once more the affable man she'd met upon her arrival.

"Good morning," he said as she came to a stop by the lab's entrance. "Ready to meet the team?"

He took her elbow. Pushing through the lab doors, he escorted her to where two others stood.

"Doctor Travis, meet Doctors Gish and Demuth. For security reasons, we ask that you not discuss your work prior to coming here." The colonel turned as footsteps sounded behind Sam. "And our final guest, Doctor Bijin. He's the lead for this project. If I'm not around, all questions should be funneled to him. Doctor, would you give us a brief tour of this lab, please?"

Bijin was short and barrel-chested, his face rounded, and his nose flat. He reminded Sam of a bulldog, until he bowed slightly, and she found his manner to be oddly formal. When he spoke, Sam heard a trace of an accent she couldn't quite place.

"Of course," he said, and then gestured to a row of terminals against the wall. "Each of you has been assigned a workstation. As you can see, there are more workstations than there are people to run them. Others will arrive soon to join our team."

He gestured to a nearby station, where an RNA replicon manipulator was mounted beside a 3D printer with an optical centrifuge. He laid a hand on the printer.

"Samples of chiral material identical to the stolen vials are being sequenced and loaded into the two machines you see here. Your job is to identify as many ways in which the material can be weaponized as possible."

When he didn't continue, Sam spoke up. "And then neutralize them."

Bijin shot her an annoyed look, his gaze flickering to Marceau and then back to Sam. "And neutralize them," he echoed.

"You'll have to excuse him," the colonel murmured to Sam. "The doctor's an old warhorse."

Straightening, Marceau stepped forward and raised his voice. "Doctor Travis is here from the Centers for Infectious Diseases. She and a small team of doctors and scientists have been working with the chiral material ever since it was recovered from Luyten's Star. She will now walk us through what their research has found. Doctor?"

Sam stepped forward. "The CID works to protect humanity from life-threatening agents of any type. This includes any potential threats that may arise from chiral life found on the planet Vermilion."

She looked at Marceau and gestured to the nearby holoscreen. "May I?"

He nodded, pushing the holo's token to her over the lab network.

As the unit flared to life, she loaded the document she'd spent the previous afternoon compiling onto the screen.

"Chirality grants pathogens a certain degree of immunity. A mirror virus or microorganism cannot infect its non-mirror host. Which, at first glance, would seem to render them harmless." She turned from the screen that displayed two simple, mirrored organisms.

Marceau and Bijin were nodding, but the other two were standing stoically, their expressions carefully blank. Marceau motioned for her to continue.

Sam turned back to the file. Reaching toward the holo, she gestured, shrinking the images and bringing up a new one.

"There are two primary ways in which chiral material can be weaponized. One is a slow-moving, brute force instrument. It's not something you'd ever consider using in conventional warfare, because it would render the battleground completely unusable by both sides," she said. "In essence, you'd end up fighting over nothing."

"And why is that, doctor?" Marceau prompted.

She turned to face them once more. "It's a weapon of mass

destruction, good only for genocide." She made a frustrated noise. "That's too small a word. Planet-o-cide? It would wipe out all life wherever you unleashed it. Chiral life would, in essence, choke out its non-chiral mirror image."

"How would it accomplish this?" Marceau asked.

"All you'd need to do is introduce a very small amount, a droplet, really, of cyanobacteria into a world's ocean," she said. "Cyanobacteria is the foundation of an ocean's food chain, and it replicates through photosynthesis, which means it wouldn't require chiral fuel to subsist. After that, it would just be a matter of time before the entire ecosystem collapses."

"You said it is slow moving, doctor," Bijin spoke up, eyes almost raptor-like in their intensity. "How slow?"

Sam cocked her head. "It'd be a few centuries," she admitted. "It would take a while for the carbon dioxide in the ocean to be converted into mirror material. After that, it would begin to draw more CO2 down from the atmosphere. After a few hundred years, standard carbon dioxide is depleted to the point that photosynthesis no longer occurs, rendering it impossible to grow crops."

"So people would starve to death," Marceau said thoughtfully, rubbing a hand along the edge of his jaw.

"That's the first set of problems," Sam agreed. "Followed by an ice age. You'd be looking at a complete evolutionary reboot."

Bijin's tone dripped with derision. "That isn't a weapon. It's a long-term strategy. Tell me, doctor," he mocked, "if your idea of 'slow' is measured in centuries, is your idea of 'fast' measured in years?"

Sam narrowed her eyes at the man, intense dislike bubbling up within her. "What kind of doctor did you say you were, again?" she asked sharply. "Because you seem awfully bloodthirsty for someone who has taken an oath to first do no harm."

The other two doctors, who had up to now remained silent, shifted uncomfortably at her verbal attack.

Bijin stepped toward her, anger written across his face.

Marceau raised a restraining hand, and the shorter man visibly struggled to control himself.

As Marceau continued to stare at Bijin, the doctor gave a short jerk of his head. "My... apologies, Doctor Travis. I have been practicing war far longer than I have medicine."

As apologies went, it didn't do much to explain his attitude, but she nodded her acceptance anyway.

"Please, doctor, continue." Marceau's voice was soft but firm.

Sam sucked in a lungful of air and, on a quick exhale, turned once more to the holo. "Fast," she muttered. "You want fast? I can give you fast. The other main way in which chiral material can be weaponized is to use it to encase an existing biochemical weapon."

"Why would that give the Akkadians an advantage, doctor?"

Sam met Marceau's eyes. "Because of the quantum entanglement Lee Stinton's cloning process imposes on the chiral pairs at a molecular level. When a biological compound like a virus replicates itself, so does its chiral twin. And all those particles are entangled too. That's why—"

She broke off when she heard an audible gasp from one of the doctors, and saw shock and a dawning awareness arise in Marceau's eyes. Unease settled in her gut.

"I... thought you'd been read into this, Colonel."

"Not to this degree, no," he murmured. He straightened abruptly as if suddenly recalling where he was. She saw a wry expression cross his face as he added, "I'm going to have to give your uncle a hard time about this, Sam. He's been holding out on me."

Bijin stepped forward, eyes alight with banked excitement. "They are truly entangled? To what extent? What would happen if we were to program a release sequence into a chiral pair? Could you plant one light years away on a distant world, and use the other as a trigger to activate it?"

Sam stared back at the man, unable to comprehend the elation that had seized him.

She felt Marceau's hand wrap around her upper arm.

"Answer him, please, doctor."

She swallowed, unease transforming for the first time into genuine fear. "I'm not sure," she admitted. "We haven't come that far in our research."

"But in theory?" Bijin demanded.

Sam felt the hand around her arm tighten, and she nodded. "Yes," she whispered. "Yes, you could."

MISSING TRIGGER

'ROSEN' BASE
AN-YANG DUST BELT
PROXIMA CENTAURI

THE OPEN HOSTILITY between Bijin and Travis made Marceau realize it had been a mistake to give the man leadership over the research team. As they dispersed to find their workstations, he pulled Bijin aside.

"We can't afford another clash between you two," he said quietly. "Please gather your things and move to the lab on the other side of the base."

Far from being upset over the order, the doctor beamed. "Excellent. I will be able to continue my work uninterrupted."

And your presence will cause no further disruption, Marceau thought, but he merely nodded his agreement.

After Bijin left, the colonel remained until he felt sure Sam had settled in and was reviewing the data on her workstation. Only then did he leave the lab.

He strode toward a nearby lift, placing his palm on its

controls. His biosignature allowed him to bypass security measures that kept Samantha Travis confined to this level.

The lift descended. When its doors parted, the gimlet-eyed soldier who exited in no way resembled the Alliance officer he had been tapped to portray.

When he spoke, his words weren't in Standard, but in the little-used Old Tongue. It was a language spoken almost exclusively within the ranks of the Junxun Tèzhǒng.

"Citizen General," Marceau sketched a crisp bow.

"Doctor Travis is cooperating?" Che asked, and the Junxun agent inclined his head in a brief nod.

"She appears a bit cautious, and has asked to confirm with her uncle, but I believe I have managed to assuage her concerns for the moment," he said.

He looked over at McGee, who stood in parade rest behind the general. "Do we have an ETA for the other scientists?"

The man who had posed as an NSA agent to retrieve Travis stepped forward. "They should arrive later this afternoon. "There are three: an Alliance pathologist and two biochemists. One is from Brower Biologics, the others from the Merki Institute on Hawking."

"Good." Marceau's breath left him in a gust of air. "The medical corpsmen we have in the lab right now posing as doctors will not be able to stand up under close scrutiny for very long."

"That is why you ordered them not to interact, is it not?" Che asked.

Marceau nodded. "Yes. Their lack of expertise would soon be evident if Doctor Travis were to engage them in conversation. Speaking of which, I know we require Bijin's expertise, but he very nearly cost us the ruse with his response to her imperialist opinions."

"Bijin may be a terrible actor, but he is loyal to Rin Zhou," Che reminded him. "And we need a biochemist to assemble the delivery mechanism for our biochemical payload."

Marceau inclined his head, acknowledging that fact. "I know

his role is vital, but I believe he'll do more harm than good if he interacts much more with Travis, so I asked him to restrict himself to our side of the base."

Che jerked his chin down in a brief nod. "Whatever it takes to complete the job."

"Five days until the summit," McGee shook his head. "That's very little time for us to pull off this operation."

"Thus our subterfuge," the general said. "If Doctor Travis believes she is working to benefit her own people, she will gladly do the work for us."

"I would be happy to provide her with an incentive to perform." The voice was low and seemed to come from out of nowhere.

Marceau turned to see Che's shadow, the assassin, stepping away from the wall. He hadn't seen her or sensed her presence until the moment she spoke.

She glided toward them, closing the distance until she stood by the general's side. A glance down showed she had pulled a karambit from its sheath. She angled the haft, examining the blade. It glinted as it caught the light.

"Deception will get faster results. Coercion may take longer than we have," Che murmured, reaching out and gently lowering the hand wielding the blade. "Her worth isn't only on her knowledge, but in the value her uncle places on her. She is his closest living relative. I'm sure she will be useful in other ventures, if not this one."

He turned back to Marceau. "Do you have any more updates for me, Citizen Colonel?"

"Yes, actually. It's why I came down here," he said with a slight grimace. "Doctor Bijin just informed me that the contents of vials one and two aren't what we'd been led to believe. They contain nothing more than simple protein chains from Vermilion plant life. It would seem our person inside the CID failed to deliver the requested material."

Anger darkened Che's eyes and a slight tic formed as one eye narrowed. Marceau braced himself, but the citizen general's rage seemed to melt away between one breath and the next.

After a beat, his lips twisted into a bitter smile. "It's at times like this that you truly regret not being able to go back and kill someone all over again." His voice held irony but little rancor.

McGee shook his head. "The programmer, you mean? I wouldn't have thought she'd be brave enough to do something like that."

"And yet she did," Che said, his gaze shifting meaningfully from McGee to Marceau. "Let that be a lesson. Never underestimate an opponent. Even a dove can turn on you if provoked."

Marceau bowed his head, acknowledging that truth.

"Please, Citizen Colonel, continue," Che said. "Did Bijin have anything to say about the third vial?"

Marceau felt the room's sudden interest, and he kept his expression carefully neutral as he replied, "That is the other reason why I came. The third vial does contain a viral pathogen, and it can be weaponized."

He stepped closer and lowered his voice as he delivered his next line.

"Travis's briefing included one vital bit of information something we were previously unaware of. The vials are paired, one chiral, one non-chiral. In order to use the third vial against those attending the summit, we must get our hands on the one it is paired with: the fourth vial."

Che's brow creased, and he pulled his head back with a frown. "Are you saying this is a two-stage weapon?"

Marceau shook his head. "Not precisely, no. But if you control one vial, you control the other."

He purposely kept his words vague, aware that others might be listening in.

Turning to McGee, he asked, "Did I hear you have a team working to acquire it?"

McGee grimaced. "One of our agents was to meet the man who purchased the vial on a mining torus in Procyon. An Alliance recon unit got to him before we had a chance to intercept him."

"So the material is lost to us, then?" Che asked sharply.

McGee shook his head. "No. This man has a properties manager who took possession of the vial. We will go after her next."

"Do we know where this properties manager is?"

"Yes, but it will be a race to see who gets there first. I'm sure the Alliance will get her location out of the man shortly."

Marceau turned to Che in alarm. "Sir, I would strongly urge you to put as many resources behind this as you can. The entire operation may hinge upon us acquiring that fourth vial."

He felt the weight of Che's gaze as the other man studied him quietly for a long moment. The general shifted his eyes to McGee and nodded once. The man stepped away, motioning to one of his people to join him at a comm console.

A signal passed between Che and his Dagger. The general waved Marceau closer. At the same time, Marceau's overlay tracked the release of a cloud of audio chaff; it inserted itself between them and the rest of the room. The tiny machines would provide an effective yet unobtrusive security screen.

"Now then, my friend," Che said. "Tell me exactly what it was you did *not* say about that missing vial. Why it is so imperative we have it?"

Marceau met his eyes, willing his superior to feel the import of his next statement.

"The vials are connected. When we plant the bioweapon inside the ballroom where the summit is being held, this final vial will act like a remote control. Whatever you do to the contents of one vial, the other will emulate. You will be able to release the bioweapon from anywhere."

He paused a beat, and then added, "And I do mean *any*where."

EPIDEMIC

Royal Ceriban Cruise Lines
The Klintis Region

Zoya Nolotov had the *Atliekan Queen*'s crew hot-racking in makeshift beds within their respective areas. It wasn't ideal, asking crew to share the same bunk with their opposite-shift crew-mates, but it reduced the amount of space needed for sleeping.

Those on the bridge were lucky; they'd had her captain's office to convert into shared quarters. Those in engineering and enviro were less fortunate. They'd had to make do with a storage closet and a partitioned-off corridor, respectively.

Staterooms on levels Amaryllis, Bougainvillea, Clematis, and Dahlia had been converted to convalescent care units.

Whose brilliant idea was it to name the passenger decks after flowers, anyway, Zoya thought grumpily, and not for the first time.

Thankfully, there were several on the staff and crew who had a bit of prior medical experience; these had been pulled in to assist with passenger care.

"How is the crew handling the new arrangements?" Josh asked. His image peered out at her from a holo at one of the bridge's stations.

Zoya tossed the doctor a wry smile. "Not any happier about it than anyone else, I'm sure. But it's a fair sight better than the alternative. At least they're more compliant than the passengers."

Tapping the console in front of her, she added thoughtfully, "You know, I learned a lot of things in the military. One of them was that when you work in close proximity to your fellow soldiers, you're more likely to appreciate how dependent you are on one another for survival. Besides, they're far less tempted to bend the rules if they know they're under close scrutiny like this."

The doctor grimaced. "It doesn't much help, having the tech to isolate everyone, if the people we're trying to save refuse to isolate."

Zoya shrugged. "Humans are going to human. That means some will cooperate while others refuse."

Josh nodded. "Yeah, well.... You know, all this is a bit like closing the barn door after the animals have all escaped, if they've already been exposed."

"True, but we can't risk any further exposure."

The doctor frowned. "Yeah, about that...." He blew out a sharp breath. "My contact at the CID confirmed my suspicions. It's a previously unknown variant of pneumatic hantavirus. But I'm beginning to think it's more than that."

"What do you mean?" she asked.

Josh rubbed the back of his neck, exhaustion written clearly on his face. "The incubation period is ridiculously short. Most viruses take a bit longer to replicate within a host."

Zoya didn't like the sound of that. The disease was spreading faster than the purple-banded kudzu that covered the rocky shores of her homeworld Beryl, back in Sirius. The weed could choke out a kelp farmer's entire crop within two stellar days.

"How is this possible?"

The doctor's lips thinned. "If this is an engineered virus."

Zoya stared back at Josh as she turned over his words in her head. "You mean engineered as in *purposely* altered to do harm? Developed to unleash on an enemy?"

His lack of response was the only one she needed.

The captain's eyes sharpened. "How many new cases?"

"Right now, we're closing in on seven thousand confirmed, and our patient zero is dead. At the rate it's chewing through those on board, there certainly won't be anyone left uninfected by the time we reach port."

HANTA IN HIDING

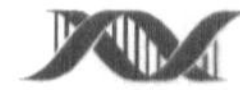

MEDICAL DEPARTMENT, CID
MONTPELIER, CERIBA

ADDY HAD JUST finished cataloging the missing vials from the L4 lab and sending Toland an update when her office comm unit pinged. She was surprised to see one of the virologists from the main complex on the other end.

She kept her expression carefully neutral as the man explained he had a file he wanted the admiral to see. The moment it loaded, Addy knew she was looking at something that might be one of the L4 compounds that had gone missing.

"You said this was sent to you from someone on a cruise ship?" she asked.

The virologist nodded. "Yes, it's from the chief medical officer aboard the *Atliekan Queen*, one of the yachts owned by Royal Ceriba. Their patient zero is unresponsive, so we can't contract trace him prior to boarding, but he did list a next of kin."

Addy leapt at that. "Can you send that along as well?"

He gestured to the data he'd projected onto the holo. "It's

appended to this file. As you can see, the antigen tests they conducted show it's a hanta. The first few patients presented a known variety, but molecular tests on subsequent patients show a completely different gene sequence. Before labeling this a novel virus, I wanted to run it past you, to see if it's anything your team might recognize. Nothing in the CID's database is a match."

"Thanks, Jon, you may have the right of it. Let me send it over to the team to look at. I'll take it from here."

The virologist nodded with some relief, and then disconnected.

"Is that what I think it is?" Harper said from where she sat on the other side of Addy's desk.

Although she couldn't see him, Addy knew Snotface was curled up asleep in the analyst's lap.

"You mean our missing fourth vial?" Addy's hands flew through her holo interface as she pulled the data on the hantavirus the yacht's medical team had sent, and brought it up alongside the missing L4 vial.

The data was identical.

"Yes. I'm afraid it is."

Harper wrinkled her nose. "On a *cruise* ship?"

Addy spared her a quick glance. "Gather up everything we've found so far. I need to report this to the admiral, and we need to get back to the base."

* * *

Micah paced TF Blue's situation room, restless and ready for action. The missing vial had not been found on the drug lord, but Micah was certain the man they'd taken prisoner knew where it was located.

The scumbag was currently enjoying the amenities offered by the SRU's lockup, two floors below Task Force Blue. A pair of Unit operators stood watch over him, ready to bust his balls if he so much as blinked wrong.

Micah hadn't heard anything from Jonathan on the way back, and had been stunned to learn his twin was not at the base when they returned. On top of that, Sam was still not responding. Both of these factors fed his nervous energy.

He'd refused Nina's offer to join the rest of the flight crew in a card game, and was currently tossing around the idea of cruising past lockup, when Valenti strode into the room.

"SCIF in five," she said, gaze sweeping the room. "Severance, with me."

Micah shot Thad a questioning glance as he walked past, but the Marine just sent him a look from under raised brows that told him the man was as clueless as he was about what was going down.

Gabe was just outside the room. The agent moved aside to let Thad and the colonel pass, and then came in, trailed by both Katie Hyer and his twin.

What's with the silent treatment? There a reason you went dark on me?

The look on Jonathan's face had him stopping in his tracks.

"What?" he demanded, looking from Jonathan to Gabe and then over to the chief warrant.

Hyer just held up her hands and then pointed to Gabe before taking a seat. The fact she'd done so without saying a single word was worrisome.

Boone and Asha must have realized the same. Boone's feet hit the ground from where he'd had them propped up on another chair, and Asha set aside the half-formed creature she'd been whittling from a piece of wood.

Yuki and Nina looked up from their game. Will set aside the deck of cards and stood.

Gabe motioned them over. His eyes swept the team before landing on Micah. When he spoke, his voice was grave. The words rocked Micah to his core.

"We have a situation. The Akkadians have Sam."

* * *

The atmosphere inside the SCIF was thick with tension, and Addy wondered if there was more going on than she knew. She and Harper were the last to arrive. As she closed the door behind her, she felt her wire disconnect from the Unit's server when Valenti activated the room's security.

"This briefing needs to be fast but thorough," Cutter informed them all. "Too many lives are depending on it—including my niece's."

Addy's eyes widened. "Sam?"

"She's been taken by Akkadia."

"This is worse than I thought, then," she murmured.

"I think you'd better clarify that right now, doctor."

Addy'd never heard Duncan Cutter's voice sound the way it did. It was as cold and hard-edged as his last name implied. She glanced across the table at Toland.

"Can you load the data for me, please, Addy?" the admiral asked.

"Of course," she murmured.

Toland turned to face those seated around the table. "Captain Moran and Agent Kinsley have identified the vials that were stolen. Two of them are inert material, simple protein chains from plants found on Vermilion. But the other two..."

Toland's voice drifted off and she turned to face the holoscreen when it flared to life.

"That's one of the stolen vials?" asked Cutter as he stared at the image.

"It is," Toland confirmed. "You're looking at a hantavirus. This particular virus is single-strand RNA. It has the ability to exchange genome segments, through a process known as reassortment."

From the back of the room, Asha spoke up. "That sounds like it would mutate pretty easily," the team's medic said.

Addy nodded. "It can. This particular virus is pneumonic in nature; it attaches to cells in your lungs. It's also a novel virus, which means Alliance citizens have no immunity against it yet."

"That shouldn't be all that dangerous, though," the medic protested. "Don't hantas respond well to antiviral meds, if the infection's caught early enough?"

Addy gave the medic a brief smile. "They do. It doesn't take long to sequence them, either, which means they're fairly easy to inoculate against. Though at the rate this one mutates, it'd take a robust medical department to keep up with it. But this isn't a normal hantavirus."

The viewpoint changed, plunging them into the virus' heart. Inside was a single helix strand, surrounded by a sea of protein.

Gabe squinted at the screen. "Is that... another RNA strand?"

Addy shot him a considering look. "Sharp eye. Yes, it is." She turned to the display. "The hanta is an RNA virus. But this RNA strand *inside* it is not. Which makes this... a trojan."

Thad leaned forward. "A virus, hidden inside a virus," he mused.

Asha stirred. "If that's not a hanta, then what is it?"

Addy's gaze swung to the medic. "It's a Khufu."

There was a collective inhale as the word *Khufu* cast a pall over the room. Addy imagined it was similar to the foreboding conjured by *Ebola* or *Zika*, back in pre-diaspora times. Like Ebola, Khufu was hemorrhagic.

Toland's smile held a wry twist to it that said she knew very well the fear those words had struck in those assembled. "In its current state, this strain of Khufu is not zoonotic. That means that it can't transfer to humans."

"Keyword, 'current state'," muttered Jonathan.

"Exactly." Toland's gaze cut to the pilot. "In the wrong hands, it can be reassorted, its gene segments shuffled and recombined to create an entirely different virus. One that *is* zoonotic, and has the potential to be much more deadly."

"How deadly?" asked Gabe.

"Sargon Fever deadly. Or worse."

Her words plunged the room into silence.

The outbreak that spread through the Sargon region of Alpha Centauri in the late twenty-three hundreds had killed hundreds of thousands of people in a matter of days before it burned itself out. The virus was so aggressive, nanomedicine simply could not keep up with it. It attacked organs and destroyed blood-clotting cells faster than the tiny medical bots could rebuild them.

"This is the vial the Akkadians have?" asked Cutter, looking from Toland to Addy.

Addy shook her head. "No. Well—" she amended as she glanced at the admiral, "yes, and no. They have the chiral version of this trojan."

Micah sat back. "That's not so bad, then, right? You said chiral viruses can't harm any of you, just me."

Toland's lips thinned. "Believe me, there are plenty of ways they could find to use that single vial against us."

Gabe's eyes were back on the image. "But that's not the real problem..." He turned to face Addy. "The *non*-chiral version's our missing fourth vial, isn't it?"

Addy stared back at him and, after a beat, gave him a faint nod. For the briefest of moments, she felt herself stripped bare under his gaze, all her fears exposed.

She blinked and turned away when Toland spoke.

"That's not our immediate problem."

She looked up to see the admiral had pulled up a second image, displaying it alongside the first.

"What you see on the left is from our records of the missing fourth vial, back at the CID," Toland informed them. "The image on the right was sent to us from a Royal Ceriban cruise ship a few hours ago." Toland paused and let her gaze sweep the table. "They're the same."

Voices broke out, people exclaiming all at once.

"What the *fuck*?" "Omi*god*...." "Holy *shit—*!"

Cutter's rose above them all. "How the hell did that fourth vial get on a cruise ship?" he asked, his gaze shifting from Toland to Addy.

Harper cleared her throat. "I don't think the vial is on the ship."

Valenti leaned forward. "Explain."

Harper glanced at Addy. "On our way here, I pulled everything we have on Jurgens, the man you brought back from Mercer. He keeps his hands clean, gets involved with high-level negotiations but never handles the merchandise himself. He has a properties manager who does that. Allegedly, she's very no-nonsense. I can't see her touring the Atliekas with Royal Ceriba. It doesn't fit the profile. I think the person who swiped the package and helped himself to that fourth vial is on the ship."

"So, whoever arranged to sell it to Jurgens cracked it open first before handing it over... and then booked a cruise to celebrate?" asked Micah.

Thad made a disgusted sound and sat back, hands tucked under his armpits. "If that's true, hoss, then it's a case of curiosity killing the thief."

"And harming a lot of other innocent people in the process," Addy interjected, sending Thad a sharp look.

"Yes, we think he's the thief who swapped the packages. He's the yacht's 'patient zero'. He's also dead," Harper added, her voice flat.

Asha stirred. "Hemorrhagic?"

Addy shook her head. "No. The trojan is still dormant and no threat to humans. Like you said earlier, he either went too long without treatment, or possibly he had cheap medical nano. The yacht is now under quarantine. Its medical department is being stretched to its limits, I'm sure. We've ordered relief packages sent to them."

Then Thad asked the question Addy had been expecting—and dreading.

"Doc... you said that thing could be reprogrammed. But the folks on that yacht are isolated. Shouldn't they be safe from any tampering?"

Addy sucked in a deep breath. "Theoretically, the virus onboard could still be altered from a distance."

Thad's brows drew down. "How?"

"By altering the virus's quantum entangled, chirally paired twin. In this case, that would be the Khufuvirus inside the *third* vial. The one the Akkadians already have."

"Let me get this straight," Cutter said slowly. "The people on that yacht have been exposed to the virus from vial number four. And the Akkadians have vial number three, which contains the virus's mirror twin. And you're saying that the Akkadians could do something to the virus they have, and it would impact the people on that yacht?"

Toland nodded. "Theoretically, yes."

"You keep saying that word," Micah muttered.

Jonathan jackknifed up in his seat, his back ramrod straight. "Hold on a minute. You're suggesting this is possible because the vials are entangled, right?"

"Yes," said Toland.

"And whatever happens to one pair partner happens to the other?" he persisted.

Toland nodded once more.

"That's clearly not true," protested Micah. "If that were the case, every time Jonathan's injured, his wounds would appear on me, and they don't."

Toland gave them a faint, wry smile. "To be frank, we don't precisely know why it's happening to these smaller organisms but not to you. The machine that created you and the other chiral pairs was lost when deGrasse was destroyed—along with most of Dr. Stinton's research. We had to begin from the ground up, so to speak, and reverse engineer a lot of it."

"I think another important aspect to keep in mind is that it was never that man's intent to entangle you two," Addy reminded them. "It was Sam who discovered that your lives were intertwined; Stinton never knew. There's no single set of instructions. I'm sure the method we've worked out is much different than what that man put you through."

Micah sat back, his gaze turning inward as he processed what they'd just learned.

"Micah's right; you've repeatedly said this is all theoretical," said Gabe suddenly, turning to Toland. "Why, Admiral?"

"Because we're proceeding very cautiously, and gathering

copious amounts of data every step of the way. We're only now reaching the point where we're ready to test Doctor Travis's theory of quantum entanglement."

"And Akkadia has Sam," Micah bit out.

"How will we know if they've figured this out?" Gabe asked.

"You mean how will we know if they tortured the information out of her?" Micah's voice was harsh.

Valenti sent Micah a quelling look before turning to Addy.

"How will we know, doctor?" she repeated Gabe's question.

Addy met Valenti's steady stare. "We'll know when the people on that yacht begin to show signs of severe, multisystem failure as a result of hemorrhagic fever."

"In the interim," added Toland, "somewhere out there is a drug lord's lackey in possession of that fourth vial, and probably very ill. Whatever medical nano she has on board likely won't do much more than provide palliative care."

Valenti looked over at Gabe. "Go. Interrogate Jurgens and get the location of that ship. I don't care how you do it. Just get it, and get it fast."

When Gabe stood, Thad looked over at Valenti, a question in his eyes. At her nod, he rose and followed Gabe out the door.

* * *

The man seated inside the interrogation room was pale with Nordic features. His ID token stated he was one Hans Jurgens, and he looked it, too—although Gabe seriously doubted that was the man's true identity.

Jurgens had white skin, white hair, and icy blue eyes. Those eyes stared across the table at Gabe with a practiced indifference.

Thad loomed just behind Jurgens, arms crossed, a silent threat. Two Unit soldiers completed the ensemble. They stood on either side of the door, hands on their weapons.

"Let's try this one more time," Gabe said as his gaze moved from Thad back to Jurgens.

The man's eyes had been roaming the room in quiet assessment. As Gabe spoke, they shifted to meet his, a bold, self-assured confidence in their depths.

"You recently acquired a vial filled with an unknown substance," Gabe said. "Did the person who sold it to you tell you it's an experimental drug? Maybe something a pharmaceutical company would kill to get their hands on?"

The man's mouth curved in a faint, mocking smile, his eyes reflecting amusement at Gabe's efforts.

He turned away, expression bored as he picked an invisible piece of lint off his suit jacket with fingers that were so thin, they were almost stick-like. "I'm afraid I have no idea what you're talking about. I don't do drugs."

"I know you don't," Gabe said readily.

At the man's look of surprise, he added, "Your reputation precedes you. I understand you have a properties manager who does the dirty work for you."

When the man merely stared back at him, Gabe leaned forward. "Let me tell you what I think happened. Feel free to step in at any time and correct me if I get it wrong. Your properties manager brokered a deal with some local, two-bit thief. The man or woman probably told her the substance had been stolen from the CID, and that maybe, just maybe, this item was something so lucrative, pharmaceutical companies everywhere were fighting to get hold of it. How'm I doing so far?"

Jurgens's smile broadened. "You should take up writing fiction, Agent Alvarez. You weave a fanciful tale. Please, go on. Your story amuses me."

Gabe folded his hands on the table. "Let's see if you find this next bit just as entertaining, then. Whatever that thief told your properties manager was wrong, and it has likely already cost the woman her life."

This evoked a reaction. The prisoner's smile was replaced by the briefest flash of concern before the mask slid back into place.

He shrugged. "For argument's sake, and because I do find you entertaining, let's assume for one minute that this fictional tale you're weaving were true. Why would you assume this equally fictional properties manager of mine would be dead? What would have killed her?"

Gabe smiled. He leaned back, flattening his hands against the table. "You see? Now we're getting somewhere."

He lifted a hand, and the holo embedded in the wall lit up. Floating within the holo was a scene that depicted a ship, emblazoned with the Royal Ceriban Cruise Lines logo, floating in the black against a sea of asteroids.

Jurgens laughed. "A cruise liner? What does this have to do with some vial you've evidently misplaced?"

"Do you have any idea how many people on average are on board one of those Royal Ceriban yachts?" Gabe asked. "Upwards of fourteen thousand. The people on board this particular ship are all dead—they just don't know it yet. And it's all because of that vial."

Alarm crossed Jurgens's face. "That sounds... unpleasant."

"Oh, it's worse than that."

Gabe turned from the holo to stare at the man. "The vial in your possession isn't some designer drug that pharmaceutical companies are fighting to obtain. Is that what those Akkadians you were meeting on Mercer told you? That they represented an Akkadian drug company who would pay top credits to get their hands on it?"

He leaned across the table, closing the distance between them. Lowering his voice, he said, "That vial contains something nations will go to war over. A very deadly biochemical weapon. And you were about to sell it to them."

Gabe paused, his gaze drilling into the man. "And that, Mister Jurgens," he added softly, "is treason."

"Now hold on." The man's eyes grew icy with anger. "I'm no traitor to the Alliance."

"Prove it," Gabe shot back. "Give us the information we need to reach your properties manager before the Akkadians do. Because I can guarantee they're as eager to get their hands on that vial as we are."

The man shifted in his seat, his eyes tracking from the holo to Thad and then back to Gabe. "You said my manager is likely already dead. Why?"

Gabe nodded to the holo. "The people dying on that yacht are proof that the person who sold you that vial opened it before handing it over. And once that seal has been broken, the experts tell me the vial itself is compromised. If your manager wasn't wearing full protective gear when she handled it, she would have been exposed. And, in this situation, exposure means death."

Jurgens swallowed hard, his adam's apple bobbing as he processed the information. Gabe waited him out, content to let the man's imagination run wild.

"You said they were dead, but they don't know it yet," he recalled with a nod toward the holo. "What did you mean by that?"

"The vial contains a pathogen that begins innocently enough, but can evolve into something reminiscent of Sargon Fever."

The man's face leached of what little color it had as he murmured, "She was a good, loyal person." He straightened. "If I cooperate fully, I want a commuted sentence."

Thad's voice rumbled from behind him. "How about you cooperate, and we let you live, hoss?"

The man's eyes cut to the Marine's and then just as quickly shifted back to Gabe. "I'll be turning state's evidence against Akkadia. You said it yourself, they're the real enemy here. I'll be helping you keep something dangerous out of their hands." His expression turned crafty. "You said this was a biochemical weapon. What if I could identify the location the Akkadians intend to target?"

Gabe's wire pinged.

{Tell them he'll get ten instead of life,} Cutter's voice sounded in his head. *{That's the best we're prepared to offer, but the deal goes off the table if he doesn't hand the intel over within the next five minutes. And if the properties manager isn't where he sends*

*us, we **will** try him for treason.}*

Gabe relayed the information.

The other man's eyes turned flinty for a brief moment. "Five, and you've got a deal."

{We accept.}

Gabe reluctantly nodded. "Deal."

Jurgens' act of casual disdain fell away like a discarded suit. In a crisp, businesslike voice, he asked, "What do you need to know?"

"Ship's location and tail number. Any security overrides that we might need to defeat to gain access to that vessel. A personal message telling her that our visit is sanctioned by you." Gabe's delivery was rapid-fire and precise.

The drug lord held up both hands. "Wait. You said she was dead. Why would you need a message?"

"She may not be dead quite yet," Gabe conceded. "She may even still be conscious enough to trigger anti-piracy protocols if we try to board. The ironic thing is that the only hope she might remotely have of surviving is to let us get our hands on that vial so we can begin working on an antigen."

Jurgens ran thin fingers through his white-blond hair. "Stars and flares, who would have ever thought I'd be working with the feds," he muttered. "Okay, here's what you'll need to bypass that ship's systems...."

Gabe looked over at Thad, making sure the Marine recorded everything Jurgens said. When the man was done, Thad nodded and slipped from the room.

Gabe turned back to Jurgens. "You say you think you know who they're targeting?" he asked.

The captive's demeanor had turned uncharacteristically solemn, almost as if he'd truly meant it when he said he was no traitor. "I'm pretty damn sure—and it's not a who, it's a what. There's been a lot of chatter on the darkside splinternet lately about a summit that's being held in Hawking next week."

{Hold,} the director's voice cut in. *{I'm coming in.}*

"Hang on," Gabe told Jurgens. "Someone wants to join us."

The man lapsed into silence, his eyes on his interlaced fingers as they waited for the director.

He gave Cutter a nod that was almost respectful when he entered.

"You mentioned a summit," Cutter said. "What kind of summit, exactly?"

Jurgens smiled thinly. "The one where five different Coalition nations are meeting to discuss defense strategies." He looked from Cutter to Gabe and then back. "I stay far away from that kind of thing, but people talk. And that summit's name has come up a lot in sectors of the splinternet that Akkadia has been known to frequent."

{Dammit. We have security from every one of those nations crawling all over the venue. There's no possible way Akkadia could get into it,} the director told Gabe.

{But if he's right....} Gabe let his mental words trail off.

"I can see the doubt in your eyes, Director Cutter," Jurgens said. He leaned forward, expression earnest. "I know you have no reason to believe a man who *purportedly* deals in illicit drugs. But I can assure you, the criminal underworld would not thrive under Akkadian rule. They wouldn't want this any more than you do."

Gabe angled the man a sidelong glance. "I've heard the way they deal with criminals is a bit harsh."

Jurgens grimaced. "I'll take due process over totalitarian rule any day."

Cutter tapped his forefinger against the table. "If this information pans out, you just earned your reduced sentence, Mister Jurgens."

He spared Gabe a swift look. *{Finish up here and meet me in the situation room. We have a mission to plan.}*

FARADAY TATTOO

SAM'S CONFRONTATION WITH Bijin and the steel in Marceau's tone when he'd ordered her to answer the doctor had left her shaken. Things quieted a bit after that, Marceau spiriting Bijin away, and the other two doctors migrating to their respective workstations.

Sam wandered past the inactive units until one of them lit up as it connected to her ID token.

I guess this is my spot, then.

She looked around at the nearly empty room and then down at the unit that sat quiescent, awaiting her command. She reached into the display's holographic interface, tapping on the icon that represented the vial she had been assigned.

As the file unpacked its data stores, Sam's gaze strayed to the hand she'd used to activate it. Encircling her ring finger was an elaborate, platinum-hued tattoo. She ran the fingers of her other hand over the tattoo's surface, debating what action she should take next.

The tattoo wasn't what it seemed; it was a precaution she'd acquired not long after being held at knifepoint by an Akkadian assassin, nine months ago. The experience had made her realize she knew next to nothing about self-defense. She decided that needed to change.

Not long after, she found the perfect person to ask about it.

Elodie Cyr had come to Ceriba for some training and had stopped by to spar with the team. Sam had flagged her down afterward and asked her advice. The special agent had given her a few pointers, but possibly the most useful thing she'd given Sam wasn't a skill; it was a tool.

"This is a breadcrumb app," Ell had said, holding up a small, silver cylinder, the kind nano was often stored in. "It's a two-stage program linked to your ID token. When activated, its single purpose is to send your location to protective services. It inserts under a Faraday tattoo, and is best worn like a ring around your finger." She reached for Sam's hand and pressed the cylinder against the base of her third finger.

Fascinated, Sam bent forward and watched as a small swarm of nano assembly bots began to weave a ring of intricate Celtic knots. "Can I assume, because of its name, that the tattoo provides some sort of shielding to keep the app from being detected by scans?"

Ell nodded. "Plus, jewelry will likely be confiscated. This will pass as decorative body art."

"How does it work?"

The NCIC agent smiled. "It's essentially a soldier with one directive, a single-minded purpose that it will strive to execute over and over again. Once activated, it will behave like a caged animal, tirelessly seeking its way out."

"That sounds a bit aggressive," Sam said doubtfully.

Ell lifted a challenging brow. "That's the point, isn't it? If you've been taken, time is a critical factor. There are certain channels, like Guard, that the military always monitors. Protective services has isolated channels they watch as well.

This app knows them all. It will piggyback off any signal—no matter how weak—jump networks, burrow into any node. It's a chameleon, able to grow and change and disguise itself, adapting to whatever system it infiltrates. Hell, it'll use a coffee machine, if it's connected to a network. It'll do whatever it takes to reach one of those channels. And it will continue to do so until protective services sends a cease code."

Sam flexed her hand and then looked up as Ell tapped a finger against the cylinder to get her attention. "Can you bend your head to one side, please? Stage two is a stash of formation material. I need to inject it into your mastoid process."

Sam did as asked, pulling her hair aside to give the agent better access to the bony knot behind her ear. "So how do I use it?"

She felt the cold press of metal against her skin as Ell replied. "Press the tattoo between the thumb and first finger of your opposite hand."

"That's it?"

"Not quite." Ell removed the cylinder and Sam lifted her head. When she met Ell's eyes once more, the NCIC agent continued.

"Once the ring is activated, slide your hand up and press it behind your ear, like this." Ell mimed the action. "That gives the app access to the formation material it needs to replicate."

"I suppose the two-step process is there so I don't accidentally activate it," Sam mused.

"Yes. They also designed the gestures to be natural enough that they pass the sniff test."

"Sniff test?"

"An action that's believable and won't out you to your captors."

Sam gave a wry smile. "And then what?"

Ell gave her a fierce grin in return. "And then you start touching things. Get your hands on every piece of equipment you can find, every lift button, every printer, every door control. It'll only take a few seconds for the breadcrumb to drop a copy of itself onto whatever structure you touch. It'll breach with nanofilament, and if there's a chink in their armor, this thing'll find it."

Sam pulled herself from the memory and looked once more around the room that had begun to feel more like a prison than a lab.

The way Doctor Bijin had reacted when she explained that the chiral pairs were entangled at a quantum level was wrong. She'd never seen an officer who served in the Alliance military respond in such a way; certainly not any of the Navy doctors she knew.

Marceau's behavior in the hallway, the network with limited connectivity, the manner in which she'd arrived—each fact taken individually might not be enough to convince her. But the body of evidence had built to a point she could no longer ignore.

Sam was convinced this was no advanced research base. Not one run by the Alliance, at any rate.

And isn't that ironic. They used the threat of my kidnapping...to kidnap me.

Her decision made, she pressed the tattoo between her thumb and forefinger to activate it, and then casually brought her hand up as if to massage the back of her neck. The action brought the tattoo into physical contact with the small, bony mastoid process behind her right ear.

The store of nano formation material inserted just beneath her skin reacted instantly to the app. She felt a small pull as the formation material found its way from her skull into the ring. It wasn't much, but it would be enough to do the job.

"Excuse me," a voice said from behind her.

Sam jumped, and turned to find one of the other scientists, his eyes widening in alarm.

"I'm so sorry," he said. "I didn't mean to startle you."

She brushed off his apology. "It's fine. What can I do for you?"

He waved awkwardly to his station. "Well, I was hoping you could help me identify the substance in the vial I was assigned. I'm unfamiliar with the description on the label, and thought you might have heard of it."

"Sure," she said readily, following him to his station.

He gestured her over to the holo, which she noted had a security-wrap of light-bending nano applied to the image it projected.

Interesting. Unless someone comes up directly behind us, no one will be able to see what we're working on.

On the heels of that thought came a less pleasant one.

Of course, they're probably monitoring us remotely, too.

Her musings stumbled to a halt when she caught sight of the file the scientist had on display.

Chemical notation of molecular chains hung suspended beside space-filling models, surface representations, and ribbon diagrams. In a separate window floated a 3D reconstruction of the vial itself, the hazardous materials icon clearly shown on its label.

It was to this that the scientist pointed. "I've not heard of this...adamantium...before. Do you know what it is?"

Sam blinked in shock. "I...excuse me?" She leaned in and took another careful look at the vial's image. "May I?" she asked, and the scientist nodded.

She minimized the image and pulled up the other samples. A quick glance to her left showed the third researcher industriously working at her station, studying a substance known as naquadah.

"I...uhm...." Sam cleared her throat.

Thinking furiously, she darted a look back at her own workstation and pulled up the information on the vial she'd been assigned, labeled thyrium.

All three substances had one thing in common: they'd been jokingly mentioned in a conversation she'd had three weeks earlier with the Center's lead programmer, Leah Harris.

The woman had shared with Sam her guilty pleasure: watching feeds from old pre-diaspora productions that imagined what life would be like hundreds of years in their future.

"It's crazy, some of the stuff they envisioned," Leah had told

Sam. "To make their stories more believable, they'd fabricate these wild discoveries. Unobtanium, they called it. And then they used handwavium to explain away the things we take for granted today, like wire communication and Starshot buoys."

Sam had laughed with her at the odd, made-up words and their obvious meanings. She'd laughed even harder at the names of some of the materials Leah had mentioned. Some had been ridiculously fake, but others like thyrium and adamantium had an aura of believability about them.

Seeing the fictional materials listed here meant Leah was involved somehow. Sam could think of no good reason for the programmer to purposely mislabel valuable test material, unless she'd been dragged into the situation against her will and had used the labels as a last-ditch effort to send a cryptic message.

"Doctor?" the scientist beside her prodded.

"Sorry. It's a… new nomenclature we've been discussing in the labs," she said, grasping at the first excuse that came to mind. "I hadn't realized we'd begun using it already. Here, let me fix that for you."

She turned back to the holo and reached for the molecular structure on display. She took her time, rotating it slowly as her gaze roamed the rest of the workstation. Her attention was caught by an icon that showed network connectivity. His access wasn't limited like her own.

She casually moved her other hand against the workstation's console, ensuring the tattoo made contact with its surface.

While the app did its thing, downloading itself and working its way into the base's system, Sam identified the chiral material as one of the L2 samples. She erased 'adamantium,' replacing it with the molecular chain's actual name, and then stepped back with a smile.

"I've reverted it back to its non-chiral label for you. That'll be less distracting, I think."

The scientist, who she now suspected was no real scientist, nodded his thanks.

Sam motioned to the woman standing in front of the other workstation. "Do you think Doctor Demuth would mind if I did the same for her?"

The man bobbed his head. "Here, let us go over there, and I will explain. She is a private person and does not like strangers to interrupt her."

Sam let him lead, trailing behind and waiting patiently as the woman listened to Gish's explanation, staring at Sam with suspicion all the while.

The woman pursed her lips, nodded abruptly, and then stepped back.

"Doctor?" Gish gestured to the station, and Sam stepped forward.

She wasted no time. With one hand, she manipulated the contents on the screen, while she pressed the other against the console, giving the Faraday tattoo the opportunity to send out more of its digital phone-home troops.

She was relieved to see that this vial also came from an L2 lab, and even more relieved to have caught Leah's mislabeling before it raised any attention.

Calling up the vial's label, she erased its 'naquadah' designation and replaced it with the actual molecular description.

"That should do it," she said, stepping back.

Demuth looked as if she'd eaten something sour, but she at least thanked Sam before practically pushing her out of the way in her haste to regain control over the workstation.

Sam nodded pleasantly to Gish. Then, instead of returning directly to her own station, she detoured to the table that held the 3D printer and RNA replicon unit. Under pretense of examining the equipment more closely, she took care that her tattoo made solid contact with each machine.

She'd just finished and was looking around the room for other equipment that might have network access, when sudden movement at the lab's doors caught her attention.

Marceau was approaching, and he did not look happy.

SLEIGHT OF HAND

AKKADIAN BASE
AN-YANG DUST BELT
PROXIMA CENTAURI

CHE WATCHED FROM his office inside the asteroid's Combat Information Center as the tau-neu stasis pods containing the three additional Alliance scientists were placed inside 'Rosen Base'. A medical corpsman would arrive shortly to release the three from stasis and escort them to another lab in the faux research facility. There, they would be given the same vial Travis had been assigned and ordered to weaponize it.

It had been Bijin's idea to acquire scientists from various disciplines and assign them the same problem. His reasoning was that different points of view combined with different skill sets might provide Akkadia with an arsenal of bioweapons. Working as a team, they would land on only one.

Che privately thought that one surgical strike, precisely delivered from an exceptional weapon, was preferable to relying on less potent ordnance. Yet the citizen doctor was the medical scientist, not Che, so he deferred to Bijin's recommendation.

Fortunately, the abandoned drug facility had plenty of clean lab rooms. They were grouped in such a way that the fictional base could be contained to a relatively small area.

Throughout the rest of the station, Che's soldiers could move freely without the need for pretense. It was bracingly, unashamedly Akkadian.

Che swiped away from the tau-neu pods, cycling his way through the various feeds that showed the goings-on around the asteroid. He knew the CIC staff just outside his doors were keeping each feed under close scrutiny, but it gave him a measure of satisfaction to occasionally see for himself that all was well.

He paused as he came to the one that showed Dr. Bijin bent over a piece of equipment. Behind the man and across the hall, Che could just make out a row of sealed rooms.

Shadowed figures moved within two of them—political prisoners whose deaths had been commuted so that they might serve the empire in a more useful manner. They would become the bioweapon's first test subjects.

Che continued flipping through the feeds until a chime announced he had a visitor.

"Come," he called, and the doors slid open to reveal Citizen Commander Li, the officer of the watch.

"Sir, we have news from Procyon," the man said with a small bow. "The properties manager has been located. The team is en route to her ship as we speak, and the fourth vial should be in their hands before the end of the day."

"Very good," Che said. "Thank you, Citizen Commander."

Li bowed himself out, but before the doors fully closed, Marceau appeared.

"Do you have news for me as well?" the general asked.

Marceau twisted his head to the side in a gesture that suggested he was hedging his answer. "I just came from Intelligence. They're confident the Alliance won't see this attack coming. They'll assume it'll take weeks before we can weaponize the vials."

Che narrowed his eyes at the man. "You do not agree."

Marceau shot Che a wry look. "Despite Intelligence's assurances, the Alliance has ordered an increased level of security around the Merki Institute on Hawking, prior to the Summit. I would call that more of a 'trust but verify' behavior, myself."

"Does this pose a problem to the operation?"

"Not one we can't overcome." Marceau motioned to Che's holoscreen. "May I?"

"By all means." Che sent Marceau the token to control it.

The base's feed was replaced by an image outside the institute, located in Midland, one of Hawking's three major cities. "Three agents have inserted into the area, as employees for the service organizations that work the institute during large events."

The image was replaced by two logos: a caterer and a cleaning and maintenance company.

"Our initial plan had been for these agents to plant the viral canisters either in the lifts that carry the delegates to the ballroom, or along the hallway that leads into it." The image shifted to a floorplan, with the areas highlighted. "It's too risky to plant anything in the ballroom itself. The number of secret service agents already on site prevents that. But now..."

Marceau hesitated, and Che motioned for him to continue.

"The agents on site now believe the heightened security compromises that plan. They think those canisters will be found."

"I take it you've come up with a satisfactory alternative?" Che asked, letting a small acerbic edge leach into his voice.

"Yes, Citizen General," the other man said with a small dip of his head. He indicated the holo, and the view changed once more.

It was as if a drone had backed away from the building, and then plunged beneath the city's streets. Che found himself staring at meters of ceramacrete and durasteel as they whizzed by. They were now in a tunnel that ran parallel to the institute.

"There is a warren of maintenance tunnels beneath the streets of Midland, and one of them runs reasonably close to the Merki Institute," Marceau said. "It is far enough away that those policing the building have dismissed it, assuming no one would go to the trouble it would require to access the institute by this means."

He pointed to the holo, and a highlight encircled an access door built into the side of the tunnel.

"Every few meters, there are access panels. Behind them run sewage, water treatment, and other lines. The team has been steadily feeding formation material into the panel closest to the institute. Nanobots are working to weave channels leading into the building. They have already breached its foundation."

"How do you plan to reach the ballroom where the summit is being held?" Che asked. "It is not on the ground floor."

Marceau smiled. "We go up through the walls. By this time tomorrow, we will have channels spaced at regular intervals along the ballroom's perimeter."

As he spoke, the holo's image altered to show the room in question. Small dots began to light up along the edges of the venue.

"With a single command, the builder bots will chew through the intervening five-millimeter substrate in a matter of minutes," Marceau said. "From there, it will be a simple matter to pipe the viral agent through."

Che frowned as a thought occurred. "What of the canisters already planted?"

Marceau shook his head. "I don't want to risk our operatives by sending them back in to remove them. If they discover the canisters, so be it. Let them think they have outwitted us."

Che flipped the holo back to the base's feed and stared thoughtfully at the image of Bijin in his lab as he considered the plan Marceau had laid out.

He gave the man a decisive nod. "Very good. I have a comm

scheduled with the minister shortly. Rin Zhou will be pleased with this update."

DERELICT SHIP

SHADOW RECON DAP HELIOS
ONE AU OUTSIDE ATLIEKAS NEBULA

DEEP INSIDE THE NSA, analysts quietly retasked two Starshot buoys to perform a sensor sweep along the coordinates the drug lord Jurgens had provided. The sensor suites within the buoys were classified, and few knew they existed. The buoys executed the sweep, and then sent the results back to NSA headquarters.

Analysts then forwarded the information to Colonel Valenti. She, in turn, pushed the data to a stealthed DAP Helios, floating silently just outside the Atliekas Nebula.

The sensor sweep had been at the highest resolution, offering exact positioning of each object within a very narrow area. This allowed the Helios to make a Scharnhorst jump with precision accuracy.

The ship the buoys' scans had found did not react in any way to the unexpected appearance of the stealthed ship, nor had those aboard the Helios expected it to. The craft behaved almost as if it were derelict, drifting aimlessly in space.

The team aboard the Helios was suited in full drakeskin gear, with supplemental ES hazmat shielding. They carried with them a case that would be able to safely contain the vial they had come to obtain.

A portable decontamination unit had been introduced into the Helios's airlock system, and everyone who entered the derelict vessel would be required to pass through it before returning to the ship.

{Five minutes out,} the pilot reported.

The leader responded with a two-click, and then motioned for her team to do a final gear check.

{Hold up. I'm seeing evidence this ship's been breached recently,} the pilot sent suddenly. *{No evidence of any other vessels in the area, but be advised. Please proceed with caution.}*

{Copy that,} the team leader sent.

The Helios settled gently against the outer hull of the other ship, and one of the team members affixed a Bravo Charlie onto its hatch. When the telltale flashed green, the team lead gave the signal, and four ghosts slipped through the airlock and onto the ship.

Five minutes later, the team lead was back on the ship's net.

{I have five dead—three crew, and two who match the description of Jurgens' properties manager and her assistant.}

The woman's voice was steady, but there was something in her tone that caught the pilot's attention.

{Bloody battle?} he asked.

{Not the kind you're thinking,} came the reply. *{Looks like the virus did a number on them.}*

The pilot exchanged a swift glance with the copilot. She then swept a hand through the ship's holo, double-checking the seal that separated the cockpit from the cargo bay.

Another voice came on the net. *{Yeah, this place has been tossed, Captain. Someone got here before we did.}*

{Check anyway,} came the terse response. *{And someone see if they can access ship's record on this boat.}*

{Already on it,} the ship's tech witch and flight engineer said.

{It's looking like.... Well, hell's bells.}

{That tells me nothing, Specialist,} the team leader said sharply.

{Sorry, ma'am. I'll forward you the feed.}

The flight engineer paused as she let the footage of the Akkadian infiltration stream to the combat net.

{I have confirmation. Repeat, I have confirmation. The vial's not here. The Akkadians got here first.}

REVEALED

Akkadian Base
An-Yang Dust Belt
Proxima Centauri

THE INFORMATION THAT Sam had gleaned from the other workstations proved something was afoot. She'd immediately recognized the hantavirus from the Center's L4 lab. This particular vial was the chiral version.

Because chiral viruses could not infect humans, it presented no danger to anyone on the base. Also because of that, the inner antigen vial had not been included. Sam worried about where its paired, non-chiral twin might be, and feared that it was on its way here to join them.

Now that there was no longer any doubt in her mind that she was being held inside an Akkadian base, she looked for ways she could throw a wrench into the works without them knowing.

The Project Rufus team back at the Center hadn't studied what it might take to break the entanglement that tied a cloned chiral pair to its original. That was scheduled for a later research phase, so that option was out.

As a physicist, Sam had her *opinions* on how to break an existing quantum entanglement between a set of organisms, but she hadn't had an opportunity to test her theory. She feared that, rather than break entanglement altogether, altering one virus would simply send the command for the other to reassort itself in the same manner.

If that were the case, the only thing she'd end up doing was rendering the existing antigen useless, and the very last thing she wanted to do was unleash a new virus on the settled worlds that had no antigen to counteract it.

But her abilities were limited. Sam hadn't lied to Marceau; although she knew a substantial amount of chemistry, the kind that crossed over into her fields of study, she wasn't a biochemist. Beyond that, there was the probability that Bijin would be able to tell instantly that she'd meddled, and she would have no good answer to give them as to why.

I really don't want to find out how they'd respond to that, she thought as she laid her tattooed hand onto the 3D printer to deposit more copies of her breadcrumb app.

The soft *whoosh* of the lab door opening had her looking up from the holo to see Marceau approaching at a rapid pace. She stood and braced herself—for what, she didn't know.

He lifted his hand almost imperiously, ordering her forward with a flick of his fingers. "Come with me, doctor."

He didn't stipulate why; he simply turned and headed toward the door, expecting her to follow.

Sam hesitated for a brief moment, indecision paralyzing her.

As if he could sense it, Marceau turned back and shot her an impatient look. "*Now*, doctor."

Not wanting to raise suspicions, Sam complied.

There is always the possibility you'll find a few new places to drop breadcrumbs, she reminded herself.

Marceau escorted her to another lab down the hall. It was empty save for Bijin, who stood beside a holoscreen that displayed the image of a laboratory glove box. Inside the box was a vial.

The moment she came within reaching distance, Bijin seized her by the arm and pulled her in front of the holo.

"What is this, doctor?" he demanded, thrusting his hand toward the image.

"One of the vials?" she asked, genuinely stumped by his line of questioning.

The stocky man rounded on her, hands on hips, jaw thrust forward belligerently. "Yes! The fourth vial! It is different from the third one. You lied to us!" Bijin's face was apoplectic, his voice just shy of a scream as he flung the accusation in her face.

Sam backed away from the man, stunned by the attack that seemed to come out of nowhere. "Ex-excuse me?" she stuttered as her gaze swung from Bijin's reddened face to Marceau.

The colonel's face was set into hardened lines, and Sam knew it would be wise not to cross him.

"The vials you claim are chirally entangled," Bijin said. "They are not the same!" He jabbed an accusing finger toward the holo.

He must have also sent the command for the feed to play, for as she watched, she saw the view widen until she could see a second glove box seated beside the first. Each one contained a vial held in place under a nanoscopic scanner.

Her gaze jerked back to Bijin as the man got up in her face once more.

"You said these vials were mirror images of each other and that they were paired. That is an impossibility!"

He was so close that spittle hit her face.

He seized her arm once more, thrusting her toward the holo. "One of those vials has a second, inner container. *What is this third vial?*" He punctuated his question with quick, vicious pulls at her arm, and she staggered as she twisted to get away from him, only to back right into Marceau.

"Answer him, doctor." The voice that came from behind her was pitched low and sounded dangerous.

"I didn't lie," she said as she took a step back from them both, her gaze bouncing from one face to the other.

She held up a hand when Bijin began to advance.

"I didn't!" she protested. "That third inner vial is something completely separate from the entangled pair. It contains the antigen for the non-chiral version of the virus."

Bijin quieted, and his expression turned thoughtful.

"Did you think we'd create something that might accidentally find its way into the general population?" she asked. "That's not how we work. We don't experiment with dangerous pathogens without also manufacturing a cure."

She couldn't keep her anger from creeping into her tone, but Bijin didn't seem fazed.

He turned his head to one side, eyeing her in that raptor-like way of his. "So that's all this is?" he demanded suspiciously. "An antigen?"

He waved a hand, and the feed changed. In this new recording, Sam saw a closeup view from one of the glove boxes. Inside the protective ES field, nano-gloved hands reached in to unseal the vial, then poured its contents into a separate container.

The vial was turned so that its neck faced the feed, and Sam could now clearly see the inner compartment. A pair of tweezers came into view. They lifted the narrow cylinder out of the vial and placed it alongside the container without attempting to crack it open.

"That right there," Bijin froze the feed, pointing to the removed component. "This is not some kind of Alliance trap? A, how you say, *booby trap*, in case it falls into enemy hands?"

The man's accent had grown stronger, but as she realized what this man had just voluntarily—or involuntarily—revealed, Sam couldn't help the look of horror that crossed her face, nor the instinctive step back she took.

"Doctor Bijin," Marceau's voice cracked sharply into the silence that followed the man's outburst. "You are out of line. Dismissed."

Bijin drew himself up, his snub nose wrinkling as his face screwed up in protest. "But—"

"Enough. Go back to your lab. Leave us."

Bijin spared Sam one last annoyed glance before stomping off.

Sam took in a careful breath before she dared look at the person who had been pretending to be an Alliance military officer who knew her uncle.

Marceau sighed. "I see this one isn't going to be smoothed over as easily as the last."

"I beg your pardon?" she asked carefully.

"I'm curious. What did Gish say to raise your suspicions earlier?" The *colonel* studied her face as he spoke. "Or has it been Doctor Bijin's behavior all along that gave us away?"

Sam's heartbeat quickened. She tried to act confused, clueless. "I... don't understand," she wrinkled her brow.

Marceau's expression told her he wasn't buying it.

"Your acting skills aren't as good as your medical ones, doctor. This charade has come to an end." He reached for her arm and pulled her toward the door.

Recalling Ell's comment about a door's controls, Sam dug in her heels when they reached the exit, and grabbed the frame when the doors slid open.

"Look, I'm getting really tired of being hauled around," she complained. "What do you mean 'charade'?" Since confusion hadn't worked, she tried for frustration and anger. Those, she could do.

Marceau turned with an impatient look. "Please, doctor. We don't have time for this."

Sam glared at him as she clung stubbornly to the frame, her hand groping blindly for the door's controls. "I don't care. I'm not going anywhere until you tell me what in the hell is going on," she said.

When she found the panel, she pressed her tattoo against it, praying that the internal mechanism was somehow tied into the rest of the base, and the app could have yet another means by which to send out its SOS.

Marceau pried her hand from the door and yanked her

forward, sending her stumbling out into the corridor. His voice was cold and hard, and he didn't bother looking at her as he marched her toward the nearest lift. "You are our guest, Doctor Travis, and will be treated as such for as long as you cooperate fully. Do I make myself clear?"

When the lift doors closed behind them, Marceau entered a code, and four new floors appeared.

Sam saw another opportunity and took it.

"Stop!" she cried out as she pushed her tattooed hand repeatedly against the controls as if to find a way to halt the lift. "Will you please just *stop* for a minute?"

Marceau made an exasperated sound. "The lift will not respond to you, doctor. Besides, there is no place for you to go on this station. You're a smart person... Let's cut the act, shall we?"

Sam dropped her hands and sucked in a deep breath before she squared off against the imposter.

"Who are you really?" she demanded.

"I'm a colonel, as I told you. And my name really is Marceau. Or at least, that is the standardized pronunciation of it."

Sam attempted to sound confused. "Then why all the rough treatment? And what is *with* Bijin, anyway? He acts as if he's working against the Alliance's interests. Or at least, as if he and I are on opposing sides."

Marceau shook his head, a chuckle escaping as he stared at her. "You really expect me to believe you're still oblivious to what's going on here, after what Bijin just did? It doesn't matter," he said. "We're running out of time, we need answers *now*. You will provide us with what we need, or we will force it out of you. It is as simple as that."

The lift doors opened onto a different world altogether. She saw soldiers clad in strange military uniforms hurry past, and directional holosigns written in a language her wire translated as Akkadian.

She'd fallen through the looking glass.

BREADCRUMBS

TASK FORCE BLUE'S combat center was located in a room adjacent to the team's situation room. The entire team was present, as were Valenti and Cutter. They were grouped around a holotank that stood in the center of the room.

Thad looked up when Micah entered, and waved him over. The colonel was standing on one side of the Marine, and the director flanked him on the other. Jonathan moved to make a space for Micah, who slid into the opening between his twin and Gabe.

A quick glance around the room showed the rest of the team were at various consoles, scrubbing through information feeds or monitoring in-progress operations. He looked down into the tank to see the Procyon System displayed.

Valenti's hands moved through it, enlarging a sector as she spoke. "Starshot data recorded a Casimir flare here, about two hours ago." She pointed to a spot just outside the Klintis Belt.

"The buoys then recorded a Scharnhorst signature an hour and a half later, originating here." Her finger slid from the outer edge of the belt inward, until it hovered near an object that had been highlighted.

She spread her hands, and their perspective changed, the view growing until Micah could make out that the object was a ship. A dotted line grew from the pin she'd dropped to indicate the Scharnhorst signature, and a window popped up to show the distance between the two.

Fifty kilometers. Exactly the distance a ship needed to be from any object before it could safely jump to Scharnhorst space.

Whoever had been there was long gone by now.

Micah's head snapped up as he pointed to the highlighted vessel. "That's the ship the vial was supposed to be on?"

The grim expression on Cutter's face would have confirmed it, but Valenti nodded anyway.

"Echo Team infiltrated. Their report just came in," the colonel said.

Micah's hand curled against the edge of the tank as he stared once more into the holo. "They beat us to the vial, didn't they."

Valenti nodded. "They did."

Jonathan looked up. "Are we going on the assumption they've taken both Sam and the vials back to Akkadian space?"

"For the time being, yes. I have Delta and Foxtrot teams running through simulations to infiltrate the two most likely locations, and we're working some back channels, trying to pinpoint exactly where they've been taken."

"Our regular sources are telling us things are strangely quiet," Cutter told them. "This behavior's atypical. More than one of them have remarked that they suspect something big or off the books is going down."

"Ain't that the truth," Thad muttered.

"One of those sources dug a bit deeper. Possibly a bit too deep, since we haven't heard back from them since," the director admitted. "But thanks to this intel, I think we can confirm what

Jurgens said."

Gabe's brows rose. "So he was right? The summit's their target?"

"Yes," Valenti said as she reached once more into the holotank. The Procyon System remained, but an image floated atop it.

Thad grunted. "Asher Dent."

Cutter looked over at the team leader before sweeping his gaze across those standing around the tank. "Yes. Akkadian, and the Coalition's minority leader. Dent also happens to be one of the people attending that defense summit on Hawking."

"Well, damn," Gabe said softly. "Would they really be that bold?"

At Valenti's sharp look, he explained.

"Harper, Hyer, and Will have been poring over everything they can find about that summit. His name came up, and I thought maybe that's how they planned to deliver the virus."

Addy shot him a considering look. "You mean, expose him to the virus and then dose him with the antigen." She nodded. "It's possible. He'd be shedding viral particles for days, if not weeks."

"I figured something like that, yes," agreed Gabe. "But I'd dismissed it as too obvious."

He hooked his hand around the back of his neck and began to pace, eyes dropping to the floor as he thought it through.

"Dent would burn his position within the Coalition forever by doing that, but it might be worth it, if it cements his position at home."

Gabe paused and looked back up at Cutter. "There's bad blood between him and the sitting minister of state security, isn't there?"

Cutter nodded. "She replaced his father years ago. Rumor has it she was the one who leaked the intel that led to his execution."

"You really think Dent's behind this?" Thad asked.

Gabe shrugged. "It's possible. A strike this big would give him enough street cred with the premier. He could use that newfound influence to have her removed. It would be poetic justice, since she was responsible for ousting his father in the first place."

There was a beat of silence as they all stared down into the holotank.

"Even if it is Dent, what are the chances he'd have a backup plan, in case we detain him? A meeting between people at this level doesn't happen without a lot of security, planned out well in advance," Jonathan murmured. "Am I right in assuming that each delegation has sent their own forces to coordinate security for the event?"

Cutter nodded.

Micah shook his head. "I'm sure the Alliance has people swarming all over the place, then."

Thad lifted a brow at that. "More than you can shake a stick at, *ami*. And now we have sensors on site that'll detect chiral particles, too."

Gabe eyed Cutter. "Whatever they have planned, they've either already planted it, or they figured out a way to deliver it that can't be detected."

Thad looked thoughtful. "My credit's on some woo-woo delivery system, if they went to the trouble to kidnap the doc."

"We're certain the intel this Jurgens gave us is accurate?" Addy asked. "Should we be considering alternative targets?"

All eyes swung to Cutter.

"All our pipelines are coming up empty," he told them, "and the asset close to Enlai who seemed to confirm what Jurgens said about the summit has gone dark."

"I have confirmation!" Hyer's voice called out from a nearby console. She stood and crossed over to join them at the holotank. Her eyes tracked to Gabe and then Valenti.

The colonel nodded. "What do you have?"

"Remember the surveillance nano I dropped on Janus this afternoon?" she asked Gabe.

When he nodded, she continued.

"Well, I just got a ping from it. Janus met with someone from the Akkadian embassy on the downlow just a few minutes ago.

You know how the surveillance nano is set to go dormant each time it senses it's come into proximity of a sensor sweep?"

Gabe made a rolling motion with his hands, and Hyer cleared her throat, muttering a quick *"Sorry"* before she began again.

"Anyway, it just came back online. At first, it sounded like he was just reporting in—standard stuff, the 'I've been interrogated by the enemy' thing. But then he asked if it had anything to with the summit operation."

She grinned widely as she added, "Pissed his handler off, mentioning it aloud." Hyer's eyes rounded when she realized what she said. Mumbling another *"Sorry,"* she eased away and turned back to her console.

Micah's lips twitched when he heard her chastising herself as she returned to her seat.

"No joking around the boss. No using the word 'pissed' in front of the director. Seriously, Katie, what the hell are you thinking?"

A quick glance at Cutter's face told him the director had heard as well. For the first time since this madness had begun, Micah saw the man's expression ease momentarily.

"Okay, then," Cutter said. He straightened and turned to Valenti. "Hawking is a go. Prep a team."

"Hang on," Addy cautioned, raising a hand. "For this particular mission, I think the weapon should dictate the team."

"Come again?" Thad asked. He braced his forearms against the tank and leaned around Cutter so he could make eye contact with the doctor.

Addy's gaze moved to Micah. "There are three individuals who have a natural, built-in immunity to any viral weapon Akkadia tries to throw at us. That's Micah, Pascal, and Sneaky Pete. Their chirality makes them immune to the virus."

Thad reared his head back. "You want me to send a ferret on a mission, *cher?*"

Addy huffed a small, annoyed sound. "Look, I'll grant that it's unorthodox, but you already use Pascal. Both animals have basic E-V comm implants. And," she added, "a ferret is small enough to fit into places—"

"Places a drone can fit just as easily," Thad countered.

"But a drone can be jammed," Addy pointed out. "*Any* signal can, except for the entangled connections our chiral pairs share."

He slashed his hand through the air. "No to the ferret. But you do raise a good point." He turned to Micah. "What do you say? You up for a feline partner?"

Micah nodded, and opened his mouth to speak, but Valenti beat him to it.

"We take a standard team, we interface with security already onsite, and we keep everyone on the search until the delegations have landed on the habitat."

She turned to Micah. "You and Pascal will go in. The rest will retreat to the perimeter and try to round up the Akkadians who infiltrated to place the weapon."

Thad shook his head, muttering, "I'm really beginning to hate those bastards."

Micah grunted. "You and me both."

The Marine straightened, slapping a hand on Micah's shoulder. "Okay, hoss. Let's get you started on some intelligence and mission prep—"

He was interrupted by the sound of footsteps pounding down the hallway. The doors split open to admit a breathless Harper. She came to a stop just as Addy began to scold her.

"I told you, you need to take it easy while you're recovering, Harper."

"This is too important, Captain." She wheeled to face Cutter. "I found Sam!"

TEST SUBJECTS

AKKADIAN BASE
AN-YANG DUST BELT
PROXIMA CENTAURI

THE AREA WHERE Marceau had brought Sam was clearly a military installation. This, more than anything, proved to her that 'Rosen Base' was merely a ruse to ensure her cooperation.

Sam stared stonily ahead as the Akkadian colonel led her off the lift. "Where are we really?" she asked.

To her surprise, he answered. "An abandoned asteroid base in An-Yang's outer belt."

"So, Proxima Centauri, then," she murmured as she took in the signs of disrepair that were a bit more evident here than in the small area they'd staged as an Alliance research center. "That's odd. Why not use a base closer to home? There are rumors about places you people have hidden within the Sargon Straits. Surely, they'd be more convenient—" she paused and looked around, "and in much less disrepair than this."

She blinked and ground to a halt as a thought occurred to her.

"Omigod. This isn't sanctioned, is it? The premier has no idea what you're doing."

Marceau shot her an annoyed look as her actions brought him to a stop as well. "I don't particularly care to drag you around by the arm, doctor, but I will if you don't keep up. Clearly, there is nowhere for you to run, and this whole experience will be much more pleasant if you cooperate."

She crossed her arms and shot him a sour look. "For whom? You? Like I care."

Marceau's expression hardened, and he stepped closer, looming over her. "Akkadians learn respect and discipline at a very young age," he bit out. "We have penalties for disrespect that you soft imperialists cannot begin to fathom."

He took her hand, turning it over in his, and then suddenly bent her small finger back at an unnatural angle.

She gasped, twisting her hand awkwardly to ease the building pressure, but he released her just before he did any real damage. Sam curled her fingers into a fist and held it protectively against her chest.

"Did you know that the empire has nano to negate the basic medical package your people enjoy?" he asked in a mild tone, as if they were discussing a much more inane topic, like the weather or her preference for tulsi tea. "You don't require every finger on this hand to do your work. Remember that."

Having made his point, he walked off.

Sam watched him go, anger suffusing her. She called after him, "You people are real bastards, you know?"

Halfway down the hall, he paused and pivoted to face her. "You really wish to test me on this, doctor?" One brow lifted, and his expression turned mocking. "I *will* resort to stronger methods to ensure your cooperation. That can begin now, if you like."

Sam sensed his contempt, knew that he considered her and all other Alliance citizens to be beneath him. The practical side of her nature cautioned her not to challenge him just yet.

As long as I'm free to move about, I have a chance of finding additional ways to drop that SOS nano, she reminded herself as she moved to follow in his wake.

His destination turned out to be a laboratory located at the end of a long corridor. Empty isolation rooms lined one side of the passage. They were distinguished by the channel, inset just outside each chamber's clearsteel wall, that indicated an ES field had been installed. It was a standard setup for laboratories that dealt with unsafe and potentially lethal materials.

"You must have been planning this since the moment we discovered what was in Luyten's Star," she mused as she paused in front of one of the rooms. "It had to have taken months to build an installation like this. I'm surprised you managed to hide from An-Yang all this time."

Marceau laughed, a genuinely amused sound. "It was already here. You're standing in an abandoned Frenzy factory."

Sam's eyes widened, and she stepped away from the isolation room. "Do you have any idea how dangerous it is to manufacture that drug? We should all be dead by now!"

Marceau lifted a brow. "I imagine the squatters who were here when we arrived cleaned the place out pretty well, years ago."

Sam shot him a look of incredulity. "Don't you people get the news in Akkadia? Coalition raids on Frenzy refineries? Hundreds of workers dead?"

She gestured vaguely around her. "There could still be ultrafine refractory droplets floating around, caused by condensation during the vapor phase. Inhale enough of it, and no medical nano in the settled worlds could scrub it from your system fast enough to save you."

Her words seemed only to amuse him further.

"If it makes you feel any better, Bijin insisted we do a clean sweep of our own before he'd set foot inside the place." He placed a hand over his heart and bowed. "But your concern over the health of my people is admirable, doctor."

"Unfortunately, you've tied my well-being to your own," Sam snapped. "Your people can all be shot into the core for all I care."

Marceau's humor fled. "You've made your point, and as you say, your survival is tied to ours. More precisely, it's tied to your performance." He gestured to the airlock entrance to the laboratory. "It's time for you to prove you're worth keeping alive."

His hand on her back propelled her forward. The two-stage system, the presence of hazmat suits, and Marceau's insistence that she don one told Sam this was equivalent to L4 containment.

This must be where the vials were being kept.

The inner airlock doors slid open, and Sam's eyes were arrested by the single prominent piece of furniture in the room: a long table upon which two glove boxes sat. She recognized them from the feed she'd seen earlier.

"You are in Doctor Bijin's world now, Doctor Travis," Marceau warned as they approached the table. "I would advise you to tread carefully."

Placing his hands on her shoulders, he turned her to face the wall that separated the laboratory from the hallway. It was apparently some form of nano-coated clearsteel; although the wall was opaque from the outside, from inside it offered a clear view of the isolation rooms lined up across the hall.

She realized with a start that not all of them were empty. A trace of glowing blue ran around the edge of three, indicating the ES field was active. Inside two were small clusters of people—three in one, four in another.

Sam received the distinct impression that what she was seeing weren't isolation rooms, but rather cages. The people inside were prisoners.

"These are our test subjects," Marceau explained. "We imported several from the homeworld for just this purpose."

"Somehow I doubt they volunteered for this," Sam said in a barely audible voice, but Marceau heard.

He laughed softly. "You would be correct. We have a prison on Eridu filled with a special breed of criminals. Some are traitors, others are those who have failed the cause. Political prisoners, you might say. And then there are enemy soldiers who need elimination."

She jerked around to glare at him. "That's against the Accords!"

The man shot her a sardonic look. "If you make it out of here alive, doctor, do you really think the Alliance will go to war with Akkadia over such a trivial thing?"

She narrowed her eyes and pointed at the isolation rooms where the prisoners were held. "I don't think any of those people would call their situation trivial, 'Colonel'."

He looked down at her in annoyance. "I would not expect you to understand. You are a product of your Geminate upbringing." He gestured to the prisoners. "This is the Akkadian way. My people are not wasteful of anything—not even those sentenced to die. They were brought to the base so that they might serve the empire one last time."

Sam shuddered at the explanation. "That's barbaric," she whispered.

Marceau shrugged dismissively. "You imperialists are all the same. You have never known what it is like to struggle the way Akkadia did when it was first settled. It breeds a spine into our people, a pragmatism we comprehend on a visceral level. I do not expect you to understand such a thing."

Marceau pulled her closer to the lab's windows, hand once more wrapped around her arm, forcing her to accompany him.

"Akkadian tradition found many uses for those who would be dead," he said. His tone sounded like he was lecturing in front of a classroom as he began to enumerate.

"Once broken, they make passable servants," he told her. "Some military prisoners were inserted onto the battlefield training ground, but most didn't fare as well as we'd hoped against Akkadian soldiers."

Sam pressed her free hand to her stomach to try to still its churning.

Marceau stopped just before the clearsteel wall and released her. He stood looking out at the prisoners across the hall, hands clasped loosely behind his back. His voice grew distant, as if he were recalling a memory.

"In ages past, if no other purpose was found, prisoners could always be used as fuel."

Sam stepped back, eliciting a chuckle from the man.

"Oh, there's no need for that any longer," he said, as if to reassure her. "But we do, on occasion, find other ways for them to serve."

As Sam stared into the isolation rooms, she realized belatedly she should have been documenting everything she'd seen since leaving the fictional Rosen sector. She remedied that now, starting with the victims in this cell. If she ever made it off this rock, she would at least have proof of the atrocities these people were committing.

Stepping forward once more, she studied the four men in the first cell. They looked broken, all hope lost.

Marceau took her arm again, leading her past the second occupied cell, where two men and a woman were held. She observed each one carefully, seeing the same dispirited acceptance of their fates.

The Akkadian stopped in front of an empty isolation room. "Doctor Bijin says the prisoners we have are too small a sample size to be considered statistically reliable. He insists that the margin for error is so great that standard deviation cannot even be measured."

Sam's gaze narrowed as she studied him, wondering where he was going with this. The expression on his face told her it wasn't any place good.

"You're the scientist. You know more about these things than I do. Tell me, doctor," he said, a triumphant gleam in his eyes, "how important is standard deviation in a test of the weapon we intend to deploy? Would seven deaths suffice? Ten?"

Movement caught her attention, and she turned to look across the hall. Her breath froze in her throat as a door opened in the back of the empty cell and three people were shoved inside. She didn't recognize the first two, but the third one....

Her gaze rocketed to Marceau. "Why did you bring them here?" she demanded.

The colonel merely raised a skeptical brow. "Really, doctor. Did you think you were the only person we acquired when we sought scientists who could manipulate the chiral material?"

He gestured to the three people Sam assumed were all Alliance citizens. She knew for a fact that one of them was.

"I will make you a deal, doctor. You cooperate with Bijin, answer his questions, assist him, and perform whatever task he asks you to perform. Do so without hesitation, and I will not include these three in our test run of the final bioweapon."

Marceau's gaze turned flinty and his hand tightened painfully around Sam's arm. "If he tells me you have fought him on this, or if I in any way sense you are trying to sabotage our goals, these three won't just be included with the rest of the test subjects." He turned her to face the group of scientists in the cell and pressed his hand against the window. "They will be the *first* ones we test the bioweapon on. Do I make myself clear?"

"Perfectly," Sam whispered through numb lips.

He must have done something to the wall to adjust its transparency, for as Linnet Thompson—Sam's peer and friend—looked up, her eyes widened in recognition.

All Sam could do was stare helplessly back at her.

ANTIGEN DROP

Task Force Blue HQ
Humbolt Base, Ceriba

After hearing that Harper had intercepted Sam's SOS, Cutter authorized a military gate override to allow a Shadow Recon flight to slip unnoticed into An-Yang space.

The ship was one of five DAP Helios vessels flown by Shadow Recon crews, all under Major Snell's command. While *Katana*'s pilot was occupied keeping the ship from being detected, the ship's copilot launched a small fleet of drones that went winging toward the asteroid belt where the signal originated.

The ship had come to rest an AU away from the asteroid they'd identified as their target, hovering invisibly beside a nearby Starshot buoy. A whiskerbeam relay provided an untraceable, real-time connection to TF Blue's situation room.

"I'm reading a faint energy signature from this area here," the drone pilot's voice sounded over the connection. In the next instant, a spot on the asteroid that was projected in the holotank lit up.

Micah knew that Daz, *Katana*'s copilot, had a delicate touch and could sneak up on anyone, anywhere. Still, he held his breath as the woman pushed her stealthed drones closer, willing them not to be discovered.

Breathe, bro.

Micah shot Jonathan a dark look. *You know what they'll do to Sam if they learn we've found them?*

No, but—

Neither do I, but I can guaran-damn-tee you it won't be good.

Jonathan's expression turned slightly amused. *And holding your breath's going to keep that from happening?*

Micah narrowed his eyes at his other self. *Fuck off.*

He turned back to the holotank when Daz spoke once more.

"I'm going to try to ease in a bit closer...."

He could tell from the distant quality of her voice that she was fully enmeshed with the drones under her control.

She delicately probed at the asteroid, gently coaxing the unwieldy rock to give up its secrets.

"Don't push this, Lieutenant," Major Snell ordered. The man paced, arms folded under his armpits, head down, as he listened to the report the pilot was feeding them.

"Copy that, sir," her voice returned. "Wait one. I'm seeing entry points."

The asteroid lit up once more as Daz identified five different vents that led into the rock's core. She had the drones drop the latest iteration of breaching nano packages onto the lip of each one.

Those in the situation room back at Blue waited silently for the telemetry to come in. All five lit up with indicators that showed airlocks at the end of each vent.

"Bingo," Daz breathed, and another sector of the asteroid lit up. "It's well hidden, sir, but you see that right there? That's the seam for bay doors, folks."

"Well done," Snell said. "Now pull those drones in and get the hell out of there. I want *Katana* back in Alliance space before anyone has a chance to spot you in that star system."

Daz sent a two-click, and the chatter from *Katana* lowered in volume as Daz reeled her drones back into the fold.

Micah turned to Valenti. "Ma'am, request permission to fly the Proxima op."

When Valenti started to shake her head, he sped up.

"I know what Captain Moran said about my chiral immunity, but if we can take this base and defuse the weapon, then whatever's been planted on Hawking becomes a non-issue."

A brief flash of sympathy appeared in the colonel's eyes, and then it was gone. "Unacceptable risk. You'll be going to Hawking."

Micah clenched his teeth before nodding reluctantly. He glanced at Jonathan. "If I'm inserting into Hawking, does that bench *Wraith*, then?"

Valenti and Snell exchanged a long look, and the Shadow Recon CO sighed and shook his head. "No. Jonathan will captain *Wraith*."

Valenti turned to Jonathan. "You'll drop Captain Severance, along with teams One through Four onto the asteroid."

"I'm sending a pair of Novastrikes to accompany you," Snell added, "full stealth."

Jonathan nodded and straightened. "Permission to join Thad's briefing, sir?"

Snell nodded, and Jonathan clapped Micah on the shoulder on his way out of the situation room.

Don't worry. We'll bring her back.

Micah met his twin's eyes. *You do that.*

As the doors slid shut behind Jonathan, Valenti turned her attention to Gabe.

"I've retasked Delta and Foxtrot. They're awaiting you and Micah down on level two. Sasha will lead the two Ranger teams, but she takes her orders from you, understood?"

Gabe jerked his head in a crisp nod.

"I'll get Johnson to fly you all over on *Scimitar*," Snell said. "Circle back with him once you've touched base with Delta and Foxtrot and have an ETA."

"I hear you know one of my former operators," Valenti said, and Gabe shot her a questioning look.

"Ell Cyr," she clarified.

Gabe's expression cleared and he nodded. "I do, ma'am. She runs the Navy's NCIC branch on Hawking."

Micah looked up at that, surprised. "I'd heard she left the teams, but I didn't know she was NCIC now. She was one hell of a sniper."

Valenti nodded but didn't otherwise address his comment. "I understand she's familiar with the institute. You both should know that the director cleared her to be read into this mission." Her gaze strayed to Micah. "Major Zander as well."

"*Fully* read in?" Micah asked carefully.

"Chiral material, yes. You and Jonathan?" Valenti's gaze swerved from Micah to Gabe. "No."

Gabe's brow wrinkled. "Why Zander?"

"He's former team, too," Micah explained. "Well, Shadow Recon, at least."

"He'll provide extra coverage, plus have eyes and ears on all traffic coming into the habitat," Snell explained. "Hopefully, his people will be able to finger the ship that delivers the goods from the asteroid base."

Gabe eyed Micah. "With your permission, then, I think Micah and I should meet up with Sasha and sit in on their mission planning."

Valenti nodded. "Granted. Sasha knows I want this buttoned down and the team ready to roll by tomorrow morning."

"Yes, ma'am."

Micah turned to follow Gabe out the door, but paused as it slid open to admit Duncan Cutter.

"I have news," the director said as he walked over to the holotank.

His expression told Micah that, unlike everything else they'd been hearing over the past two days, this might actually be good news.

Cutter dipped his hand into the tank, and moments later,

Addy's face peered back at them.

"Captain," the director greeted, "can you please tell the team what you just told me?"

Addy's gaze swept those assembled, a tired smile playing about her face.

"I thought you might want to hear something positive for a change," she told them. "I've been working with a team to cultivate an antigen for the yacht's hantavirus victims using Sam's notes. I just got word. We did it! It's on its way to the *Atliekan Queen* now."

Gabe stepped toward the tank. "Does that mean that we can declare that part of the situation resolved, then?" he asked.

Addy's smile wavered as she shook her head. "I wish I could tell you otherwise, but we won't be able to do that until we know for sure the Akkadians on that base haven't figured out how to manipulate the virus through its chirally entangled partner."

Her last words had Micah freezing, his hand on the door frame.

"What are you saying, doc?" he asked.

Addy's gaze met his. "Just what I've said before—no one who's been exposed to that fourth vial is safe until the third vial's contents are back in our hands."

MISSION PREP

Task Force Blue HQ
Humbolt Base, Ceriba

BEFORE JOINING GABE with Sasha and the rest of the Hawking team, Micah stopped in to see how Sam's rescue mission was progressing. He found the team—along with SRU Teams One through Four—in one of the VR suites set aside for combat mission prep and dry runs.

The room was more crowded than Micah had seen in a long while, with a dozen warriors joining Thad, Boone, and Asha on the VR course. He spied Jonathan leaning against the far wall; his twin's eyes were slitted in concentration as he watched the teams' progress.

Micah moved to join him, his own eyes roaming over the newly configured room.

The space was covered with ActiveFiber, the same material that clad *Wraith*'s interior. The walls, the thick mat underfoot, even the room's ceiling were coated centimeters thick with the malleable material. Just as *Wraith*'s interior walls could be reconfigured with a simple mental command, so too could this area.

Harper had found recordings of the abandoned base that was their destination buried in an after-action report that had been declassified by An-Yang a few years earlier. The report was dated more than ten years back, when a team of operatives from Shang's Controlled Substances Enforcement Agency had gone in to shut down the illegal drug operation.

The VR room's ActiveFiber material had been programmed to match the base's rough dimensions, and as Micah looked on, he could see warriors climb shafts, creep down hallways, rappel from cavernous hangars, and slide past various obstacles, engaging enemies that only they could see.

It was eerily silent. The fifteen people working the virtual Hogan's Alley were all clad in special haptic response suits and were communicating strictly over their combat net.

As he watched, one of them staggered as his suit's haptic inputs responded to invisible blows dealt by an adversary. In another corner, three soldiers' helmeted heads snapped around in reaction to the approach of enemy forces neither Micah nor Jonathan could see.

Micah cocked his head, considering that last thought.

Are you jacked in with the sim? he asked his twin as he came to rest beside him, unconsciously mimicking his other self's stance.

For answer, a link appeared on his overlay.

When he tapped the flashing icon, he was allowed to join as an observer, the feed being sent to them from the VR simulation emulating the one the teams would send to his twin on *Wraith*.

The feed compiled multiple different points of view from various operators, prioritizing them by their hierarchy on the team, as well as who was sending what over the wire. Beneath it all was laid the virtual 3D rendition of the abandoned asteroid.

Micah knew it was likely that things had changed there in the intervening years, but it was better than nothing. The base's bones would remain the same regardless.

It was good enough; it had to be, for Sam's sake.

As he watched, one of the SRU teams came under heavy fire from fictional Akkadian soldiers who were holed up behind a barricade hastily erected from rugged durasteel alloy shipping containers in the vast cargo bay. His eyes moved to another feed when he saw SRU Team Three breach a lab where another set of equally fictional Akkadians held a group of scientists hostage.

His gut clenched at the thought that this scenario was all too possible a reality.

Don't you have a mission planning session of your own to attend? His twin's words slid into his brain, a mental murmur.

Yeah, but...

Jonathan jostled his elbow. *Don't be getting any ideas and going team guy on me now.*

Micah coughed, knowing Jonathan's words were an attempt to rouse him from his worry over Sam. *Don't think there's any danger in that happening. I just have the right genes for this, is all.*

He stayed another few minutes, watching the figures move around the cushioned mats, and then turned to Jonathan.

Bring her home.

His twin's eyes shifted from the virtual course to meet Micah's. He nodded. *Always. Be careful, bro.*

Micah kicked up one corner of his mouth. *Always*, he parroted back.

With one last look at the simulation in progress, he pushed away from the wall and slipped out of the room to find Gabe.

The NCIC agent and Foxtrot's team lead had opted to delay a sim run-through until they arrived on Hawking, so Micah found himself seated across from Gabe over a briefing table. Spread out in front of them was a flat 2D projection of the Merki Institute.

The woman seated beside Gabe speared Micah with gray eyes. "Let's run this one more time. You enter here." She pointed. "Two Geminate Protection Detail MPs will be waiting. Once you clear them, you'll be greeted by two Coalition Protective Services people at the secondary security station. They will walk you through the ballroom."

The display changed to another 2D representation, the city block surrounding the institute. With a wave of her hand, Sasha turned the flat image spread across the table into a 3D holo that rose above it.

"Kai, Emma. You will be stationed here, and here," she instructed the two snipers. She shot Gabe a quick glance. "Alvarez and I will take positions here, and here."

She gestured, and another two icons lit on the holo, flashing to identify their respective positions.

"Connor, Franks, Noland. You three are in full drakeskin. You have the perimeter. We rotate, four hours on, four off."

Heads nodded all around.

She swiveled once more, and her eyes caught Micah's. "We'll sweep the building the night we arrive, and then again the next morning. Hopefully these jackasses will be kind to us and do something stupid."

There were grunts and a few *Oo-rahs*, but then one of them said what was on everyone's mind.

"Hope is not a plan."

Sasha nodded at that. "And that's why, when we arrive, we're doing this all over again, only with our local assets. Alvarez?" Stepping back, she ceded him the floor.

Gabe took over, using quick, concise terms to update those present on the people who would be waiting for them on the Hawking end.

Sasha's eyes flickered up, a tell Micah was sure she did on purpose to let everyone know she was checking her chrono.

"Okay, everyone, sack time. We leave at 0600 tomorrow." She glanced at the one person at their table who had yet to speak.

Johnson, who piloted the DAP Helios that would courier them over, gave her a slow nod. "We'll be ready, ma'am."

Sasha slapped her palms against the table, pushed back, and stood. "That's it, then. Dismissed, people."

NIMITZ BASE

NIMITZ BASE
PORTSMOUTH
HAWKING HABITAT

SCIMITAR CROSSED THE threshold of the open hangar in full stealth. As silent as its namesake, the sleek vessel slipped from the black into the cavernous, nearly empty space like a shark slicing through the sea.

It was weird for Micah to be a passenger on a Helios instead of its pilot. Although there was little likelihood that they'd need a flight engineer for this run, he'd taken the crew chief's cradle and webbed in.

The overlay readout that appeared as he jacked into the ship was oddly incomplete, and it took him a moment to realize why; the portions of the SyntheticVision feed that were blank were the pilot's readouts.

Johnson brought the ship to a stop using thrusters to nudge the Helios onto a cradle set off to one side of the bay. As the doors closed behind them, he powered down, turning to face

Micah and the rest of his passengers.

"I'll be here when you're ready to leave," he told them, and then gave Micah a pilot-to-pilot nod. "If you need any space cover, you let me know."

Sasha, Foxtrot team's lead, motioned Micah over to where she stood beside the weapons' locker with the team. They were in the midst of a gear check, the loadout for the team varying as widely as each member's individual skillset. Sasha had two tactical vests in her hand, and Gabe was checking the action on a projectile weapon, Pascal by his side.

The former special agent looked up as Micah came to a stop beside him.

"You ready for this?" Gabe asked, and Micah gave him a brief nod.

"Here," Sasha said, handing him two tactical vests. "Large one's for you; smaller one's for him," she lifted her chin in the direction of the large hunting cat, who rose to sniff the drakeskin-clad vest.

{Why need this?} he asked, batting at it with a massive paw.

Sasha rolled her eyes and muttered, "Stars and flares, whose idea was it to give a working cat an E-V wire?"

Pascal turned baleful green eyes on her. *{Heard that.}*

She scowled down at him. "I know."

The big cat turned to Micah. *{Why?}* he repeated.

He knelt to feed Pascal's legs through the vest's arm holes. "It'll protect vital organs from a direct hit. I hear it still smarts like hell if you're hit with a projectile, but the synthsilk in the vest will diffuse the strike and keep it from being fatal."

The cat was silent, digesting this in whatever way a large predator like him would, while Micah sealed the vest along his spine.

Gabe held a small disk up to show Pascal. "This," he told the cat, "will make you invisible. You understand what that means?"

{Am a cat, not an idiot.}

Micah's lips twitched as he bent once more to affix the disk to the back of the vest. "Sorry, dude. No offense intended."

The disk had been Will's idea. Hyer had helped him cobble the tech together from a commonly used nano package, and then tied it into Pascal's E-V wire.

Basic light-bending nano was common throughout the settled worlds. Corporations often used the tech to protect intellectual property from theft. It used refraction to bend incident light waves around an object. It could disguise a prototype, or mask a sensitive area like a testing bench, making it impossible to distinguish anything within its shroud.

This tech wasn't mobile, and it lacked the refinement of a drakeskin's stealth. It couldn't render a person invisible, yet Will and Hyer had found a way to adapt it for just such a purpose by tying into Pascal's E-V wire.

The big cat's comm implant was simple; it didn't thread throughout his body like the nanofloss filaments of a SmartCarbyne lattice, it was restricted to a few delicate fibers inserted into the cat's brain. It did allow the capture of neural data, though. That data could then be sent to the disk, which in turn controlled a swarm of light-bending nano.

As Pascal's neurons fired, sending messages to his limbs, the implant's feed allowed the device in Micah's hand to predict which way the big cat was going to move and where he would place his paws. It would then direct a magnetically controlled colloid cloud of light-bending chaff to cloak Pascal's movements.

It wasn't perfect. In strong light, a wave-like ripple outlined his form whenever he moved, giving away the cat's location. In the subtle lighting of a darkened ballroom, however, Pascal would blend into the shadows without issue.

{So I disappear like humans on mission?} the cat asked. *{Not very useful for hunting game. Prey uses scent more than eyesight.}*

His apparent disgust elicited a surprised laugh from Sasha.

"Cat's got a point. Too bad what you're hunting in there has no scent."

Micah shot her a wry smile as he grabbed his own vest and shrugged into it. "Yeah, but he knows the type of cylinder they'll most likely use to aerosolize it. That's better than nothing."

Since she hadn't been read into the chiral aspect of the mission, Micah couldn't tell her the real reason only he, Pascal, and Sneaky Pete would be allowed entrance to the venue.

Like Thad, he had his own worries about including the ferret in the mission, but Valenti had sided with Addy on that, overruling the Marine.

Micah's answer must have sufficed, for Sasha just shook her head and bent to rummage around in the weapons locker once more.

Micah looked up as a small holoscreen on the bulkhead beside the locker chimed an alert. The screen then projected the ship's external feed.

Micah could tell by looking that the hangar's ES field had dropped, and its atmosphere had been restored. Three people who had been awaiting their arrival were now on approach.

Sasha looked from the feed to Micah. "How many years ago was it that you and Zander worked together?" she asked with a head tilt to indicate the screen.

Micah glanced at the image of the tall, dark-haired man closing on *Scimitar*'s aft hatch. "Must have been about four, maybe five years, now, I think. Rafe captained this ship for a good ten years before Johnson took over. I was with him for seven."

Sasha grunted. "Kickass pilot," she remarked. "I remember when he left Shadow Recon. You folks lost a good man."

He nodded. "I'll bet the Nimitz CO was pretty pleased when he accepted the promotion to command the base's wing, though."

He looked away from the feed and down at the tac-vest and drakeskin suit he wore, mouth twisting into a wry smile. "I remember dropping your team to a few places, back when I was his copilot." He shook his head. "Never thought I'd be doing things from your end."

"About that," Sasha turned to face him. "I know I said it in the briefing, but I'll say it again. I get that you and the cat here are immune to whatever bioweapon the Akkadians have on them, but you're not immune to *this*." She patted the P-SCAR rifle that hung on a three-point sling around the neck of the specialist first-class who was standing beside her.

Sasha's eyes drilled into Micah. "No heroics. Identify the bioweapon, neutralize it, and then get the hell out of there and let us do the rest. Capiche?"

"Capiche, ma'am."

Sasha's stare edged into glare territory, and Micah wondered if he'd overstepped with that last bit. Before he could say anything, she turned back to the weapons locker, where she grabbed a flechette and a spare set of clips.

"I hear you qualified as Expert on the range," she said.

He nodded. "Yes, ma'am. Major Snell requires all Shadow Recon to requalify regularly."

"Good." She handed him the flechette and spare pair of clips.

He slid it into a holster that rested in the hollow of his lower back, just below the kidney.

Next, Sasha handed him a small, palm-sized backup CUSP and a spare battery. The CUSP, he tucked into an ankle holster. The battery went into one of the vest's pockets, alongside the clips.

A chittering noise broke the silence, and he saw Foxtrot's leader close her eyes as if in pain.

Opening them once again, she shot Gabe a displeased look. "I'm with Severance on this. Ferrets have no place on this mission."

Gabe merely nodded. "I understand your position. It was the colonel's call after...certain things were discussed."

{This chiral shit's getting harder to pass off,} Micah warned.

Gabe sent him a hooded glance. *{I know. Just do the best you can.}* He paused and scrubbed his chin with one hand. "I've had a talk with Sneaky Pete, impressing upon him the seriousness of this situation. He knows we expect him to be quiet, and he knows what he's looking for."

"Stars and flares, I hope so," she muttered, shaking her head and stalking back toward the cargo bay doors.

"Good thing we have one of these for him, too," Gabe said to

Micah, holding up a disk similar to the one Pascal now wore.

Micah shook his head. "Good thing Will added audio chaff to it. Something tells me he doesn't understand 'quiet'."

Gabe chuckled softly.

They both turned when they heard Sasha ask Johnson to lower *Scimitar*'s aft ramp.

"Ready for this?" Gabe asked.

Micah twitched his head in a response that could mean just about anything. He knew the other man wasn't referring to the mission. In about thirty seconds, he'd be coming face to face with someone who'd flown combat missions with him—with *Jonathan*—for seven years.

"You sure you'll be able to fool him?" Gabe persisted.

Micah shrugged uncomfortably and ran a hand through his hair. "The two most obvious differences between me and Jonathan are superficial things," he said with more confidence than he felt. "Okay, so our hair parts differently. I can explain that as a bad haircut. If he notices that I'm now right-handed, I'll tell him I've been practicing working with my non-dominant hand."

Gabe nodded, satisfied.

Micah wished he could settle his own doubts as easily.

We'll see how well I can sell it soon enough, he thought, following Gabe down the ramp.

Rafe reached out a hand as Micah approached. Micah slapped his into the other man's open palm, and Rafe pulled him close to thump him on the back.

Releasing him, he muttered, "Crazy-ass 'Head' Case, living up to your call sign, I see. What? You think you're a team guy now, or something?"

Micah rolled his eyes but ignored the jibe, turning instead to face the others as Rafe and Gabe shook hands.

Gabe turned to Sasha, motioning between Rafe, Micah, and Ell. "I guess most of you are already acquainted?"

Sasha nodded. "Our paths have crossed a few times, yes." She inclined her head toward the man who stood beside Ell. "Though this is a new face."

Gabe smiled and turned toward Ell. "Want to introduce us to your bloodhound?"

The compact woman shot Gabe a quelling look that stopped just shy of an eyeroll. "I'm sure he appreciates the comparison, too," she said in a dry tone. "Charles, meet the guy who recruited me to criminal investigation, Gabriel Alvarez."

Gabe smiled. "Couldn't let the opportunity pass. The Unit's loss was our gain."

Charles murmured his agreement as he shook the agent's proffered hand.

Next, Ell turned to Sasha and gave her a brisk, no-nonsense nod. "Captain, good to see you again. Meet Charles Quinn." She turned to Quinn as the man reached to shake Sasha's hand. "I'd tell you her last name if I could pronounce the damn thing."

The leader of Foxtrot barked a laugh and let out a spurt of Russian. Ell responded in kind.

Micah looked over at Gabe and Rafe, and the three exchanged knowing smiles.

"I forgot Ell's dry sense of humor," Micah said.

Rafe laughed. "And the fact that she speaks Russian—along with about three other languages." He shook his head.

They were interrupted by Ell, who turned and poked Micah in the shoulder.

"Zander tells me you were the one who helped seal that magnetosphere breach we had here a few years back."

Rafe slid an amused glance Micah's way. "No, Ell, I told you he blew plasma out his ass to seal the breach. Get your story right."

*Yeah, but it wasn't **me** who flew it. I didn't even exist at the time.* The bleak thought flitted through Micah's mind as Ell and Rafe continued to discuss an event that occurred prior to Micah's creation in Luyten's Star.

Ell shot Rafe a longsuffering look. "Facts, Zander. I deal in facts, not wise-ass pilot speak." She turned back to Micah. "At any rate, thanks for plugging that hole while I was chasing down the Akkadian assassin who caused it."

Micah blinked. "Wait. What? That whole thing was Akkadia's fault too?"

Ell's gaze turned quizzical and something approaching humor flared in her eyes as she exchanged a look with Rafe. "You could say that. Or you could just say it was the result of a bad paint job," she added.

Quinn choked, and Micah realized some sort of inside joke had just passed between their three hosts. Before anyone could ask about it further, Ell held up a hand.

"If you happen to run into Thad when you get back, ask him to tell you the story. I'm sure you can loosen him up over a few beers." Her comment had a ring of finality to it that seemed to draw the social exchange to a close.

Rafe motioned for the group to follow him, and Micah fell into step beside him, Sasha on his other side. The two four-person teams that made up Delta and Foxtrot trailed along behind, while Gabe walked with Ell and Quinn.

The major waved them over to a table that had been set up just inside the doors that led from the hangar into Nimitz Base. He gestured around them.

"We put you in our secured hangar, across the base from the rest of the wing," Rafe told them. "We were also told this op's top clearance only, so we have countersurveillance and jamming apps running."

Ell looked at Sasha as she took a seat. "This is going down at the Merki Institute?"

When Sasha nodded, Ell pulled out a portable holoprojector. "I've been in that building a few times. I'll walk you through the setup, and then we can hop a flight to the Belly Band for an initial recon."

Quinn caught the confused look that crossed the face of one of Sasha's team members. "Belly Band's the nickname locals gave the ring that circles the middle of Hawking's McKendree cylinder," the man explained. "It's a quick twenty-minute flight from here, and then we ride the elevator down to Midland."

"And that's where this Merki Institute's located? In Midland?" Sasha queried.

Rafe nodded. "Second largest city in the habitat. Set up right against Olympic Lake and a nice stretch of forest land, about fifteen thousand hectares' worth."

The team leader nodded, expression thoughtful.

Clapping his hands together, Gabe's gaze swept the group. "Okay, then. Let's get this briefing started."

LIVE FIRE

Akkadian Base
An-Yang Dust Belt
Proxima Centauri

WITH MARCEAU HOLDING both Linnet's life and those of the other Alliance scientists in his hands, Sam felt she had no choice but to go through the motions of cooperating with Bijin.

The medical scientist had samples of both the chiral and non-chiral versions of the hantavirus projected onto a holo above the glove boxes. He used a nanoprobe to pierce the protein envelope that enclosed the chiral virus. As he did, the view jumped to show the RNA material inside.

Bijin manipulated the probe, pushing through the material until he came to the Khufuvirus, floating among the protein strands.

"Ahhhh," the man breathed in apparent satisfaction. "Now this, I can work with." He glanced sharply at Sam, and then over to Marceau. "I need assurances."

Marceau stirred. "What kind, doctor?"

"I need to know that no anti-tamper sequence has been introduced into the strand that will cause it to terminate if manipulated in the wrong way."

Marceau looked toward the airlock, and Sam saw one of the soldiers stationed outside straighten when the colonel caught his eye. He went over to the cell that held Linnet, and placed his palm beside the controls for the ES field. His other hand rested on his weapon.

Marceau turned. "You think the Alliance may have failsafed the virus?"

At Bijin's nod, Marceau glanced over at the cell where Linnet was being held. His next words were directed at Sam. "If it disintegrates when Doctor Bijin touches it, so will Doctor Thompson. Are we clear?"

She swallowed. "Yes."

Marceau inclined his head toward Bijin. "Tell the doctor what he needs to know."

Sam sucked in a lungful of air. "Begin at the juncture between the third and fourth segment in the strand."

The doctor didn't acknowledge her; he merely turned and bent over the glove box once more. He slid a sidelong glance her way, and the crafty look in his eyes made her want to throw up.

Sam knew all too well how easily this virus could be reassorted into a devastatingly efficient killer. A killer like Marburg. Ebola. Lloviu. Sargon. She had been holding out a fleeting hope that Bijin might be more of a generalist than either a virologist or a biochemist.

However, the way he transferred the viral material out of the vial and into an RNA manipulation unit and began working it put paid to that possibility.

She bit her lip as she watched Bijin bring up a different image on the screen, a modified Sargon virus he'd clearly been working on. Her hands clenched in impotent rage when she spotted the extra gene-modified variant he'd added—the viral equivalent of pouring accelerant onto flames.

"Now this...." Bijin's voice was low but filled with a

satisfaction that bordered on glee. "This will work very nicely, indeed."

Monsters.

Sam's brows drew down in puzzlement when the man went against her expectations and added a sequence that rendered the entire thing inactive. When she saw him bring up another screen that showed an enzyme she knew would cleave the sequence back into action, she understood.

This was his trigger mechanism.

She followed his movements as he brought up the other vial on his scope. She knew he was checking to see if the material was indeed entangled at a quantum level.

Sam silently castigated herself once again for letting that critical bit of intel slip. It didn't matter that she'd believed this was an Alliance research facility at the time; she should have known better than to mention it.

She looked on as Bijin inserted a probe into the non-chiral sample, deftly maneuvering past the outer envelope and through the RNA material until he came upon the mirror Khufuvirus.

Sam's heart sank, and Bijin chortled with satisfaction at what the holo showed.

The mirror virus had indeed been transformed to match its entangled twin.

Bijin wasted no time transferring the newly reassorted virus into a culture bath. Once completed, he sent it over to an RNA replicon machine.

The man turned, satisfaction written on his face. "It is done," he told Marceau.

The colonel looked shocked. "That quickly?" He looked from Bijin to Sam and then back. "If altering a virus is so easy, then why did we go to all this trouble to obtain it? Why not simply do the same thing from within your lab on Eridu?"

Bijin dismissed the question with a scoffing sound. "You do not understand, Citizen Colonel. It is not the manipulation of the virus that is so difficult. It is the entanglement of the particle itself that is the masterpiece here." He cocked his head, a grudging admiration showing in his eyes as he looked over at Sam.

He hummed, rocking back on his heels as he sought to explain it in words the colonel might understand. "It is like shooting a firearm. All you do is pull the trigger and the weapon fires. Simple, yes? So why the need for soldiers, or sharpshooters? Just have an SI do it."

Marceau scowled. "It takes extensive training to properly handle and discharge a firearm. If the target is moving, it takes exceptional hand-to-eye coordination. An experienced, battle-tested soldier develops an instinct for it that no SI can master."

Bijin nodded sagely, crossing his arms over his chest as if Marceau had just made is point for him.

Sam realized that he had.

Marceau didn't connect the dots, however. "Doctor. Elaborate."

Sam would have laughed at the colonel's annoyed growl had the situation been any less dire. Instead, she willed them to ignore her and keep talking. The longer they talked, the greater her chances that help would arrive before something deadly was unleashed out into the cosmos.

Bijin sighed long and loud. "Fine. It is like this. What I just did? Reassorting a virus? That is something a student learns how to do in school. Equivalent to a novice soldier's first week at a shooting range."

He turned back to the holo and pointed to the image of the chiral supraparticle. "Knowing that a certain type of material can be inserted inside another without it being rejected as a foreign body, having the vision to build it into a supraparticle shell, using that shell to safely hide a material that most certainly would be rejected by its host, and then doing so successfully?"

Bijin bowed to Sam, the lowest bow she had seen from any of the Akkadians thus far.

"That, Citizen Colonel, is the work of a virtuoso."

Sam felt the eyes of both men as they turned to regard her. Bijin's were admiring, almost envious. Marceau's were thoughtful. She hated them both.

When the replicon beeped, signaling the sample was ready for use, her gut twisted. She took an involuntary step toward the unit, but checked her motion when Marceau lifted a brow in silent challenge.

Bijin hummed to himself as he bustled around the lab, filling a canister full of aerosolized colloid nano with the viral agent. That task complete, he turned and presented the canister to Marceau with a much smaller bow.

"Citizen Colonel, I believe we are ready for our first test."

Marceau waved Bijin forward, and the doctor went over to a bank of panels Sam hadn't noticed before. As they lit up, she could see one of the consoles was connected to the isolation rooms' environmental systems.

He pulled one of the rooms up on the holo as he inserted the cylinder into the console. With a glance back at the colonel, Bijin said, "Initiating test now."

* * *

The Akkadian operatives who accompanied Bijin to his laboratory didn't follow him inside. Instead, they took up stations on either side of the airlock. That gave them an excellent view of the experiment about to take place.

The citizen doctor had ordered the prisoners separated into two groups; he'd told the soldiers that one would be the control, the other the first experimental wave.

Neither man knew what the doctor was talking about, but that was nothing unusual. Ever since they'd arrived and been assigned to his support staff, they'd been subjected to a running commentary that meant less than nothing to them.

At first, this had seemed to annoy Bijin, but then the citizen doctor had muttered something about being able to increase the sample size if they didn't work out. That seemed to have restored the man's good humor somewhat, and this relieved both of the soldiers.

Being assigned to escort a medical scientist might seem to be menial work, something their counterparts back home would scoff at, but their participation in this pivotal event would go in their records, and after Asher Dent was defeated, their careers would be assured.

The first soldier stared across the hallway at the prisoners behind the ES field. Too cowed and beaten to be a threat, they moved with a numb lethargy, hopelessness etched into their faces.

"How does one disperse a bioweapon like this without being killed along with the intended victims?" one asked the other softly, his voice barely above a whisper.

The other looked oddly at him. "You sound as if you aren't willing to make the ultimate sacrifice for the cause."

"It's not that," the first hastened to assure him. "It's just... surely they must have a way to keep this weapon from turning on its wielders, yes?"

A haughty expression crept over the other's face as he recalled what he had overheard Bijin tell Citizen Colonel Marceau earlier that day. Nodding toward the cells, he said, "The mixture is oxyphobic."

"Oxy— What? It is afraid of air?"

His perplexed tone had the other soldier puffing his chest out in self-importance. "No, oxyphobic means it reacts in the presence of oxygen."

The first soldier leveled an accusing look at his companion. "You have no idea what you are saying. You're just parroting what you overheard."

The other shrugged. "I heard enough to know that the virus is inert until it is aerosolized." He nodded at the ventilation system in the sealed rooms. "Once it is introduced into the air ducts, then we will see who knows what he is talking about."

They watched as Bijin approached the clearsteel wall from within the lab. A portable device sheathed his hand and forearm, while his other hand was buried in the holo projected just above it as he input a string of commands. He looked up at the men in the first cell one last time, nodded in satisfaction, and then triggered the sequence.

The soldiers turned back to the cells to watch.

At first, nothing seemed to happen. After several minutes had passed, the four subjects huddled together began to cough. One by one, they collapsed onto the floor as their bodies began to succumb to the viral agent.

The control group looked on in horror as the clearsteel sheeting separating the two rooms gave them an intimate view of the gruesome results of an airborne version of a hemorrhagic virus.

Sobs erupted from the woman as one man turned to the side, dry heaving in reaction to the sight. Another pounded furiously on the clearsteel wall separating them from the soldiers standing guard.

"Murderers! Bloody fecking murderers!"

PANDEMIC

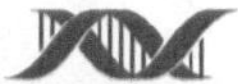

Royal Ceriba Yacht *Atliekan Queen*
Atliekas Nebula Park

THE FIRST INDICATION the captain had that things had turned south was when Josh pinged her to report they had their first casualties since their 'patient zero' had expired.

*{We need to get back to port **now**,}* he said, and she could hear he was approaching full-blown panic.

"Just calm down, Josh, and tell me exactly what's going on."

She knew she didn't need to speak the words to be heard, but she found that in situations like this, she thought with greater clarity if she repeated aloud the conversation that was going on in her head.

"You're saying that you've given them the antigen that the Navy captain sent us from the CID, but it's not working?"

{That's exactly what I'm saying. But it's not just that.} Josh's words were clipped as he rushed them out as quickly as he could think them. *{It's altered. I just took a sample from one of the deceased—stars know there is plenty of material to work with.}*

That last was said with an odd timbre, and the captain was suddenly glad Josh had opted not to use the holo.

"Okay, then. Which destination did the CID say we needed to head for?"

There was a pause on the other end.

{They didn't.}

"What do you mean?"

{Look, Captain. All I'm saying is that if we don't get these people more qualified help very soon—and I mean **immediately**—*there's going to be no one left alive to bring this ship into port. Any port, anywhere.}*

"Stars, Josh, you're laying the drama on a bit thick, aren't you?"

{No, Captain. I'm really not.}

* * *

A comm came in from the Novastrike squadron shadowing the *Atliekan Queen*. The NSA analyst monitoring the feed stepped into the situation room where Cutter, Addy, Toland, and Valenti sat.

"We have a problem, sir, ma'ams," the analyst said. He gestured to a nearby holo, and the feed he'd just intercepted came online. "It's the *Atliekan Queen*. Captain on that ship has turned for the nearest port and is pinging the CID with an urgent request for medical assistance. Says they're experiencing heavy casualties."

Addy exchanged a swift glance with Toland before she returned her attention to the holo.

"Play it," Cutter ordered, and the analyst turned back to the screen.

"This is Captain Nolotov of the Atliekan Queen, *requesting a redirect to the nearest port with advanced medical facilities, and a liaison with someone in the CID,"* they heard a woman's voice say. *"Repeat. This is Captain Zoya Nolotov..."*

"Nolotov is former Navy, sir," the analyst spoke quietly over the feed as the ship's captain restated her initial transmission. "Captained the destroyer *Audacious* out of Puller-Moore in Sirius. Twenty years served, excellent record." He pulled up Nolotov's Navy record on an adjacent screen.

Addy had been stationed on Puller-Moore for one tour. The Naval base was attached to Heliodore, the McKendree cylinder that orbited the dog star.

Cutter nodded to the analyst. "Thanks, Mack. Now I need your opinion. Can we speak candidly with Nolotov?"

Mack's gaze swerved to the holo. He stared consideringly at the woman pictured there for a few beats before he nodded. "Yessir, I believe we can."

Cutter blew out a breath. "Good." His gaze cut to Toland and then Valenti before ordering, "Keep this feed scrambled. As of right now, it's need-to-know. I may need those Novastrike pilots to relay some hard messages going forward. Do you understand what I'm saying?"

Mack's face may have paled slightly, Addy couldn't be sure. But the man's mouth firmed, and he nodded.

"Perfectly, sir. Here are the tokens for the feed. I'll leave them with you."

Cutter sat back as the analyst exited the situation room. The feed paused, and the director looked first at Toland and then at Addy.

"Am I ready to hear this?" he asked them.

Toland shook her head. "I suspect none of us are, sir."

Cutter stared back unblinkingly, and then turned to face the holo.

As Nolotov's message began to play, Addy felt sick. She didn't need the appended files from the ship's doctor to tell her what this was. The images of the dead and dying told her in clear, certain terms. Still, she took her time studying the viral samples the doctor had obtained for them.

Her jaw worked as she saw what the virus had been reassorted into.

"Sargon Virus," she said quietly.

Cutter turned his head, brow lifted in silent question.

"A particularly virulent form of Sargon," Toland qualified.

Addy pointed. "And they added an accelerant."

Cutter looked at them both. "What does that mean?"

"It's a gene-modified variant that causes the infection to spread more rapidly." Toland's voice was curt. "It's essentially digesting its victims from the inside out. When it's done, it seeks another host for it to replicate."

Cutter blanched at Toland's raw words. He dropped his head for a moment, absorbing what she'd just told him.

"Bottom line?" he asked, his eyes meeting theirs once more.

Addy commanded her wire to run a few simulations on her overlay, altering the parameters in various ways, hoping against all hope that she could find a way to save at least some of the people on that yacht. Each model continued to show an aggressively exponential spread that gave her the same outcome every time.

That ship was quite literally a floating death trap.

Toland's low curse told Addy she'd come to the same conclusion.

"I...." Addy's voice broke. She cleared her throat and tried again. "We can get the CID's mainframe to run the models again. We can't just doom almost fourteen thousand people to their deaths without double-checking these models." She turned her head, seeking to deny what the simulations told her.

"Doctor?" Cutter's voice was uncharacteristically gentle. "Addy, look at me."

You're a Captain in the Geminate Navy, she told herself fiercely. *For stars' sake, grow a frickin' spine, Moran!*

Her mental pep talk didn't alleviate the churning in her gut, but it did allow her to turn and look him in the eyes.

"Addy, *we* aren't dooming anyone to their deaths," he said. "Don't lose sight of who has done this to them. Akkadia just declared war, and these people...."

He faced the holo once more, the grim cast of his features evident even in profile. "These people may be our first KIA."

KIA. Killed in Action.

Addy shuddered but did not disagree.

"I'll need you to be absolutely sure." Cutter directed his words to both Addy and the admiral, his tone quiet but resolute. "But once you are, you need to let me know. Let me be clear, that is an *order*."

It was the admiral's turn to stare at the holo, expression fierce. She nodded. "We will not allow them to suffer."

DEADLY SHIPMENT

Akkadian Base
An-Yang Dust Belt
Proxima Centauri

Che watched Bijin's test from his office, Dacina at his side. His eyes were glued to the holo with morbid fascination. One thing was clear: the deaths on Hawking would be dramatic and not easily forgotten.

Rin Zhou would be most pleased.

Shortly after the experiment's successful conclusion, his wire pinged.

{The doctor has successfully concluded his field tests,} Colonel Marceau told him. *{He has officially signed off on the bioweapon being ready for real-world use.}*

{Excellent. Please extend my congratulations to the citizen doctor,} Che responded.

Marceau sent him a nod. *{He is packaging the weapon into smaller payloads at the moment. Once that is completed, we will bring you the trigger, and then I will personally supervise the* *weapon's transfer to the shuttle. It should be ready to depart within a few hours.}*

The connection dissolved, and Che turned to his Dagger. "And what do you think of the weapon?"

Dacina's face was blank as she stared at the feed from the isolation room. "It is... difficult... to see the honor in such a kill," she said finally.

Her words startled Che.

"Do you know," he said slowly, "this is the first time I have ever heard you voice a criticism of a tactic of mine?"

Dacina's dark eyes met his steadily. "But there you are wrong, my general. This," she indicated the holo feed, "is not your tactic, but the minister's."

Che's attention sharpened. Had there been a thread of disdain in Dacina's voice?

Her expression remained as impassive as ever, and she offered nothing more on the subject.

He dismissed her odd behavior, turning instead for his office door. As it opened, he saw Li snap to attention, and realized that news of the test had probably spread throughout the base like wildfire.

With great ceremony, he bowed to Li. The citizen commander returned it.

"Prepare the message," Che instructed quietly, and Li nodded.

In order to provide Rin Zhou with complete deniability, it had been decided that a single encrypted burst would be sent, informing her they had completed their first task and a viable bioweapon was now in their hands. As previously agreed, a second message would not be forthcoming.

The events would unfold on Hawking in a very public way, the news nets flashing the attack across the settled worlds within minutes of it happening. Rin Zhou would learn of it at the same time the rest of Akkadia did—and it would provide her with an extra measure of deniability.

Che waited while Li relayed the instruction to the comm

officer, and he felt the electric thrill that ran through the room at the citizen commander's words.

With great ceremony, Che turned to face those within the CIC. "The weapon has been tested. Our mission here is a success."

Cheers went up through the room, and Che allowed it to continue for a beat before bringing the command center team back in line.

"Our work is not yet complete," he warned them. "Only diligence can prevent success from slipping past on the edge of a breath."

Those assembled bowed their heads and then turned back to their workstations, the ancient Akkadian proverb weighing heavily on their shoulders.

The process of replicating enough viral material to fill the cylinders that would become weapons took another few hours. Finally, Marceau signaled when the task was complete, and Che exited the CIC to see the shuttle off.

Marceau and Li were standing by the ES field, observing final flight preparations, when he and Dacina arrived in the hangar bay. Through the ES field, Che could see the pair of Hydra Mark IV fighters that would accompany the shuttle. When he dropped a pin on his overlay to query each ship, a readiness report showed their pilots already on board.

He came to a stop beside Marceau, and the man straightened into parade rest.

"Well done, Citizen Colonel," Che said.

The man dipped his head as he accepted the praise, and then handed him a portable clearsteel container. Inside, Che could see a small canister.

"What's this?"

"Your trigger," Marceau told him. "It holds the mirror version of the bioweapon."

Instinct had Che thrusting it away from his body.

The other man shook his head. "That is entirely safe. Bijin explained—and Travis confirmed—that it is impossible for this to infect a human."

"Then how do I arm the weapon?"

Marceau's lips pulled back in a feral grin. "Oh, the weapon is already armed. To pull the trigger, all you need to do is twist the lid until it clicks."

Li looked on. "Impressive," he murmured. "I suppose now, as they say, it's all over but the shouting."

Che grunted, not entirely sure where Li's words came from, but getting the general gist of their meaning. "There is always work to be done in the shadow of success," he agreed.

"You will find none of the men slacking, I assure you, Citizen General. We will wrap the operation, and those who come after will never know we were here."

Che nodded as the hangar's warning klaxons sounded and the great bay doors began to slide open. "Very good, very good," he said absently, his attention on the three ships that had begun to maneuver on thrusters toward the black.

"How would you like to dispose of the Alliance scientists?" Marceau asked, drawing Che's attention once more.

The general pursed his lips, thinking. "Cutter's niece will return to Eridu with us. I've been assured the memory of her time here can be wiped. We will use her as a bargaining chip to obtain concessions from Cutter. As for the rest?" He shot Marceau a hard look. "We leave no witnesses. You know this."

"Indeed. It will be as you say." Marceau bowed once more and then paused, his eyes on the departing ships as the bay doors sealed once more. "*Bad ba shoma ba shed*," he said, rendering the traditional farewell-into-battle. "May the winds be with them."

STRIKE FORCE

Calabi-Yau Gate
An-Yang Heliopause

THE PROXIMA CENTAURI gate flashed with brilliant color as it disgorged a small Alliance diplomatic ship the NSA had ordered to visit the Geminate embassy on Shang that day.

They'd also arranged to have the gate's operations room locked down so that only those with the highest clearance would be present for the ship's transit.

Jonathan knew that those who programmed the gate had to be aware that the small vessel had invisible tagalongs. Each gate passage was carefully calibrated based on the transiting vessel's tonnage. The information was used to calculate the amount of energy needed to keep the gates' apertures open on either end.

Ships either submitted to a gate's weight-and-balance check prior to entry into the lanes—or risked not making it to the other side in one piece. The fact their transit passed without incident was telling.

Then there was the courier's captain. She hadn't said a word about the three stealthed vessels that were tucked uncomfortably close to her ship's outer skin, yet Jonathan knew the courier's proximity alarms must have been going nuts. The woman had to have muted her ship's SI, or she would have surely been deafened by its warning klaxons.

By previous agreement, the ships sheared away from the courier the moment they cleared the gate, thrusters pushing them well clear of the smaller vessel before it exited the no-wake zone and lit up its fusion drive.

As the two Novastrikes formed up alongside *Wraith*, Yuki flushed a constellation of small, equally stealthed drones from various ports along the ship's length. They encompassed the formation in a sensor shell she controlled. The perimeter they formed would augment *Wraith*'s own impressive sensor suite and that of her fighter escort.

All three ships turned toward the rich buildup of hydrogen that had accrued along Proxima's heliopause. They had a bit of time to kill, and the dense wall of gas would allow the Navy vessels to top off their fuel reserves before the upcoming engagement.

As the ships plowed through the hydrogen cloud, their MXene coatings worked as sieves, funneling the gas into each vessel's respective storage tanks.

Jonathan watched the Helios's gauges and waited patiently while Will pulled up the activity of the red dwarf at Proxima's core. They'd timed the jump to coincide with a medium-sized CME that would be accompanied by an X-thirty-five solar flare event. The emission would easily obscure the flares brought on by three Casimir bubbles dissipating fifty kilometers from the asteroid that was their destination.

{*Thar she blows,*} the flight engineer sent. {*It'll reach here in four hours, seventeen minutes, mark.*}

{*Blackbird One copies,*} the Novastrike on Jonathan's left wing sent.

{*Blackbird Two copies,*} came the echo from the Novastrike on his other side.

{Scharnhorst flight time to destination,} Will's voice pierced the ship's net once more, *{is three hours, ten minutes, mark.}*

Jonathan switched over to *Wraith*'s ship-wide combat net, relaying to Thad and the teams what Will had just calculated. *{Seven-seven minutes to translation, folks,}* he informed the men and women seated in the Helios's cabin.

Thad grunted. *{Heads-up,* amis. *Gear check at thirty minutes from the pocket. Set your chronos.}*

A flurry of double-clicks hit the combat net, and then the channel went silent, the warriors doing whatever it was they did prior to an op.

Jonathan had seen over the years how varied that could be. Some grabbed additional shuteye, others played poker. Still others meditated, read a book, or watched an entertainment vid. He glanced over at Yuki, whose hands were buried in the cockpit's holo but whose eyes were closed in an almost zen-like state as she directed the drones that surrounded the ships.

He knew without looking that Nina would have a light mental touch on ship's weapons, ready to go live at a moment's notice— at least until they entered Scharnhorst space. With nothing able to penetrate a Casimir bubble, she would be able to stand down during the more than three-hour transit.

The time passed without incident, and all three ships jumped from realspace into their respective bubbles as the chronos zeroed out.

Travel through Scharnhorst space was an exercise in isolation. Nothing could get to them, and they couldn't interact with anything outside the bubble. The mechanics of the transit were best left to the ship's SI, so Jonathan unwebbed and stretched.

"Coffee?" he asked Yuki as she yawned.

"Don't mind if I do," she said, reaching for her own webbing.

As they left the cockpit and entered the crowded cabin space, Jonathan's eyes met Thad's, and he quirked a questioning brow at the Marine. He made a drinking motion with his hand, and Thad's chin lifted in a silent yes as he rose to follow.

"Geminate Navy at its finest, hoss," Thad's voice rumbled from behind him as they stepped into the galley.

Yuki snickered quietly at the comment, and Jonathan grinned. "Yeah, man. Hurry up and wait."

The time seemed to crawl, but finally, they reached the thirty minute mark. The flight crew returned to their stations as the unit operators moved back toward the ship's weapons cache.

Jonathan could hear the rumble of Thad's deep voice, delivering orders while each soldier checked their loadout. Flipping *Wraith*'s internal feed up onto one of the cockpit's smaller holoscreens, the flight crew watched as the four SRU teams geared up.

Spare batteries and extra magazines were stuffed into pockets. Flash-bangs, frags, and sticky grenades were tucked into tac-vests alongside carbyne-jacketed rappelling lines with nano-coated grappling hooks. Cylinders with LockPik and Crowbar hacks went in alongside the larger Bravo Charlie breaching canisters.

{That's quite the arsenal.} Will's thought floated to him on their isolated cockpit channel.

Nina grunted her agreement. *{And may they rain down a helluva lot of whoop-ass onto those Akkadian bastards for what they're trying to do to us.}*

{Amen, sister,} Yuki murmured.

There was one addition each team carried with them: a compact L4 glove box, rated for the containment of a Level Four pathogen.

Jonathan's brain shied away from the thought of carrying a contagion that toxic back home with them, but he knew the alternative was far worse. He was also well aware of the portable decontamination unit sealed to *Wraith*'s aft cargo hatch.

His mind returned to his duties as the chrono marched down to zero. The teams had formed into clusters by insertion group, and the first one stood ready to deploy, beside the ship's portside hatch.

{Lock and web. Entering realspace... now,} Jonathan called out, and he felt *Wraith* shudder slightly as the Helios shed its Casimir bubble.

Blackbirds One and Two appeared on his overlay, the Novastrikes peeling off to hold station on either side of the asteroid while Jonathan moved the Helios toward the first vent identified by Daz the day before.

He sank deeper into the merge, his eyesight now one with the ship's SyntheticVision system. The asteroid grew slowly before him, *Wraith*'s predictive systems highlighting the indentation that hid the first vent, its opening little more than a slit tucked deep within the shadows. He used thrusters to feather *Wraith* to a stop a scant meter away from the indentation.

{We're a go for insertion,} he told Thad.

TF Blue's leader sent him a two-click. Shortly after, a notification flashed on his overlay, telling him the Marine had cycled open the hatch.

Jonathan split his view so that he could see the harnessed figure of a drakeskin-clad soldier being spooled carefully out, a Bravo Charlie held in one hand.

Jonathan flipped over to the isolated channel the team was using in time to hear a woman's voice say, *{Ten centimeters... five... and hold.}*

There was a beat of silence, and then, *{Bravo Charlie active. I'm dropping into the vent. Feed coming at you in five.}*

The feed from the Unit soldier's optics showed a long, narrow shaft with handholds welded to one side. The woman descended more than a dozen meters before the vent stopped abruptly at a hatch.

The soldier's arm came into the feed, another BC in her hand. Jonathan saw the moment the breaching canister's light flashed green, indicating it was safe to enter.

{We are green. Repeat, condition green,} the advance scout called out.

Instantly, three more bodies passed through *Wraith*'s hatch and into the shaft. Jonathan watched the telltales flash from red to green, indicating *Wraith*'s hatch had been sealed, but waited for visual confirmation before moving.

{Hatch is sealed,} Will reported, and on the heels of his words came Thad's *{Go! Go! Go!}*

Jonathan nosed *Wraith* up, sending her gliding silently across the surface of the asteroid to the next insertion point.

The drill was repeated three more times before Jonathan brought the ship to a stop at their final location: the asteroid base's massive docking bay doors.

{See you on the flipside, ami,*}* Thad called out as he, Boone, and Asha dropped from the ship's hatch.

{Good hunting,} Jonathan replied, but the Marine had already cut the connection.

* * *

Bijin's testing of the viral weapon had been halted at Marceau's order—not out of compassion, but expediency, Sam was sure. It was more important for the doctor to fill the requisite number of canisters with the bioweapon than it was to confirm the test was repeatable.

Thank God for small mercies.

That left her alone in the lab with only the watchful eye of a pair of guards to keep her company for the remainder of the day.

She'd been hesitant to test her boundaries at first. As time went on, she'd screwed up enough courage to try to approach the equipment. The soldier nearest her had raised his pistol, barking out the order that she step away. She'd done so, hands raised.

Then she'd moved restlessly about the perimeter of the room, seeking anything she could use as a weapon, eyes probing the area for weaknesses. She found none.

Eventually, Marceau returned. She wondered if she imagined the banked triumph in his eyes, but refused to engage him in conversation beyond a demand that she be able to join Linnet and the other two scientists.

Marceau ignored her, hustling her through the lab's airlock and back to the quarters she'd been assigned. She immediately tried to access the room's door, and found exactly what she'd expected: it was locked.

The night passed and the next morning came without anyone coming to her door. Sam tried the base's network only to find she'd been completely cut off. She wondered fleetingly if they'd just abandon her here, now that they'd extracted the information they needed.

Fear of being left to freeze or to run out of air rose in her mind. She pushed it aside, willing herself to find a way out.

She walked through the room—her prison—once more, seeking weaknesses that she could use to her advantage. She discovered a small DBC unit that had been tossed carelessly into one corner of the room's single utilitarian desk. The unit functioned, however it had only one brick of formation material attached to it.

She had the unit handshake with her wire, and then began probing at it, seeking a backdoor she could exploit. She knew if she could hack her way in and get it to accept alternative forms of matter as formation material, she might be able to print herself a weapon.

It was a long shot. Both the reprogramming and the actual creation of the weapon would be a slow process—if it was even feasible. Any number of things could go wrong, not the least of which that she could get caught at any point along the way.

She had nothing better to do, however, so she settled back onto the bed, resigned to long hours of tedious work.

That came to an abrupt halt when she heard alarms sound in the distance.

Her head snapped up just as the overhead lights began to strobe in a universal warning that something was amiss. She smiled in grim satisfaction.

Help had arrived.

PITCHED BATTLE

WRAITH REMAINED ON station, hovering mere meters above the access point where Thad, Boone, and Asha had inserted into the base. Yuki had a sphere of sensors working the section of nearspace surrounding this side of the asteroid, and Jonathan had both of the Novastrikes' sensors up on secondary screens.

So far, it seemed their arrival had gone unnoticed, just as planned. Everyone knew that wouldn't hold for long.

Nina had her weapons trained in two directions, both at the asteroid and outward, prepared to engage any aggressors who might suddenly appear. Will had both hands sunk into his console, his face a mask of concentration. His fingers swept through the holo before him, an intricate weave of gestures and jabs, pushes and grabs as he sought something Jonathan couldn't see.

He grunted, the sound breaking the silence that had

descended upon *Wraith*'s cockpit since the teams had deployed.

{Talk to me, Specialist.} Jonathan sent the words softly, not wanting to jar the man from his absorption.

Will's head jerked up anyway. He blinked rapidly, his eyes refocusing on his surroundings. And then he grinned.

{I'm in,} he announced.

* * *

The vent Thad had chosen for an entry point sat two meters above a catwalk that ran the full length of the bay. Even better, it was tucked into an unused corner of the hangar; the entire area was cast in deep shadow.

The three infiltrators slid from the vent, landing on the mesh walkway with quiet thumps masked by colloid audio chaff. Thad motioned for Boone to cover them.

{You're up, cher,*}* he told Asha.

The medic knelt and extracted a carbyne-jacketed rope. After a quick look around, she nodded to an area up ahead where a support beam would hide them from the Akkadians they could see milling about on the far side.

After attaching the rope to the catwalk's steel frame, Asha clipped a set of handholds to it and fast-roped down. Thad waited for her to position herself where she could provide covering fire before he followed her to the bay floor.

{Your turn, ami,*}* he called up to Boone.

The sniper rose, closing the distance on silent feet. He slung his rifle over his shoulder and reached for the rope. Thirty seconds later, he was down.

With a sharp tug and a mental command, the carbyne rope released, falling into Boone's waiting hands. He coiled it as he crossed over to where Thad and Asha crouched, and then handed it to the medic, who tucked it away.

{Okay, exactly as we rehearsed,} Thad told them. *{Boone, you're scout. I'll bring up the rear. If you see anything—}*

He was cut off by an incoming message, a brief, encrypted

burst from *Wraith*. He knew those onboard wouldn't break op silence without good reason.

{Go,} he barked.

An icon appeared.

{Will managed to hack into their systems.} Jonathan's voice sounded inside his head. *{Want us to contact the other teams?}*

{Negative. I'll do it from this end. Tell Will I owe him a beer,} Thad replied as a connection request appeared on his drakeskin's combat HUD.

He toggled it, and information came flooding in, along with secured visual feeds. Will had tagged the vials' location; he'd also found where Sam was being held, as well as the three Alliance scientists.

Thad's mouth thinned into a hard line as he saw the notation that they'd been marked for elimination.

He passed the information along to Boone and Asha, and then reached out to the leaders of teams One through Four. He added two quick instructions to the comm burst.

{Team Three, the L4 lab's in your sector. Team Four, rendezvous with Three. There are two vials inside, and six prisoners to extract.}

The brief EM signal could pinpoint their locations for the enemy, he knew, but the tactical information provided by Will's hack into the base was worth the risk.

Four sets of two-clicks confirmed receipt of his transmission, then Thad went dark once more, his only link now the low-powered one that he, Boone, and Asha shared.

{Sam's nearby,} he sent, highlighting the room two levels up where she was being held. *{Let's go spring the doc and do a bit of vermin extermination along the way, what do ya say?}*

{Oo-rah,} Asha said, her tone sounding much more bloodthirsty than usual.

* * *

Jonathan sat back with a satisfied smile. *{Good work,}* he told

Will. *{That ought to cut their time inside significantly.}*

Will shrugged off the compliment, but his face held a slight smile as he returned his attention to his console.

Jonathan felt a mental tap, and widened the pathway he and his chiral twin shared.

Now a good time? Micah asked.

Sure. The teams just infiltrated. You know how it is, he told his doppelganger with a mental smile. *We're just the taxi service, hanging out, waiting for them to return.*

There was a pause. *Any news yet?*

Jonathan could sense the concern in the other man's words.

Yeah, Will hacked into the base and located Sam. The team's on their way to spring her now.

The relief that came across their connection was palpable, but then turned to quick annoyance. *And you didn't think to lead with that?*

Well, I—

Jonathan stopped as a sharp exclamation from Yuki brought his eyes rocketing to his readouts.

Gotta go, he shot the words toward his other self.

He barely noticed Micah's mental retreat as *Wraith's* proximity alarms began going off.

He plunged back into his merge with the ship, his awareness of the cockpit melting away as the blackness of space enveloped him once again. His overlay began to populate with information as Yuki fed him datastreams from her drones.

{Four Hydra Mark IVs,} she sent, the words delivered in a clipped, staccato-like tone. *{Two converging on Blackbird Two, the others are going after Blackbird One. Novastrikes are maneuvering to engage. I don't think they know* Wraith's *here, Cap.}*

Jonathan sent *Wraith* hurtling toward the nearest Novastrike even as he asked, *{Where the hell did they come from, Lieutenant?}*

He felt more than saw her headshake.

{Don't know, Cap. Katana *didn't report seeing any when she*

was here earlier. Likely, the big belch from that star over there hid their EM signatures from us, just like it hid our transition out of Scharnhorst space from them. Took 'em a while to notice us. Not sure what tipped them off, either.}

Jonathan's eyes narrowed as he saw the ships arrowing toward Blackbird Two. *Wraith* interpreted that as his desire to investigate further, and the ship's SI magnified that sector of space.

{Their headings indicate they came from there and there,} Will joined in, dropping pins on the locations where *Wraith*'s drones had initially picked them up. *{Hidden behind a few smaller stones.}*

Jonathan didn't bother acknowledging; he was too busy analyzing the situation before him. His gaze swept from one engagement cone to the other, nearly one hundred eighty degrees opposed, with respect to the asteroid.

What he saw wasn't encouraging. Two of the Hydras had already engaged Blackbird Two and were slinging railgun fire at the fighter. The Novastrike's pilot sent the ship into a dive to dodge the initial salvo, and then put the vessel through a series of random jinks to evade the second Hydra.

As Jonathan watched, Blackbird Two flushed a cloud of chaff, and its drone complement went into point-defense mode, firing lasers at the metal slugs the Akkadian ship was slinging at its armored hide.

{Nina! Steel!} Jonathan called out, and the gunner went weapons-free, engaging the Hydra that was the fighter's biggest threat.

{Reconfiguring,} Yuki announced, and Jonathan saw the drone swarm that surrounded *Wraith* shift as the lieutenant manipulated the complement under her command.

She recalled some of the sensor drones and exchanged them for more effective point-defense and electronic countermeasure platforms. The Dazzlers went winging toward each of the four Hydras, a small but mighty part of *Wraith*'s arsenal.

One from each pair immediately began producing powerful

jamming signals, while the other emitted decoy EM meant to draw smart weapons toward them and away from the ship they had been programmed to target.

Jonathan saw tracer fire and then felt the deep *foomp foomp* that accompanied the firing of *Wraith*'s RAU-19 railguns as Nina let loose with a stream of steel-jacketed slugs. Yuki's point defense lasers joined those of Blackbird Two as they battled the Hydras' onslaught.

A lucky hit rocked the Novastrike just as its pilot was jinking, and Jonathan saw the ship kick over into an uncontrolled tumble.

{Ah, damn,} he heard over comms. *{Shoulda zigged instead of zagged.}*

{Status!} Jonathan barked as he sent *Wraith* into a slip that would give them a least-time intercept to the hail of bullets raining down upon the Novastrike.

The pilot's voice sounded tense. *{Took a direct hit to the interlock between the nav controls and the drive. Both aft and port thrusters inoperable.}*

{Cap, there's a small rock directly in his path. It's too big for his ship's magnetic sweepers. He's going to need to eject,} Will warned on their private ship's net.

{Copy,} Jonathan responded, and then switched back over to the combat net. *{Ben, you see that rock about to hit you? Get the hell out of there. We'll cover you.}*

A two-click hit the net just as Jonathan saw a puff of air expelling from the fighter's cockpit and a small figure go jetting outward. Five seconds later, the rock impacted the Novastrike.

Yuki sent a pair of point defense drones to provide cover for the pilot while Nina dealt with the Hydras. Jonathan spun *Wraith*, and the gunner let loose with a tungsten sabot that embedded itself into the Hydra's flank.

The fighter was too well-armored for the sabot to pierce its hull, but the fighter's pilot would surely know his bell had been rung.

While he was shaking that off, Nina let loose with another

spate of railgun fire, concentrating on three of the Akkadian fighter's known weak points.

The Hydra's partner began harrying them in retaliation. Nina growled a low *{Bugger off,}* and then flung a tungsten sabot at the second ship.

The fighter broke away, allowing Nina the precious few seconds she needed to nail the first ship.

She let out a mental whoop as the fighter's accel abruptly dropped, and it shot past at a steady velocity on a heading from which it did not deviate.

Unfortunately for the Akkadian piloting the ship, that heading would intersect with another large rock in exactly three minutes.

{He's too busy shitting his pants to do much else, I'll bet,} the gunner said smugly.

{Good. Do it again,} Jonathan ordered, pointing *Wraith*'s nose at the remaining Hydra.

He brought them in low, giving her a good look at the fighter's underbelly as he split his attention long enough to check on Blackbird One.

{How you doing over there?} he asked.

{Yuki sent me a present,} a female voice responded. *{Damn those Dazzlers are nice, but a Banshee? They make nice holes in ships, didja know that?}*

Jonathan chuckled. *{I take it you're not in any immediate danger?}*

{Nah, just playing tag with this last joker, bouncing him between the two Banshees Yuki sent. He's running scared. Just do me a favor and fish Ben out of the drink, will ya?}

{Roger,} Jonathan replied.

He gave Nina a mental heads-up that he was about to maneuver, and then turned the ship toward the pilot's transponder blip, his attention still partially on the Hydra that *Wraith*'s gunner had engaged.

As he watched the way the Hydra moved, his gaze intensified. He waited to be certain he wasn't imagining it, but *Wraith*'s SI had noticed the same thing.

Maybe it was pilot fatigue. Maybe the pilot was injured and had handed over some of the nav to his ship's control. Whatever the reason, Jonathan saw a repeating pattern emerging.

He nudged Nina. *{Pilot's got a tell.}*

He studied the Hydra for another few seconds, mentally anticipating the moves the other ship was about to make, and then projected a specific location on the Hydra's spaceframe onto Nina's targeting reticle.

{Put a slug right here in ten seconds... mark.}

Nina didn't waste time with words. Leading the ten-second mark, Jonathan saw tracer fire. At ten seconds, the Hydra's radiation shadow shield shattered when it steered right into the artillery Nina had unleashed, pieces scattering into the void as the fighter's fusion drive went into auto shutdown.

The four members of *Wraith*'s flight crew held their breath as they awaited the Hydra pilot's next move. A tense second later, the craft exploded.

*{Dammit. I **hate** when they self-destruct,}* Will muttered. *{Tell me you saw the pilot eject before that?}*

Jonathan shook his head slowly, his gaze searching the debris for the pilot, but there weren't any pieces large enough to be an escape pod.

{Damn Akkadian policy,} he muttered. *{There is no reason for a pilot to go down with his ship like that.}*

{They consider it the ultimate sacrifice, Cap,} Yuki murmured. *{It's a shitty mindset.}*

Jonathan took a deep breath as he focused once more on the situation with Blackbird One. *{You doing okay over there?}*

{One suicide boom, one running for the gate,} the Novastrike's pilot said in a tone that was part annoyed and part furious. *{Clear over here. You get to Ben yet?}*

{Headed there now, Lieutenant,} Jonathan assured her, as he sent *Wraith* surging toward Blackbird Two's black box transponder signal.

Yuki's drone made it there before *Wraith*'s sensors did, and he heard her drag in a harsh breath.

{Cap....}

Her one-word comment trailed off, and Jonathan felt his own breath leave his lungs at the gut-punch visual that assaulted his eyes.

It looked like a piece of shrapnel from the damn Hydra's self-destruct had impacted the escape pod's durasteel surface.

The pods were sturdy enough to withstand some pounding and local stellar micrometeorite dust—at least long enough for a rescue to take place. But the section of armored plating that had impacted the pod must have done so with violent force, and with an incredibly sharp edge. A one-in-a-million shot.

The plating had cracked the pod open, leaving it vulnerable to the cloud of debris that had followed in the shrapnel's wake.

Yuki's feed showed where Ben's arm had been severed, and evidence that his flight suit attempted to seal the wound to keep him from bleeding out. It also showed a nonworking ES field, the generator pierced through by yet another piece of debris. And it showed the man's eyes, staring sightlessly into the black.

{We have a tau-neu pod,} Will reminded them. *{Let's see if we can't get him into stasis. There may still be time for the docs back home to revive him, if we can get him in there quickly enough.}*

His words prodded Jonathan forward, and he maneuvered the Helios alongside the pod, as Will and Nina unwebbed and went aft to retrieve the body.

{Damn,} Yuki whispered. *{Sometimes I hate this job.}*

* * *

The teams on the station remained unaware of the pitched battle happening in nearspace around the asteroid. They had enough on their hands.

Units One and Two met with a phalanx of soldiers just outside the area Will had identified as the base's CIC. The coordinated resistance was surprisingly effective, causing the teams to upwardly revise their estimation of the people staffing the base. These weren't standard Junxun regiment soldiers; they were Tèzhǒng, Akkadia's answer to the SRU.

That warranted another brief EM burst to update the rest of the teams who had infiltrated—and it was detected. It tripped klaxons and sent lights strobing throughout the base.

The Akkadians knew they were here.

This made it harder for Three and Four to approach the lab where the Alliance prisoners were being held, but they were Unit soldiers, and 'easy' wasn't in the job description.

They coordinated their efforts, laying a decoy trail to lure away those guarding the lab. Some took the bait; others didn't. The Akkadians who remained guarding the cells ended up very dead as two fireteams converged on them, dispatching them with brutal efficiency.

Unit Four's leader toggled her drakeskin to visible and stepped toward the isolation room holding the three scientists.

"Are we ever glad to see you," the woman breathed.

Team Four lead's drakeskin combat HUD positively identified her as Linnet Thompson, biochemist.

"Do you know if you were exposed to the pathogen?" The leader projected her voice into the passageway.

Linnet shook her head. "The asshole who had Samantha Travis used us as leverage. He threatened to use us as guinea pigs for their new weapon, but never did."

Four's leader nodded, took a swift moment to debate logistics, and then stepped away from the ES field hemming them in place. She looked around and spied the two-stage airlock three meters away.

{Connors. Break out the spare suits, and lay them out for our guests. Whitcomb. Drop a LockPik on that room's ES controls, but don't activate it yet. Then move back and set up an ES barrier on the other side of that airlock.}

As the two soldiers moved to carry out the instructions, Four's leader turned back to the prisoners to explain what they were about to do, but she saw Linnet nodding.

"Good plan," Linnet responded. "We'll get geared up, pass

through the airlock's decontamination, and then meet you in the hallway."

On the other side of the asteroid, Thad, Boone, and Asha silently worked their way from the hangar bay to where Sam was being held. They used an access shaft adjacent to the nearest lift to get to the right level, but there wasn't much cover to be found in the passageways that led to her room.

So far, it hadn't turned out to be an issue. They'd encountered no one along the way. That held for another two intersections—and then intruder alarms began to blare throughout the compound.

Seconds later, a group of Akkadians came barreling around the corner. The wall of soldiers had their weapons out and were purposely taking up the width of the passageway to prevent stealthed adversaries from slipping past.

{Up!} Thad ordered, and both Boone and Asha engaged their suits' organogel threads and swarmed up the bulkheads.

{They're trying to flush us out,} Asha sent as she and the sniper clung to either side of the passageway where wall met overhead.

Thad didn't bother responding; he engaged his SmartCarbyne lattice and used his Marine augments to give him the boost he needed to launch himself over the phalanx of oncoming soldiers. The move allowed him to just barely clear the heads of the two in the center.

{Engage!} he ordered as he landed in a crouch behind the line of Akkadians.

The soldiers he'd just leapt over had felt the air stir as he'd passed over them and had already begun to turn, bringing their weapons around to aim at an invisible foe.

Both Boone and Asha had the five soldiers down before anyone, including Thad, had an opportunity to fire.

{Leave some for me next time,} he grumbled as he rose to standing once more.

He helped Boone slap a nano ziptie package onto the three soldiers he'd knocked out, freezing them in place and rendering their wires inoperable. The two Asha had shot hadn't been so lucky; their dead eyes stared up at Thad, and he found he didn't really have a shit to give about the loss of life.

{Come on,} he ordered. *{Scan shows she's just around that bend.}*

The sound of footsteps advancing told Thad another cluster of Akkadians were between the team and Sam, and that they'd heard the weapons' fire. As they came into view, it was evident they anticipated an attack from stealthed opponents; they were warily sweeping the corridor with their firearms, while guarding the officer who stood before Sam's door.

{Shit. Situation's about to turn hostage on us, Cap,} Boone warned.

Thad cursed silently as he stared the man in front of Sam's door. *{I know.}*

The man's uniform projected the digital salad of an Akkadian colonel.

"They'll be coming for her here. Find them and eliminate them!" He barked the order, and his troops went racing down the hall, straight toward the team's drakeskin-clad forms.

Thad had an instant to decide how he wanted to handle the situation. He knew if he engaged these men, that would give the colonel the precious seconds he needed to take Sam hostage. He also knew Boone was the one of the best sharpshooters the Navy had.

{Boone, get into position to take out that colonel,} Thad sent.

The sniper nodded, moving once more to scale the bulkhead while Thad and Asha engaged their oncoming adversary.

The combat HUD built into Thad's drakeskin suit showed Boone's outline clearing the oncoming soldiers, its predictive systems limning the sharpshooter in the green of a 'friendly'. Thad had just enough time to catch a glimpse of the sniper as he engaged his suit's 'sticky' threads, pressing his back to the bulkhead and bringing his P-SCAR up to his eye.

And then the first soldier plowed his face into Thad's fist.

Thad followed it by hooking a hand behind the man's neck

and driving his knee up into the Akkadian's gut. A quick look up had Thad sidestepping to avoid a flurry of flechettes fired by the man's partner. Yanking the soldier forward into the path of the weapon, Thad used the unconscious man's body as a shield. A second round impacted, and the man became dead weight.

Thad rushed another Akkadian, his partner's body hitting him with a wet smack. At the same time, Thad aimed a savage kick at the man's knee joint, shattering it.

A quick look showed Asha had dispatched her two soldiers with surgical efficiency, as the two neatly drilled holes in their foreheads attested.

"Drop your weapons or the director's niece dies," a voice called out.

{How do you want to play this?} Boone asked.

{You got a clean shot, hoss?}

{Not as clean as I'd like,} he admitted. *{If you could provide about thirty seconds of distraction, it would give me a chance to move forward about fifteen meters....}*

{Done.} Thad sent a mental command, and his drakeskin suit decloaked. "Sorry to disappoint you, *ami*, but the lady's comin' with us," he said as he slowly advanced.

The colonel's grip tightened on the pistol he held at Sam's temple. "Your partner. Tell him to reveal himself, too."

Asha crossed to the other side of the bulkhead before decloaking, a move that would split the man's focus even further. "Sorry to disappoint, *Colonel*, but his partner's a 'her'." The medic's voice dripped with disdain as she reappeared.

The colonel jerked his head toward Thad. "Both of you, together. Hands where I can see them."

Asha rolled her eyes and gave a loud sigh, which elicited a shaky laugh from Sam. The sound caused the colonel to loosen his hold on her, allowing her to pull slightly away and for Boone to get off a shot.

Unfortunately, the colonel reacted swiftly to correct the error, moving to pull Sam back. The shot burned a neat hole into the bulkhead just beside the man's left ear.

{Dammit!}

* * *

When Sam saw Thad and then Asha appear, she knew Boone must be somewhere nearby. The suppression app Marceau had slapped onto the side of her neck the moment her cell door slid open blocked her entirely. She could neither send nor receive any signals with her wire. That left her with nothing more than verbal and physical cues to communicate her intent.

She'd purposely snickered at Asha's comment, shifting her body away from Marceau as she did so. As she'd hoped, it briefly broke the man's concentration, and he'd glanced over at her.

Also as she'd hoped, Boone took the shot, but Sam realized her mistake the moment it passed harmlessly by her captor. She'd actually caused Marceau to move out of the sniper's line of fire when she'd pulled away.

Later, when questioned, she would be unable to explain why it was this that set her off—but it did. Fury consumed her, a wrath over the test subjects who'd died a horrible death, and an incandescent rage for all the unwitting victims Akkadia intended to kill in its quest for power.

Sam braced the way Ell had taught her months ago, and pushed off her front leg with all her strength as she twisted her torso, bringing her elbow up in a vicious strike that clipped Marceau under the jaw.

It startled the man. He loosened his grip, and Sam staggered out of the way, leaving them clear to take another shot.

"Non-lethal!" she blurted out.

Just in time, too. Boone's next shot drilled into Marceau's shoulder instead of through his heart.

The three converged on the man, Thad's CUSP delivering a brutal pulse plasma shot that sent him to the floor, his face in a rictus of pain. The Marine had the man ziptied and shoved to one side before the paralysis from the shot wore off.

"You okay, *cher*?" Thad asked, coming up beside Sam while

Boone stood guard over the colonel.

Asha had pulled out her medic's kit and was busy running a scan, but Sam was too preoccupied to tell her she was fine.

"No! They've already shipped the vials." She jabbed a finger at Marceau, her hand shaking with anger. "And *he* knows where they went."

STEALTH ESCAPE

AKKADIAN BASE
AN-YANG DUST BELT
PROXIMA CENTAURI

DACINA CAME RACING into Che's office, dark eyes flashing, weapon drawn. "We must leave. Now."

Che looked up, startled by her sudden, fierce appearance, but not alarmed. He knew the depth of the Dagger's loyalty; she was deadly, but not to him. Never to him.

"What is this?" he asked, and was even more surprised when she crossed to his side.

"We must leave," she repeated. Her words were low, but they were intense and held the same steel his own voice held when barking orders to troops.

His gaze swept the feeds as he sought the answer on his wire, but nothing he saw seemed amiss.

"Dacina—"

"We have been found," she told him. "Alliance unit troops have infiltrated the base."

She stepped toward his office door and turned with an urgency he'd not seen in her before. That and the news of their unwanted visitors propelled him forward.

He reached back for the clearsteel case containing the weapon's trigger, and followed her out the door.

They walked through the CIC at a steady pace, but once the doors to the outer passage slid shut behind them, she urged him forward. She broke into a fast trot and, with a quick look around, Che did the same.

Dacina darted down a side passage, her hand slapping at a panel inset into the bulkhead. It slid open, revealing a maintenance tunnel Che had never noticed. She beckoned him inside.

{This will take us to an auxiliary shaft that runs parallel to the hangar bay,} she said as they sped through the small enclosure. *{I have a small vessel awaiting us. It will require a hard burn.}*

She shot a worried look over her shoulder, and her voice sounded doubtful.

Che almost laughed. *{Do not concern yourself over me. I may be old, but do not label me grandfather just yet, Dacina Zian,}* he chided. *{My lattice will suffice.}*

In truth, he was amazed at the amount of thought his Dagger had put into an escape plan such as this. His amazement grew when he caught sight of the sleek shadow ship used by Akkadian assassins that she had somehow appropriated for this mission. How and when she'd snuck all this onto the base were questions he intended to get answers to once they were safely away.

He pulled to a stop beside her, a single thought intruding on his consciousness. "You say we have been invaded, yet I've seen no evidence of such. How is it that you know and the rest do not?"

She shot him a look that was a blend of devoted daughter and impatient warrior. "I am of the assassin's guild. I live in the shadows."

A connection appeared over his wire, and when he accepted it, he realized he was seeing her personal feed. The recording showed nothing but a pair of soldiers standing guard in front of one of the laboratory entrances. In the next instant, both of them slumped to the deck, victims of an invisible assault. When their bodies began to levitate partially off the deck, sliding backward into the lab, Che shut it off.

He turned to her, his expression grim. "I am in your debt. I should not have doubted you."

She bowed deeply. "You owe me nothing, my general."

Turning swiftly, she lifted a hand, swiping at a keypad only she could see.

"I have set a worm within the base's mainframe," she said as an access panel slid open on the ship. "There will be nothing left for them to find that would connect you to this mission."

Her words—her deeds—rendered him speechless.

She stepped back to give him room and gestured for him to precede her into the craft. "It will be a tight fit," she warned. "This is no pleasure ship."

Che grunted at that. He knew better than most that the ship was little more than basic life support seated atop a powerful fusion drive. His nuts shriveled at the thought of the radiation he was about to be exposed to; it might render him sterile if he went too long without treatment.

Eh, who wants children at my age anyway, he thought with mordant humor. *If I want progeny, I can always have them cloned.*

His gaze strayed once more to the assassin who had to practically climb over him to reach the ship's controls.

Then again, there is more than one way to gauge family....

* * *

Yuki and Will had just sealed the tau-neu pod when *Wraith*'s proximity alarm went off.

{Brace!}

Jonathan sent the mental shout as he slewed the Helios away from the plume left by the ship that had just rocketed past them.

{Plasma-pissing pulsars!} Blackbird One shouted. *{Do you know what that was? Holy crap on a comet! That was—}*

Her voice cut out as a brilliant blue flare presaged the forming of a Casimir bubble.

{One of those mythical shadow ships from the assassins' guild?} Jonathan finished. *{Yeah, looks like. And they're gone, with no possible way for us to tell where they went.}*

Will whistled. He'd somehow made it back to his flight engineer's cradle and was already pulling up the data from *Wraith*'s records. *{Eighty gs? That's a helluva lot of stress, even with a lattice fully engaged. Whoever it was wanted to make damn sure we didn't get a shot off before they transitioned.}*

Jonathan shot a look over his shoulder and gave the man a brief nod. *{Yeah, which means they knew we were out here. Also means they know we've infiltrated the base.}*

{What do you want to bet the person responsible for all this was on that ship?} Will asked after a moment.

Nina's voice was sour when she replied. *{I don't take sucker bets. My credit's on them slagging all the evidence before they left, too. They'll be back in Akkadia soon, leaving the rest of these poor fools here to take the blame.}*

Yuki's voice held a trace of sadness as she lifted her hand from the tau-neu pod and pushed off for her cradle once more. *{Let's hope things are going a bit better in there than they did out here.}*

DEATH TRAP

Situation Room
Parliament House
St. Clair Township, Ceriba

An urgent request from the prime minister pulled Duncan away from TF Blue's situation room, where battle reports flowed in from the teams in Proxima. An SRU lieutenant delivered the summons, and then flew him down to Parliament House, where the Alliance's top leaders had convened.

He was now in a different situation room, a room that held the same hushed quality of a memorial service. Duncan stood with his hands pressed into the hardwood surface of the conference table, his head bowed as he fought to maintain his composure. The report coming in from the destroyer keeping pace abeam of the *Atliekan Queen* made that a difficult feat.

"Based on the captain's reports, engineering and bridge crews have had to barricade themselves in to keep the passengers at bay," Duncan spoke quietly into the silence.

Beside him sat the governor-general, and beside her, the

prime minister. The governor-general's expression was grave, but the prime minister's face was frozen in shock, as if he couldn't quite believe what he was hearing.

"They're panicking," the governor-general said in a low voice. "With so many deaths, you can see why."

"Is there *any* way out of this, Amara? Any other option?" Duncan asked.

Toland pressed her lips together until they were nothing but a bloodless line. "No, Director. The Akkadians corrupted the data at the Proxima base, and left no samples behind. Until we can get our hands on that virus, we can't be certain how they've reassorted the gene sequences."

"And that means?" The question came from Fleet Admiral Wake, the man in charge of the Alliance Navy.

Duncan saw a tic begin to form as Toland clenched her jaw.

"Without any kind of blueprint, the best we've been able to do is send them antiviral nano for existing hemorrhagic fevers, hoping they do some small amount of good."

"But it's not working?" Duncan asked.

Toland shook her head. "No, sir. It is not."

He felt his chest go tight as he thought through the ramifications of what they were considering.

He looked over at Wake. The man had a decent poker face, but Duncan could see a banked agony behind the man's eyes.

"*Redoubtable* has a pair of Novastrikes on standby," Wake told Duncan quietly. "All you have to do is say the word."

The governor-general drew in a breath. "Whatever we decide, this goes no further than this room. I want this close-held until we've had a chance to contact next of kin."

Duncan nodded his understanding, and then looked up as the captain of the destroyer broke in again.

{The ship hasn't deviated from this heading. She's still on course for port,} Redoubtable's skipper was saying. Duncan could hear the tension in the man's voice. *{If you want us to take action, we'll need to do it soon. They're due to arrive by the end of the day.}*

Duncan met Wake's eyes. "Give the order," he said, his voice heavy.

Wake nodded. Toggling the holo, he addressed the destroyer's commanding officer. "Captain Ensminger. You are ordered to fire upon that yacht. She is not to reach port. I repeat, she is not to reach port."

There was a beat of silence. Ensminger's face stared back at them, his expression calm. The only thing that betrayed his inner turmoil was the hard swallow he had to force before his words would come.

"Understood, sir."

As the holo went blank, Duncan heard the governor-general's voice whisper, "May God have mercy on their souls—and on ours for ordering it."

* * *

The captain of the *Atliekan Queen* sat in her chair on the bridge as she spoke to the Novastrike pilot who had been her shadow for the past day.

{You still out there, Dover Three-two?} she asked.

{Yes, ma'am,} replied the voice of the young man flying the Novastrike thousands of kilometers off her starboard bow. *{Everything okay over there, ma'am?}*

She looked over at the feed from the corridor leading to the bridge, and saw the pile of bodies that lay motionless. Blood dripped from their eyes, their noses, their ears.

She flipped to the feed still open in medical, saw Josh's dead body propped up in his chair where he'd expired while trying desperately to send data to the CID.

"Been better," she whispered, swallowing hard.

Somehow, enviro had been breached, as had engineering. She supposed it was now just a matter of time before the virus made its way onto the bridge.

She'd begun to feel feverish an hour earlier, and her comm

officer had collapsed with a groan just before that. When she'd reached over to touch him, he'd screamed, the pain from that simple contact more than he could bear. He was unconscious now, and she wondered how much longer he'd be around.

{So, Dover, huh?} she replied with forced joviality. *{Are you with the one hundred and first, then? Last I heard, they were based on* Redoubtable. *They still call her the Banana Boat?}*

{Yes, ma'am,} the pilot's voice said, a note of surprise in his tone. *{Pardon me for asking, but were you Navy?}*

{I spent a few years in the service. Racked up a few hours in that spaceframe you're flying, too. Mind if I ask your name?}

{Slater, ma'am. Captain Rich Slater.}

She nodded and took a moment to wipe the sweat from her brow. It was getting hotter in here—or was it the fever?

{Nice to meet you, Captain. Name's Nolotov. Zoya Nolotov.}

* * *

When the yacht's captain had initially pinged him, Slater had been polite, but quietly impatient. Privately, he thought that shepherding a cruise liner wasn't the kind of job a Novastrike pilot should do.

He'd been surprised by her callout of *Redoubtable*'s nickname. That knowledge wasn't something he expected a glorified bus driver to know. And her name... now, why was it so familiar?

{So, Captain Nolotov, did you serve on Redoubtable *before you retired, ma'am?}*

When the woman's voice came back, she sounded winded, as if she'd just come off a sprint. *{Not the Banana Boat, no. I spent most of my time on the* Audacious.*}*

{Hell of a destroyer, ma'am, with a great record. Were you deployed on her during the Zosher incident?}

The woman coughed a laugh. *{I **captained** her during that shitstorm.}*

Slater looked at the image of the yacht on his holo with new respect. *{Ma'am, the stories of that battle are what caused me to want to be a Novastrike pilot. I had holos of all the ships that were there, plastered everywhere in my room when I was a kid.}* The words tumbled from him in unabashed hero worship. *{What you did there was truly brilliant. Did you know we study your maneuvers? Wait'll I tell the squadron back on the Boat.}*

He was gushing, and he didn't care. The babysitting job he'd abhorred was turning into a pretty sweet gig after all.

A flash over his comms caught his attention.

{Sorry, ma'am, got to bounce to another frequency for a bit. Be right back.}

{Take your time,} she responded. *{I have nowhere to go.}*

The brief comm flash contained a link to an encrypted feed from Parliament House. When he accepted it, he found himself facing five people he never thought he'd meet, virtually or otherwise.

The conversation was brief, a handful of minutes at most. But what they told him had Slater reeling.

He asked for confirmation twice, unable to believe what they were telling him to do. To his stunned horror, his orders did not change.

When the connection dissolved, he found himself staring once more at the vessel that filled his visual frame. The image blurred, and he blinked. Only when he felt the runnels of wetness trailing down his face did he realize his tears were the reason the visual had begun to warp.

"Oh stars. Oh stars," he softly chanted as he reached mentally for the connection to Zoya Nolotov. *{Ma'am, are you still there?}*

He was glad the conversation was over the wire; he knew he could never have forced the words from his mouth otherwise.

{Still here.} Her voice was fainter. *{You know, Rich, I've been doing a bit of thinking....}*

Her voice faded away, and he waited silently for her to continue.

{My comm officer here on the bridge, he just passed. He was a good man, a friend. His death, it wasn't... pretty.}

Slater cleared his throat. *{Captain—}*

{I was thinking. You know, I cheated death in the Zosher incident. This isn't how I envisioned it would go down. Do those Novastrikes still carry a load of Banshees?}

Slater's throat convulsed.

{Yeah,} he sent after a moment. *{Yes, we do.}*

{Good. Now here's what—}

{Captain,} he interrupted, *{would you do me a favor? Could you switch to visual?}*

A holo connection request appeared on his HUD moments later. Slater accepted and stared back at the woman, sitting up as straight as his pilot's cradle would allow.

He snapped her a sharp salute, tears brimming in his eyes. She returned it, an unutterably weary and haunted look in hers.

"A favor of my own, Captain?" she said as she lowered her hand.

"Anything."

"I have a brother. We're very close. This will devastate him. If it's ever allowed... will you look him up?"

"Ma'am," Slater nodded, unable to say more.

"Fair skies and tailwinds, Captain." Nolotov gave him a faint smile and then cut the connection.

Slater pulled back on the Novastrike, sending the ship in a loop that would place him on a direct intersect for the yacht. With a steady hand, he reached into the cockpit's holo and armed his ship's Banshee missiles.

The Novastrike's fire control system confirmed it had a lock and he squeezed his eyes shut, although it didn't help any; the SyntheticVision link tied into his optics relayed the telemetry of the salvo as it bore down on the *Atliekan Queen*.

"I'm sorry," he whispered aloud, tears running freely down his face. "I'm so, so sorry..."

SECURITY SWEEP

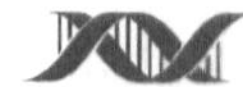

MERKI INSTITUTE
DOWNTOWN MIDLAND
HAWKING HABITAT

INTEL FROM THE strike force in Proxima came in just as Micah, Gabe, and the two spec-ops teams landed at Hawking's Midland spaceport.

We got her, bro.

Jonathan's words released the knot in Micah's chest he'd been carrying around ever since he first heard she'd been taken.

Sam's unharmed?

Jonathan's mental tone held genuine amusement. *Unharmed, pissed, and with a mean elbow.*

A... what?

The guy holding her captive? She clocked him with an elbow strike under the jaw, Jonathan sent. *Thad said it was a thing of beauty.*

Micah grinned as he envisioned the petite blonde in action.

Didn't know she had it in her. How'd Wraith *fare?*

There was a beat of silence.

They had a small fleet of Hydras on patrol that were lying doggo, Jonathan admitted, and Micah heard a trace of self-recrimination in his mirror twin's voice. *Their energy signatures were masked by the flare, just like ours when we arrived. Sensors didn't pick up on them, and they managed to launch a strike.*

Micah ground to a halt in alarm, eliciting a concerned look from Gabe. He waved the agent on and resumed his walk toward the spaceport's exit.

Well, you're obviously alive. Are **you** *unharmed?* he probed.

Me? Oh, sure, I'm fine. Crew's all fine.

Jonathan didn't sound fine, though.

You scratched the paint job, didn't you?

He leveled the accusation at his twin in an attempt to inject some levity into the mental conversation.

Aw, hell.

Jonathan paused, and Micah braced himself to receive bad news.

They got one of the Novastrikes. Pilot ejected, and then the idiot Hydra pilot had to go and suicide on us. It was too close to the escape pod, and shrapnel shredded it.

Micah's gut clenched in sympathy. It was tough watching a comrade fall.

Do we know him? he asked.

Not sure. Does Ben sound familiar?

Micah wracked his brain, but couldn't put a face to the name. *Not to me, no.*

Well, he's in stasis. Hopefully he'll pull through.

Micah felt Jonathan wrench himself mentally from that train of thought.

Anyway. Sam says to tell you the bioweapon left the base for Hawking sometime yesterday. They've encapsulated it into aerosolized cylinders that look like this.

An image appeared in Micah's head, one of the side benefits of their shared quantum state.

He nodded. *We guessed it might be something like that. Already have Pascal and Sneaky Pete dialed in and looking for something along these lines.*

He looked around for Gabe. Spotting the man, Micah waved him over.

"You hear from Thad?" he asked.

TF Blue's second-in-command shook his head. "No, should I have?"

Micah held up a finger, silently signaling him to wait a moment. *Hey, is Thad going to be giving Gabe a sitrep?* he asked his mirror twin.

Yeah. But things are a bit of a mess over here, so give him a minute, Jonathan told him.

I'll give him the short version for now, and Thad can fill him in when he gets freed up.

Jonathan sent a mental nod. *He says go ahead.*

Micah let his connection to his doppelganger fade, and gave Gabe a summary of the Proxima operation. He'd just finished the briefing when they stepped out of the spaceport and into the sunny skies of a Midland afternoon.

The day was a warm one inside the McKendree cylinder, and the atmosphere generated a surprisingly blue sky.

Gabe lifted his chin. "I'm always surprised to see clouds floating by in a habitat this size," he said as they caught up with Ell, Sasha, and the rest of the team.

Quinn, Ell's assistant, also tilted his head skyward and squinted. "Well, there's a lot of atmosphere between here and the other side."

Gabe nodded, conceding the point. Then he stepped closer and lowered his voice. "We have news. I'll brief you on the way."

The conversation switched to the combat net that had been established before leaving Nimitz. This way, they could loop Rafe in as well.

The major had remained behind to set up a flight plan for his fighter wing—one that had increased their presence within the habitat's surrounding nearspace.

Half an hour later, with the team fully briefed, Micah found himself standing across the street from the Merki Institute, with a large hunting cat by his side, and a ferret on his shoulder. He tilted his head back and looked up at the building, his eyes following it to the top. Somehow, he'd never envisioned a skyscraper inside a habitat.

If the institute was trying to impress, he'd give them top scores. It was an imposing structure.

{We're a go for Menagerie,} he heard Sasha say over the net.

Micah responded with a two-click, wincing internally at the operation's code name.

It was Rafe's suggestion—one Micah vowed he'd repay him for once the op had concluded.

Today's undertaking was recon only, and would be followed by a briefing back at Nimitz. The intel from the team in Proxima suggested the attack wouldn't occur until the summit began the following morning.

It also suggested that Akkadian agents had infiltrated service organizations supporting the summit. Ell had Quinn running those agencies through another round of security checks, hoping to identify the operatives before the event launched.

Micah stepped off the curb and ducked under the barricade that barred pedestrians and transports from breaching the perimeter that Protective Services had set it up in concert with Coalition forces the day before, in preparation for the event.

{Heading in now,} he informed the team as he crossed the street and walked to the entrance.

He knew snipers from both Delta and Foxtrot had eyes on him, and his overlay sparkled with icons indicating the cloud of surveillance microdrones that floated around him.

As much as was possible, the team was taking no chances with this op.

He nodded a greeting to the two Alliance Navy MPs standing watch over the front doors. Their SIs challenged his ID token, and he waited patiently while they scanned it.

The soldier on the right moved aside with a nod. "You're

cleared to enter, Captain."

"Thank you, Sergeant," Micah said.

He stepped out of Midland's sunny afternoon into the subtle elegance of the institute. A blast of chilled air hit him, and he mentally adjusted his suit to compensate for the differential.

Sneaky Pete chittered his displeasure with the blast of air, and curled his tail around Micah's neck.

Micah lifted a hand to steady the animal while he glanced around, seeking likely places for aerosolized canisters to be stashed. Dappled light filtered in through large, paned windows, casting long shadows against the marble floor. Low, cushioned benches lined the walls, and comfortable sofas sat in small clusters on either side of the lobby. The area was bare otherwise, barring an ornate chandelier that hung in the center of the open, three-story space.

{No likely candidates in the lobby. Too big an area to aerosolize,} he sent.

{Agreed. Protective Services has ruled that out as well,} Gabe replied.

Micah's boots made no sound against the floor as he crossed the polished tiles, thanks to the cloud of microdrones enveloping him. Another pair of MPs awaited him at a kiosk that looked like some sort of reproduction concierge station straight from Old Earth. On the other side of that were two more agents—his escort, if he had to guess.

The MPs at the secondary checkpoint made short work of his ID token, and, like the soldiers outside, didn't bat an eye at the ferret clinging to his neck or the cat that paced silently beside him.

He'd been correct; the pair that awaited him were his assigned escort.

The shorter of the two stuck out his hand for Micah to shake. "Brad Torgen," he said, "Coalition Secret Service." He nodded to the tall, rangy woman who stood beside him. "Corporal Ginder, Ganymede Protection Detail."

"Thanks for the escort and the tour," Micah greeted. "You said you had a list for us of the people who've had access to the ballroom where the summit is being held?"

The corporal nodded. "We do," she said, and an invitation to join the Protective Services' net appeared on his overlay.

Micah had a sector of his wire already partitioned off and ready to accept the PS net. Once connected, he accessed the file that awaited him and scanned the names on the list. They matched the names that Ell had already fingered and Quinn was running traces on.

He glanced between the sergeant and the corporal. "I understand you've been monitoring them?"

"Yes, and so far, they've done nothing suspicious." The man looked frustrated.

"Cheer up, the day's not over yet." Micah let a touch of sarcasm leach into his voice.

Ginder snickered, and Micah took the opportunity to introduce the animals accompanying him.

"This is Pascal," he indicated the big cat beside him, "and Sneaky Pete." His hand landed atop the ferret's head.

The female agent leaned in, peering at Sneaky Pete. "Interesting. I've heard of working dogs and cats, but never a ferret. So, they say you have a nose like a bloodhound, eh?"

She looked back at Micah. "I suppose its head is pretty much all nose anyway, now, isn't it?" With a chuckle, she stepped back.

{Rude, rude, ruuuude,} the ferret said, chittering indignantly at the woman.

Ginder stared back in fascination at the trilling noises the ferret was making, and Micah was glad they had restricted the animals' E-V comms to team members only.

Ignoring Pete, he smiled at Ginder. "Yes, they have an extraordinarily well-developed sense of smell. We're hoping they'll be able to find something we've missed."

He looked down at Pascal. "Ready to get to work?"

The big cat chuffed and paced forward a few steps, turning and shooting a look back over his shoulder at Micah.

Torgen laughed. "I take that as a yes. Come on, then.

Ballroom's this way."

He gestured, and Micah fell into step beside the two agents. They led him to a bank of lifts at the far end of the lobby, where he could see one had been held open for them.

As the doors closed and the lift began to rise, the ferret suddenly stirred from around his neck.

Nose in the air, Sneaky Pete sniffed, and then chirruped. *{Up! Up! Want up!}*

He balanced on his hind paws, and rose until his front paws were braced on top of Micah's head.

The captain could see in the burnished copper of the lift's doors that the ferret was staring intently upward. As he watched, Pete lifted a paw, reaching toward the lift's ceiling.

Micah exchanged a puzzled look with the two protective service agents. "Any idea what might be up there?"

Ginder shrugged and exchanged a look with Torgen. "Safety cables, maglev SC batteries?"

"Light fixtures?" the Coalition agent chimed in. "Why, does he smell something?"

"I don't know."

Micah stepped to one corner of the lift and steadied Pete with one hand so that he could tilt his head up without getting a face full of ferret. As he moved along the lift's perimeter to inspect the ceiling, he groped inside his tactical vest for the recon drones he'd packed for just this situation. With the flick of a wrist, he released the small swarm.

The tiny machines synched with his overlay, and he sent them winging upward before continuing his visual inspection of the ceiling. His eyes stopped at a seam that looked like it might be an access panel.

He pointed. "There. Let's see if we can't get that open."

They stopped the lift at the next level, and one of the agents exited long enough to locate a chair. She hauled it inside, and Micah nodded wordless thanks as he stepped up onto it.

His fingers probed the edges of the panel until they found a section that moved. He pressed it, and the panel slid open.

Sneaky Pete stretched his body to peer inside. Micah felt the ferret wobble, and he placed a hand on the animal's flank to stabilize him.

{Yup, yup, something here. Yup.}

The ferret flowed into the darkened crevice, chittering to himself as he sniffed around. They heard a scraping noise, and a few seconds later, the ferret's head popped out.

To Micah's astonishment, his paws were wrapped around a cylinder that matched the image Jonathan had sent.

"Well, I'll be damned," he heard Torgen say.

As the ferret pulled it further into the open, the guards instinctively backed away.

Micah unslung the bag he'd hooked over his shoulder and rummaged inside it for one of the mini clearsteel cases it contained. Reaching up, he took the small, silver cylinder from Sneaky Pete's paws.

{Found a cylinder,} he sent over the team's combat net as he inserted the offending object into the case and activated its ES field. *{Can we get them to evacuate now?}*

He heard the surprise in Gabe's voice when the man replied.

{That was fast.}

{It was Pete who detected it, and I'm not entirely sure how,} he replied.

{Smelled it.}

The ferret wriggled down from the opening, settling once more around Micah's shoulders.

*{You **smelled** it?}* he repeated, ignoring the chorus of questions being shot at him over the combat net as he focused on the ferret. *{What do you mean, smelled it? What did it smell like?}*

The ferret scrunched up his face. *{Icky sweet, like funny cloud around man's head outside cage. Make Snotface loopy.}*

Micah patted the ferret's head as he absently slid the access panel shut and stepped down from the chair. He hardly noticed when Ginder dragged it back out into the hallway, and the lift resumed its ascent to the institute's ballroom level.

{Gabe?} he sent on a private path. *{I need to check in with Sam about this. Pete's saying he recognizes it from somewhere, but his description sounds like it's from a lab, and I'm not entirely certain it's the CID he's talking about.}*

Gabe's mental tone was sharp. *{Are you talking about a memory from deGrasse?}*

Micah's hand returned to the ferret. *{Yeah,}* he replied slowly. *{I think I am. Hang on, let me get Jonathan to ask Sam a few questions....}*

After a few minutes of back-and-forth with his doppelganger, Micah was back with Gabe.

{You're not going to believe this.}

{Try me.} The agent's voice sounded impatient.

{Pete smelled Frenzy on the cylinder.}

There was a moment of stunned silence from the other end. *{He smelled **what**?}*

{Sam says that one of the lab workers back on deGrasse was arrested for possession of Frenzy. A review of the feed showed he'd been vaping it while cleaning out the animals' cage.}

{Yes, but—} Gabe's mental voice broke off. *{Hang on, bringing the team in on this.}*

Micah's icon tag changed from private to multi-user, and he could feel by the quality of the signal that they were once more connected to the full combat net.

Gabe brought them quickly up to speed, adding, *{I understand the Proxima base is an old Frenzy processing plant. Could trace elements still be there?}*

{That was a decade ago,} Sasha countered. *{Surely, squatters would have raided all the stock.}*

{If they didn't, the Akkadians would have scrubbed it clean before working with a virus this deadly,} Ell added. *{You don't do that kind of thing outside a clean room.}*

{Maybe one of the lackeys down the line ran into a hidden stash when they went in to sterilize the place,} Rafe suggested, *{Or maybe it has nothing to do with the base at all.}*

Quinn came on the line, his voice thoughtful. *{You might be *on to something, Major. Even in totalitarian regimes like the Akkadian Empire, there is a robust black market, and trafficking in illegal drugs like Frenzy. I'll add that to my search filter as I scrub through these names again.}*

{Okay, so I'm clear to share this with the protection detail?} Micah asked.

{Yes.} This came from Gabe. *{And summit security is working on evacuation.}*

The two agents shot him an incredulous look.

"You have got to be shitting me. Frenzy?" Disbelief rang in Torgen's voice as they exited the lift. He shot the large cat a look. "Can he smell it, too?"

Micah looked down at Pascal.

{Yes. Wrong-sweet.}

{Can you use that smell to find more of the cylinders?} Micah asked.

For answer, Pascal turned and began to slink down the hall. *{Going hunting.}*

"Guess he can," Ginder murmured as she watched the cat disappear down the hallway just as service staff and security personnel began to head toward the lift where they stood. She shot Micah a look. "We've been told to evac. Are you sure you're okay being in here?"

"We've been given experimental vaccines," he lied. "How long will the evac take?"

"Not long," Torgen said. "This level's going to take the longest, since this is where the summit's being held."

"I'd better catch up to Pascal then, before he runs into anyone."

As if on cue, they heard a shriek coming from around the corner.

Micah exchanged looks with the agents and then began running toward the sound.

A LUCKY BREAK

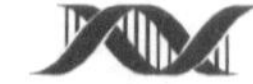

MERKI INSTITUTE
DOWNTOWN MIDLAND
HAWKING HABITAT

MICAH ROUNDED THE corner at a run, but came to an abrupt halt when he spied Pascal pacing around a caterer's cart. The big cat's head was lifted and his jaw slightly open in classic flehmen response as he scented the air.

Three people stood frozen beside the cart as Pascal continued to circle it.

"Get. This. Creature. *Away* from here," a woman demanded shrilly. She was wearing a business suit and teetering on a set of ridiculously high stilettos. Her face was contorted in a combination of anger and fear.

"The institute's events director," Ginder told him.

"And a royal pain in the arse, too," Torgen added under his breath.

"You both need to evacuate and let me handle this," Micah told them.

Ginder shrugged. "We've already been exposed to one cylinder," she said, not moving.

Micah didn't waste time arguing; he strolled forward, his focus entirely on Pascal. *{You smell something?}*

Pascal abruptly stopped, his eyes zeroing in on an object on the cart. *{Might smell something,}* the big cat's whiskers arched. *{Might not. Need to scent.}*

He rose up onto powerful hind legs, his front paws settling onto the maglev cart. It began to shift under the new weight, and Pascal dug his claws into the soft material skirting the lower half. It tore with a loud ripping sound.

The event director shrieked once more, but fear of the sleek, darkly furred animal kept her at bay.

Micah left her for the two agents to handle while he steadied the cart for the cat. *{What do you smell?}* he asked.

{There.} Pascal pawed at a set of serving utensils, and one went flying.

{Careful!} Micah called out, but the cat ignored him, reaching for the one remaining on the cart.

{Here.} A massive paw landed on top of an ornate salad tong, its handle easily two centimeters in diameter at its end.

As Micah reached for it, he realized one of the catering staff was edging toward the exit. "Stop him!" he pointed, and Ginder unholstered her directed energy pistol.

A single shot, and the man was down.

Micah pulled the heavy metal utensil from between Pascal's paws and examined it carefully. Torgen joined him as he flipped the piece over in his hands.

"Look," the man said suddenly, pointing to where the heavy fork flared. "I'll bet the entire end piece is threaded."

Micah looked at it more closely. "I think you're right."

He looked up and saw that Ginder had the man cuffed. Three additional Protection Service agents had joined her.

He palmed the heavy piece. "Now would be a good time for the rest of you to evacuate." He nodded toward their captive. "See what you can get out of him, too, maybe?"

Torgen nodded, and he and Ginder rounded up the civilians in the corridor as the Coalition team led their captive down the hall.

Micah waited until the floor was cleared before kneeling and carefully unscrewing the tong's handle. Another cylinder slid into his palm, and he placed it in the clearsteel case alongside the first one.

{That's two. Any news from the base yet?} he asked Gabe. *{Any idea how many of these they've planted?}*

{Not yet. Keep searching. If they get any information out of the guy, the animals can reconnoiter and confirm.}

At least one of their sources was cooperating. The Coalition agents' questioning of the caterer who had tried to escape led to the discovery of two additional vials before the search was called off at the end of the day.

Several hours later, a weary Micah led Pascal out the front entrance and over to where Gabe and Sasha stood.

Foxtrot's team lead nodded to the small, furry bundle in his hands. "Looks like he's had all the excitement he can take for one day."

Micah looked down at Sneaky Pete. "Yeah, guess he's earned a nice meal and a good, long nap."

"Speaking of which," a voice behind him said, and Micah turned to see Rafe, flanked by Ell and Quinn. "I know a place that serves killer steaks, and they deliver to the base. How about we place an order, round up the team, and head back for that debrief?"

An hour later, the team had reconvened in the secured hangar back at Nimitz Base. They spent the meal dissecting the day, going over everything that had occurred.

Micah picked at the remains of his meal, his mind on the day's events. His head jerked up when Gabe's fork went clattering to his plate.

The man tossed his napkin aside in disgust. "This feels... off," he stated, his words echoing Micah's own thoughts.

"You're thinking the whole thing's too easy, aren't you," Rafe said.

Gabe lifted a shoulder in a half-shrug, his eyes distant. "Maybe, maybe not."

"But your instincts are pinging, aren't they," Ell said knowingly. "Mine are too."

They were interrupted by a notification from Task Force Blue's headquarters. When Gabe accepted it, Harper's voice came on the line.

{The director would like to speak with you,} she informed them. *{You guys have access to a holo?}*

Two minutes later, Duncan's face stared back at the team from the portable holo they'd set up.

"I've spoken to the team in charge of security for the event. Based on today's outcome, they believe the threat to have been neutralized, and plan to proceed with the summit as scheduled tomorrow."

Gabe looked back at the holo, his jaw working. "I can't help but feel this was some sort of decoy or diversion."

Ell's eyes tracked between Gabe and Cutter's image. "He's right, sir. It's a tactic Akkadians would use, too. They're a cagey lot."

Cutter grimaced. "The colonel and I agree with your assessment, but the Coalition does not. However, we think they're making a mistake, which is why we want you to continue to pursue all leads."

He looked at Micah. "I had to pull a few strings to get you admitted to the summit tomorrow, Captain. Officially, you'll be part of the Alliance Protective Detail. Unofficially, your job is to try to figure out what their next play is—if they have one. No joy on the animals, though."

Micah straightened abruptly. "Sir, they're the ones who found the canisters, not me."

Cutter's hand rose. "The official line is that they're not allowing them entry. Unofficially, someone named Torgen reached out to us and offered to help get them in under the radar. You know this guy?"

Micah nodded, relaxing back into his seat. "He was with us when Pete and Pascal found the cylinders."

"Ah," Cutter said. "You have a believer on your hands, then. Good. If you can get them in without being seen, you have my blessing."

Micah nodded, his gaze straying to Gabe's as the holo came to an end.

"That's it, then." The special agent stood, his gaze landing first on Sasha, then on Rafe. "You have teams that will patrol throughout the night?"

Both nodded.

"Very well." He turned to Micah. "You'll be inserting first thing in the morning, and I want you fresh. Get some rest."

SHADOW SHIP

Midway "Belly Band" Ring
Hawking Habitat

THE SHIP CAME in silently, its ultra-black coating and layers of high-performance electromagnetic shielding making its signature virtually nonexistent. Its pilot timed thrusters to match nearby ships when she could, and kept the bursts to a minimum when she couldn't.

She managed to slip in between the watchful eyes of those on patrol by dint of a bit of careful timing, swinging inside the arc of a shuttle that was docking just as it passed between her and the departing Novastrike.

The ship settled up against the ring at a maintenance hatch and used its own version of a Bravo Charlie to hack its way past Hawking's security and access the ring's interior.

Two figures slipped inside, the smaller of the two urging the other to work off the cramps that assailed his body from remaining in a single position for hours on end. A small backpack was hauled inside, its contents a simple change of clothing and a set of hacked ID tokens that had been acquired at great cost.

Thus, Citizen General Che Josza emerged into Alliance space clad in workman's coveralls, an assassin by his side.

{Come,} she murmured, a hand at his elbow. *{We have little time.}*

{Why did you bring us here, Dacina Zian? Are we once more to be found at the scene of a failed operation?} Che asked. *{If we are found out, we are dead. You know this. Better to have died in battle, on the station, than to be executed for treason back on Eridu.}*

Dacina shot him an inscrutable glance. *{All is not lost, my general. Trust me.}*

SUSPICIOUS FIGURE

DOWNTOWN MIDLAND
HAWKING HABITAT

GABE WATCHED FROM across the street as Micah entered the institute the next morning. The increased level of security surrounding the event should have eased his mind; instead, he couldn't shake the fear that they were being played somehow, and he was going to be just a hair too late to figure it out.

They'd received word that the ship carrying Asher Dent had been delayed. The vessel developed a small magnetic field flutter in its tokamak, so the delegates were being transferred to another ship. The arrival would put them a few hours behind, and Gabe couldn't help but wonder if this was the window of opportunity the Akkadians would use to strike.

As he walked, his eyes sought the locations for the sharpshooters they had hidden around the building. He saw a pair of Delta soldiers patrolling the perimeter, their drakeskin armor covered over by Alliance MP uniforms. He knew another pair was mixing in with the crowd behind the stanchions, their armor masked by civilian attire.

He and Sasha were dressed in discreet suits, a compromise they gauged would allow them to blend on either side of the stanchions.

Gabe kept one eye on his overlay, his other scanning the crowd as he strode along the far side of the institute, opposite its entrance. He felt like Pascal, all coiled energy, pacing back and forth, waiting for something to happen—what, he did not know.

Movement caught his eye a few blocks away. The figure's actions were furtive as it slid into an alleyway. The action was enough to trip his radar.

He took off after the person, reaching out to Ell and Sasha on a private channel. *{I may have spotted something,}* he sent, dropping a pin on the alleyway his target had disappeared into. *{Going to investigate.}*

{Take someone with you,} Sasha suggested. *{Risa is nearby. I'll send her your way.}*

She highlighted the woman's icon on the team's net.

{Tell her to hustle. I can't lose this guy.}

Gabe sped up, reaching the corner just in time to see the man descend a set of sunken stairs. The area map Ell had supplied indicated they led to a subterranean tunnel system.

{Ell, you said summit security decided the tunnel system was too far away to be a factor?} he asked.

{Yes. It's a few dozen meters away, through durasteel-laced ceramacrete. They figure the amount of work it would take to tunnel through all that would be high-profile, and ruled it out.} She sounded as if she were quoting from a report.

{This is your turf. Do you agree with that assessment?}

She paused. *{Not to sound trite, but where there's a will, there's a way. You and I have both seen enemies go to great lengths to accomplish their goals.}* She paused. *{Also, I don't think they were taking a bioweapon into consideration when they wrote that report. How large would a tunnel need to be to deploy a weapon microscopic in size?}*

{Agreed.}

He reached the stairs and, after a quick glance behind him to see if he could spot Risa, began to descend.

He failed to notice the figure that detached itself from a nearby wall. It waited for the Delta operator to pass after him, and then slipped from the shadows to trail behind.

* * *

Micah's frustration built as he paced the back of the crowded ballroom. The press of bodies was stifling, and he adjusted his suit's temperature for the third time since his arrival.

{This is ridiculous,} he reported. *{This room is crammed, and this is just the protective detail people. It's already next to impossible to get a search done in here. Once the brass arrives, you can forget about finding anything.}*

There was no way he'd bring the animals into this situation. Sneaky Pete would freak out, and Pascal would likely swipe at someone with unsheathed claws out of sheer annoyance.

{Unless we can clear the room, the animals are a no go,} he added. *{I'm not doing much good in here, either.}*

{Copy that. We'll keep the animals back with us,} Quinn replied.

Sasha's voice came on the line. *{I've been trying to convince summit security to give us one last shot at that room since Dent's ship is delayed, but no luck so far. Just do the best you can. Maybe we'll get lucky—or they'll slip up.}*

Micah could tell Foxtrot's leader didn't believe it any more than he did, but he sent her a two-click, and turned back to the ballroom with a sigh.

* * *

Ell listened in on the chatter from the combat net while her attention roamed the streets below. For this op, she'd once more donned the mantle she once wore as a Unit sniper.

She lay prone along the rooftop of the bank building across the street, her sniper rifle's smartlink system connected to her drakeskin's combat HUD. As her gaze swept those milling about on the street, her rifle's reticle automatically followed. If she stopped to examine a suspicious person, the weapon's sights locked onto them as well.

She hated using it, and had never done so when she'd been active duty, but she'd been NCIC now for two years, and the situation's sudden escalation hadn't allowed her the time to fully knock the rust off her skills.

Her gaze landed on the alleyway entrance down which Gabe had disappeared. She hadn't heard from him since he'd descended into the tunnels, and she was beginning to get worried.

Ell heard a noise behind her and rolled, bringing her weapon up, but there was nothing to see. The barrel of her rifle tracked the shadowed wall of the building that abutted the bank as she sought the source of the sound.

A shadow separated itself from the wall, and resolved into a figure Ell had not seen in two years: the Akkadian assassin she'd hunted halfway across Hawking, only to have her slip through the team's net.

The assassin stepped slowly forward, hands raised as if in surrender.

Ell knew better than to fall for that. Her finger moved toward her rifle's trigger.

Then the woman called out in a voice low and filled with urgency, "Sergeant Cyr, wait! I'm here to stop the bioweapon."

UNEXPECTED ALLY

Downtown Midland
Hawking Habitat

GABE'S TRIP DOWN into the tunnel wasn't proving to be fruitful. His quarry had disappeared.

He nodded toward one of several locked doors that lined the walls. "He must have gone through one of those," he told the Delta operator standing beside him.

The specialist looked as unhappy as he felt.

"We could go after him," Risa suggested. "I have a set of LockPiks on me."

"No," Gabe said. "Most of these probably lead to basements in nearby buildings, and we have no idea which one he used. I'm not willing to break into private property without good reason. He could be legit for all we know."

Risa nodded her understanding and fell into step with him as he called up the area map.

"According to this, we should be abeam the institute right...here." He came to a stop and studied the tunnel wall.

All he could see were a few small access ports.

He stepped up to the nearest one. Placing his palm on the panel's handle, he pressed it, only to find it locked.

He leaned back and motioned to Risa. "I'll take that LockPik now."

Risa strode forward and applied the nano package. The panel swung open, and they peered inside, but saw nothing more than a junction box for a sewage line.

"Well, shit," Risa muttered.

Gabe barked a short laugh. "Literally."

She shook her head and sealed the box up, and they headed back toward the surface.

As they walked, Gabe pulled out the cylinder that held his surveillance microdrones, and sent the command to recall the swarm.

He thought he'd found something when they first descended, and the drones had registered a brief hit almost immediately. Oddly, the blip seemed to come from behind him, not in front. He'd tasked a few of the drones to investigate further, but their scans showed nothing more than a tunnel rat scurrying into a crevice.

Marking it down as a sensor glitch, he'd sent them forward to join the rest.

Risa hadn't had any more luck with her drones than he'd had with his.

"Sorry this didn't pan out, sir," she said, her hand outstretched to catch her drone swarm as they dropped back into their container.

"Not your fault." Gabe shot one last thoughtful look at the tunnel's walls. On impulse, he reached out to Rafe.

{What can I do for you, Agent Alvarez?}

Gabe's hand stroked his jawline. *{Did I hear that your wife has something to do with Hawking's cylinder maintenance?}*

There was a startled note in Rafe's voice when he replied. *{Yeah, Cass is their chief engineer. You run into a maintenance problem down there?}*

The agent's eyes traveled the length of the tunnel. *{Not maintenance. I need her to do a scan. There's a subterranean tunnel a few blocks away from the institute. Protective Services dismissed it as a possible threat, but I'm not so sure about that.}*

{You want her to investigate?}

{I'd like her to scan the ceramacrete between the tunnel wall and the institute, see if she finds anything suspicious.}

Rafe grunted. *{You see anything that set off an internal alarm?}*

{Nothing concrete.}

Rafe laughed, and Gabe grimaced. *{Sorry. Bad pun.}*

{I'll get her right on it,} the major assured him. *{Might take a few hours, though, so don't be surprised if you don't hear back from either of us immediately.}*

{Understood.}

Gabe cut the connection and then, after a final look around, motioned up the stairs. "Come on. Let's get back topside."

* * *

Across the street, on the bank's roof, Ell kept the assassin centered in her reticle as she thought through how she wanted to handle this stalemate.

The matter was taken out of her hands as the woman began to slowly step forward.

"Don't. Move," Ell ground out, and the assassin instantly arrested her progress.

"Sergeant Elodie Cyr. *Special Agent* Cyr," the woman tried again. "We have been adversaries before, but in this, we are allies." She made a show of carefully and slowly pointing to the institute, her palms remaining open, her feet rooted to the spot. "You know there is a faction that has targeted the summit. You suspect there is a bioweapon. Those policing the event believe you have found all the cylinders... You have not."

Ell motioned the assassin away from the shadows. After a brief hesitation, the woman complied. When she stepped into

Hawking's bright sunlight, Ell could see that she was clad in Yinshen light armor, the Akkadian equivalent of drakeskin.

"If we really are on the same side and you truly do want to stop this bioweapon, then why are you jamming my wire?" Ell demanded.

The woman's eyes were dark and unreadable. "I needed time to speak with you, to present my case."

"Why me?"

The assassin cocked her head. "You are *zhídé de duìshǒu*. A worthy opponent."

Ell lifted her gaze from the reticle to look the woman in the eye. "You called me that when you were here before."

The assassin inclined her head ever so slightly. "It is an honor few receive."

"Why me?" she repeated.

"Your assistant, Quinn. He knew of the beads." The assassin turned her head, and the light caught her hair. Woven into the brown strands were beads of a similar color. They blended in, unnoticeable if one didn't know to look for them.

"So?"

Unaccountably, a quick smile graced the assassin's face, and her eyes flashed in amusement. "He is wrong on most counts. You will tell him I said so. But there is one thing he has correct about us. We live by a strict code of honor. There is no honor in a kill like the one planned here."

Ell's eyes narrowed. "I'm not buying it. You'll use any means necessary to carry out your orders. Akkadia killed fourteen thousand on that yacht—what's a few dozen more?"

The assassin's head jerked up. "What yacht?"

"Didn't you know? The seal on that last vial was broken before your people got hold of it. It ended up infecting a cruise ship. When your scientists altered it, it changed within those people, too. Fourteen thousand innocents, some of them children. All dead."

The assassin's expression didn't change, but Ell could feel a strange tension ripple through her.

"We did not know."

"It makes you no less culpable."

"It makes *them* no less culpable."

Ell cocked her head at that, but before she could ask what the woman meant, the assassin made a fluid motion with her hand.

Ell tensed, readying herself for an attack that never came. Instead, her wire came back to life.

"Contact your Quinn. Only him, please. Ask him if an Akkadian assassin would condone the use of a virus such as this to kill."

Ell pinged her assistant, relieved to hear his voice flood her mind.

{Yeah, boss? You need something?}

{Need an answer, quick. What would an Akkadian assassin think of this bioweapon? I mean, they use poisons, don't they?}

There was a brief silence.

{Boss? That's an odd question—}

{Just answer it.}

{Well, the way the virus works, it's not really the kind of weapon an assassin would use. It doesn't fit their profile,} he replied, but his voice sounded uncertain.

{Elaborate,} she ordered, and she could tell her tension had telegraphed itself to him by the way his own responses sped up.

{Yes, they use poisons, but they're quick ones.}

Quinn paused a beat, and when he came back, his voice sounded a bit out of breath.

{All their kills are fast—unless there's a blood vengeance at stake. Plus, they've never been into mass murder. They like to do things one on one, up close and personal.}

{Thanks.} Ell ended the comm and stared at the assassin, who was standing perfectly still, hands raised in the air, patiently awaiting the verdict. "Say I believe you. How do we stop this?"

The assassin let a data chip fall from her hand to the rooftop's ceramacrete surface. "The agents responsible will be at this location, but it must be your team that apprehends them, and you must bring Asher Dent as witness. He must see the treachery firsthand."

The assassin's eyes burned into hers. "If I see others, the deal is off. I trust only you and your people."

The silence stretched between them, and Ell risked another look down at the chip that lay on the ground at the woman's feet.

"Well, damn," she whispered after another long moment. "Now what the hell am I going to do with you?"

"You're going to tell her to lie face-down and place her hands behind her back so I can cuff her," a hard voice said. Quinn stepped through the roof's door, his weapon trained on the assassin.

A look almost of amusement crossed the woman's face. "Tell Agent Alvarez his instincts are correct. The attack will come from below."

In the next instant, she vanished.

BLINDSIDED

AKKADIAN SAFEHOUSE
MIDLAND
HAWKING HABITAT

THE TEAM THAT Colonel Marceau had assembled for the Hawking mission was made up of professionals handpicked from the Tèzhŏng's best operatives. They were holed up in a safehouse near the institute, and it was here that Dacina had led Che the night before.

Their middle-of-the-night arrival was noted immediately. Had it been anyone other than him, Che knew the trespassers would have been dispatched with quiet efficiency. Instead, the ostovar leading the group bowed them inside and quickly cleared a room for Che's private use.

It was now the morning of the planned attack. The ostovar in charge had just intercepted an update from a lookout and sought Che out to give his report. A lesser soldier trailed behind, carrying a ceremonial coffee set.

Che waved for the ostovar to join him and shot Dacina a

questioning look. She refused as always, preferring instead to stand guard at his back.

The lesser soldier began the prep work, setting out the materials for the ritual grind-and-pour. Tradition dictated that business not be conducted until the first sip had been properly addressed, and so they waited in silence for the soldier to complete the weaving of the water over the grinds.

With a bow, he placed the cups before his superiors, and awaited Che's sign.

The general waved his hand before the steaming cup on a slow inhale, scenting the bitter aroma. He nodded his approval, and the soldier gathered the ritual service. With another bow, he departed.

Che gestured to the ostovar's coffee, and the man accepted the invitation, his hand cupping the steam so that he might breathe the bean. The two completed their first sip, Che hiding a grimace as he nodded to the man.

He'd forgotten the hardship of deployment; the grind was never fresh, the flavor harsh.

"Please," Che said, "begin your report."

The ostovar wasted no time with pleasantries, jumping straight into the topic. "The canisters with the virus have been inserted into the channels we drilled through the tunnel. They are seated behind the ballroom's walls, and will remain dormant until activated."

Che felt the assassin shift behind him, and wondered about it. Her movements were always deliberate, detected only when she wanted them to be.

He made a mental note to ask her once the ostovar finished his update.

She had disappeared earlier that morning, no doubt to confirm for herself that their location was secure. His Dagger was nothing if not diligent.

To his utter shock, she spoke.

"And they will be enough to eliminate your target?" she asked in a low voice.

Surprise registered briefly on the other man's face, but at Che's nod, he answered the question.

"We will wait until the ballroom doors have been sealed, and everyone is seated. The virus should permeate the enclosed space within thirty minutes after the canisters are activated," the ostovar said. "At that point, Asher Dent, and everyone else attending the defense summit, will have inhaled enough of the virus for it to qualify as a lethal dose."

The assassin stepped back into the shadows and did not disturb Che or the ostovar any further.

Once the ritual coffee was complete, the ostovar took his leave. As the door closed behind him, Che rose and walked over to the window of the safehouse. He looked out upon the quiet side street that fronted the apartment building, his mind on Dacina's unusual behavior.

"Why did you speak up just now?" He turned from the window and saw that she'd glided silently toward him.

"It was necessary to protect you."

He frowned, not understanding, so he asked the other question on his mind.

"Where did you go this morning?"

Dacina stepped closer. "They know about the tunnel. They know there are additional cylinders."

Che shook his head. "It is not possible."

The assassin stared back at him, eyes gone dark. "I have been shadowing Marceau's team. One of them slipped and allowed himself to be seen entering the tunnel."

"Why did you not tell me of this sooner?"

"I waited to see what would come of it," she said evasively. "Our people are good, but so is the team they have sent in to oppose us."

She looked away momentarily and when her gaze returned to his, he saw an openness there that he hadn't seen on his Dagger's face since she was a young student.

"The minister's plan has failed," she declared softly. "I have seen with my own eyes the truth of this. But do not worry, my general. I have a plan."

Che's heartbeat began thundering in his ears as the implication of her words sank in—and then he realized the pounding he heard wasn't from within, but from the apartment door being breached.

The look in her eyes betrayed her lack of surprise.

"Dacina, what have you done?"

She pulled him from the window just before it shattered. He reached instinctively for his firearm as Alliance troops dropped in through the opening, but found his holster empty.

They trained their pistols on him, and Che registered with some shock that Dacina was offering up his, along with her arsenal, to the intruders. Never had he seen her willingly part with her arsenal.

{What I do, I do to save your life, my general.} Her words rang inside his head, filled with conviction. *{I would do it again a thousand times.}*

A woman stepped forward to accept the weapons from his Dagger, her eyes filled with a wary respect.

"Is the Citizen Representative here?" Dacina asked, and the woman nodded.

"He's out on the street, behind a protective barrier. Once the apartment's secure, we'll bring him in to meet with you."

Che fought to keep an impassive face as his Dagger inclined her head at the other woman's words.

"Very well, Agent Cyr. Please tell Representative Dent that Citizen General Josza awaits his pleasure. We have all the records he will need to prove Rin Zhou Enlai's treachery to the premier."

* * *

Gabe looked up as Ell and one of the Delta operators escorted a man and a woman down the stairs.

{This her?} he asked, and Ell gave a subtle nod.

{She told me the guy with her is Che Josza. Says he has

information to indict the minister of state security for this whole operation, and implied it was completely unsanctioned.}

Gabe grunted and stepped back as two Foxtrot soldiers hustled bound Akkadians out the door and into a waiting impound vehicle.

"That's the last of them, sir," Quinn said as he stepped from the back room.

"Thanks." Gabe gave the NCIC agent a nod, and then pinged Sasha. *{You're up. Bring Dent in.}*

The apartment door opened a second time to admit Asher Dent, the Coalition's minority leader. Sasha, flanked by two of her team carrying P-SCARs, stood just behind him.

The man came to a sudden halt when he laid eyes on the assassin. They narrowed when he registered the man beside her.

"Representative Dent," Gabe said, stepping forward. "This woman claims she knows of an Akkadian plot to release a bioweapon at the summit today."

Gabe saw shock appear on Dent's face at the news.

The man whipped his head around. "Is this true?" he asked the assassin.

{You know, that looked like genuine surprise,} Gabe heard Ell say thoughtfully.

Gabe murmured his agreement.

The assassin dipped her head. "It is true."

"By whose order?" Dent sounded angry.

He took a step toward the assassin, only to be stopped by two Delta operators.

The man turned to face Gabe. "You think I had something to do with this?"

"You could have been inoculated against the viral agent used in the attack," Gabe said mildly.

Fury blazed in Dent's eyes. "I would be just as dead as everyone else, I assure you." He turned back to the two Akkadians standing under guard. *"Who ordered this?"*

"Rin Zhou Enlai." The general's voice was quiet, but Gabe

could clearly hear the strain in it.

"And you expect me to believe this?" Dent scoffed, then turned to Gabe. "This man is Enlai's puppet."

The assassin stirred, and Gabe saw a flash of anger in her eyes.

"The citizen general is loyal to the premier," she insisted. "This action is not sanctioned, and General Josza has taken great care to document his findings. Why else would he send me to warn you?"

Dent's expression turned thoughtful. "You have evidence?"

"The *citizen general* has evidence," the assassin emphasized. "Obtained at great risk."

The general raised his hand, and the assassin subsided. "What evidence we have, we freely offer, Citizen Representative. The Dagger is correct. There is no honor in an attack such as this."

The man's expression was inscrutable, but something about the way he gestured for the assassin to present the evidence made him seem weary.

Gabe stepped forward as the assassin placed a data chip in Dent's hand.

"We still have a bioweapon to disarm, Mister Representative," Gabe said. "I assume you have no problem sharing that information with us?"

Dent turned to him. "No," he said after a moment. "Not at all."

The general cleared his throat. "You will also be wanting the trigger for the weapon. It is in a clearsteel case in the room behind me. Please. Handle it with great care."

Gabe turned and nodded to Quinn. The agent stepped forward with a unit to clone the chip, but before his hand closed about it, the room was rocked by a massive explosion that knocked everyone inside to their knees.

{Foxtrot Three, report!}

Sasha's voice shot across the combat net, but there was no answer.

She motioned to one of the soldiers who had accompanied

her, and the woman held her P-SCAR at the ready before triggering the door open.

She darted out, only to come up short.

{Impound vehicle's been hit. Foxtrot Three and Four are down. No sign of the Akkadians.}

TO SAVE HAWKING

OLYMPIC PARK, MIDLAND
HAWKING HABITAT

THE ASSASSIN'S SUDDEN appearance, and the data chip she'd left behind when she subsequently disappeared, had been enough to convince the summit's event coordinators to evacuate the building.

On the heels of that had come the news that *Wraith* had just transitioned from Scharnhorst space just outside Hawking's no-wake zone, and docked at the Belly Band. Thad had the task force and all four SRU teams on standby, ready to deploy.

Micah sent Jonathan the feed from the combat net, and they all watched as the raid on the Akkadian safehouse went down. Because they were monitoring *all* the feeds, they saw a lone Akkadian—one the raid had missed—step out from behind an adjacent building and throw the grenade at Foxtrot Three.

Micah was on his feet and running right before the rumble from the explosion several blocks away made itself heard. Another soldier's combat HUD showed the Akkadians overpowering the stunned operatives as the terrorists made good their escape.

{We're on our way down,} Thad's voice rumbled in his head.

{Copy. I'll meet you at the elevator.}

Micah pushed through the crowd until he found a familiar face within the Protective Services detail. He waved Ginder forward.

"That explosion—" she began.

"Akkadian terrorists," he told her. "Make sure that *no one* goes back in that building!" He pushed an address to her wire. "We need medical support. There are soldiers down at this location."

"Wait!" she called after him, but Micah just raised a hand as he raced through the city streets.

Thad's voice sounded on the combat net. *{Alvarez. Sitrep.}*

Micah listened with half an ear as Gabe updated them. He pushed past an ever-enlarging crowd as curious and panicked people streamed from nearby buildings, all wondering what had caused the big boom they'd just heard.

Gabe's voice came back onto the net. *{Our friendly Akkadian assassin tells us that the ostovar leading the terrorist cell had instructions to sow as much chaos as possible and then slip away in the confusion.}*

{Any idea what is meant by that?}

There was a pause.

{There is some disagreement,} Ell chimed in, *{but the assassin believes they'll head inland instead of to Portsmouth.}*

{Inland,} Thad repeated.

{That's habitat-speak for away from the end of the cylinder.}

Micah's attention sharpened at that. *{What kind of chaos could they create? What would be big enough to cover their retreat?}*

An alert came over Hawking's public net, overriding every other EM signal.

{Alert! Alert!} the recorded voice said. *{Olympic Park Forestry reports several fires. Repeat, there are several confirmed fire*

incidents at Olympic Park. Alert! Alert!}

A string of low curses sounded over the combat net.

*{That is **not** good, Thad,}* Ell's voice broke in.

{I know, cher.*}*

* * *

The crowd thinned, and Micah broke into a run. He could feel Jonathan's presence inside his head, a silent companion, standing by to jump in if needed.

{ETA two minutes,} Micah told Thad. *{You have any connections with the habitat's firefighters?}*

{Workin' on it.}

By the time he met up with Thad, Boone had commandeered a skimmer, and the three were loaded and waiting. Boone slid over so Micah could fly.

"Go here." Thad pushed coordinates to him, and Micah turned the small vessel's nose toward it.

They overflew a narrow finger-like lake that stretched beyond visual range across the habitat's cross-section.

Olympic Lake, Jonathan supplied. *Goes around the entire circumference.*

Beyond that, a long green strip of pastureland ran the length of the cylinder, bordered by acres and acres of woodland. Micah could see smoke billowing up from several places within the dense, forested hills.

Reports are coming in, Jonathan added. *They're saying the fires were started with flash-bangs.*

Thanks, bro. I'll update Thad.

A few minutes later, and Micah could see the coordinates led to a clearing where a steady stream of drones, shuttles, and Firestrikes were departing. Each vessel was laden with firefighters or fire retardant nano, or both.

He brought the skimmer down at the far end of the glade, where they would be out of the way of departing ships. Thad was out the door before the little vessel had fully stopped. Micah powered the skimmer down, set its parking brakes, and followed him out.

"What's the plan?" he asked.

"If we can tap into the drone feed, we might be able to spot those *couyon* before they get too far. And when I get my hands on them, I'm going to—"

"Wait in line while I kick the shit out of them," a new voice cut in.

The woman striding toward them was lean and hard-bitten. The fire chief had the look of someone used to fighting an enemy that had no compassion and took no nights off.

"You the one who asked for the feed?" she barked.

Thad nodded.

"I'm not re-tasking them for you under any circumstances until these fires are under control, so don't even ask."

"Understood."

She gave a curt nod, and with it came an invitation to join the Forestry Service's feed.

Micah flipped through the various drones that were aloft, familiarizing himself with the terrain from an aerial point of view. He accessed Hawking's pub net and pulled up a map of the forest, laying the drones' eyes overtop.

"Look at this." With a mental swipe, he added a line that showed the progression of the fires.

It wasn't perfect; the Akkadians must have had the backup plan in place prior to today. But if one discounted the first kilometer or so of forest land that ran along the lake, the later fires did seem to point in a particular direction.

"If we assume the assassin's not leading us astray, and they really are on their way to the south end, then—"

"Then we can project where they'll be." Thad looked thoughtful.

"I have three packages of surveillance microdrones on me," Boone said, patting his tactical vest. "If we can release them while we're in flight, we might be able to pinpoint their location."

The fire chief held up her hand. "I'm sorry. I can't let you overfly an active fire. It's too dangerous."

"We'll be—"

"Not to you," she interrupted. "To my firefighters."

Thad stood straight. "I work Air Attack on Ceriba, *cher*. I know my way around a fire."

The woman squinted at Thad. "And him?" She jabbed a thumb in Micah's direction.

"Best damn Firestrike pilot you'll ever see," Thad supplied.

She grunted and waved to a Firestrike sitting on the line. "Too bad you're not habitat-rated. Fire's one of the worst things that can happen inside Hawking, and I'm short a pilot."

Micah stared down at the Firestrike, noting the bladder attached to its belly, and an idea began to form.

He nodded to the large, rounded tank at the end of the small runway. "Is that filled with fire retardant nano?"

She nodded.

"The red goo? The kind that sticks to every surface and is impossible to get rid of?"

Thad looked over at him. "You got an idea, hoss?"

Micah jerked his chin toward the container at the end of the airstrip. "It'd be awful hard to hide, dressed in fire retardant red. Be even easier to find someone covered in it, especially if we add some trackers into the mix."

The woman shot him a stern look. "Not so fast. You aren't licensed. Flying to fire on a planet is not the same as flying inside a habitat. Our airspace is limited, and we have at least two plasma tubes that generate our magnetosphere cutting their way right across your flight path."

We could do it if we gestalt.

Oddly, Jonathan's words sounded closer. Micah understood why when he heard a second skimmer closing fast.

Thad looked up. "Good. About time."

Micah just managed to stop his jaw from falling open. *{It's one thing to break protocol when we're in two separate star systems. Does Valenti know about this?}*

The Marine shot him a sidelong look. "Hoss, when boots are on the ground during an op, I call the shots. And right now, we need to stop these *couyon* before they further endanger the hundreds of thousands of lives on this habitat."

Jonathan brought the skimmer down beside the first one, and Thad took the woman aside to negotiate their use of the Firestrike. Five minutes later, Thad was back. A second after that, Micah saw an access token for the Firestrike show up on his overlay.

"Load in. I want to be airborne in five."

Micah sat as pilot, Jonathan copilot. Thad and Boone were webbed into the flight engineer and gunner's cradles respectively, while Asha was clipped to a tether beside the Firestrike's port hatch.

Jonathan established a ship's net and brought the others into the connection.

{How much red goo you got in that bladder, hoss?} Thad asked as he came online.

Jonathan pulled up the specs. *{Five thousand liters.}*

The Marine grunted. *{That ought to be enough.}*

Micah brought the ship online, and with a light touch, pulled back on the controls, lifting the aircraft off the grass strip. From this elevation, they could see the thickening clouds of smoke.

Doesn't look good.

Micah felt the quick glance Jonathan sent his way. *Agreed.*

He looked down at the controls. The decommissioned Novastrike had the same SyntheticVision system all Navy ships used, though this one was years out of date.

Instantly, his vision became one with the ship. Below, it was filled with the greens of the tree crowns they skimmed. Above, it was the blue of the sky, mingled with clouds and smoke and the plasma tubes the fire chief had warned about.

Crashing into one of those would make for a very bad day.

Along with his expanded senses came the growing awareness of his other self. As Micah slid deeper into his merge with the ship, the clarity of his chiral connection became sharper, more defined, his every sense elevated.

Thad's voice intruded into their link. *{Air Attack is coordinating the fire runs and is on this frequency.}*

An icon blinked over the ship's net, and Micah tied the comm channel into the Firestrike, bringing its chatter in low under their own ship's net.

{They're running a corridor here and here. Swing to your left and give them a wide berth. Then head for these coordinates.}

The Marine dropped a pin on an area beyond the most recently reported fire, along the estimated track of the Akkadians.

{Copy,} Micah sent, and the Firestrike nosed over in that direction.

* * *

As they flew, Jonathan pulled up the feed from the fire drones. It showed the fires progressing at a rate of ten kilometers an hour, and in places where it broke out into the grasslands bordering the wooded terrain, the fires leapt ahead, racing closer to twenty kilometers an hour.

The first fire had been reported forty minutes ago. It was sobering to see the speed at which the flames spread.

Let's get these jokers tagged so we can help douse these flames, Jonathan sent.

You'll get no argument from me.

As they closed on Thad's mark, a proximity alert sounded. In an instant, Micah's world shrank to one of sensor returns, instrument panels, and control surfaces as he and Jonathan merged more fully with the ship.

He immediately noticed the difference in their connection. It was at once the same and yet infinitely deeper than their chiral connection, a melding of their two consciousnesses into one.

The fidelity was such that their enhanced senses immediately intuited the surface-to-air missile that had just been launched at them from below.

{{Incoming!}} the Jonathan/Micah merge shouted. *{{Brace for maneuvers!}}*

In the same instant and without conscious thought, the Micah/Jonathan merge side-slipped the Firestrike, and the missile rocketed past. It was a move no human could have replicated.

Boone was on it in an instant, the ship's lone operational laser slicing through the missile as it wobbled, seeking to acquire lock once again.

{{There they are,}} Jonathan/Micah sent, and a heat map showing five figures appeared on the main screens.

Micah/Jonathan sent the ship into a corkscrewing dive as another missile launched, pulling up just short of the trees' canopy.

There, a barrage of automatic fire pinged against the hull. The merge saw a telltale light indicating Asha had popped the port hatch. She and Thad were braced on either side, their P-SCARs aimed down at the terrain below, laying down covering fire.

{Can that big brain merge manage to drop our load on those yahoos without getting us blown out of the air?} Thad asked.

{Or we could just keep playing shoot-the-Firestrike until they run out of ammo,} Asha quipped.

You maneuver, I'll handle scan.

Micah wasn't sure where the thought originated from, him or Jonathan. At the moment, he didn't really care.

The merged man sank more deeply into the connection, and with it came a hyper-awareness of the hillside below. The part that was Jonathan brought up the image of a tree that had split down the middle. He rotated it and then tagged its base.

Five-second burst, the Jonathan merge sent.

Micah saw immediately what his other-self meant. The merge knew they were communicating too quickly for the team to follow, so they consciously slowed their thoughts long enough to transmit to Boone.

The sniper nodded his understanding, and the Micah part of the merge called out for the team to brace once more.

Will need to be fast, the Jonathan part warned.

May get bumpy, the Micah part agreed.

The merge turned the ship into a modified strafing run, and the Firestrike went hurtling down toward the Akkadians taking cover beneath the trees. At the last instant, with ground fire streaking up to meet them, Micah/Jonathan whipped the Firestrike up into a knife edge, the ship skidding between two trees as Boone let loose with the laser.

A series of well-placed short bursts toppled a tree on top of where the Akkadians huddled. They scattered, and the Firestrike kept pace, the Micah part of the merge slaloming between trees as the Jonathan part handled the release of red fire retardant.

A steady stream poured out, coating the terrorists. Immediately, the tracking nano Asha had injected into the bladder began to light up, and Thad connected with Gabe to pass along the trackers' telemetry.

Time slowed, and then resumed its normal march as Micah separated from the merge, his thoughts his own once more.

DEBRIEF

MERKI INSTITUTE
MIDLAND, HAWKING

THAD DROPPED MICAH off at the Merki Institute before he and the team headed back to Ceriba on *Wraith*. Three virologists from the CID's Hawking branch were waiting in full hazmat dress, and Torgen had spirited both Pascal and Sneaky Pete in through a side door. All that remained was for Micah and the chiral animals to run a sweep of the ballroom.

It was unfortunate the Akkadians had been clever enough to clad the canisters in mimetic material programmed to project its surroundings onto its own surface when probed. It would have been much more convenient to simply scan the walls to identify their locations.

The virologists had shot down Protective Services' suggestion that they cut into the composite sheeting to reveal the space behind the walls. Though everyone assumed the canisters were situated down low, where wall met floor, no one was willing to risk cutting into one if their intel was incorrect, or if they guessed wrong.

That left the low-tech animal detection method. Micah could tell the virologists weren't thrilled with this unorthodox approach.

Stepping into the ballroom, he set Sneaky Pete down by the nearest wall. "Okay guys, you know the drill."

Pascal began prowling the perimeter of the room, head lifted, lips pulled back slightly as he scented the air. The ferret alternated sniffing the wall and the baseboard, tiny hands patting the surfaces.

He came to a sudden stop. Patting the wall, he sent, *{Bad-sweet, here, here!}*

Micah bent to examine the wall, marking where Pete had laid his paw. He pulled a laser cutter from his pocket and began working it around the ceramacrete surface.

{Careful, sir,} one of the virologists called out.

Micah ignored him, prying the plug he'd etched from the wall. Behind it gleamed a dull metal shape. He reached in, extracting a cylinder that exactly matched the ones they'd found yesterday, and placed it in the glove box one of the scientists held open for him.

{That's one down, ten to go,} Micah sent.

{Nine,} he corrected, as Pascal called out that he'd found one, too.

{How's it going in there?} Rafe's voice intruded on the search inside Micah's head.

{Three down, seven to go,} Micah reported as he knelt by the next spot Pete indicated.

{Thought you might be interested to know we found an Akkadian shadow ship snugged up against one of the access ports on the backside of the Belly Band.}

Micah sat back on his heels. *{No shit? Is that how the assassin got here? Those ships aren't big enough to have carried the entire terrorist group. Don't only seat one, two at most?}*

{Yes, and Asher Dent is demanding that we hand it over. He and General Josza are heading back to Akkadia soon, and they'll be

towing it behind the diplomatic ship.}

Micah stood as Pascal swung his head over to look at him. *{Hope someone manages to get some good scans of it before we do that. What about the terrorists?}*

{Dent wants them extradited to Eridu, but we used the ship as a negotiation point. Since the attack occurred in Alliance space, they'll be tried here.}

Micah handed the next canister off to the virologists. *{I'm surprised the Coalition didn't want a piece of that.}*

{Oh, they did. They're sending representatives to Parliament House to contest the decision.}

{Popular guys,} Micah muttered, moving to the next spot where Pete was patting at the wall.

{It doesn't matter who doles out their punishment, I suppose, as long as it happens. Speaking of which, do you have any idea how long it took the Olympic Park firefighters to remove that red goo from the prisoners?} Rafe's voice shook with laughter.

{They're lucky we used the fire retardant on them, instead of the stuff that depletes oxygen. Don't think they would have survived that,} Micah retorted.

{Don't think the settled worlds would have missed them, if you had.} There was a pause. *{So, you're letting Yuki handle* Wraith *all by herself these days?}*

Micah had wondered if Rafe would ask about who was piloting the ship Micah normally flew. It felt odd to keep Rafe in the dark about his cloning, especially since Thad had just blatantly violated the ghosting mandate that kept him and Jonathan from appearing in public together.

Despite this fact, Micah knew he still didn't have clearance from Valenti to let Rafe in on the facts about Micah's existence. That meant he couldn't know Jonathan had been the one to fly the Helios to Hawking.

He phrased his response to Rafe's question with care.

{Well, after me, she knows Wraith *best—but she's not alone. Snell asked us to help train a new Shadow Recon pilot, a chief warrant, named Hyer. My guess is that Snell sent her along, and*

she's flying left seat.}

Contrary to conventional spacecraft, the Helios pilot sat right seat, and the copilot sat left.

{Ah, gotcha,} Rafe responded. *{Soon as you're done there, bring the menagerie and head to the hangar. Everyone's regrouping there.}*

{Will do.}

Rafe dropped the connection, and Micah did a swift count of the recovered canisters, realizing they'd completed the task while he and Rafe conversed.

"We'll take it from here, Captain. Thanks for your help," one of the virologists said.

Micah nodded and then turned to Pascal and Sneaky Pete. "Ready to go?" He reached down for the ferret as Pete patted his pants leg with a paw.

Pascal stropped Micah's legs, depositing black fur on his pants in the process. *{Yes. And that was a three-steak job.}*

"I'll be sure to pass that along to Colonel Valenti when we return. Did you do another sweep, just to make sure you didn't miss anything?"

The Ceriban hunting cat shot him a look from baleful green eyes. *{Cats don't miss.}*

"Humor me, and I'll get the colonel to throw in another steak."

Pascal huffed but obligingly strolled the perimeter one last time.

Micah knew the assassin's information reported ten canisters, but he preferred to 'trust but verify' before giving the heads-up to the other teams to come in and check their work. He knew none of the star nations' protective service details would be comfortable letting their charges in without first having eyes on, themselves.

The big cat's jaw dropped open as he scented the air. He padded slowly about the room, pausing occasionally, his head swiveling. After a complete circuit, he came to a stop once more before Micah.

{Was extra careful. Six steaks.}

* * *

Sam envied the team's ability to grab sleep wherever and whenever they could. The almost six-hour journey from the base where she'd been imprisoned had seemed interminable.

Then there had been the unexpected three-hour stopover at Hawking, where she and the Unit teams were told to lay low and not leave the ship. Thad had yet to explain what went down there, but when he returned, with Asha, Jonathan, and Boone trailing behind, the Marine had a satisfied look on his face.

Finally, they were on their way back to Ceriba.

The Marine's laugh broke into her reverie, and she looked over to meet his amused gaze.

"Bit impatient are you, *cher*?"

At her confused look, he pointed to her knee, which was bouncing as if it had a mind of its own.

She blew out a breath. "I'm… just ready to put this all behind me. And I have a lot to go over with Admiral Toland and the rest of the CID."

"Yeah, about that…."

His humor fled, and Sam felt herself tensing.

"There's been an incident. The colonel asked me to brief you before we landed."

He began to tell her about the thief who had stolen the vials, only to keep one for himself. As the tale unfolded, Sam felt horror grow within her. Alongside that horror came a terrible guilt.

* * *

Rafe had a ship waiting at the Belly Band to deliver Micah and the animals back to the hangar, where the team was waiting for them aboard a Nimitz Helios. Ell was there too, at Valenti's request.

Their return flight was a quiet one, everyone taking the time to decompress in their own way. They'd just landed back at Humbolt Base when Jonathan touched Micah's mind.

Welcome back, brother. Come by the hangar in a few? Need to show you something.

He didn't elaborate, but Micah could tell there was something more going on.

Be right there, soon as I drop off the animals.

He let the connection lapse as he parted ways with the team, Sneaky Pete in his arms and Pascal at his heels.

"You did good today," he murmured as he rubbed the ferret's head.

{No more bad-sweet?}

He laughed. "Nope, you got 'em all."

Harper was waiting in the bullpen to take the ferret off his hands.

"Director's on his way down in half an hour," Hyer called out from the situation room. "I got pizza. Oh, hey, boss! Welcome back."

"Did someone say pizza?" Gabe groaned as he settled into a chair.

Hyer grabbed a few slices and slapped the plate down in front of him.

"Thanks," he said around a huge bite.

She shrugged it off. "Just don't let the colonel see you eating it."

"Why's that?" Micah asked, grabbing a slice off Gabe's plate.

The agent scowled and moved it out of Micah's reach.

"Because a certain crew chief pulled double duty last time, and I found tomato sauce smeared all over the comm console the next morning," Valenti said as she entered.

Gabe sat up, but Valenti waved him back down.

"Eat your pizza." She dropped a set of plas sheets on the bullpen's center table. Tapping them with one finger, she nodded toward the SCIF. "Half an hour. Grab food, a shower, a nap. Just don't be late."

Heads nodded as the colonel exited the way she came.

Micah moved toward the lift. "I'm going down to the hangar. See you in a few."

Gabe, mouth full, made a shooing gesture with his free hand.

Down in the hangar bay, Micah stared up in frustration at *Wraith*'s lowered ramp.

What do you mean, I can't come up? She doesn't want to see me?

Inside was the one person he'd come down to see. The woman he'd been quietly worrying about for the past several days. If he hadn't been literally the only human in existence who could disarm those bioweapons without risk to himself, nothing would have kept him off the Proxima mission.

Jonathan's mental tone was sober. *She doesn't want to see anyone. She's blaming herself for the deaths on that yacht, bro.*

Micah dragged a frustrated hand through his hair. *It's not her damn fault. No one blames her.*

There was a pause.

Just give her a few minutes. Thad's with her. Let him work some of his Cajun magic on her.

Micah blew out a breath. *Yeah, okay.* He looked at his chrono. *We're due in the SCIF in twenty minutes.*

We'll be there.

Micah started to walk away, but couldn't bring himself to go far. He braced against *Wraith*'s hull and dropped his head as he let the events of the past several days wash over him.

Jonathan came out and tapped him twice on the shoulder with his fist. *Heads up, brother.*

Micah turned and met Thad's stare as he walked Sam down the ramp. His gaze dropped to the petite physicist who'd saved his life back on deGrasse. The utter defeat he saw in the eyes that stared dully out at the hangar tore at his heart.

He started toward her, but stumbled to a stop when Thad silently shook his head.

A connection sprang up from TF Blue's leader, and Micah accepted it.

{Don't think she can take much more right now, ami.}
{She's not responsible—}
{She doesn't see it that way. She made a deliberate choice to allow the Akkadian scientist to alter the virus in order to save the lives of three Alliance prisoners. In doing so, she killed everyone on that yacht.}

Thad's choice of words caused hot anger to flare in Micah.

{That's a pile of shit and you know it. She had no idea that vial had been compromised.}

Thad shook his head. *{You know it, and I know it. That's not how she sees it.}*

{Well, did you tell her she's wrong?}

Thad sent him a derisive look. *{Hoss, what you think I've been doing for the past half hour?}*

More than anything, Micah wanted to wrap Sam in his arms, erase the pain he saw etched on her face.

He approached as they waited in front of the lift. He didn't say a word as he came to a stop beside them, just reached over and grasped her hand.

Thad released her as they stepped inside, and Micah enveloped her in a hug. It was then that Sam began to cry.

{I'll update the colonel,} Thad said. *{I'd say take your time, but try not to take too long. Join us in the SCIF when she's ready.}*

Micah nodded and when the lift doors opened, he maneuvered Sam into one of the breakrooms, shutting the door behind them.

* * *

The SCIF doors opened to admit Micah and a subdued Sam. Micah caught Cutter studying his niece covertly as they entered, and knew the man would note her lowered head and red eyes.

His gaze shifted to Micah, who gave him a subtle nod.

Cutter relaxed slightly, understanding the unspoken message behind the nod. Sam was far from all right, but she was strong and she would recover.

Admiral Toland and Addy were the last to slip in, the doctor sparing Sam a quick glance before taking her seat.

The room was the same one Micah had entered just four days earlier, but it seemed as if a lifetime had passed since he had first heard the chiral material had been stolen.

Cutter nodded at Ell as the NCIC agent glanced curiously around. "Thank you for joining us, Agent Cyr."

She gave him a wry look. "I'd say it's a pleasure, but I have a feeling the reason you invited me here is to ask me questions I don't have answers to."

"Fair enough, but it's as good a place as any to begin. Not everyone can claim to have been visited by an Akkadian assassin—and survived to tell the tale," Cutter quipped. He straightened and looked around the table.

Micah knew it was a signal that the briefing was about to begin; he was proven correct when the director continued.

"Our analysts have pieced together a bit more information based on what Josza and our mysterious assassin provided. Apparently, the entire operation was indeed a rogue attempt by Rin Zhou Enlai to rid herself of a long-time adversary."

Cutter nodded to Harper, and the analyst took up the tale.

"Enlai is currently missing, presumed dead," she told them. "Asher Dent has been recalled home, and the premier has installed him as the new minister of state security."

"What of Elodie's new friends?" Thad queried.

"Che Josza landed on his feet. He's been promoted to Dent's right-hand man."

"And the assassin?" Micah asked, curious.

Harper shook her head. "She's faded into the woodwork again."

"She seems to have a very strong loyalty to the general," Gabe said.

"I think she also has a bit of a pragmatic streak. She told me you were close to figuring the whole thing out," Ell responded. Her gaze grew thoughtful. "She also said something about there not being any honor in this kind of weapon."

Micah shook his head. "Strange thing, hearing an Akkadian talking about honor."

"And the people we captured on that base?" Thad asked.

Cutter's smile turned predatory. "An-Yang is handling that. The news from our embassy is that Akkadia wants to extradite both Marceau and Bijin, but the Shang government has refused."

"Were they able to get anything more out of the base's mainframe?" Jonathan asked. "Will said whoever wiped it did a pretty thorough job."

Harper let out a breath. "Nothing. All we have is what General Josza's assassin copied for him."

"Speaking of Josza, did anyone else get the feeling that he was a bit shell-shocked through the entire takedown?" Micah asked.

Gabe nodded. "I think Ell's assassin might be the one who convinced Josza to out Rin Zhou in the first place."

Micah saw the former Unit sniper frown at Gabe's reference, but then Valenti tapped on her plas sheet, drawing his attention.

"We still have plenty of loose ends to tie up," the colonel reminded them. She nodded to Sam. "The sealed document, apparently from Assistant Director Sullivan, is one of them."

Sam looked up at that. "It passed the new AdS/CFT encryption. It's scientifically impossible to bypass that."

Harper frowned. "But not *humanly* impossible."

Thad leaned forward. "What do you mean?"

"Someone could have forced Sullivan's hand. Sullivan could be a mole. Sullivan could have thought he was approving the seal on one thing when it was actually another." Harper ticked off the options in rapid succession.

Sam thought about that for a moment, and then nodded.

Jonathan stirred and looked to Gabe. "What about the asshole we chased through the Planck Centre?"

Hyer spoke up for the first time. "Clint Janus has vanished. He's a no-show back at his job with Brower Biologics. The last readings I got off his spike had him on Leavitt Station, and then *poof.*" The chief warrant's hands expanded, miming an explosion. "He went totally off-grid."

"I'd say that puts paid to our suspicions that he's an Akkadian agent," Cutter murmured.

"Well, actually...." Hyer glanced at Harper, who nodded for her to continue. "I've been looking into that. I don't have everything to prove it just yet, but it looks like the weasel's related to Asher Dent, several generations back."

She looked over at Jonathan. "If that's the case, and he was on deGrasse, and he's now gone back to the dark side, I'm thinking it might be a very bad thing that he got a glimpse of you at the university, sir. Especially since he seemed to somehow realize that you were... well," she nodded at Micah, "not him."

Sam's head shot up. "Saw who?" She looked over at Jonathan.

Micah sat up. *He saw you, and you didn't think to mention it?*

Jonathan looked uncomfortable.

Valenti lifted a hand. "We've already had this discussion, and yes, it appears Janus suspects that the captains Case are chiral twins."

"Oh, this is bad," Sam breathed. "Very, very bad."

Micah put a hand on her shoulder and squeezed lightly. "It's okay," he began, but she shrugged him off.

"No, it's not." She turned to her uncle, her agitation plain. "This could turn into a major national threat."

He leaned forward, expression concerned. "In what way?"

Sam swallowed hard. "We have to assume that everything Marceau and Bijin did on that secret base was somehow transmitted back to Akkadia. Until now, Janus had no idea the chiral clones Stinton created survived. With the information I gave them on that base, they now know quantum entanglement with chiral pairs exists. If Janus takes this news with him back to Eridu? They have to suspect that it's possible to create the same thing in *living* pairs."

Her haunted gaze swept the table.

"You can't begin to imagine what they might do with that knowledge," she added quietly. "But I can."

A word from LL Richman

Thank you for reading *The Chiral Protocol.* I hope you enjoyed the adventure. Turn the page for a preview of the final book in the trilogy, *Chiral Justice.*

If you don't mind, please take a minute to leave a short review. Not only would it make this writer a very happy person, but your review also makes a real difference. It's an effective way you can help to keep this series going. The more reviews, the easier it is for new readers to find these tales!

Connecting with you as a reader is also one of the most rewarding things about writing. I'd like to invite you to join my VIP Reader's Group at bit.ly/biogenesiswar. There, you'll receive the latest news about new books and deals, plus receive free content and exclusive excerpts from upcoming books.

PREVIEW: CHIRAL JUSTICE

Power works by division, influence by multiplication.
Power, in other words, is a zero-sum game:
the more you share, the less you have.
Influence is a non-zero-sum game:
the more you share, the more you have.

~Rabbi Lord Jonathan Sacks

PART ONE: DISCOVERY

TURNING THE ASSET

PREMIER'S BRIEFING, STATE ASSEMBLY HOUSE
CENTRAL PREFECTURE, ERIDU
AKKADIAN EMPIRE (ALPHA CENTAURI A)

THE PRISONER'S HEAD hung forward, his restraints the only thing keeping him from collapsing into the slick of bodily fluids pooling at his feet. The lone patch of illumination was centered on the chair, yet something about the recording suggested a cavernous space extending into the darkness beyond.

Che Josza wasn't watching the holographically projected image; he was watching the man riveted to the frozen scene before him. Asher Dent, the new Akkadian premier.

"This is the Alliance's vice chief of Joint Operations?" asked Dent.

Che nodded. "Yes. Harris Carlisle."

The premier flashed him an approving look. "Excellent."

Asher Dent had made good use of the political fallout from a failed bioterror attack on the Coalition of Worlds' Defense Summit eighteen months earlier. Having been one of its targeted victims, he was the only Akkadian that the settled worlds knew was uninvolved with the attempt to decimate the intelligence community.

Dent had used that political currency to trade his seat as the Coalition's Minority Leader for the reins of the Akkadian Empire. The botched operation by the previous administration had provided the leverage needed to 'retire' the aging premier and lay the blame at his heir-apparent's feet.

It hadn't mattered that the premier's daughter had no prior knowledge of the failed attack. Asher Dent had an ironclad alibi; he would have died with all the rest had the viral agent not been neutralized in time.

With Dent at the helm, Akkadia enjoyed an unexpected leniency within the Coalition. Sanctions held against the Empire by other star nations were relaxed, tariffs lowered.

If they only knew, Che thought. *They have exchanged a sleeping fox for a ravenous wolf.*

Che's own appointment to the ministry had been whirlwind—and utterly undeserved. Had Asher Dent known the truth behind Che's own involvement in the bioterror attack, Che was certain he'd be resting with his ancestors now, instead of serving as Minister of State Security.

The previous minister—his superior, Rin Zhou Enlai—had been convicted of crimes against the state, and subsequently been made to disappear. She yet lived, but Che wondered if she wouldn't rather have been gifted an honorable death.

"How long before he breaks?"

The premier's question pulled Che back to the present. He glanced over to see if Dent had noticed his wandering attention, but the man's focus was entirely on the prisoner that Che's senior interrogator had recently acquired.

"I was told a single session secured his cooperation," Che replied.

Dent frowned at him. "Truly? That is... a surprise. Although..." The premier's fingers drummed a soft pattern on the table's surface as his attention returned to the man on the screen, "I would expect no less from the Tèzhŏng."

The Tèzhŏng was the elite intelligence branch of Akkadia's

state army. It had been Che's responsibility once upon a time to train these warriors, to forge them into the ultimate weapons of the State. Part of him wished for those days, simpler times with a singular goal, when the weight of duty was a much easier burden to bear.

But his words betrayed none of these thoughts, his voice calm and measured as he spoke. "You'll soon see why. It's evident the man never had any form of resistance training."

Dent's lip curled in a sneer of distaste. "Yet another reason our citizen soldiers are superior. The militaries of other star nations cannot compare."

"I'm not certain we should judge all of the Geminate Navy by this measuring stick," Che cautioned, thinking of the men and women they had encountered eighteen months ago inside the Hawking Habitat.

He inclined his head toward the holoscreen. "Carlisle may have served in their military, but he is no warrior. It is to our benefit that he managed to rise to the rank of general, but he is clearly a career bureaucrat, not a soldier. He cares more for recognition than respect. These political ambitions were what led us to choose him over other targets."

Dent shot him a look. "That just serves to prove our military superiority. He never would have made it to that position here on Eridu. Resistance training is mandatory for our soldiers. We both know this. You were the leader of the Junxun; I was one of your students."

Che lifted his coffee in wordless acknowledgment. "One of the best."

The recording began to play, though it was difficult to tell. The man being turned into an Akkadian agent remained slumped in his chair, pasty skin glowing in the harsh light. Carlisle was in his mid-fifties, with the telltale softening of a man who'd spent recent years behind a desk.

Footsteps sounded over the feed, echoing off the bare metal walls of the empty warehouse. A pair of boots stopped short of visual range, their toes just touching the pool of light surrounding the subject.

The man didn't stir.

"You know, I've always thought it strange how something as basic as clothing can so easily be used against a prisoner," Dent mused as he continued to watch the screen with rapt absorption. "Yet, time and again, I've seen how the simple act of stripping someone naked ends up being the chink in their armor."

"That's a fitting metaphor," Che agreed. "That thin layer of fabric is a sort of emotional shield. Removing it renders the subject bare in more ways than the obvious."

A sharp slapping sound broke through the conversation. Che saw a short leather crop in the hand of the agent in charge, and watched the restrained man flinch when it met her bare palm.

"So, General Carlisle." The woman addressed the man, her face hidden from the holorecorder's field of view. "Are you ready to cooperate now?"

The prisoner lifted his head, and Che saw blood dripping from the man's nose. He worked his mouth, and Che knew the man was gently probing his broken front teeth with his tongue.

He winced, then nodded once.

Che saw the agent lean forward, light haloing the back of her head.

"I can't hear you, sir. Will you cooperate?"

"Yessss." The word was hissed, pain-filled, as cold air slid over the tooth's jagged remains, firing the exposed nerves.

The woman gestured one of her men forward. The soldier crouched beside Carlisle and attached electrodes to the man. The prisoner jerked in his restraints, panicking. Promises of fealty quickly devolved to epithets, and then pleas for clemency.

Che looked away. He knew what would come next; he'd performed the same interrogation himself countless times as he'd risen through the ranks. Agents like these did the work for him now, removing him from the process and providing a thin film of deniability on the off chance they were discovered.

He used to find satisfaction in the hands-on brutality of the work. There was a gritty immediacy to it all that he could still vividly recall. The blood dripping from the man's face, mixed with the piss that he'd just voided, would give the air in the room a sour, slightly metallic smell, Che knew.

Now... it sickened him.

This next phase wasn't calculated to break the man; that had already been accomplished. It would serve to guarantee his compliance. The psychological effects of this particular brand of torture, targeting his most vulnerable core, would sear an important lesson into the man's brain. Memory of this event would serve as a reminder of the consequences he could expect, should he ever entertain the thought of refusing his handlers.

Actions like this were necessary, for once an asset was restored to his position behind enemy lines, the individual invariably fell into a false sense of security. The man would receive one final round of torture, conducted in his own office one week from now, specifically to disabuse him of that falsehood.

The interrogation team cleared the pool of light, and a stream of water hit the prisoner, hosing him down. In the next moment, Carlisle's body arched as an electrical stimulus poured into it. The military-grade carbyne nanofloss augmentation that ran through his skeleton served as an excellent conductor; the man's face twisted in a rictus of pain.

Blood foamed at Carlisle's mouth as he began to seize. From the corner of his eye, Che saw Dent lean forward, despite the fact that the drama playing out before them had occurred several hours earlier.

"Don't lose him," the premier growled, and Che heard Dent's words echoed by the agent on the other end.

Once released from the current, Carlisle slumped forward. The feed ended as operatives cut him loose and then dragged his unconscious form away.

"That session ended an hour ago. Carlisle has already been treated by medical," said Che as he shut off the recording and turned to face his premier. "He'll be returned from his 'vacation' this evening, and will resume his duties with the Geminate Alliance tomorrow."

"Very good. How long after that before we enact Obelus?" the premier asked. He stood, signaling to Che that his time was up.

Che followed the man's lead. "It shouldn't be long. Our people are moving into position now."

Dent nodded and started for the door, but then came to a stop at the minister's next words.

"Carlisle isn't the holdup. It's Clint Janus."

The premier turned, his expression icy with displeasure. "I understood he'd successfully cloned a working proof of concept. I was told that our assets inside the Alliance made the swap a few days ago, and that the clone is already in position."

"He is—or rather, he was." Che worked hard to keep his expression blank. "Janus has allowed the pawn to slip its leash."

A STRANGER'S PLEA

THE HILL – FINE DINING DISTRICT
DOWNTOWN MONTPELIER, CERIBA

MICAH CASE PAUSED in the middle of the crowded Montpelier district known as The Hill and inhaled deeply as a savory smell teased at his nose. The dark-haired Shadow Recon pilot looked around, but pinpointing the origin of the mouth-watering aroma was an impossible feat. He was literally surrounded by bistros and curry houses, marisquerías and trattorias.

The dining district, located in a town just south of the capital city of St. Clair Township, was a popular destination, as evidenced by the crush of people flowing past him.

He inhaled once more, and his stomach growled. That earned him a light elbow jab from his companion.

"Don't they feed you up on that base, Captain?"

The warmth in her voice danced through his mind, a bright glow dispelling the darkness that had sunk its claws into his soul at the end of his last mission.

The sight of two bodybags carried by the remaining four members of the special forces team was seared into his brain. They'd come in hot, both Nina and Will, *Wraith*'s gunner and flight engineer, had stood at the end of the Helios's ramp, laying covering fire inside the cargo bay of the derelict space station as the men and women of SRU Team Six raced toward them.

Micah had had his own troubles, fending off two technicals—improvised fighting vessels the smugglers had launched against them. Still, he'd kept one eye on the team's approach, saw the frag grenade the enemy had fired, watched Tank launch himself toward it to shield the others.

Six inserted. Three retrieved.

Unacceptable.

A hand tapped him on the sleeve. He looked down, his blue eyes meeting laughing green ones.

"Don't they feed you up there?" Samantha Travis repeated. She tugged lightly on his arm, silently encouraging him to resume their stroll.

Micah took the hint and began maneuvering them once more through the dinnertime crowd. He made an effort to shake his morbid thoughts, to stay in the present with the woman who held his heart.

"There's food and then there's culinary artistry." He strove to inject a lightheartedness he didn't yet feel into his tone as he spun his finger around to indicate the various eateries. "Trust me. What the Navy serves and what I'm smelling here? Not even close."

"Well, we are surrounded by the best that Montpelier has to offer. I wonder..." Her brows arched in playful challenge. "You think that might be why this area's also known as Restaurant Row?"

"Watch it, wiseass."

Sam bumped her hip against his as he snaked a hand around her waist.

"That's *Doctor* Wiseass to you."

Micah grinned, and he felt the last of the chill in his soul retreat under the shine of Sam's exuberant spirit.

It felt good to be planetside for a change, with Sam by his side.

The light from the white dwarf above Ceriba kissed Sam's

hair, the strands glinting gold in the waning light. His fingers twitched, and he resisted the urge to tuck an errant strand behind her ear.

Instead, he tugged her closer, and she settled comfortably against him as he let the murmur of voices from the crowded street wash over him. The sounds mingled with the chirping of the birds flitting through the trees at a nearby park as they meandered through the small borough.

They'd both been busy of late, him flying special forces teams to the Badlands, her with a time-sensitive chiral experiment. The moment he'd been cut loose, he'd pinged Sam to see if she could get away for the evening. She'd eagerly accepted.

A small street vendor cart filled with shawarma caught his eye, the meat's juices making quiet sizzling sounds as spatters of the liquid dripped onto the searing hot plate below.

Reaching for Sam's elbow, he pulled her to a stop. "Come on."

He nudged her toward the street vendor and extended a token, silently pointing to one of the skewers of meat.

"We're on our way to dinner. You'll ruin your appetite," she scolded.

The vendor smiled and handed it over, despite Sam's protest.

Micah lifted one eyebrow as he regarded her. "Woman, have you seen me eat? Besides, our reservations aren't for another hour, and you know that place is always jam-packed. We'll be lucky if I survive that long."

Sam rolled her eyes, but didn't refuse the skewer of meat he held out to her, pulling the topmost piece off and popping it past her lips.

Mouth full, she switched to a more private method of communication. *{Sometimes, I find myself forgetting that none of this food will sustain your chiral body.}*

Micah shot her a sardonic look. *{I don't. Can't afford to.}*

When he saw her stricken expression, he saluted her with his skewer and sent a reassuring smile. *{It does come with a few perks, you know. I can't get sick... and I can eat all I want and not have to worry about packing on the pounds.}* To illustrate his point, he tossed a piece of the spicy meat into his mouth.

The smells hadn't done it justice; the savory flavor that coated his tongue was sheer heaven. Sam agreed, if her moan of pleasure was any indication.

He inclined his head toward the nearby park. "Come on. Let's get out of the crowd and go enjoy these in peace."

The park incorporated the same tasteful architectural lines as The Hill. Surrounded by a colonnade, its entrance was a graceful, arched trellis, tumbling with a waterfall of colorful flowers. A park bench sat just inside, and he angled toward it, their entry briefly interrupting the birdsong.

"How's work coming along?" he asked, sparing Sam a glance once they'd settled onto the bench.

She popped another piece of meat into her mouth and chewed thoughtfully, waggling a flattened palm back and forth before letting it drop.

{Eh. We're taking it slow, trying different methodologies as we work our way up from simple organisms. Creating quantum-entangled chiral clones of complex, multi-celled organisms like a Trichoplax is much more involved than when I was working with molecular compounds.}

{A trick-o-what?} Micah slid the last chunk of meat off his skewer with some regret, wishing he'd purchased more than one.

Sam sent him an image of something that looked a bit like a disk-shaped blob with fuzzy tendrils as she licked the juices from her fingers. *{A simple sea animal. It only has six cell types, which is why we chose it.}* She brushed her hair from her face with the back of her hand as a light breeze stirred her short, blonde locks. *{By comparison, your basic fruit fly has fifty cell types. Humans have hundreds.}*

Micah grunted as he processed her words. He wadded up the napkin he'd used to wipe his fingers, and then looked around for a recycling receptacle. "Someone needs to uninvent those things."

{What? Chiral clones?}

"No. Fruit Flies."

That earned him a laugh. She dropped her napkin-wrapped skewer into his waiting hand, and rose to follow as he walked toward the exit.

{Sometimes the quantum entanglement between the two chirally-paired mirror organisms is complete,} she continued. *{But sometimes, it's not there at all.}*

The puzzlement in her tone had him glancing sharply at her as they reentered the flow of the crowd.

He considered his words carefully before responding, keeping their conversation a mental one, more for security reasons than efficiency, now that they'd finished their snack.

{It's... difficult to wrap my head around how slowly you're progressing when I think about—}

She cut in, her words scathing.

{About what that sorry excuse for a chief scientist did to you back on deGrasse? I suppose you could say he 'got lucky' when he chirally cloned Jonathan and brought you into this universe. But the fact remains he experimented on you without permission.}

She turned to face him, heedless of the press of the crowd, her eyes snapping.

{That was more than unethical. It broke every rule in the book. There's no possible way to precisely duplicate the methods he used. We may have his research notes, but his lab perished when deGrasse blew up, and we lost a lot in that explosion.}

She turned and resumed walking. *{I won't pretend the mental connection you and Jonathan share due to your quantum entanglement isn't unique and worth studying. But we sure as hell aren't going to skip the important interim steps to get there, like he did. And as a reminder, we're doing it so we can better understand and assist you, **not** so we can make more of you.}*

He pulled her to a stop, laid his hands on her shoulders, and turned her to face him. "I know that, Sam. I'd never think otherwise."

She stared back for a beat, and then her gaze softened. She tucked her hand through his arm, and they resumed walking.

"Thanks. What he did was horrid," she added in a soft voice, "but I can't say I'm sorry, when it brought me you."

They walked in silence for a while.

A small cluster of swantail flitters erupted from a nearby bush as they passed, catching his attention. The colorful butterflies were native to his home planet of Beryl; they brought back warm memories of family picnics from when he was a child.

"I didn't know you had these on Ceriba," he said, craning his neck to follow their flight.

"What, the flitters?" Sam followed his gaze. "I remember a newsnet cast about it several years back. They migrate in large swarms, don't they?"

"Yeah, it's called a kaleidoscope, I think. The southern migration's a pretty big deal back home."

Sam made a noise of agreement. "Well, if I remember correctly, they were having some trouble with the pollinators here on Ceriba, so the conservatory decided to introduce them into the ecosystem to help balance it a bit better."

The flitters disappeared behind one of the buildings, and Micah turned his attention back to the street. "Reminds me of home."

He saw Sam slide a glance his way. "You don't talk about your homeworld much."

Micah hesitated, and then lifted his shoulder in a half shrug. "Jonathan and I don't go back as much as we used to prior to Luyten's Star. Kind of awkward, not being able to tell them there are two of us now."

"Understandable," she murmured after a moment.

Micah's mouth tipped up into a wry grin. "When Mom complains about us not visiting, we blame your uncle. Since the... incident... at Luyten's Star coincided with the creation of Task Force Blue, he makes a convenient scapegoat."

Sam laughed. "Fair enough."

The clink of glass and the murmur of patrons reached Micah's ears as they passed by an open-air café. The chatter reminded him of the two people who would be joining them at their destination.

"Hey, you sure you're okay with Thad and Ell joining us for dinner?" he asked Sam. "He kind of invited himself along tonight."

Thaddeus Severance was the commander of Task Force Blue, and an imposing man. A former active-duty Marine turned special forces soldier, Thad could make hardened veterans quail in their boots.

Despite his foreboding aura, the warrior had a quick wit and a ready smile that flashed white against his ebony face for those he counted as friend, and that included Micah. He trusted Thad to have his six, no matter what, when, or where.

Ell—Elodie Cyr—was a bit harder to read, but no less trustworthy despite that fact. She'd been a sniper on Thad's team for many years, until an injury forced her down a different career path. Now a special agent for the Navy's Criminal Investigation Command, Ell had been instrumental in the takedown of the Akkadian terrorists that had targeted the Defense Summit on Hawking eighteen months ago.

A dimple formed in Sam's cheek at Micah's mention of Thad and Ell.

"I think Mister Tall, Dark, and Dangerous might have a thing for...." Sam's voice trailed off as she sought the words to describe the woman Thad was bringing along with him.

"Small, silent, and deadly?"

Micah's comment earned him another ripple of laughter.

"Accurate." She lifted a finger, one eye narrowing in contemplation. "Elodie Cyr is one scary lady when she wants to be."

"Never known a sniper who wasn't a bit scary. Boone's the same way," he reminded her.

Sam dropped her finger, tilting her head at his mention of the task force's sniper. She shot him an appraising look. "True. I'm sure you've known your share of them, too. You flew recon on missions for how many years before the task force was commissioned?"

Micah smiled, but didn't comment.

After a beat, she let it go, and he silently thanked her for it. Some things he was cleared to discuss with her; others, he was not.

As the white dwarf gave up its last light and sank behind a mountain range in the distance, Micah drew Sam closer, noticing her shivering in the breeze.

After a few more steps, she came to a stop, pointing across the busy street. "There it is."

Micah spotted a marquee hanging above an establishment's entrance and read the name off the tasteful, holographically-extruded sign. "The Rieger. Never heard of it."

"It's fairly new. I hear they have some pretty good handmade pastas. Someone back at the CID told me we needed to try their signature Hanna cocktails, too."

"Cocktails? You mean, like, sweet drinks with tiny umbrellas?" He shook his head. "Nah. Think I'll leave those fancy things to you ladies."

Sam rolled her eyes. "Got news for you, Micah Case. A Hanna cocktail's what they used to call a 'man's drink,' made from liquors the Reiger's owners distill themselves."

He didn't miss the heavy sarcasm she laid on the phrase 'man's drink,' and a grin tugged at his lips. "Oh yeah? Now you're talking."

Sam ignored him as she began to tick them off. "There's the Sage Advice, the Smokin' Choke, the Settle Down, and my favorite, Cortez the Killer. Mezcal, tequila, mango, a healthy dose of habanero, and a little bit of lime." She shot him a look he knew better than to cross. "That sound like a girly drink to you?"

He held up his hands. "Ma'am, no, ma'am."

They waited with the crowd for traffic to clear and then crossed the street. Just as they stepped up onto the sidewalk, Micah heard someone shout his name.

"Captain Case!"

Micah turned, and the crowd parted just enough for him to

see a man rapidly approaching. He tensed, reaching out instinctively to his mirror twin.

Brother....

Trouble? The response came instantly, the connection as clear as if his other self were standing beside him instead of at his post, up at the base.

Don't know. Do we know who this is?

He sent Jonathan a mental image of the man as he jolted to a stop before them. The stranger was young, of average height and looked vaguely familiar. He seemed unusually anxious, his eyes shifting left and right as if seeking danger in those milling about.

"Captain Case," the man repeated, stepping close and lowering his voice. "Doctor Travis. You have to help. Please, you're the only ones who can."

Sam's eyes widened, and she inhaled sharply at the stranger's use of her name. *{How does he know who we—}*

Her words cut off abruptly as a bloody trail grazed the man's forehead.

The stranger's body jerked in reaction, and he staggered back a step, bumping into the people nearest him. A woman turned, her irritation over being jostled morphing into horror as two more holes silently appeared, one in his abdomen, the final one near his heart.

She screamed and quickly backed away as he fell to the ground. "He's been shot! Somebody help!"

Cries of *"Shooter!"* and *"Run!"* mingled with the press of bodies as people nearby panicked, stampeding to get away from the unseen threat.

Micah grabbed Sam and shoved her against the recessed alcove of the restaurant's entrance, urging her into a crouch.

"Stay down!" he yelled over the shouts of the crowd. At the same time, he initiated a combat net, the mental connection snapping into place. *{Shots fired, downtown Montpelier!}*

His words were sent simultaneously to all the members of Task Force Blue.

{We're two blocks out. Ell's going high.} Thad's mental voice

sliced through Micah's mind.

{I need a visual,} the former sniper's voice cut in, slightly breathless. *{Can you give me access to your optics?}*

In lieu of response, Micah patched Ell into his wire.

{Good. Let me see the vic.}

Micah set his eyes on the young man bleeding out, three meters away. *{He was facing us. It was odd, not the standard two to the chest, one to the head.}* He added, *{If I didn't know better, I'd say this was done by an amateur, but from some distance away.}*

{Reverse angle of street,} Ell instructed. *{Just a quick look, and then get back under cover.}*

Based on the placement of the shots, Micah had a good idea of the shooter's location. From where he crouched over Sam, he let his gaze sweep the street, his eyes darting from rooftop to rooftop, looking for the shooter—but he saw nothing.

{Got it. Thanks.}

Thad's voice returned, barking out a quick, *{Sitrep!}*

Sam tried to rise to get to the fallen stranger, but Micah pulled her back, forcing her to remain still.

"Don't move," he ground out, when she resisted his hand.

"Micah, I don't think there's a shooter. Not one here locally, at least."

"Holes don't just mysteriously drill themselves into a person's head and chest," he countered.

"They could, under certain conditions."

Her words made no sense, but in the heat of the moment, Micah didn't try to parse their meaning.

He continued to cover Sam with his own body as he relayed what he could see of the street in staccato bursts of information. Something about what she'd said snagged his attention, though, and he found his gaze returning to the downed man.

She's right. We didn't hear any gunshots.

The fallen man was, surprisingly, still alive, though Micah could see the life draining from him by the second. So could Sam, and she redoubled her efforts to get free, her doctor's instincts and medical training demanding she go to him and treat his wounds.

When the man met Micah's eyes, he gasped a word that speared Micah with a cold terror.

"Chiral." Then his gaze sought Sam's with a pleading intensity. "Prisoner." He took a shuddering breath, blood bubbling from between his lips. "Stop them...."

The man's eyes glazed over, fixed in the distance.

"Dammit, Micah, let me *go*." Sam elbowed him in the solar plexus, attempting once more to get to the fatally wounded man. "Micah, I'm telling you, the only danger is to that poor man!"

"Want to elaborate on that a bit, *cher*?"

Sam jerked as a deep bass rumble sounded above them.

Thad had arrived.

An ebony hand reached down; Sam grasped it, and the Marine pulled her to her feet. Micah saw an icon flash over his wire and realized Thad had added Sam to the team's combat channel.

{Ell doesn't think anyone's out there. She's checked out the most likely spots, but the single microdrone we had between us isn't showing any residual IR heat signature.}

Sam shot Micah an impatient look and moved toward the man lying on the sidewalk, three meters away. *{Told you so. I need to get to him before someone tries to steal his body or alter the evidence.}*

{She has a point.} Thad slanted a meaningful look at the once-empty street. After several minutes had passed without additional bullets fired, a few brave souls were beginning to stir, morbid curiosity overcoming their fear. Some were on an intercept with the body.

If they wanted to keep a lid on this incident, they'd have to move fast.

One look at Sam's expression suggested she was on her own communications network. If Micah had to guess, it was with people back at the CID.

Thad moved to follow Sam. "We need to keep everyone back.

Damn, I hate that we're out here with no gear."

Micah felt much the same. This was supposed to be a night off; no one had kitted up for that.

Ell showed up, and something unspoken passed between her and Thad. The former sniper nodded and then stepped forward to flash her NCIC special agent's badge at those in the restaurant, assuring them that things were under control.

{Local LEOs are going to be all over this, and that's pissin' me off, hoss,} the Marine admitted as he lifted a hand and shot a warning look at an especially bold bystander. *{You say he mentioned you by name?}*

"Yeah," Micah replied. "Me and Sam both."

Sam looked up from her cursory exam. Her eyes slid to the people standing in a loose semicircle around them before returning to him and Thad. "I need to get the body into stasis. I've contacted Admiral Toland, and she's dispatched a critical care team; they're on their way."

He nodded. "Copy that."

Admiral Amara Toland was the officer in charge of the Navy's chiral project, based at the CID's main offices here in Montpelier.

It wasn't long before Micah heard a shuttle coming in on a fast intercept. As it came to a stop, medical personnel spilled out, two of them pushing a stasis pod between them.

Seconds later, the strobe of flashing lights signaled the arrival of two police cruisers converging on the street. Thad waved Ell toward them.

{That badge of hers is coming in handy tonight,} Micah commented.

Thad grunted as he stopped another curiosity-seeker from trying to get a better look at the victim. *{By the time this wraps up, I'm going to owe that woman a lot more than a nice dinner.}*

The medics stopped in front of Sam, and she beckoned impatiently to one of them. He handed her the medical bracer he had tucked under one arm. Shoving her hand into the gauntlet, Sam's fingers danced over its controls as she brought the unit to life.

The medics staffing the stasis pod bent to lift the body, but she snapped a quick command, halting them so she could conduct her exam. The pod hummed softly, hovering between them while the two medics waited.

Sam's gauntleted hand traveled from the entry wound in the man's forehead to the ones in his chest, the bracer cataloguing each injury as she went. She ended the exam by placing her hand against the man's neck. After a second, she nodded and motioned the medics forward.

They lifted the body into the unit and sealed the lid. Micah could just make out a faint blue glow emanating from the pod when the unit cycled on, signaling the body had entered stasis.

The crowd that had stuck around to gawk dissipated quickly once the body had been removed.

As the medics piled back into the shuttle and Sam retraced her steps back to them, Thad motioned Micah closer.

"What in hell went down here?" he asked in a low voice.

Micah scrubbed a hand through his hair. "Damned if I know. We'd just crossed the street when the man ran up to us. He called us by name, but before he could say anything else, he was shot. That's about it—except projectiles that cause wounds like his usually travel fast. We should have heard a sonic crack, and we didn't."

Thad nodded. "That tracks with what Ell found—or rather, *didn't* find. No evidence of a shooter."

"If there was no shooter, then how'd he die?" Micah didn't try to hide the skepticism in his voice.

"I can think of one way." Sam's gaze was troubled, and Micah could see her mind working, analyzing. "Right before he died, the man said something... something that might explain it."

"What was it, *cher*?"

She looked Thad in the eye. "Chiral."

Want updates?

Join my reader's group to hear news of upcoming books, behind-the-scenes glimpses of life with a physicist, and views from the cockpit. And cats, because the feline overlords insist. Sign up at bit.ly/biogenesiswar.

TERMINOLOGY

ActiveFiber Coating – a coating used to layer the bulkheads of ships and space stations. It has self-healing properties, similar to self-cleaning fabrics used for shipsuits, and its structure can be rearranged with simple programming. The fiber is infused with nanobots, which can absorb contaminants within an area, break it down into its constituent parts, and reuse the material.

The Bulk – the many layers, or branes, that comprise hyperspace, the area of extradimensional space outside the dimension our universe inhabits.

Calabi-Yau Gate – This method of folding space is powered by siphoning dark matter out of a Ricci-flat manifold. The manifold, a special curvature within the Bulk, is a place where the vacuum energy of space can be accessed. Once converted to Casimir energy, it is then used to bend the Bulk, allowing for instantaneous travel from one location in normal spacetime to another, regardless of distance. The amount of Casimir energy differs, based on the amount and direction of the bend.

Colloid Nano – Colloids are extremely tiny insoluble particles that are so light, they remain suspended in air. When grafted onto nano, colloid nano clouds can be released.

Thanks to brownian motion, the force of the particles in the air around them is greater than the force of gravity attempting to pull them down, therefore they float and are susceptible to the activity of air currents.

Colloidene Nano – A colloidene is made from a colloid particle, but formed just like single-layer graphene. Patterned in a honeycomb lattice, it employs some of the click-assembly techniques used in chemistry.

Pre-loaded common codes, or 'bricks', give nano creation a jump-start. The result is a nanobot, programmed to rapidly alter existing nano to whatever the person controlling it needs it to be.

Crowbars and LockPiks – Both are lock-picking programs, although LockPiks are covert, where Crowbars are overt.

A Crowbar is a brute-force version that borrows click-assembly techniques used in chemistry to rapidly alter the properties of existing nanolocks. Pre-loaded common codes, or 'bricks', give the Crowbar a jump-start, pushing a cascade failure into the lock that cracks it wide open. In the process, it renders the lock useless.

In contrast, a LockPik is a slower and more subtle app that works to subvert a lock while maintaining its program integrity so that it can be reset back to original specs after the LockPik's use

DBCs – A digital-to-biological converter capable of printing complex, synthetic, biological material from detailed molecular diagrams transmitted to it.

DUET Wires (aka "the wire") – DUET is a little-used acronym for communication nanocircuitry implanted in the brain.

DUET stands for Direct Uplink Evanescent Telecom. Much to the dismay of the corporation that invented the tech, that name never took hold. Commonly known simply as 'the wire,' a DUET implant must wait until the brain has reached a certain development level. At that point, a web of nanoscale tendrils is deployed at critical spaces within the brain: information inputs at dendrites, and data outputs at synaptic terminals.

Evanescent (E-V) Nanocircuitry – E-V nanocircuitry is the foundation upon which the DUET system was launched. The core communication unit embedded in the brain makes use of the optical phenomenon of evanescent modes with imaginary wave numbers and a poynting vector of zero to achieve the mathematical equivalent of quantum tunneling for the instantaneous transmission of information.

Ford-Svaiter nodes – F-S nodes use the concept of focusing vacuum fluctuations with parabolic mirrors to induce a quantized field wherein evanescent nanocircuitry can be used to establish instantaneous communication. An F-S node is encased inside a Starshot Buoy. Buoys are seeded throughout a star system in a pattern known as the Starshot Constellation. All inhabited star systems have deployed Constellations.

MAC –Magic-Angle Carbyne is the strongest material known in the 25th century. It is fashioned from two single-layer, honeycomb lattices of carbyne, twisted so that they sit at a specific angle relative to one another. MAC is two times stronger than graphene or carbon nanotubes.

MXene – A high-temperature, 2D, laminar molybdenum carbide material that functions as an ultrafast sieve. Alliance Navy ships are coated in the material. When in motion, the material pulls $H(0)$, ultra-dense hydrogen that dark matter is made of, from the interstellar medium for use as fuel. The $H(0)$ is stored in CNT-reinforced receptacles lining the ship's hull.

No-wake zones – The biggest reason for a no-wake-zone around a space station is because of the amount of neutron radiation generated by a ship's fission drive. A minimal dose of 4.4 GW of neutrons will deliver a lethal dose at half a kilometer in 1/5 of a second. As a result, all ships are manufactured with very thick, effective anti-radiation shadow shields. As a precaution, all ships must maintain mandatory separation when operating fusion drives.

Ricci-flat manifold – a special curvature of space found in the Bulk, also known as hyperspace.

Scharnhorst Drive – Interstellar drive that generates a Casimir bubble. This allows the drive to both harness and magnify the Scharnhorst effect, a phenomenon in which light travels faster than *c*. The drive allows a ship inside its bubble to travel at triple the speed of light.

SmartCarbyne – A self-repairing version of MAC, used as the building material for space elevators.

SmartCarbyne Nanofloss – This adaptation of SmartCarbyne is a lattice of ultrafine SC filaments, implanted to reinforce bone, muscle, and sinew. This
military augmentation is usually given to fighter pilots and special operations soldiers.

It was originally adapted for military use to protect pilots in high-*g* maneuvers. An accelerometer embedded in the pilot's wire controls the deployment of the nanofloss into an SC lattice, woven into the soft tissues of vital organs. When experiencing acceleration greater than what the human body can withstand, the SC lattice automatically hardens, protecting the pilot.

Spike – Special operations electronic breadcrumb trail, only useful at short range. Each spike has a unique geometric signature. That signature is contained in the Alliance military database. An app registers the negative space created by each spike on whatever surface it resides. Once a person or item has been spiked, the search app keeps track of the void that particular spike makes, pinpointing its location while it remains in range.

Tau-Neu Chambers – Stasis chambers where all atomic function is held in suspension. The term comes from the Latin symbol, tau, [τ] which in physics and engineering represents the time constant. Neu, or the Latin 'nu', represents the molecular vibration mode, v_x which, in stasis, is zero.

Ziptie – a nano breach application for use in restraining people. Once placed onto exposed flesh, the app immediately unpacks itself, blocking an individual's wire from transmitting a call for help, and rendering the victim temporarily immobile.

WEAPONRY & ARMOR

CUSP – Compact Ultra-Short Pulse pistol uses a pulsed, laser-induced plasma to either paralyze, flash-bang, flash-blind, or deliver searing pain, depending on the weapon's setting.

P-SCAR – Pulsed Special Combat Assault Rifle.

RAU-19 – Railgun mounted on DAP Helios attack craft.

Banshees – Each Banshee fighter-bomber mounts a five-centimeter laser, and is capable of strafing runs. In addition, each USV carries a pair of missiles, their yields varying by Banshee model type.

Dazzlers – Dazzlers emit decoy ECM and jam signals, robbing enemy vessels of their ability to coordinate their attack.

Drakeskin armor – A carbyne-reinforced synthsilk skinsuit used by special operations forces when infiltrating hostile territory.

Drakeskin stealth suit – A drakeskin suit with a nanoweave embedded into the topmost layer of fabric that is tunable to the environment, providing visible-spectrum stealth. The underlayers are made of metamaterials, which use transformation optics to shield the wearer from view by controlling electromagnetic radiation and guiding incident waves around the wearer.

MAJOR PLAYERS
in the
BIOGENESIS WAR UNIVERSE

The Geminate Alliance – The ships that set out to settle the binary systems of Procyon and Sirius initially formed their own governments, but after the first century of colonization, began the loose governmental alliance known as the Geminate Alliance.

After the invention of the Calabi-Yau gates, this alliance was merged into a cohesive parliamentary government.

The Coalition of Worlds – The Coalition isn't a governing body, but rather an alliance of independent star nations, for the advancement of peace and collaboration between the settled worlds. Its members include the Sol, Alpha Centauri, and Proxima Centauri star systems.

Sol's member nations are Terra, Mars, Venus, and the Ganymede and Europa colonies. Alpha Centauri B's star nation is Zoser. Alpha Centauri A (Rigel Kentaurus) is the Akkadian Empire. Proxima Centauri's member nation is the Shang dynasty.

The Coalition's articles state that all eight governmental bodies are equally represented, however, some are unofficially regarded as more equal than others.

The star nations within the Sol system hold the lion's share of influence.

The Akkadian Empire – Akkadia is the Coalition's weakest and hungriest member, due to the hardships the lone terraformed planet, Eridu, suffered. The resulting disparity in both trade and commerce caused a repressive culture to rise up and govern the planet and its people.

Akkadia is known throughout the settled worlds for its oppressive government and its extensive spy network. A state of cold war exists between Akkadia and the Geminate Alliance, as well as most of the Sol nations.

The Akkadian government is notorious for its tendency to steal the intellectual property of other star nations, appropriating it in commercial endeavors where its conscripted labor force can manufacture and then undercut the owners of the original IP in production.

Akkadian Junxun Tèzhŏng – Akkadia's elite intelligence branch of the State Army, those chosen as Tèzhŏng are sent through a crucible of deep indoctrination that refines its members into surgically efficient killing machines. Most Tèzhŏng operatives focus on a specialty, with the most elite being its assassins, the Shinobi.

ACKNOWLEDGMENTS

This book was particularly challenging, and I owe a very special thanks to a biochemical scientist who checked the passages in this book that dealt with viruses and RNA sequencing.

I've said it before: the hard sciences have an incredible number of niche specialties, and though many scientists share a basic understanding of the other branches, in no way can they be considered expert.

This story very quickly outpaced my grasp of biochemistry. I owe John a huge debt of thanks for helping me straighten my science out in this book. Any mistakes you may find are entirely my own.

I have a host of beta readers who help me spot inconsistencies, two of which have years of military service under their belts. Their input in this series has been invaluable. Steve and Dawn, thank you so much for your service.

Manie, Doug, Marti, and James, your feedback made this story better, and for that I'm grateful.

No manuscript of a hundred thousand words is going to make it to print without the eagle eye of a proofreader and the expertise of an editor, I don't care how meticulous a writer you are.

Crystal and Jen, thank you for lending me your keen eyes.

Lastly, I want to thank Marty for keeping the cats fed and the food coming, and for the very first time, trying your hand as a beta reader, too. Thanks. You're the best!

ALSO BY LL RICHMAN

The Biogenesis War Series

The Chiral Agent

The Chiral Protocol

Chiral Justice

Chiral Agent/Chiral Conspiracy audiobook set

Chiral Protocol/Ambush in the Sargon Straits audio set

The Biogenesis War Files: The Early Years

Operation Cobalt

Ambush in the Sargon Straits

The Chiral Conspiracy

ABOUT THE AUTHOR

L.L. Richman has a diverse background, balancing a career as a film director with evenings spent running a linear accelerator.

Physics is a big part of Richman's life—particularly radiation physics. Whereas most people keep plates and cups in their kitchen cabinets, Richman's are filled with radioactive materials, lead-lined gloves, and a Geiger counter.

A self-proclaimed 'NASA brat,' some of Richman's earliest memories are of following her father through the Johnson Space Center, of being inside Mission Control (but not while it was active), of fast planes and astronauts.

Richman went on to become a pilot, and can often be found flying a Piper Cherokee, or photographing Deep Sky Objects (DSOs) late at night.

For more information on upcoming releases or the latest news on space science and technology, like LL Richman's Facebook page, or join the Biogenesis War Friends and Fans group.

www.ingramcontent.com/pod-product-compliance
Lightning Source LLC
Chambersburg PA
CBHW051557100726
47898CB00001B/127